To Live in His Fear

To Live in His Fear

DAN SALTER

RESOURCE *Publications* · Eugene, Oregon

TO LIVE IN HIS FEAR

Resource Publications
An Imprint of Wipf and Stock Publishers
199 W. 8th Ave., Suite 3
Eugene, OR 97401

www.wipfandstock.com

PAPERBACK ISBN: 979-8-3852-6396-7
HARDCOVER ISBN: 979-8-3852-6397-4
EBOOK ISBN: 979-8-3852-6398-1

11/05/25

For Chris and Angela,
Whose honest wrestling with truth
reflects a faith both thoughtful and deep.

Contents

PART 3 | THOMAS MORE

PART 4 | MARY TUDOR

PART 1

Black Joan

But this is human life: the war, the deeds,

The disappointment, the anxiety,

Imagination's struggles, far and nigh,

All human; bearing in themselves this good,

That they are still the air, the subtle food,

To make us feel existence, and to shew

How quiet death is.

John Keats from *Endymion, Book II*, l.153–159

Prologue

An oppressive heat hung beneath the noonday sun. Though the window stood open, the dense, humid air pressed heavily into the dimly lit bedroom. On the bed, a young woman writhed in agony—pale, slick with sweat, her tangled hair plastered to her cheeks. The midwife whispered encouragement, her voice taut with urgency, but the laboring woman's mind was elsewhere, half-anchored to the sounds rising from Tower Hill beyond the window.

The crowd outside shifted restlessly. Murmurs rippled through the heat. Somewhere near the back, a lone voice shouted for the traitor, but the weight of the day smothered any echo. The sun burned down, punishing the heads and backs of those gathered.

On the bed, the woman arched again. Her breath came in gasps. Once, not long ago, she had been reserved—watchful, thoughtful, her presence felt more through quiet intensity than through charm. Now she grimaced in silence, her lips trembling. A faint moan escaped her as she turned her face toward the window.

The gates of the Tower clanged open. The murmuring swelled, then fell suddenly silent. She heard it all—the rustle of garments, the distant ring of armor. He was coming. The man who had broken her. The man whose child she now bore. They were bringing him to the block.

In her haze of pain, her mind tangled the outside world with her own struggle. The midwife's cry—"Push now! I see the head!"—wove with imagined voices from the hill.

Then, the silence. She knew what it meant. The condemned man had reached the block. A final speech began—distant but distinct through the hot stillness. She could just make out the words, carried on the wind:

"The Lord God Almighty makes clear through his Word the righteous path. England has strayed. I die today not for sin but for faithfulness. . . ."

The woman's lip twitched—not in agreement. She had once heard that voice up close, had seen its sharpness. That speech was for strangers.

Her eyes fluttered. She cried out again as the baby emerged. Then came the sudden cry of new life.

Outside, a single sound rang out—dull, heavy, final.

The axe had fallen.

Inside, the newborn's cry rang clear. The woman did not stir.

The midwife leaned close, fingers at her neck, checking for a pulse. Then gently turned to the small bundle she had wrapped. The child—a girl—mewled and blinked.

The midwife laid her gently beside the still body of her mother.

1

Where the Pain Begins

It was July 1516, and the sun hung higher than Thomas Cranmer would have liked. The cloistered court of Jesus College shimmered with heat, its stone walls throwing it back like judgment. He paused in a patch of shade, sweat already darkening his scholar's collar.

He had walked these stones for more than a decade now—since he was fourteen. Not out of ambition, but because his mother had nudged him toward theology with quiet determination, and because the family name—solid, if not noble—could afford a place.

His first tutors were harsh—more rod than reason—and from them he learned not only a thirst for truth but for order. For clarity that could endure pressure.

Now, at twenty-five and newly made a fellow, he should have felt settled. Respected. Instead, unease traced through his thoughts—quiet but insistent. Something beneath the surface had shifted. He couldn't name it, but he felt it.

The plodding stability he once prized had begun to unravel.

"Thomas Cranmer!"

Roger Cressy's voice rang out from across the green, cheerful and unburdened by academic gravity. He trotted toward Cranmer with the easy gait of a man who had made peace with mediocrity so long as it came with good ale.

"Jesus College's quiet wonder—twenty-five years old today and a freshly minted fellow! We must celebrate, my friend."

Cranmer smiled despite himself. "Does the sun shine brighter for you on my birthday, Roger?"

"It shines because our good God approves of drinking in your honor."

They set off across the courtyard, Cranmer adjusting his stride to match Roger's buoyant pace. He had grown used to his friend's irreverent warmth. Roger was no theologian—not really—nor did he pretend to be. But his quick tongue and steady heart had earned him a measure of favor at the college—traits Cranmer found increasingly rare in Cambridge.

As they walked, Roger glanced sideways and said, almost too casually, "There's more to this than your birthday, you know."

Cranmer frowned slightly. "More?"

Roger's grin widened. "You know the inn south on Hills Road—The Dolphin? The one run by that pair of sisters. One of them—Emilie—has taken rather kindly to me. We've been talking."

"I see."

"And we thought"—he cleared his throat with exaggerated innocence—"that you might enjoy meeting the other."

Cranmer stopped. "The other—sister?"

"She's called Joan. Sharp as whetted steel. Not like most others."

"I didn't ask to be set up."

"No one said you did. But Emilie insists she's worth knowing. I agree. And you—well, let's be honest, you could use someone who doesn't live in a scroll."

Cranmer exhaled slowly and resumed walking. "This was your plan all along."

Roger chuckled. "Only partly. The rest involves ale. That part's foolproof."

He glanced up at the hazy sun and added, more dreamily, "You know, if all goes well, we could make a fine foursome—Emilie and me, you and Joan. There's talk of my uncle securing a post for me in Waltham, something with the church there. If I marry, he'll pull the strings."

Cranmer turned his head sharply. "You're already planning my future?"

Roger laughed. "Only loosely. A fellowship isn't forever, Thomas. Why not start fresh—with good women, quiet country, honest work? We could both marry and leave the dusty colleges behind."

Cranmer gave a dry smile. "You paint it like Eden."

"Then you be Adam," Roger said cheerfully, "and I'll bring the apples."

The Dolphin had become one of Roger's favored retreats in recent months. Since a former soldier and his sisters had taken over the establishment, it had shed much of its previous disrepair. The floors were swept, the air bore the scent of fresh stew, and the patrons, though still common, kept their boots cleaner than they had in years past.

Cranmer hadn't been there in weeks. He preferred the quieter corners of the college library. But something in Roger's face that day—a glint of mischief, perhaps, or earnestness—nudged him forward. He sensed, though he could not say why, that this visit would not be like the others.

The Dolphin was livelier than usual. A trio of minstrels in the corner struck notes that were only vaguely in harmony, but the melody was familiar enough to draw soft murmurs of song from patrons scattered at tables. Ale flowed liberally. Bread and cheese passed in greasy fingers. The place smelled of woodsmoke and broth, faint lavender trailing from a freshly scrubbed floor.

Cranmer followed Roger inside and was immediately struck by the change. This was no longer the disheveled haunt it had been a year ago. It had shape now. Purpose.

And then he saw her.

Behind the bar, sleeves rolled past her elbows, dark hair pulled back, face shadowed and still—a young woman moving with deliberate, economical grace. She didn't look up at first, focused on wiping down tankards, but something in the way she moved—some internal rhythm of control and tension—arrested Cranmer before he understood why.

Roger raised a hand in greeting. "Joan!"

She looked up. There was something guarded in her expression, the poise of someone who had learned not to expect much from strangers. Her eyes met Cranmer's only briefly, flickered away, then returned as if compelled to measure him again. Not with flirtation, but with curiosity sharpened to a fine edge.

"You've brought the scholar," she said, not coldly—but with a dry note that hinted at weariness more than judgment.

Roger grinned. "Fellow, now. A day freshly ripened."

Joan's brow arched. "Then he'll want more than ale. We've stew on, and Emilie's bread hasn't burned yet."

"God's mercies are new each morning," Roger said, crossing to the counter. "This is Thomas Cranmer."

Joan offered a nod, neither cold nor warm. "Joan."

Cranmer inclined his head. "I'm honored."

"Wait until you've eaten."

From the kitchen doorway came a voice, bright and buoyant. "You brought someone new?"

Emilie entered, wiping her hands on her apron. Where Joan held a quiet edge, Emilie radiated warmth. Her curls had resisted restraint, and her eyes crinkled at the corners when she smiled.

She moved toward them, giving Roger a light swat on the arm. "You didn't say he was handsome."

Roger clutched his chest. "And I thought we had something real."

Emilie laughed and turned to Cranmer. "Welcome, sir. You'll find the stew better than the music."

"It's a pleasure," Cranmer said, unsure whether to bow or simply nod. He did a bit of both.

Emilie's smile widened. "A modest scholar. How refreshing."

Joan had returned to her work, but Cranmer could feel her awareness lingering, like a pressure just behind his shoulder. Something in her silence made Emilie seem even brighter.

He followed Roger to the table, but his thoughts remained divided between the two sisters—one full of light, the other full of shadow.

Roger had once referred to her—perhaps half in jest—as Black Joan. He'd added quickly that the name wasn't for malice—never that—but for gravity. 'She's better than most of us,' he'd said. 'Just carries the world more quietly.' The name had stuck with Cranmer, not as gossip, but as a puzzle. A stillness that drew rather than repelled.

The table in the corner had been cleared for them—Roger's request, no doubt. Joan brought stew and bread with the efficiency of someone watching the room while working it. She didn't sit but hovered briefly near the hearth, arms crossed, as if undecided whether she belonged at the table at all. Emilie lingered to chat, her laughter like a breeze that moved through the corners Joan left undisturbed.

Roger talked enough for all three, recounting an encounter with a dean who'd confused Aristotle with Augustine, then debating himself aloud about whether that had been intentional. Emilie responded with playful jabs; Cranmer smiled but spoke little. His eyes, when they weren't fixed on his food, returned often to Joan.

She rested one hand on the back of a nearby chair, her bowl in the other, posture straight as if ready to leave mid-bite. She didn't sit, but the words she spoke anchored her there nonetheless. Her spoon moved with quiet precision, her gaze lowered. When she did speak, it was without preamble.

"Is theology ever simple?"

The question came as Roger was mid-swallow and Emilie mid-laugh. They both paused.

Cranmer looked up. "Simple?"

She met his gaze now. "I mean—does it ever offer clarity? Or only more questions in finer robes?"

Roger chuckled, half-choked. "Careful, Joan. You're picking a fight with a fellow."

Cranmer held up a hand. "No. It's a fair question."

He hesitated, the spoon in his fingers forgotten.

"Clarity may come," he said slowly, "but often only after much unlearning."

Joan nodded once, then looked back down. "That's what I thought."

"Have you studied?" he asked.

"No. I've listened."

"To whom?"

She didn't answer. Instead, she tore a piece of bread and dipped it into her broth.

Emilie glanced at Cranmer. "Our brother listens a lot, too," Emilie offered brightly. "But he mostly just stares off like he's not even here."

Roger raised his cup. "To seeing and still liking what you see."

Cranmer lifted his own, more from reflex than conviction. Across the table, Joan's fingers paused on her spoon, as if the toast had touched something too close to name.

A quiet moment passed, broken only by the clatter of crockery behind the bar.

Emilie leaned in slightly, her voice brighter. "Come now, Joan. Master Cranmer isn't here for brooding talk. Why don't you just relax and get to know each other?"

But Joan did not speak, and Cranmer continued to feel the lingering ache behind her words.

Roger whispered something to Emilie, who nodded immediately. Without explanation, they rose and slipped toward the back archway, vanishing through the kitchens.

Cranmer half-rose instinctively as they disappeared, a flicker of discomfort tightening his chest. He glanced at Joan, uncertain whether to stay or follow.

"I apologize," he said, lowering himself again.

Joan raised her gaze to him—not angry, not even surprised. "It's fine," she said. "They have their ways."

The clatter of something behind the kitchen door interrupted them. Then it opened slowly, and Roger and Emilie reappeared—Roger flushed, sleeves rolled; Emilie careful in her grip on one end of a wooden board.

On it sat a thin, pale man—legs ending just above the knee, wrapped in white linen. His shoulders hunched forward, hands gripping the edge of the board, as if bracing against being seen.

"We thought it might do him good," Emilie said softly. "He hasn't come down in days. But he said he'd try."

Joan was already moving, clearing a space near the hearth. "You could have warned me," she said to Roger under her breath—not rebuking, but controlled.

Roger shrugged, uncomfortable. "Didn't want to make it a thing."

Cranmer watched in silence, the mood shifting around him. What had felt like a warm, if uneasy, evening now felt sacred and precarious.

Joan brought a cushion, slid it behind Matthew's back, then placed a small stool beneath the board's edge to keep it steady. Her touch was careful, practiced. She didn't smile. She didn't speak. But she stayed beside him.

Matthew's face was expressionless. He stared into the fire, unmoving, as if unsure where or even who he was.

Roger tried to recover the atmosphere—made a joke about missed birthdays and lukewarm stew—but it fell flat. Emilie offered a tired smile, then retreated to the kitchen again.

Joan stayed beside her brother a moment longer before returning to the bar. She moved quietly now, wiping tankards, restacking bowls. Her stillness wasn't one of peace—it was something heavier, like waiting for a room to exhale.

Cranmer watched her, his earlier arguments about providence and pain now shriveled beneath the rawness of what he had just seen.

He approached slowly, not wanting to startle her.

"You ask difficult questions," he said quietly.

She didn't look up. "Do you expect easy ones in a town like this?"

"No," he said. "But I don't expect them from many."

At that, she looked at him—sharply, the lamplight catching in her eyes. "Then you're not listening very well."

She returned to her work, wiping down the bar with quick, even strokes.

Cranmer hesitated, then said with a gentle, practiced tone, "Sometimes suffering is part of God's will. A path we're given to walk."

Joan's hand froze mid-wipe.

She turned toward him slowly. Her voice came flat, but her eyes were lit with fury born of long-held grief. "Don't. Don't you dare offer that nonsense to me."

Cranmer blinked. "I didn't mean—"

"Yes, you did. You meant to calm me with something safe. But don't confuse your safety with truth."

She leaned closer, her voice now tight. "If you're going to speak of God, then speak of a God who needs to be questioned. Don't hand me a God who ruins lives and calls it purpose."

He stood still, the moment piercing.

"Thank you for the meal," he said softly.

She said nothing.

As Cranmer stepped out into the darkening street, the air cooler now, he found the words still burning at the back of his throat. Not a question, but the beginning of an accusation he didn't have the courage to admit.

Cranmer didn't sleep. He lay still in his room above the college court, staring at the grain of the ceiling beam while Joan's voice replayed—sharp, exact, unrelenting. Her words had drawn blood, and he knew it was not undeserved.

He had begun to believe his answers served others. Tonight, he suspected they served mostly himself.

A knock jolted him from the silence.

He rose and opened the door to find Roger leaning against the frame, smelling of ale and night air, shirt rumpled and collar askew.

"She wants to see you," Roger said. "Joan."

Cranmer blinked. "Tonight?"

Roger nodded. "At St. Mary's. Out front."

Cranmer reached for his cloak.

Roger paused, squinting at him through a wobbly grin. "You've made an impression. Not sure if it's a scar or a halo. But she doesn't invite people lightly."

Then Roger turned and wandered down the stairs, half-singing a hymn—wrong tune, slurred words, and all.

Cranmer stepped into the night.

Great St. Mary's stood quiet beneath the stars, the tall windows dark, its doors closed but not locked. Cranmer approached without hurry. The air had cooled, though the day's warmth still clung to the stones. The sound of his steps on the worn path echoed softly against the church walls.

He saw her seated on the low steps beneath the entry arch, her posture drawn inward, hands resting in her lap. She kept her gaze fixed on the stone path.

"You came," she said.

"You asked."

Cranmer sat beside her, leaving a careful space between. The hush of Cambridge night settled around them like a veil.

Joan drew a slow breath. "I didn't call you here to finish a fight," she said. "I called you because you flinched."

Cranmer turned to her.

"All the others—your fellows, your masters—they don't flinch. They quote. They fold pain into doctrine and smile when they're done."

She looked away. "But you flinched. You felt it. You didn't fight back."

She was quiet again, her gaze tracing the curve of a stone near her foot. Then: "I don't go inside. Not anymore. Not since Matthew."

She went on, "People say churches are where answers live. But all I ever hear in there are echoes of other people's comforts. Nothing that stands."

"But you still come here," Cranmer said. He didn't mean to the stones or the steps. He meant in the reaching—the reaching for God.

"I don't come to pray. I come to think. And to test whether God is listening. If he is, he never interrupts."

Cranmer turned toward her. "You still believe he is?"

She looked at him now, not with anger but with something like grief. "I have to. Otherwise, I'm furious at no one."

He had no reply. But for the first time, he didn't try to find one.

They sat without speaking for some time, the hush between them neither heavy nor light, but honest. Joan leaned forward, her hands clasped as though holding something she couldn't see.

"My father used to say," she began quietly, "that when you hit your thumb with a hammer, you don't step back to admire its craftsmanship."

Cranmer gave a small nod, unsure yet where she was going.

"That's what I feel in church. Everyone so desperate to say God is good, God is wise—God is weaving something beautiful. But none of them seem to cry out when it hurts, when it makes no sense. Not really. Not like Matthew. Not like I do."

Her voice dropped. "And if God needs defending more than he needs to be confronted, then maybe he isn't . . . as good as you think."

Cranmer studied her, but the words in his mind—learned, trained—stayed where they were. He could not find the thread that would tie them into anything she would believe.

She was quiet for a moment longer, then added, "You saw him. You saw the shell of what used to be Matthew. But you didn't see what he was before."

"I don't want excuses," she said, more to herself than to him. "I want to know how a God who could prevent this suffering—this horror—chooses not to. Not just for Matthew. For every soul he watches suffer without that suffering moving him to help."

He tried to speak. Tried to begin somewhere. "God's will is . . ."

But Joan sighed and stood. "Another time," she said. "If you want."

She turned to go but paused. "Do you . . ." she began, but then dropped her shoulders with a slight shake of her head. She had come to speak, but the words were too many, and her strength, at that hour, too little. "Another time," she repeated, and then walked into the night, her figure quickly lost to shadow. Cranmer remained seated on the stone step, chilled now by the absence of her presence—and warmed, somehow, by the clarity of her pain.

2

Minds to Win

The Spanish ambassador was not accustomed to waiting.

But Hugh Chedsey made him wait.

He did so not from malice or arrogance, but from calculation. He had learned that men who were kept waiting—even men of considerable influence—arrived at conversations already tilted forward, already seeking advantage lost to time. And when they sought, Chedsey offered.

He entered the chamber a quarter hour late—deliberately so.

The ambassador didn't rise fully—just enough to claim formality without granting respect. His Spanish was clipped, precise, like a blade sheathed too tightly.

"Señor Chedsey."

"Your Excellency," Chedsey said smoothly, bowing just enough. "I trust you received our packet from the northern coast."

"I did. And you trust your men too much. They were watched."

Chedsey smiled faintly, eyes not leaving the ambassador's. "Good. Then the king's men will report a shipment of cloth and salted fish. And nothing more."

The ambassador's lips twitched. Not quite a smile.

Chedsey took a seat without invitation. The flicker of disapproval on the Spaniard's face pleased him more than it should have.

"Your man in York has made progress?"

"He has," Chedsey said. "But he grows impatient."

The ambassador let the pause hang.

"Impatience is a virtue only when it costs someone else."

Chedsey's smile was forced. "England shifts too quickly. A queen on her throne, and still the king keeps looking—as if marriage were a garment he might replace when worn. And still the bishops bow to him, not Rome. We must unsettle their trust before they redraw the lines of loyalty."

"And Cambridge?"

Chedsey's fingers drummed lightly against the arm of his chair. "A nest of puffed-up piety. But I have ears there, too. A few mouths, even."

The ambassador leaned forward. "You still think it can be done?"

"If the Church moves with conviction and the crown wavers even a little, yes."

The ambassador nodded slowly. "Then we will keep our eyes on your puffed-up nest. And you will keep us informed."

"With pleasure," Chedsey said. He rose and bowed again, slightly less this time.

Outside, the early morning fog crept through the alleys of London. Chedsey welcomed the fog. It blurred lines, blurred allegiances. He'd once believed himself righteous. Now he believed only in winning.

Hugh descended the ambassador's steps with a calm that didn't reach his shoulders. At the corner of the street, just beyond the archway, a portly man with a ruddy nose and a woolen hat waited beside a nervous horse.

"Did he suspect anything?" Richard Morgan asked, wiping his nose with the back of his glove.

"Suspect?" Hugh mounted in one smooth motion. "Of course he suspects. That's why he agreed."

Morgan swung up also, awkward in the saddle. The horse stamped once, ears twitching at sounds not present. "I still say we should have waited. Let the Spaniards make the next move. We're risking too much— getting too deep."

"We're not deep enough," Hugh said, urging his horse forward.

Morgan didn't reply at first. Then quietly, as he turned to follow: "I sometimes think we're not just deep. We're lost."

They rode in silence until the fog swallowed the embassy behind them. Then Hugh spoke again.

"Our Holy Roman Emperor Charles will need Cambridge. If we win the minds, the hearts will follow. That's always been England's way—reason first, loyalty second."

"And what if the minds won't be won?"

"Then we discredit them. Buy others. Replace what can't be swayed."

Morgan shifted in his saddle, his voice quieter now. "Until?"

Hugh smiled, eyes fixed on the road ahead. "Until we've prepared the stage for the Emperor's claim. England will not rise; it will sleepwalk into Spain's embrace."

"And if someone wakes it up?"

"Then they'll find themselves very alone."

Cranmer found Joan outside The Dolphin seated near the well just off the road. The sun had just begun to lower toward the treetops, casting long shadows across the dirt, and the hum of late activity from inside faded as he approached. She didn't rise but looked over as he came near.

"Didn't expect you tonight," she said.

"I wasn't sure if I should come," he replied, standing awkwardly near her.

"She watched his awkwardness for a moment.

"Would you care to sit?" she finally invited. "Or would you rather walk?"

"Oh, yes, of course. My mind is full, and sometimes I forget myself." Cranmer began to sit, but as he did, Joan stood.

"Let's walk," she said. "I spend too much time at the inn in one spot. The walk will be good. It is a lovely evening."

Cranmer fell in step next to her as they turned north on Hills Road toward Cambridge.

"The evening is amazingly cool. For summer. Unusual," Cranmer said haltingly. "I often walk the streets in the evenings. It helps me think. Some days I . . ."

"I'm not much one for small talk, Thomas. So why did you come? What has been on your mind?"

"I wanted . . . well, you said, 'Another time,' and . . ."

"And this is another time," Joan finished.

They walked in silence. Joan inhaled and asked, "Do you know how many theology students and 'men of God' pass through our little inn? Priests, abbots, vicars . . . a bit of ale, a few laughs, and then their eyes start darting to the stairs. As if holy orders gave them license."

Cranmer said nothing.

Joan continued, "They preach restraint, justice, and compassion. But when no one is watching, they reach for what they want. Not one of them . . ." she paused, looked at Cranmer, then said, "Not one of them ever asked my brother what had happened to him. Not one."

Cranmer turned to her. "What did happen?"

She was quiet for a moment, then spoke. "Matthew left home when I was still a child—to serve God and king. He believed in both, foolishly and fully. He was sent north, to York, to fight. In a battle, a war hammer swung by some mercenary Scot caught Matthew just above the knee, sending him into a ditch. At the same time, another of his own troop fell with his horse backward right on top of Matthew—crushing his other leg, snapping it like tinder. The king's army, nevertheless, was victorious. But by the time they had dragged Matthew back from the battlegrounds to York, the corruption in the wounds and the violence of the break led that butcher turned surgeon to hack off both his legs not far from his hips. And yet, the pain never left. Nor did the silence from the ones he served."

Cranmer's brow furrowed. "So the king . . .?"

"Forgot him," she said. "Matthew wasn't useful anymore."

Her voice hardened. "I remember his first night back. I sat outside his door and listened to him weep. He called out to God for help, for death, for something. But God? God didn't answer. God may have been too embarrassed to answer, to show his face after letting it happen."

Cranmer breathed in, slow and steady.

"I'm sorry for your brother," Cranmer said gently.

She looked at him. "You're not the first to say that. But you're the first who's looked as if you meant it."

"I am sorry for him and for your distress. I fear I let you down yesterday not supplying an answer—a satisfying one. I just want to help you see God, to try to explain . . ."

Joan sighed. "Will this be deeply theological or possibly practical?"

"I would hope both. Theology shapes belief, but belief works itself out in life."

"So then tell me, how does the practical case of my brother, for example, backtrack into your theology?"

He lowered his eyes. "I lost my father young. I believed, somehow, it was part of God's direction. That if I studied, obeyed, served, it would all come to make sense. That there was a plan."

Joan's voice was soft now, but fierce. "And has it?"

He hesitated. "Not yet."

She stared at him, and tears began to well. "You're different from the others. It doesn't register with most theologians. They don't ask the hard questions."

He met her eyes. "But you do."

He paused, then followed, "And you expect an answer."

"Not just an answer," she despaired. "I want the truth."

The ache hung between them. Cranmer took a steadying breath. "My father died when I was twelve. My early education was under a schoolmaster, my father's friend, who believed Latin grammar was best learned not by the brain, but the backside."

Joan gave a thin smile. "Surely you are not going to compare my brother's suffering to a student's thrashings."

"No, no," Cranmer said quickly. "Please, hear me out. That cleric was an Oxford man. It was assumed I too would go to Oxford. But my father died. My mother, through her own acquaintances and happenstance, steered me instead to Cambridge."

Joan glanced at him, one eyebrow slightly raised. "And so?"

"And so, here I am—to speak with you now. To wrestle with your questions. To help, perhaps, in your path back to God."

Her brow furrowed deeper. "I thought you were making a point, not offering a destiny."

"The point is—my father's death was a tragedy. It could have embittered my mother. But what if . . . what if God, knowing the whole weave of lives, used that tragedy to shape not only my path, but others'? What if he orchestrates events not to cause suffering, but to bring restoration?"

Joan's mouth tightened. "No offense to your mother, but maybe she simply didn't think too hard. Accepting calamity without questioning God misses the point. Why must we suffer to begin with? If God is all-powerful, why doesn't he prevent it?"

Her agitation made her stride quicken. Then, realizing it, she slowed again.

Cranmer stayed quiet for a few paces, then said, "What if the greatest good is not earthly comfort but restored communion with God? If our relationship with God is the highest good—and it is severed by sin—then perhaps every act of his providence, even the painful ones, aims to heal that breach."

Joan walked with head bowed. Her voice, when it came, was low and worn. "So the horrors of my brother's life were for good? For whose benefit? Mine, maybe? But what of him?"

Cranmer swallowed. "One more thing," he said slowly. "God wills to guide, not to force. He defines what is good—but he invites us into that. Evil in the world twists and harms—but even then, faith can reach through the carnage. So faith follows—even when reason falters. God's mercy is never far, but it lies wrapped in the cloth of faith."

They walked on in silence, past Christ's College, where the road curved west toward Great St. Mary's. The horizon darkened with the deep purple of oncoming night.

Finally, Joan stopped. Her face was turned away, but Cranmer caught the gleam of unshed tears.

"You give much thought to these things," she said softly.

"I must," he replied.

She looked back at him, a bittersweet smile flickering. "You are not what I expected."

Before Cranmer could answer, she turned slightly, glancing at the fading light. A flicker of worry crossed her face.

"I left Emilie alone," she said. "Too long."

They turned, retracing their steps.

For a few paces, they said nothing.

Then Cranmer ventured quietly, "Thank you—for trusting me with your questions."

Joan gave a faint smile without looking at him. "Not many can listen to them without rushing to condemn them."

They walked a little farther.

"Emilie's probably laughing with the stable boy by now," Joan added, a wry note slipping into her voice.

But as The Dolphin came into view—and the sound of unfamiliar voices rose—Joan's steps quickened. As they neared, two horses stood tethered outside. Voices and laughter spilled faintly into the dusk.

Joan slowed. "Guests."

Her voice carried a new tension—half practical concern, half instinctive alarm.

Inside, a burst of laughter rose again, unmistakably Emilie's, mingled with deeper, unfamiliar tones.

Joan hesitated at the threshold. "I must go," she said, but then slowed. "Again—thank you."

She stepped inside, disappearing into the warmth and noise.

Cranmer stood for a moment longer, alone in the road. He took a step toward the door, then stopped.

Give her time, he thought.

He turned and walked slowly back up Hills Road, the night gathering behind him.

The moment Joan pushed through the door of The Dolphin, Emilie lit up.

"Oh, good!" she cried, darting forward before Joan could even close it behind her. "I want you to meet these gentlemen."

"I'm sorry for leaving you alone," Joan said, glancing around the room—and pausing as she saw the two strangers who had risen at her entrance.

"I'll build up the fire and find some food," she said, nodding briefly toward the men and turning toward the kitchen.

But Emilie intercepted her, barring the way with a wide, mischievous smile. "No, no, no—you must stay. Just for a moment. Listen first."

Joan narrowed her eyes. Emilie's matchmaking schemes were notorious. She gave her sister a look that plainly said, *I am not interested*, but, as always, Emilie breezed past it.

Steering Joan by the elbow, Emilie turned her toward the men.

"My sister, Joan," Emilie said brightly, "a wonderful English patriot."

Joan's brow furrowed at the strange introduction.

"And these gentlemen," Emilie continued, "are Master Hugh Chedsey and Master Richard Morgan—both devout Christians and fine patriots, come seeking the wisdom of Cambridge."

"Well," Joan said evenly, "patriots and Christians—that must make you very hungry. Let me find you something."

She tried again to turn toward the kitchen, but Emilie clutched her arm with a pleading look. "Just hear them for a moment," she whispered urgently.

Joan sighed.

"It is certainly a pleasure to meet you," said Hugh, his voice smooth as oiled parchment.

"Yes, a pleasure!" echoed Richard, grinning broadly. "We hadn't expected such attractive amusement during our journey . . . our mission . . . to Cambridge."

Joan raised an eyebrow. "Attractive amusement?" she repeated coolly. "With what, exactly, are you amused?"

Richard flushed. "Oh—only meant to compliment! Little pleasures along the road, you know—brighten the mood—ha!"

Emilie giggled obligingly.

Hugh gave a strained smile, masking a flicker of irritation at his companion's clumsiness. "You must forgive Richard," he said, turning back to Joan. "His enthusiasm often outruns his manners. We are here on serious business."

"So," Joan said, folding her arms, "what brings patriotic Christians to Cambridge these days?"

Hugh stepped forward slightly, taking up the thread with polished ease. "Concern, my lady. Concern that His Majesty's bold style may—unwittingly—begin to overshadow his humble allegiance to the Church."

"You need not call me 'lady,'" Joan said crisply. "Titles don't quicken my pulse."

At the edge of her vision, she saw Emilie give a tiny start, but Joan ignored it.

Hugh inclined his head, the model of gallant deference. "A lady, in my eyes, is measured by grace, not station. And by that measure, you surpass many of courtly birth."

Joan offered a thin smile that did not touch her eyes.

"And what is it you do at court, Master Chedsey?"

"I serve as secretary to Cardinal Wolsey," Hugh replied smoothly.

At his side, Richard made an awkward little movement—small, but noticeable.

Joan caught it and filed it away.

"And is the Lord Chancellor himself discontent with the king?" she asked.

Hugh widened his eyes in mock alarm. "Discontent? Heaven forbid. We serve His Majesty faithfully. But even loyal hearts must sometimes pray he will not, in his vigor, stray from the holy path."

Joan studied him a long moment, weighing the polish of his speech against the unease she felt beneath it.

"You've come to Cambridge, then," she said, "because London has run out of wise men?"

There was a small gasp from Emilie, but Hugh only chuckled. "Wisdom, my dear Joan, often needs clearer air than London's courts can provide."

At that, Joan gave a true smile—cool, amused, but not wholly unkind. She recognized the game, and Hugh played it well.

"How about some food?" she said at last, stepping back.

The door creaked faintly as a late wind stirred it.

"I'll see what I can manage," Joan said. "Our kitchen is not as grand as court."

Hugh bowed his head graciously. "It is grand enough for any true man of God."

Emilie beamed at him, utterly delighted.

Joan slipped toward the kitchen, her mind already turning—half to the meal, half to the dangerous dance beginning to unfold inside her own walls.

The door swung shut behind her, muffling the sounds of laughter from the common room. Joan leaned her palms against the worn kitchen table, letting the stillness press into her bones.

The hearth had gone cold again. She didn't bother to rekindle it. The night's breath seeped in through the cracks in the walls, and the candles flickered low, throwing long, restless shadows across the floor.

For a moment she simply stood there, staring at nothing.

But duty stirred. Sighing, she pulled bread from the larder and began slicing it with mechanical care, setting it out with some cold meat and a jug of ale onto a battered tray.

She had barely placed the cups beside it when the kitchen door creaked open behind her.

Emilie slipped in, cheeks flushed with excitement, her whole presence humming with barely-contained energy.

"I'll take it," she said brightly, already reaching for the tray. "They're asking after you."

Joan hesitated.

"They'll manage," Emilie said. "You look worn through. Go get some rest."

For a moment, Joan held the tray between them, feeling the gulf in understanding widen. But at last she let go.

Emilie gathered it up with a small victorious smile and bustled back toward the common room.

Left alone, Joan pressed her hands once more to the table's worn surface.

Hugh Chedsey.

She didn't like the way his words had slid through the room—too polished, too easy. And Emilie, dear foolish Emilie, had lapped it up like a kitten at cream.

Joan closed her eyes briefly. *Lord, if you are there, keep her safe. Keep us all safe.*

The whispered prayer startled even herself.

It was not faith that had pulled it from her—it was habit, or perhaps something older than habit, a memory of reaching toward the sky when nothing else could reach back.

She shook her head, pushing the feeling away. She could not afford to be soft now. Not with strangers in their midst. Not with a sister whose heart raced too quickly after flattery.

The night pressed deeper against the walls. In the common room beyond, the laughter faded to murmurs, then to the scrape of chairs. Emilie had shown the men to their rooms.

Joan snuffed the candle by the door, leaving only one guttering flame near the hearth.

She moved toward the stairs, her body weary, her mind refusing to quiet.

The Dolphin slept uneasily around her as she climbed to her room, one hand trailing the rough-hewn railing, her thoughts pressing against the silence she left behind.

Cranmer walked slowly through the Chimney, Jesus College's gatehouse, the soft thud of his boots against the stones swallowed by the summer night.

He was perplexed. This meeting with Joan had been infinitely better than the first. Though she had not surrendered her questions, the tears—oh, the tears—had told him she had begun thinking rather than merely flailing against pain.

And yet . . . so much remained unsaid. So much he wanted to tell her—about providence, and suffering, and the fierce, steady goodness of God even amid wreckage.

He paused outside his lodgings, staring absently at a twisted elm that rose stark against the dusky sky. Now and then, a passerby slowed, curious to see what had captured his attention, but finding only a silent man watching a silent tree, they moved on.

Cranmer did not move. He barely breathed. His mind was not on the tree. Rather, Joan filled it. The more he stood there, the more unrest flooded his heart.

He was no mindless youth. At twenty-five, he was a Master of Arts, a fellow of Jesus College, his path angled sharply toward a doctorate—perhaps even Holy Orders. His life was ordered, disciplined: the books, the teaching, the parsing of truth one Latin clause at a time. And Joan . . . Joan was a serving girl at a roadside inn.

Still—her mind. It flashed at times with a brilliance that startled him. Her soul burned behind those searching eyes. Her beauty—God help him—her beauty stole his breath.

He was not like Roger Cressy, ready to trade academia for marriage without a second thought. He couldn't simply abandon it all. His calling was real—wasn't it?

Yet equally unthinkable now was his life untouched by her presence.

A chill brushed him. He thought, for the briefest moment, of what it would mean to love her openly. Fellows at Cambridge could not marry. Holy Orders would bar him forever. If his heart bent too far, he could lose everything he had spent a decade building.

He pushed the thought aside, angry at its presumption. He was not speaking of love. Not yet. He wanted—needed—only to see her again. To talk again. To know more.

He would find her again. At The Dolphin. With Roger, perhaps. Or even alone. He would talk with her, and perhaps, if mercy allowed, he would glimpse whether her soul, too, had been touched by his.

For tonight, that would be enough.

Cranmer turned and climbed the worn steps to his rooms, the heavy wood door groaning slightly behind him as it shut out the restless night.

3

The First Move

THE MORNING LIGHT PRESSED through the warped glass of The Dolphin's front windows, striping the floorboards in long, golden shafts. The inn stirred slowly to life—creaks from the upper rooms, a soft clatter of pans in the kitchen, the faint yeasty scent of rising bread.

Emilie moved briskly through the common room, cheeks pink, smoothing her apron for the third time. She fluffed cushions that had no need of fluffing, then stole another glance toward the stairwell.

Joan was wiping down the tables with steady strokes, methodical and precise. She didn't look up. But her eyes—when they flicked toward her sister—were not unwatching.

Footsteps on the stairs. Emilie whirled.

Hugh Chedsey descended first, every inch as composed as the night before. His doublet was brushed clean, collar sharp, expression polished. Richard Morgan followed—less refined, tugging at his wrinkled sleeves, blinking like a man not quite adjusted to daylight.

"Good morning, ladies," Hugh said, his voice honey-smooth, as if they were guests in *his* house rather than he in theirs.

"Good morning, sirs," Emilie answered brightly, bobbing a curtsy. Joan gave a nod and turned back to her cloth.

"Ah, breakfast," said Richard, sniffing like a hound.

"I'll fetch something," Joan said, already disappearing into the kitchen.

Hugh gestured Emilie to a seat before pulling out a chair for himself with practiced grace. Richard thudded into his place with a grunt and seized a hunk of bread from the basket Emilie had just set out.

They made conversation while waiting—light, harmless things. Hugh steered it easily: the fine gardens at King's, the sad state of roads in Norfolk, the tedious rituals of minor courts. Richard chimed in occasionally, eager but out of step. Emilie laughed too often and too brightly. Hugh, by contrast, smiled in moderation—as if weighing each reaction before offering it.

When Joan returned balancing a tray, Hugh half-rose in courteous reflex. Richard did not.

"Your hospitality," Hugh said, eyes lingering on Emilie, "is a balm to weary travelers."

"We're glad to have you," Emilie beamed.

Joan set the tray down more firmly than necessary. More bread, cheese, porridge bowls. Her gaze flicked to Emilie. A silent signal passed. Emilie didn't meet it.

Breakfast unfolded with strained civility. Hugh continued his gentle parade of pleasantries. Emilie floated along. Richard ate loudly. Joan barely touched her food.

The sunlight shifted, slanting deeper into the room. Joan stood, collected empty cups, and left again without a word.

The front door creaked open.

"Looking for me?" Roger's voice called cheerfully from the entry. His tone shifted mid-sentence as he stepped in and spotted the guests.

Hugh and Richard rose. Emilie—nearly glowing—turned to him with breathless excitement.

"Roger, these gentlemen are Master Hugh Chedsey and Master Richard Morgan," she said. "They've come from London to seek counsel from Cambridge's finest."

Roger gave a short laugh. "Then they've missed their mark by a fair half-mile. I'm no more than a fellow scraping a living from stubborn students."

Joan emerged from the kitchen with another tray of ale, setting it down without flourish.

"Master Chedsey is secretary to Cardinal Wolsey," Emilie added with pride, as though announcing royalty.

Roger lifted an eyebrow. "Cardinal Wolsey's secretary? Cambridge *is* moving up in the world."

"One of his secretaries," Hugh corrected smoothly. "I serve within his broader court."

"Ah," Roger's smile thinned. "Still—a man of influence."

Richard, meanwhile, had seized a hunk of bread and was chewing noisily.

"We hope to consult with a few of Cambridge's theological minds," Hugh continued. "Obtain their views on certain . . . troubling matters."

"Such as?" Roger asked easily, though a note of carefulness tightened his voice.

Hugh leaned in just slightly, as if confiding among friends. "His Majesty's recent . . . vigorous independence regarding Church matters. We wonder whether the learned men of Cambridge view it as strength— or straying."

Joan, moving quietly past with a fresh pitcher, murmured, "Since all the London clerics were otherwise occupied."

Roger laughed aloud. "Trust Cambridge to be the land of second resort."

"But perhaps," Hugh said, smiling thinly, "clearer air allows clearer thought."

"Hmm," Roger mused. "You don't want theological debate, then— you want political sentiment."

"Insight," Hugh corrected quickly. "Nothing more."

Roger tapped a thoughtful finger on the table. His instincts, honed by years of subtle academic maneuvering, prickled sharply. This smelled of danger. Still, there was no harm in gathering his betters for a polite conversation—so long as they all kept their heads.

"I might arrange something," he said at last. "Late afternoon at Christ's College library. A few of us should be free by then."

Hugh rose slightly and bowed his head. "You have my gratitude."

Roger smiled affably but inwardly added, *Don't mistake my courtesy for commitment.*

Joan set down a plate of warm bread and a small wheel of cheese. Roger pulled up a chair without ceremony and joined the breakfast already underway.

The conversation shifted to safer topics—student pranks, unruly tutors, the stubborn donkey that had recently broken loose in the market and caused no end of chaos. Even Hugh laughed at the story, though his laughter was more studied than spontaneous.

After a little while, Roger rose, brushing crumbs from his doublet.

"If I don't round up a few of our scholars now," he said, "you'll find only the drunk and the dead left this afternoon."

He nodded to Hugh and Richard, clapped Emilie lightly on the shoulder, and cast a quick glance at Joan—who met his gaze with a subtle flicker of warning.

Then he was gone, the door swinging shut behind him with a soft thud.

Emilie bustled around the common room, her exaggerated cheerfulness clattering louder than the plates. Joan watched in silence, unsure whether to envy or distrust the brightness in her sister's face.

Richard was engaged in a lively monologue about London taverns to no one in particular. Hugh, meanwhile, leaned back in his chair, watching Emilie with a leisurely, appraising gaze.

Joan collected a few stray cups and plates herself, nodding toward the kitchen.

"Come help me a moment, Emilie," she said lightly.

Emilie hesitated, glancing toward the common room. Hugh's voice drifted in, low and musical. At his small smile, she gave a girlish shrug and followed Joan through the kitchen door.

The door swung shut behind them, muffling the voices.

Inside, the air was cooler. Stillness pressed close, thick with the smells of bread and damp wood.

Joan turned. "Be careful," she said plainly.

Emilie blinked. "Of what?"

Joan gestured toward the other room. "Of *him*."

Emilie gave a short, nervous laugh. "Hugh? Joan, he's been nothing but kind."

"Exactly," Joan said. "Too kind. Too smooth. Men like that don't wander into roadside inns by accident."

Emilie bristled. "You're always so suspicious. Always finding fault."

"And you're always too quick to believe pretty words."

Emilie busied herself with folding a cloth, hands moving faster than necessary. "You think I'm naïve."

"I think you're young," Joan said. "And he's not."

"I can handle myself."

Joan didn't argue. She just stood there, fingers resting lightly on the edge of the table, watching her sister's half-turned back.

Her voice softened. "I'm not trying to stop you from living, Emilie. Just from being misled."

Emilie didn't answer.

Joan waited a moment longer, then let it go.

From the common room, Hugh's voice floated in again, smooth as poured wine.

Emilie straightened her shoulders. "They're probably wondering where I went."

Without looking back, she slipped through the door, the sound of her skirts brushing the frame as she vanished.

Joan stood in the stillness, the air thick with flour and the ache of knowing she hadn't gotten through.

Late morning light filtered through the panes. The coals in the hearth had burned low. Joan was gone—off to the kitchen or out back perhaps— and Richard had taken himself upstairs, muttering about needing sleep.

Hugh noted both absences with quiet satisfaction.

Now he sat angled toward what was left of the fire, one arm draped easily along the chair. Emilie perched opposite him, her hands folded primly in her lap, eyes bright.

"As I was saying," Hugh resumed, "when the Cardinal grew tired of the Duke's narrow-mindedness, he turned to me."

Emilie leaned forward. "You advise Cardinal Wolsey yourself?"

"I do," Hugh said with just enough humility. "In matters that matter."

Her hands tightened. "Truly?"

He smiled. "It's not so grand as it sounds. Only trust earned over time. And conviction."

A quiet thrill passed through her.

"Politics is very much like chess," Hugh explained. "Have you played?"

"Chess?" Emilie wrinkled her brow. "I don't like how the horse moves. I'd rather play skittles. It's exciting."

Hugh chuckled. "Skittles has its place. But chess—chess teaches power. Every piece has rules—even the . . . horse. Some sacrifice. Some protect. The trick is seeing the board three moves ahead."

Emilie tilted her head. "Sounds lonely."

"Only if you lose."

She laughed lightly, unsure, and Hugh let the silence rest.

"So politics," he said softly, "is very much like chess. Cardinal Wolsey fancies himself the king. But it's the quiet pieces that matter—the ones no one watches."

He leaned in slightly, voice lowering.

"You, my dear Emilie, would dazzle at court."

Her eyes widened. "Oh, I wouldn't know the first thing—"

"But you would," he interrupted gently. "Court is full of women with lineage but no wit. You have both wit and beauty. And charm besides."

Her cheeks flushed.

"You flatter me."

"I don't," he said, his tone shifting—quieter, almost intimate. "London would suit you. The dances. The evenings by candlelight. Music spilling through open halls. Power hidden behind fans and laughter."

Emilie's breath caught, a smile flickering across her lips.

"You would shine there," he said again, softer now.

And with that, he leaned back—just slightly—watching as the net drew in a little closer around her heart.

The afternoon sun slanted across the dusty road as Hugh and Richard made their way toward Christ's College. The shadows of chimneys stretched long across the lane.

Richard trudged a half-step behind, swiping at his brow. "I still don't see why we're wasting time with scholars," he muttered. "You said we came for influence—not sermons."

Hugh slowed just enough to glance at him. "And how do you imagine influence begins, Richard? With banners?"

Richard frowned, "With money, usually."

"Money follows belief," Hugh said calmly. "And belief follows fear."

They walked on in silence a few steps. Then Hugh continued, voice low and firm. "The soul of England is not loyalty to Henry—it is faith. Stir faith, and you stir the people. Stir the people, and the king bends—or breaks."

Richard scratched his jaw. "And if the scholars see through us?"

"They won't," Hugh's tone was sharp now. "We do not mention Spain. We do not mention Charles. We speak only of the Church—of sacred order, of the danger of pride. Let them clutch their Bibles and panic about Rome. Let them start the landslide."

He looked ahead, toward the gothic peaks of Christ's spires. "All we do is tilt the first stone."

Richard still looked uneasy. "And if someone puts it back?"

"Then we make sure he's not standing when the next stone falls."

They reached the bend in Queen's Road, the college crest coming into view.

Hugh stopped and turned to him. "You won't come to the meeting."

"What? Why not?"

Hugh offered a mild, almost apologetic smile. "Because you speak like a drunk soldier playing chess with his fists. These men think in footnotes and layers. You'll ruin it."

Richard reddened. "So what do I do?"

"Return to The Dolphin. Find Joan and Emilie. Bring them to the college library in—" he checked the sun "—two hours."

"Why them?"

"Because the room we're in needs anchors." Hugh's tone cooled. "And because Emilie listens when you smile."

Richard scowled, but nodded.

"Two hours," Hugh repeated. "And mind your tongue."

Richard turned back the way they'd come, shoulders stiff.

Hugh watched him for a moment, then turned toward Christ's College, straightening his collar and setting his expression to thoughtful humility.

The next move had begun.

In a quiet study room off the library at Christ's College, four scholars sat beneath high mullioned windows while Hugh Chedsey paced with measured poise.

The air smelled of parchment and old oak. Volumes lined the walls like silent judges.

"Every court of Europe watches our king," Hugh began, hands clasped loosely behind his back. "Every indulgence, every overreach ripples outward—not only through politics, but through the Church's standing."

John Nicholson leaned forward. "You're suggesting His Majesty's sins are a threat to Christendom?"

"I suggest," Hugh said carefully, "that a king's soul is never private. His choices shape doctrine as much as decree. If he casts off restraint, what will others cast off after him?"

Stephen Gardiner's fingers tapped once on the table. "Are you asking for theological clarity, Master Chedsey—or inviting a mutiny in robes?"

"I'm asking," Hugh said smoothly, "for perception. If Cambridge sees what London whispers, perhaps the bishops might take courage and speak truth to the king."

Nicholson's eyes narrowed. "You say that as though the Church rules the Crown."

"I say it as one who serves the Lord Chancellor," Hugh replied. "If the king dismisses spiritual counsel, then the Church must raise its voice."

Nicholson straightened. "No. The king is anointed by God. If he errs, he answers to God—*not* to a clerk."

Hugh smiled thinly. "Is it error if he exalts himself above Rome? If he tears at sacred unity for the sake of pride?"

Nicholson slammed his palm down. "And who decides that? You? The Emperor?"

Hugh coughed to hold his temper. "Do not the leaders of the Church derive their authority from God as surely as the king does? Is not the Church a higher calling still?"

Nicholson bristled. "The king must weigh many things—even if the clergy do not."

Hugh's voice sharpened. "Do you now presume to teach me politics?"

Nicholson's reply came swift. "No more than you presume to teach me religion."

"Enough," Gardiner said quietly. "We came to listen, not quarrel."

But Nicholson had risen. "I see where this leads. I will not sit here while agents of Spain stir disloyalty in God's name."

Hugh raised a hand. "You mistake me."

"No," Nicholson said. "I see you exactly."

He gathered his notes and strode out.

The door closed behind him with a flat echo.

Silence held a moment longer.

Hugh turned slightly, composing himself. "My apologies. I did not intend offense."

Gardiner gave a noncommittal nod. Roger said nothing.

Cranmer sat back, unreadable.

Hugh turned toward him. "Master Cranmer, you've been silent. May I ask your view?"

Cranmer hesitated. His eyes flicked to Gardiner, then back to Hugh. "The Church's authority is sacred," he said carefully. "But the king's is ordained as well. We owe reverence to both."

"Indeed," Hugh said, voice like silk. "So what happens when one violates the other?"

Cranmer paused again. "Then the wise man waits before speaking."

Gardiner let out a short breath—not quite approval, but something like it.

"You are prudent," Hugh said, dipping his head. "And perhaps that is what the Church needs most."

Hugh turned to Gardiner. "Perhaps we might meet again. I'd value your insight."

Gardiner's smile was thin. "Tomorrow morning. There's an inn near Silver Street—meet me there at sunrise."

Hugh inclined his head, satisfied. "I will. This has been enlightening."

He bowed slightly and left with Roger following behind.

Cranmer rose to go, but Gardiner's voice stopped him.

"A moment, Thomas."

He turned.

Gardiner's tone dropped low. "You answered well. Chedsey wants to pull you into a game. Don't let him."

Cranmer stiffened. "You think he's dangerous?"

"I think he's hiding something. And I think he's watching to see who listens too easily."

Cranmer nodded slowly. "You want me to be careful."

Gardiner gave a brief, approving glance. "That—and aware. If he speaks again, let him. Hear him out. Just don't forget who's speaking."

He paused at the door, then added, "There's a snake in our garden. I'd rather not be surprised by where it slithers next."

Gardiner turned and left, his robes trailing behind him like a shadow.

Cranmer stood alone, surrounded by the hush of books and the ghost of a quarrel.

After a moment, Cranmer stepped out into the fading light—and stopped.

Hugh was waiting near the edge of the courtyard, Richard at his side. And Roger stood there too. But beside them—unexpectedly—stood Joan and Emilie.

Joan caught his eye, calm as ever, and gave the barest nod. Emilie was looking about with wide, eager interest.

A quiet surprise passed through Cranmer—then, oddly, a sense of steadiness. Whatever else the day had held, their presence, unlooked for as it was, seemed to steady something in him.

He exhaled slowly and walked toward them.

4

Tinder

"EMILIE AND JOAN HAVE come to dine with us!" Roger's voice rang out as Cranmer stepped into the college courtyard.

Hugh turned at once, smiling as if the thought had sprung from his own heart. "My idea, actually. I thought our company deserved a touch of beauty."

Emilie laughed, light and sparkling, her hand brushing Hugh's arm in passing. The gesture was unstudied—perhaps even unconscious—but it sent a ripple through Roger that he tried not to show.

"The inn was quiet," Emilie said, glancing between them all. "We brought Matthew his supper, locked up, and thought we'd find our way to you."

"And I'm most grateful," Hugh said smoothly, eyes on her face with too much comfort. "Your company will improve our appetites, no doubt."

"Where shall we eat?" Roger asked, voice a bit too loud, as if trying to reset the tone.

"The Lion Hotel's just around the bend," Cranmer offered. "Good food. Private tables."

"Perfect," Hugh said, already offering Emilie his arm. "Shall we?"

Roger darted to her other side. Joan, trailing slightly behind, met Cranmer's eyes with a flicker of amusement that passed like the shadow of a smile. Before he could step forward to join her, Richard Morgan inserted himself with an eager bow.

"May I?" he asked. Joan looked at him, her expression unreadable, then gave the smallest nod. Cranmer fell into step behind them all, unpaired.

The Lion Hotel's dining room was warm and crowded with the hum of conversation and clatter of pewter mugs. They found a long table tucked near the far hearth, the smoke curling lazily above them.

To any casual observer, the group would have seemed lively and merry. Hugh, flushed with triumph from his earlier meeting, dominated the conversation, spinning grand tales of court intrigue and foreign embassies, each story carefully shaped to cast him as either daring, clever, or indispensable. Emilie hung on his every word, her laughter bright and unguarded.

Richard tried gamely to add to the fun, tossing in clumsy jokes, most of which earned polite chuckles—or indulgent smiles from Emilie. Roger made several attempts to steer the conversation to Cambridge matters, or to draw Emilie's attention back to familiar things, but each effort fell flatter than the last.

At the quieter end of the table, Joan and Cranmer exchanged few words aloud, but their glances spoke volumes. More than once, Joan caught Cranmer's gaze holding hers, both of them half-lost in the noise, but not of it.

The first time, a roar of laughter from the others jolted them apart. The second time, Cranmer leaned slightly across the space between them and asked, under his breath, "Have you thought more on what we discussed?"

His voice was soft but, unfortunately, timed with a sudden lull in the table's clamor. Every face turned toward them.

"What's this?" Emilie cried, leaning forward eagerly. "What are you two plotting so seriously?"

Cranmer reddened, fumbling for an excuse. "It's nothing. Only . . . theological matters. Not fit for such a table."

"Oh, do tell," Richard urged, grinning.

Joan set down her fork and spoke evenly, her voice cutting through the gathering noise. "We were discussing God's role in the savage butchery of my brother's legs."

A sharp, awkward silence fell. Even Hugh's smile faltered.

For a few heartbeats, the only sound was the crackle of the fire.

Finally, Roger coughed and pushed back his chair. "I fear I must leave. I have a tutoring session this evening—with a first-year so dull he needs twice the coaching."

The flurry of rising bodies and murmured farewells broke the tension.

In the shuffle, Cranmer bent toward Joan again. "The reason I asked is that I have found an article—something that speaks to your very question."

Joan's eyes lit with earnest interest. "I would love to see it."

Her eagerness struck him with a sudden thrill—and a twinge of fear.

"I could fetch it. We could . . ." He trailed off, uncertain.

"I'll go with you," Joan said without hesitation. "I can't recall when I last visited Jesus College."

Roger, gathering his cloak, overheard. "Excellent. I'll walk with you."

Cranmer's heart sank a little, but he nodded, schooling his face into polite acceptance.

Meanwhile, Hugh had risen and was offering his arm once more to Emilie, who accepted it with shining eyes. Richard, faithful shadow, hurried to join them.

The party split in the street outside—the night alive with laughter on one side, and a quieter, more perilous hope on the other.

The walk from the Lion to Jesus College lasted only a few minutes. Roger hurried ahead a few paces, checked the angle of the sun, and gave a rueful shake of his head.

"I must leave you here," he said, pausing at the next crossing. "I'm already late." He glanced back at them with a grin. "Take care, you two."

With a quick wave, he vanished down a side street.

Cranmer and Joan continued on together, the evening air cool against their skin as they passed under the looming shadow of the college chapel and into the quieter grounds behind the Cloister Court.

"I'm glad you are interested in getting some resolution through men who have grappled with these questions before," Cranmer said, glancing sideways at her.

Joan gave a half-smile. "Truthfully, Thomas, it was only half interest. I had more concern in simply leaving that tedious frivolity behind."

Cranmer laughed—a soft, warm sound. "Ah! Then we are of one mind."

Joan sobered again almost immediately. "But I do want to know. I do want to learn how God . . ." She broke off, struggling. "Oh, I just grieve for my brother."

Cranmer's voice gentled. "I'm sorry for your brother. But God is not to blame for the actions of evil men."

Joan smiled bitterly. "I used to try to defend God too. 'Evil in the world, caused by Adam's curse, brings oppression to the good man.' But do you not on other occasions also praise God for being almighty and all good? Have you never once reflected on how irreconcilable those two thoughts are? The God who is all-powerful and all-good should want to care for 'his children' and should be able to do so—no matter how many evil men strike against them.

"And yet wars come, and the follower of Christ is hacked to pieces. The tempest rages, and the pure souls washed clean of sin are flung into the deep as their ship strikes the rocks. Plague, hunger, fire—all tormentors of God's children who nevertheless dutifully and blindly sing with the Psalmist, 'The Lord is my Shepherd; I shall not want. . . . Surely goodness and mercy shall follow me all the days of my life.'"

Cranmer turned toward her fully, his brow furrowed. "But you would not doubt God's goodness?"

Joan smiled again—a soft, sad smile—and shook her head slightly, not in reply but in pity.

"My dear Thomas," she said quietly, "tell me how not to."

They reached the steps leading into the building that housed Cranmer's rooms and paused.

"If you'd like to wait here," Cranmer said, gesturing toward the low stoop, "I'll retrieve the article from my rooms."

Joan cocked her head at him, incredulous. "You would leave me here? Why can't I go with you? Is there some rule?"

"No rule actually written," Cranmer said, flustered, "but . . . presumed, certainly."

"No rule, then," Joan said, brushing past him toward the heavy wooden door. "This way?"

Cranmer hurried after her, heart hammering. "Joan, we can't—"

"Shh!" she whispered back with a mischievous glint. "Someone might hear you." Then, "Up or down?"

"Up," he said helplessly, and she mounted the narrow staircase without hesitation. Cranmer followed, half in terror and half in wonder, leading her to the quiet seclusion of his rooms above.

Inside Cranmer's rooms, the quiet wrapped around them like a cloak. The heavy scent of parchment and old wood filled the air, comforting and familiar to him—but now touched with a foreign tremor he could not name.

They spoke at first of simple things—Hugh, Emilie, Roger, Cambridge. Cranmer fetched a candle from the shelf and lit it carefully, his hands unsteady, while Joan wandered idly around the small space, her fingertips grazing the worn spines of the books.

Finally, he found the volume he had been seeking: a collection of Chrysostom's homilies. He opened it to a marked page and gestured her toward the padded reading chair by the hearth. She sank into it without hesitation, her face half-illumined by the wavering candlelight.

Cranmer drew a plain wood chair alongside her, angling the book for her to see.

"Here," he said, clearing his throat. "Chrysostom's comment on the passage in Acts—when Paul's nephew discovers the ambush." He traced the line with his finger: "*Such are God's ways of ordering: the very things by which we are hurt, by these same are we benefited.*"

He looked up—and found her watching him, not the page.

"Thomas," she said quietly, "isn't Chrysostom the one who claimed God didn't merely permit Job's suffering, but desired it? That Job lashed his children into submission to discipline them just as God does to us? So Matthew's legs were taken because God needed to teach him a little more humility or something? What would we think of an earthly father who did the same?"

Cranmer blinked, caught off guard.

"You know Chrysostom?" he asked. "You . . . study?"

She smiled, small and wry.

"For some reason, my father thought women needed as much education as men. So that I might serve ale more learnedly, I suppose."

Cranmer turned back to the book, half-opening his mouth to defend the old theologian—but Joan laid a hand lightly on his arm.

"I'm not interested in debating," she said simply.

Cranmer closed the book slowly. The weight of her voice, the fire contained within it, stirred something deeper in him, something nearer to admiration—and longing.

He set the book aside. "I'm sorry," he said. "I thought you wanted to see—"

"I wanted to leave that dinner party," she said bluntly, then hesitated, her gaze softening.

"And I wanted to talk with you. Not about theology alone. I needed to know if you were different. If you were true. If you were not like all the others who smile and deceive."

Cranmer opened his mouth—but no words came. His mind and heart warred so fiercely he could scarcely coordinate breath to speech.

"Sincerity is—" he tried, and faltered. "I would—I mean, last week . . ."

She laid a hand on his forearm, steadying him. Her touch was light but sent a jolt through him stronger than any lecture or prayer had ever done.

"There's something I must ask you," Joan said. "And I need truth." Her eyes searched his, unflinching.

"Why did you come to The Dolphin last Friday?"

He stared at her, startled, before the memory rushed back—the ale, Roger's coaxing, the sense of celebration that had dissolved into confusion and awe at the sight of her.

"I came . . . to celebrate my birthday," he said, feeling foolish even as he spoke it.

"With whom?"

"With Roger. We planned . . . ale, a quiet evening. Nothing more."

"No plan to romance two sisters?" Her tone was light—but her eyes were sharp.

"Romance?" Cranmer nearly laughed for the absurdity. "No. Roger—he mentioned you on the way. I think he hoped for a double courtship." He hesitated, then added, almost helplessly, "But romance? No. I—"

He broke off, lowering his head. The confession felt raw, naked.

Joan's hand slid from his arm, but not in withdrawal. She folded her hands loosely in her lap, studying him.

"Good," she said at last. And then, softer: "Now . . . what do you feel?"

The room seemed to shrink around them. The candle sputtered in its pool of wax. Cranmer lifted his gaze.

"You are," he said hoarsely, "the most intriguing . . . the most beautiful woman I have ever known."

No smile played at her lips. Slowly, silently, she leaned forward—and brushed her mouth against his.

It was not a kiss of conquest, or demand. It was a breath. A hope. A question.

Cranmer froze, the ground vanishing beneath him. He smelled her hair, the faint scent of lavender and the faint smoke from the hearth.

Their foreheads touched. For a long breath, neither moved.

Then Joan's hand slid to his arm—light, then firmer—as she drew him into an embrace he didn't resist. Her body, slight and strong, pressed into him, and her lips found his again—this time surer, deeper.

For one shattering moment, passion swept all thought away. The years of discipline, of cloistered study, cracked under the simple, overwhelming reality of her nearness.

He pulled her closer without thinking. And then—

Awareness slammed into him like a breaking wave.

He tore away, stumbling backward, until the far wall stopped him.

"Joan," he gasped, his hands splayed against the stone behind him as if he could press himself through it. "Joan, I can't—I can't—"

His whole frame shook. He dared not look at her.

A light touch on his shoulder lifted his head. Joan stood there, calm and sorrowful and radiant.

"Thomas," she said, her fingers brushing his lips before he could speak. "It wasn't a test." Her voice trembled slightly, but she did not falter. "Had you accepted it, I would not have stopped. I would not have wanted to."

She drew a deep breath, steadying herself. "But now . . . now I know you. And I trust you."

For a moment, neither moved.

Then she lifted herself slightly, kissed him once on the cheek, and stepped away.

"Goodnight, Thomas," she said.

And before he could answer, she was gone, leaving him alone in the flickering candlelight, with his heart torn open—and changed.

The Dolphin's common room was dim and empty when they entered. Richard yawned extravagantly, stretching his arms overhead. "Think I'll turn in," he said, and without waiting for a response, he clomped up the stairs and disappeared.

Emilie, still flushed from the evening's attention, turned eagerly to Hugh. "What a wonderful night," she said, her voice rich with delight. "It felt like . . . like dining at court. You were so kind to pay for everything."

Hugh smiled, stepping closer. His hand rose to caress her cheek, his touch light but possessive.

"Emilie," he said warmly, "you were born for court. You should be waltzing in London's grand halls, turning every head."

Her eyes widened, the dream blooming instantly. "But—how could I ever?"

"I will take you," Hugh said, voice low and full of promise. "You'll meet dukes and duchesses, earls and countesses. You'll dance and laugh and live the life you deserve."

"You would? Truly?" Her hand fluttered to her chest, the necklace of her imagination already clasping her throat.

"I swear it," Hugh said smoothly. "As soon as I finish this mission, I'll send for you. London is waiting."

Emilie beamed, glowing under his gaze. Hugh caught her hand and pressed a kiss to her knuckles, lingering just long enough to feel her breath catch.

"You'll be the envy of every court lady," he murmured.

She giggled—soft, breathy, adoring.

With a magician's flourish, Hugh produced a small gold necklace from his pocket—a modest piece, with tiny enameled flowers, more quaint than grand.

"I wish I had something finer," he said, "but traveling, one carries only a few treasures. This was my mother's. And her mother's before her. I want you to have it."

Tears sprang instantly to Emilie's eyes. She turned around without hesitation, lifting her hair.

Hugh clasped the necklace around her slender neck and, with slow deliberation, pressed a kiss to seal it.

Emilie turned back to him, radiant, her fingers touching the necklace reverently. "Your mother's! Oh, Hugh, I'll treasure it forever."

"Come," he said softly, his hand finding hers again, "sit with me. Let me tell you of all the wonders waiting for you."

But he did not lead her toward the fire. Instead, he drew her gently toward him. She came without resistance, her hands sliding up around his neck.

"You will dazzle London," Hugh whispered, his lips brushing hers. "And perhaps," he added, almost teasing, "we might let the heavens borrow us for a little while tonight."

Emilie gave a soft, trembling laugh—the sound of a heart already lost.

Hugh lifted her easily into his arms and carried her up the stairs, the necklace glinting in the firelight behind them.

Late the next morning, Emilie finally came down from her room. She found Joan busily cleaning the common room, humming softly—gaily, even. From the stairs, Emilie watched her sister's strange lightness, her broom dancing along the floor as if it, too, shared her mood.

"Well, good morning!" Emilie called.

Joan looked up, wiping hair from her face, and smiled—a smile so rare Emilie nearly missed a step.

"Good morning! Sleep well?"

"I slept wonderfully," Emilie said, skipping into the room. "You seem to have had an equally fine night."

Joan set her cloth aside and dropped into a chair. "I did, Emilie. And in the grand scheme of things, I have you to thank—you and Roger."

Emilie's curiosity bloomed. She dropped into the seat opposite her, clasping Joan's hands between her own.

"Is this about Thomas?" she asked, her eyes dancing. Then, slyly, "How much time did you spend with him last night?"

Joan breathed deeply. "Now, Emilie, not every excitement must be so . . . earthy."

Emilie made a face. "Earthy?"

"I mean sensual," Joan said firmly. "I slept here last night, just as you did. But . . . I learned something about Thomas. Something I can admire—about his sense of virtue. No, not just that. About goodness. Honesty. He makes me see a kind of order, Emilie, as if the whole world isn't just men grabbing what they can before the light goes out."

She stopped, pressing her fingers together, unable to summon clearer words.

Emilie's attention slid away; she had news of her own.

"Joan, I think . . . I'm—in—love!" She blurted, clenching her teeth and hunching her shoulders in excitement.

"In love? With Ro—no, not Roger—oh no, Emilie, not Hugh?" Joan's voice flattened into disbelief, but Emilie rushed ahead.

"Joan, listen. I know you're going to say it's too fast. That I don't know him yet. But that's not true. All my life I've dreamed of living the way Hugh lives. His confidence, his daring, the places he'll go—I've dreamed of him before I even met him."

"But—"

"And he loves me, too. Look—" Emilie looped a finger through the necklace she wore, lifting it into the light. "This was his mother's. He gave it to me! That's how much I mean to him."

Joan leaned back, folding her arms. "So what now? You're going to run off with him to London?"

"I'm not going to 'run off,'" Emilie said defensively. "He has work to finish. When he's back and settled, he'll send for me."

"Send for you?" Joan said, unable to keep the sharpness from her voice. "For what? To be his mistress?"

Emilie recoiled. "He wouldn't give a mistress his mother's necklace!"

"Emilie, no man woos a mistress by calling her one," Joan said, voice low and hard. "They charm. They flatter. They promise. They lie, Emilie. And a trinket and a sweet word don't make a promise true. You know that's his mother's necklace how? Because he said so?"

Emilie pushed back her chair and stood. "I tell you I'm in love, and you answer by calling my love a fraud."

"I'm asking how you know he's not!" Joan stood too, unwilling to let her sister walk away unchallenged. "People who love—truly love—spend time learning each other. You've known him what—two days? You're in love with a dream, Emilie. Not with him."

"And you?" Emilie shot back. "You just said you loved Thomas's virtue and . . . and honesty and . . . what do you know of him?! Oh, forgive me—you've had two whole days more. Infinitely more time, of course."

"That's chalk and cheese!" Joan cried. "You're comparing two things that can't be. I'm not pledging my life to Thomas. I'm not planning to follow him across England on the strength of a story. His words aren't embroidered with flattery and pride. They're about substance."

"Substance?" Emilie scoffed. "Hugh came to discuss Church and king—the two forces that rule the world. Thomas hides in a stone dungeon with dusty books. Don't speak to me of substance!"

Joan stared at her for a long moment, something breaking silently inside. She knew, with a sinking clarity, that she could not protect her sister from the heartbreak already speeding toward her.

She sat down heavily, her voice dropping.

"Alright," she said. "I'm sorry. I know love can be beautiful. And I love you, Emilie. I care about you more than anything. I just want you to be sure. All I'm asking is that you give it time. Let the dream wear off. See if the man underneath is real."

She waited, and slowly Emilie's shoulders dropped, her anger dissolving into stubbornness.

"I know this is right," Emilie whispered. Then, after a breath: "But you needn't worry. Hugh's going to Oxford, then London. There's time. We'll correspond. I'll see him again. I'm not running off."

Joan nodded, though her heart screamed warnings she could not shape into words.

"Alright. Just be careful. Think past your dreams. Make sure his life . . . is real."

She opened her arms, and Emilie stepped into them. Joan held her tightly, fiercely, feeling as though she were holding onto something already slipping away.

"I'm so happy," Emilie whispered against her shoulder.

Joan closed her eyes, trying to will herself into believing it.

That evening, Roger pushed open the door of The Dolphin and stepped inside. A few students from the colleges were scattered among the tables, nursing ale or a bite of supper before a long evening of study. He paused, scanning the room carefully.

"Good," he muttered. "They're gone."

Then, spotting Emilie behind the counter, he called out, "They are gone, right?"

"Yes," said Emilie, wiping a mug dry. "They're gone." Her voice was clipped.

"You want some ale?" she asked, already reaching for a tankard.

"Of course!" Roger said, rubbing his hands together and sliding into a chair. "Glad they're on their way. They can plague Oxford now, ha!"

Emilie slammed the tankard onto the table in front of him.

"They are not a plague," she said flatly, and turned away.

"What? Emilie . . ." Roger called after her. "I apologize. They just stirred up . . . some high emotions. Dangerous questions, you know."

He lifted the tankard to his lips and grimaced. "This ale's cold."

"The fire's over there," Emilie called from across the room without turning. "I'm a little busy. You'll have to mull it yourself."

She vanished into the kitchen.

Roger frowned, grabbing the tankard and carrying it to the hearth. He pulled a hot poker from the embers and plunged it into his drink, letting it hiss and sizzle. Why was she so cross?

Two days ago, she had laughed with him—no, *at* him, but fondly. They had kissed, had dreamed aloud. Surely that meant something— didn't it?

But now . . . now she was acting as if he had insulted a lifelong love. Roger's stomach knotted.

"Skittles, Roger?" someone called from the back door.

"Huh? Sure—uh, no. No, not now."

Two days ago everything had seemed so certain. She was his destiny, wasn't she? They had shared smiles and secrets, even that mad picnic by the river when—

He closed his eyes.

Who was this Hugh Chedsey to crash into their lives like a bolt of lightning, striking clear skies without warning?

But Chedsey was gone now. *He* was real, and he was *here*.

"Emilie!" he called out suddenly, louder than he meant. The room went still. Heads turned. The kitchen door creaked open, and Emilie stood there, a rag still clutched in her hand, her smile gone.

The heat climbed his collar. He hadn't meant to turn this into a performance. He had meant only to call her back to *him*.

But now she waited, silent, and he had to answer.

"Emilie, could you . . . could you sit with me?" he asked, his voice small.

Every eye in the room turned to Emilie. She hesitated, then crossed the room without a word and slid into the chair opposite him.

Roger swallowed hard.

"I'm sorry," he said. "I didn't mean to insult them. I know you had . . . we all had . . . a good evening last night. I guess I just . . . I got a little lonely. A little jealous for your attention."

He reached for her hand, but she drew it back, resting it in her lap. Her eyes softened, but they did not fall.

"Roger, I'm sorry too," Emilie said. Her voice was kind but distant, as if speaking from another shore.

"I shouldn't have snapped. You're a good man, Roger. You deserve . . . happiness."

Roger's heart thudded.

"But you need to know," she said, "that Hugh and I . . . last night we spoke. We shared . . . our feelings. We're in love."

The words fell between them like stones into deep water.

Roger's mouth opened but no sound came out. He blinked, cocked his head, squeezed his eyes closed as if shutting the world out could change it. When he opened them again, Emilie was still there, still watching him gently—but already too far away to reach.

"Please understand," she said. "I'm not rejecting you. I'm just . . . following my dream."

Roger could only stare, wordless.

Emilie smiled faintly, patted his hand as one might soothe a hurt child, pressed a kiss to his forehead, and left him sitting there—his ale cooling, his heart cooling faster.

The kitchen door swung closed behind her.

Roger sat in the stillness, a man, who had been sure of everything two days ago, was now sure of nothing at all.

5

The Edge of the Thread

OVER THE NEXT FEW days, Roger convinced himself that Emilie didn't really understand what she felt—and that, with time, she would return to herself. Of course a naive girl's imagination would spin out of control when some London high-society fop tickled her fancy. It would pass. It had to.

He consulted Cranmer, and then Joan. They agreed—with enough silence from Hugh and enough patient presence from Roger, the fascination would dissolve like a mist.

And so he lingered. The Dolphin saw more of Roger Cressy than the colleges did. His studies suffered, but Roger reasoned it a worthy exchange if only it kept him in Emilie's orbit.

He arranged dinners, picnics, casual strolls—always with the company of Cranmer and Joan. Always safe. Always respectable. Any suggestion of being alone with Emilie brought a polite, if firm, refusal: she was practically engaged, after all. She wore Hugh's mother's necklace. She had promised herself elsewhere.

Cranmer and Joan didn't mind helping. Joan wanted Hugh's memory erased as badly as Roger did. And Cranmer, kind-hearted, hoped to ease his friend's suffering—and perhaps draw his mind back toward study and steadiness.

But they didn't push Emilie. And even in Hugh's absence, Emilie's dream did not fray. She carried on their one-sided romance without effort, spinning futures from the golden thread of her own fancy.

A month slipped by.

Roger remained the soft pillow, ever ready to catch her when she fell. But she never fell. She never even wobbled.

Her certainty pressed Roger toward despair.

"But back on the day you told me of your . . . attachment . . . to Hugh," Roger said at a late summer picnic, "you said you weren't rejecting me. How am I to take that?"

Emilie sat straight-backed on the blanket, pulling linen napkins from the basket with careful precision.

"Exactly as I said it, Roger. You're a dear. I'm not rejecting you because you're mean or ugly or a bore. I'm simply in love with Hugh."

She bobbed her head, punctuating her logic as if closing an account.

"But even so, you are rejecting me," Roger pressed, the words thick in his throat.

Emilie laid her hands primly in her lap and sighed at him.

"Are you truly sure you would feel better if I admitted it bluntly? Let's not twist knives, Roger. Let's just move forward, shall we?"

Roger dropped his eyes to the blanket. From the corner of his gaze, he saw her fingers busy themselves again with the food.

"So, Thomas," Emilie said brightly, glancing up. "I heard you struck a pleasing chord with the Cambridge community with your lecture on God's providence."

Cranmer stole a glance at Joan, then answered modestly, "Well, it's a subject not often spoken of, but necessary nonetheless."

"And your conclusion?" Emilie asked.

"That God provides," Joan said dryly, beating Cranmer to the answer. "Any other ending would have thrown the 'Cambridge community' into dismay."

Emilie frowned. "Well, of course God provides. I meant—what new thing did you say that pleased everyone so?"

"God doesn't always provide," Roger muttered under his breath.

"What? Roger, what are you saying?" Emilie sat back on her heels, aghast.

"He doesn't," Roger said, this time louder, his voice roughened by frustration. "Or more to the point—he does with some, but others are left to fend for themselves."

Cranmer glanced again at Joan. The conversation was veering toward territory he had been hoping to explore with her—but not like this. Still, with the challenge made, he could not let the moment pass.

"God's providence lies in coalescence with his will," Cranmer said carefully.

"Exactly," Roger replied. "And God wills good to some, while others he leaves in ruin."

"I take it you missed Thomas's lecture," Joan said lightly.

Roger didn't smile. "Yes, I missed it. But I've heard the arguments a thousand times. Augustine, Gottschalk, Aquinas . . . they favor a God who sows blessings here, withholds them there—all by unseen whim."

"Caprice?" Cranmer exclaimed, bristling. "I don't find Augustine to preach capriciousness at all in his vision of God's grace and salvation!"

"How then," Roger started, but Joan interrupted with a wave of her hand.

"Gentlemen, if you plan to dust off ancient swords and duel among bones, might I suggest you retire to a library? Emilie and I would like to enjoy the clear sunshine."

"Pardon us," Cranmer said quickly, bowing his head.

"Upon what subject would you ladies prefer to converse?" Roger asked stiffly.

"Well, let's see now. . . ." Emilie began, but Joan spoke first.

"The subject is not disagreeable. It's the endless digging for some dusty theorem that spoils it." She turned back to Thomas. "Roger says God favors some with good fortune and others he ignores. Is that how you see it—*here and now*?"

Cranmer hesitated. For a moment, the question felt like an attack—just as when they first met. But when he looked into her eyes, he saw no mockery, no trap—only pleading, only need. She truly wanted an answer.

Encouraged, he said, "It is a matter of God's will—a will that is perfect and entwined with the good of all faithful followers."

"Yes, you spoke to me of that," Joan said, her voice softer.

Cranmer pressed on. "That will — God's desire for relationship with his children—sometimes must permit evil. Not cause it but allow it. Sin has tangled the world, and in the tangle, suffering threads itself into the pattern. But even so, every thread is caught up in the patchwork toward ultimate good."

Joan, who had scarcely breathed through his explanation, now let out her breath in a slow, tight exhale.

"Yet that still doesn't satisfy," she said.

"Joan, we cannot perceive the whole," Cranmer said gently. "We can't see every road. We trust his purpose because we know his heart."

Emilie shrugged. "So we leave it to God. That's fine. As long as we don't do terrible things, we'll be fine. I'm sure everyone loved your lecture. I even heard some of the—"

"No!" Joan's voice cut sharply through the afternoon stillness. Her eyes flashed at Emilie, then softened as she turned back to Thomas.

"I want to know why. If it makes sense in the great tapestry, it should still make sense in a single thread. If God wants relationship, why can't he just make it so?"

"God doesn't quite work that way," offered Roger sullenly.

"Why not?" Joan demanded, sitting upright now. "What about the garden? Adam and Eve? He made everything good there, didn't he?"

"But sin occurred," Cranmer tried.

"Sin," Joan repeated bitterly. "So God destroys sin. So God casts Satan into oblivion. So God puts his hand over the world and stops the bleeding. Why not?"

"Because that would be too easy," Roger said, still brooding.

"No," Cranmer said, firmer now. "Because love must be chosen. I could force a child to obey me, but true relationship — true love — grows only by choice. Even when the reason for suffering eludes us, we trust him because he invites us into love, not slavery."

Joan stared at him, her mouth set but her eyes searching. For a long moment she was silent.

Then, almost as if her body gave way before her mind did, she lay back on the blanket. The others resumed small conversation, but Joan barely heard them. The sky spread endless and pale above her, the clouds drifting like slow thoughts.

Frustration wound around her chest like a corset. Since childhood she had craved answers—not from idle curiosity, but because her soul demanded order, demanded meaning. Why had Matthew come back broken? Why had her parents withered in silent despair? What was the sense of it all?

She wanted to believe Thomas. He gave her a God who might love, who might make sense of things. But still—the corset squeezed tighter.

She let her hand fall lazily to her side, brushing the grass, and her fingers found the soft head of a dandelion, gone to seed.

Without thinking, she plucked it. She turned it idly between her fingers, staring up at the sky.

"I look to the right," she said quietly, "and there's pain. I look to the left—pride. Ahead—death. Behind—regret."

She held the dandelion gently to her lips and blew. The seeds lifted and scattered, rising slowly, caught by the faint currents above.

Still watching the sky, she whispered: "There must be purpose. Some way, there has to be sense. Where do I find God in all this?"

The white seeds drifted higher, spiraling against the blue.

Cranmer watched her, saying nothing. Something in the sight—Joan lying back, the dandelion seeds spinning upward, her internal struggle—struck him deeper than he could explain.

He didn't understand why, but the sight of her—so vulnerable, so determined—would haunt him.

For now, though, the image slipped unspoken into his memory.

Joan turned onto her side, her back to them all. The sky stretched on, bright and unanswered.

Emilie careened from the kitchen, tray in hand, weaving through the maze of tables before collapsing into a chair. The tray slammed against the wood, upsetting the tankards. One clattered to the floor, spilling what little ale remained.

It had been another month since the picnic—another month with no change in Emilie's resolve.

No letter.

No message.

No word from Hugh.

But her devotion to the dream had not dimmed. She refused even to acknowledge doubt.

At the sound of the crash, Joan rushed from the kitchen, kneeling beside her.

"What's wrong? Are you hurt? Are you sick?"

Emilie's eyes were closed. She tilted her head back and exhaled slowly. "Oh, I'll be fine." She tried to rise, but with a hand to her stomach, she winced and sank back into the chair.

"You're going to bed," Joan said, already reaching for her. "I'll send for a physician."

The two college students nearby, their meal long forgotten, backed toward the door with the careful unease of men dodging drama.

Joan slid her arm under Emilie's for support, but Emilie resisted. "Joan, wait. Sit for a minute."

"No," Joan said, half command, half plea.

"Joan . . ." Emilie swallowed. "I think . . . I know . . . I'm—I'm pregnant."

Joan froze.

Her expression did not change, but slowly, as if under a spell, she sat beside her sister.

"The night after our dinner with Hugh," Emilie said softly, preempting the storm. "The night he gave me this." She touched the necklace at her throat.

Joan sat still, her hands pressed flat against the table, her shoulders rigid, her eyes fixed on nothing.

Everything changed in an instant.

Until now, it had been just Emilie's dream—a foolish thing, yes, but dreams, at least, dissolve. This was different. The dream had scratched its claw into the real world and drawn blood.

A child.

A child!

The inn, Matthew's lingering needs—they were already more than Joan could manage. And now this?

And Emilie? An unwed mother—sure to be scorned, shunned, and thrown to wolves. All because of one man's charm, and one night's illusion.

"I'll go to Hugh," Emilie said suddenly, her voice regaining strength. "He'll understand—he'll know what to do—"

"No!" Joan snapped, loud enough to echo off the walls. "No, Emilie! You won't go to that filthy, arrogant—"

"Joan!" Emilie cut her off. "He didn't force me. We went upstairs together. We both wanted it. And he doesn't even know! He can't know. I'll go to him, explain why I had to come early, and he'll accept me. With open arms."

Joan's voice dropped, but her fury did not. "Used you. He used you, Emilie. Can't you see that?"

"No!" Emilie rose a little in her seat, trembling. "No, Joan! You didn't talk with him! You don't know! You turned your nose up at him the moment he walked through the door. He had work—important work. He loves me. He'll take care of me. You'll see."

"He was here two days!" Joan's hands slammed the table. "Two days, Emilie! If he had stayed a month, he could still have gone to London, filed his report, planted a garden, and promised the same things to a dozen other women."

Tears welled in Emilie's eyes, then spilled.

"Why are you so cruel?" she sobbed. "Why do you hate for me to be happy?"

Joan's voice cracked, softening. "I want you to be happy, Emilie. I want that more than anything. I just—"

"You're jealous." The accusation came sharp, bitter. "You're jealous because all you have is that boring, milksop Thomas. You go on and on about dusty theologians. You want more. You want someone like Hugh— with wit, with style—but he wanted me."

Emilie pushed herself up from the chair, anger flushing her cheeks. But as she rose, a spasm of discomfort made her wobble. She clutched her stomach, steadying herself against the table.

"I'm going to lie down," she said, her voice still brittle with anger. Without waiting for Joan's reply, she turned and climbed the stairs, her steps slower than her words had promised.

Joan sat staring at the table, feeling the air thicken around her.

What now?

She couldn't let Emilie run off to London—pregnant, alone, and blind—chasing the shadow of a man who'd already vanished. But how could she stop her?

She did want Emilie to be happy. But happiness built on illusion would crack, and Joan knew how painful the fall could be.

And Emilie was wrong about Thomas, too. Their afternoons in the past weeks had been filled with poetry, walks, shared silences. She had never felt more known.

That's what she wanted for Emilie. Not grand entrances and gleaming promises. Not Hugh.

She exhaled, slow and tight.

Pregnant.

She had to tell Thomas. Thomas—and Roger. They would have to help her find a way.

Joan locked the front door of The Dolphin, turning the heavy iron key with a final click. Emilie lay upstairs, out of sight, fragile and furious. Joan pressed the key into her apron pocket, steeling herself.

The autumn air met her like a slap as she set out along Hills Road. The countryside already wore the thin veils of coming winter.

Each step struck the earth with hollow finality.

*Trust—trust—trust—*the word beat against her mind, keeping pace with her strides.

Not comforting. Not strengthening.

Demanding.

Was she to trust and do nothing?

Was the tragedy of Emilie's state meant to be God's will?

Was this struggle now—this desperate effort to act—somehow a fight against God himself?

Trust—trust—trust.

Her jaw clenched.

Fine.

Trust that this action mattered.

Trust that God would meet her along the way.

She quickened her pace.

The day still hung to the edge of afternoon, but the graying sky warned of shortening days. A sharp breeze slipped under her shawl, making her shiver.

As she turned onto Hobson's Lane, something in the corner of her eye snagged her. She stopped cold. Down Petty Cury, under the dimming lamps, two men laughed softly.

She blinked. Then recognition flared. One of them was Hugh Chedsey.

Her body moved before her mind gave consent—one step, then another, faster now. She hurried down the street in a rush of tight breath and pounding heart.

"Good evening, Master Chedsey," Joan said as she reached them.

Hugh turned, bleary-eyed, already flushed with drink.

"Well . . . well, hello, Miss . . . um . . . Lan . . . Lancer?" he slurred.

"Ladner. Joan Ladner."

"Yes, well . . . a pleasant surprise. Oh—this is Stephen Gardiner. Stephen, Miss Joan Ladner."

Gardiner gave a stiff nod—polite, but unmistakably cold, as the sort of man who knew serving girls were best left unnoticed.

Joan returned the nod coolly.

"Of The Dolphin, yes," she said. "You wouldn't have seen Master Cranmer, would you? I have urgent need to speak with him—about my sister."

This last she directed at Hugh, letting the weight of the word *sister* hang between them.

Gardiner shook his head. "I'm sorry; I have not."

He gave Hugh a quick, silent look of caution, then tipped his hat with mechanical politeness.

"Good evening, Miss Ladner." And he was gone.

Hugh smiled lazily.

"And how is your sister?" he asked, his tone too light.

"Strange you should inquire," Joan said sharply. "Have you not been receiving her constant correspondence?"

Hugh chuckled, dropping his gaze.

"She is . . . prolific, isn't she. Care for a drink?"

"I would not," Joan snapped. "But I would like to know why, in the midst of your so-called lofty mission, you thought nothing of ruining a woman in mind and body—and then leaving her to drown alone."

Hugh stared at her a moment—then grinned wider.

"Are you certain you won't have that drink?"

"I am."

"Well . . ." He shrugged. "I will."

And with that, he crossed the street to a nearby tavern and pushed through the doors of The Hound.

For a moment, Joan stood stunned—then anger flared through her again, hot and reckless.

She crossed the street.

The tavern was dark when Joan stepped inside. It smelled of old wood, smoke, and spilled ale. It was a low room—crowded close with shadows. A battered counter ran along one wall, and Hugh leaned into it, speaking with the grizzled proprietor.

From the doorway, Joan called out, her voice ringing across the gloom:

"You can't drown this in ale. You can't turn your back and pretend you're not responsible!"

"Lover's quarrel," Hugh said to the tapster, winking as he sauntered to a table.

The old man behind the counter laughed a dry, broken laugh.

Joan marched after him. She stood until he raised his eyes to hers—mocking, indifferent.

Then, without preamble, she said, "She's pregnant. With your child."

For a moment Hugh said nothing. Nothing at all.

Then the smile dropped. The mask cracked.

"You don't want to tangle with me," he said quietly. The words were soft, but the hatred behind them struck Joan like a blow. "I'll rip your heart out."

Joan's throat tightened. She stayed standing. Breathing hard, eyes wide, but standing.

Hugh watched her struggle—eyes narrowing, voice lowering.

"You bring me accusations?" he hissed. "My child? How would you know that? Your precious sister probably found another bed the next night. Cheap whores do what they must."

Joan's hands clenched at her sides.

"You are despicable," she managed to choke out. "You pretend to be a gentleman—you're nothing but a leech, a devil—"

The chair Hugh had been sitting on crashed backward as he leapt to his feet.

"You—" he roared, stepping toward her, "gutter sludge! Ale-slinging tramp! You think you have the right to judge me?"

Joan stumbled back as Hugh advanced.

"You and your precious sister—waiting by the roadside for any fool who might toss you a necklace or a coin—maybe charge for it next time!"

His voice rose higher, harsher. Other men in the tavern turned and watched—no one moved.

"She probably never had a real man before!" Hugh sneered. "She should have paid me for the honor!"

Joan took another step back—then another—until Hugh caught her. He seized her arm, wrenching her close.

"You filthy little crow," he spat. His hand shot up, clamping over her mouth as she tried to scream.

To the old man behind the bar, Hugh said coolly:

"You have a room, don't you? So my wife and I can settle our differences."

The old man gave a toothless grin and nodded toward a door in the back.

Joan twisted, fought, tried to cry out, but Hugh's hand smothered the sound. He dragged her backward, step by step.

Used to such scenes, the proprietor shuffled over, opened the door, and with a casual flick of his hand, ushered them inside.

The door shut behind them. Inside, the dark waited.

6

Ash and Ember

Night had fallen by the time Joan stumbled out of The Hound. The ordeal had lasted only minutes, but an hour had passed before she could gather herself enough to rise, to move, to walk. Her legs barely remembered how.

Her head swam with shame, fear, and disbelieving rage. Each breath scraped against her chest like a dry, broken thing.

She staggered down the road back toward The Dolphin, the cobbles shifting beneath her feet. The air bit against her face, but she scarcely felt it.

Trust, the word echoed again — not a heartbeat now, but a hollow tolling.

Trust—trust—trust.

Had she trusted wrongly? She had set out only hours before, believing her cause was just—that she could fight for Emilie, for rightness, for hope. Where had that trust led her?

She had not even gone to seek Hugh. She had set out to find Thomas. To find a plan. To find help.

Now, her soul felt as if it had been turned inside out—shamed, bleeding, and laughed at.

And Emilie still needed her.

She pressed a hand to her stomach, steadying herself, forcing herself forward.

The Dolphin loomed up out of the dark like a drowned wreck. The windows were dark. Even the hearth inside had gone cold.

Joan fumbled with the key, her fingers slipping against the iron lock, before she finally managed to lift the bolt and push the door open.

The common room yawned before her, shadowed and silent.

She lit a taper with trembling hands, shielding the weak flame from the draft as best she could. The flare of the lamp brought little comfort.

The room seemed wrong somehow, smaller and hollowed out. Even the walls, which had once held warmth and memory, now crouched around her like grave markers.

"Emilie?" she called, her voice catching.

No answer.

She called again—softer this time, almost unwilling to shatter the silence.

Still nothing.

Joan stood there, wavering, then crossed to one of the heavy chairs by the fireplace and dropped into it, her limbs too heavy to carry further.

She set the lamp on the table and let her head fall into her hands. The fire inside her, the rage and will that had carried her through the evening, guttered like a dying flame.

What would she tell Emilie? How could she speak of what had happened? Would Emilie even listen? Would she even care?

Joan sat there for a long moment, cold and small in the vast silence.

Finally, gathering what little strength she had left, she forced herself up.

She climbed the stairs slowly, gripping the rail, each step a small battle.

She reached Emilie's room and knocked softly, hesitated, then pushed the door open.

The bed was neatly made. The room was empty.

Confused, Joan stepped inside. On the coverlet lay a folded sheet of paper, bearing her name.

Her hands shook as she picked it up.

> *Dear Joan,*
>
> *I'm sorry for speaking harshly with you earlier. I didn't mean to attack Thomas. I was simply angry and confused that you should be so against the life I hope to start with Hugh.*
>
> *Believe me when I tell you that you simply do not know him as I do. He will welcome our child and me. I know it! I must see him and share this wonderful news with him.*

I have made arrangements for a cart wagon and leave for London now.

Forgive me for leaving the inn to you, but Lyla Pennington's daughter has agreed to help out.

Please do not be concerned for me. All is well and will be even better once I arrive.

I love you, dear sister! I will write soon of my arrival.

Your devoted sister,
Emilie

Joan blinked against the sting in her eyes. The words blurred and swam, mocking her with their easy cheerfulness.

Emilie was gone. Gone—chasing her dream. Gone—believing in a man who had already shattered one life and would surely destroy another.

Joan stood there, the note trembling in her hand, feeling the last threads of her strength slipping away.

For a long moment, she could do nothing but stare at the empty bed.

Then, with a slow, shuddering breath, she folded the note once more, laid it back on the coverlet, and sank onto the bed's edge.

The lamplight flickered weakly against the walls, and the silence pressed in around her.

She felt utterly, utterly alone.

Rain had soaked the countryside all night, and by midmorning only a misting drizzle remained. Cranmer and Roger sloshed down Hills Road toward The Dolphin, their boots caked in mud, their cloaks hanging heavy with damp. The rain had ceased, but the air itself felt sodden, as if the earth could no longer distinguish between water and sky.

Late the previous evening, Stephen Gardiner had found Cranmer in a hall at Jesus College.

"I met one Miss Joan Ladner, seeking you," he had said, one eyebrow lifting with idle curiosity.

Cranmer, wondering why Joan would have been searching for him, scarcely registered the unspoken question. He slept fitfully that night, having determined to rise before first light to set out for the inn.

Roger, pulled from his bed in groggy protest, followed reluctantly, unused to such early exertion.

They reached The Dolphin chilled, soaked, and miserable.

Roger banged on the door with the flat of his hand.

"Emilie! Joan! Open up! It's Thomas and me—we're cold and wet and . . . need a fire."

The door creaked open before the last words fully left his mouth.

Joan stood there, a ghost of herself, her dress wrinkled, her hair falling loose around her shoulders, her eyes wide and hollow. It was clear she had not been to bed.

Cranmer's heart lurched violently before he could form a word. He stepped in without waiting, reaching instinctively to steady her, but Joan turned away, retreating to the hearth where a meager flame flickered.

"What happened?" Cranmer asked, his voice low, urgent.

Joan knelt before the fire, poking at the embers as if she hadn't heard. Her movements were slow, mechanical, as though her body had outlived her will.

Roger closed the door, glancing uncertainly between Cranmer and Joan.

"Where's Emilie?" he asked. "Is she ill?"

"In a way," Joan said, without looking up. Her voice was dry, cracked like old parchment.

"She's gone."

"Gone?" Roger blinked. "Gone where?"

Joan rose stiffly to her feet, every movement stiff with exhaustion.

"I found a note," she said. "She left for London."

"Now? She just left?"

"Yesterday evening. I came home late, and she was already gone. She waited for me to leave so I couldn't stop her."

Roger stood frozen for a long beat, then pulled out a chair and slumped into it heavily. Cranmer remained standing, rigid, his hands clenched behind his back.

"I . . . I just don't make sense of it," Roger muttered, running a hand through his wet hair. "Two months, she waits—certain he'll call for her. Then she runs off . . . at night?"

Joan sighed, long and low, a sound more animal than human.

"She had a little extra reason," she said. "Yesterday she nearly fainted serving guests. When I pressed her, she confessed . . . she's with child."

The words fell like stones into the room.

Roger sat bolt upright, fury igniting across his face.

"Not . . . not me . . . Who—Hugh!"

He surged to his feet, fists balled.

"That . . . that filthy coward! I'll tear his head off—"

He paced wildly, spitting curses.

"She went to him?!" he demanded.

Joan nodded, her eyes fixed somewhere far beyond the room.

"We argued," she said. "I tried. I failed."

"You should have told us!" Roger cried.

"I meant to!" Joan snapped, a flash of life breaking through her numbness. "I left her upstairs, locked the inn, and went to find you."

Roger stopped, caught between rage and confusion.

"And?"

Joan's voice dropped to a whisper. "When I returned . . . she was gone."

Roger punched the air in frustration.

"I'll catch her. I'll ride to London. I can reach her before nightfall!"

"No," Joan and Cranmer said together, instinctively.

Cranmer glanced at her—then continued.

"Gardiner told me Hugh has returned to Cambridge."

"What?" Roger whirled on him. "And you didn't tell me?"

"I . . ." Cranmer faltered. "My mind . . . was on Joan."

He looked at her again—and this time saw not only exhaustion but something deeper: a hurt that seeped from her very bones.

"I have to find Gardiner," Roger muttered, yanking open the door. "I have to know what he knows. Then to Emilie."

"You'll lose your fellowship!" Cranmer called after him.

"I don't give a damn about my fellowship!" came Roger's reply.

The door slammed behind him, leaving only the crackling of the tiny fire.

Cranmer turned back slowly to Joan.

She stood by the hearth, arms crossed tightly against herself, trembling.

Cranmer pulled a chair close, offering it silently. But Joan made no move to sit. Instead, she swayed—and collapsed against him, burying her face against his chest.

He caught her, steadying her trembling body in his arms.

For a moment they stood locked together by the fire—until he felt her knees begin to buckle.

Gently, Cranmer guided her into one of the chairs, sinking down into another beside her, never letting go.

She folded into him, her cheek resting against his chest, her breath stirring the damp cloth of his tunic.

His hand moved slowly through her hair, each stroke an unspoken vow.

"We'll find her," he whispered. "It will be alright."

Joan stirred, pulling back just enough to meet his eyes.

"I saw Hugh," she whispered.

He nodded, tightening his arm around her.

"It's alright," he said.

"No," Joan said, voice breaking. "I . . . I tried to scold him for what he'd done. We were in an alehouse. He . . . he took me—"

She gasped, the words choking her.

"I fought him, Thomas. I fought him—"

Her body shook in his arms.

Cranmer's own breath came harsh and fast, trembling with a fury he had never allowed himself to feel. The urge to find Hugh—to destroy him—rose fiercely within him."

He closed his eyes, forcing the storm down. Not for himself. For her.

"Hush," he murmured. "You don't have to speak of it."

She clung to him more tightly.

For long minutes they sat together, silent except for the crackling fire and the distant ticking of the rain against the windows.

At last, Cranmer found words—but they broke apart in his throat.

"This . . ." he tried. "God will . . . God must . . ."

Joan's fingers found his lips, stilling them.

"Just hold me," she whispered.

And he did.

He held her as if he could shield her from the past, from the future, from the aching brokenness of the world itself. He held her because it was all he could do—and because letting go would have broken him too.

Joan fell asleep almost immediately in his arms. With Cranmer there, she could—for the first time since Emilie's flight—let go. Her body surrendered to the warmth of the fire, and to the steadiness of his presence. She slept with the slack stillness of someone emptied.

Cranmer drifted in and out. He watched the fire dim to coals. The crackle of burning wood faded, replaced by the softer pulse of their breathing.

Then, hours later—something was burning. Not just the logs.

He shifted. His eyes itched—dry, grainy. He blinked several times and tried to rub them clear, but the irritation deepened. A sour, heavy staleness hung in the air. At first, he thought it was the hearth smoke trapped by a closed flue. But then his lungs tightened.

He sat up sharply. The fire hadn't changed. It still burned quietly. But the air was heavier now—smoke-soaked and acrid, curling up into the rafters. And something else.

A shifting flicker—a faint light against the back wall of the stairwell. Not the golden flicker of hearthlight. This was orange. Violent.

Cranmer reached for Joan, shook her lightly.

"Joan . . . Joan, wake."

"Mmmm," she stirred, groggy.

He spoke more urgently. "Do you smell that?"

Joan blinked. Then suddenly jerked upright, eyes wide. The smoke filled her lungs—dry, foul, real.

"Oh no . . ." she whispered, rising unsteadily. Then she saw it.

The faint pulsing light across the staircase wall grew sharper, brighter—flickering like a silent scream.

"Thomas!" she gasped. "A fire! Upstairs! Matthew's there!"

Cranmer was already moving. But halfway to the stairs, the full heat of it hit him. The hallway above was ablaze—walls climbing with flame, the floor itself licked with fiery teeth.

"Matthew!" Joan screamed. She surged forward.

"No, Joan!" Cranmer caught her, pulling her back.

She fought him, wild-eyed, desperate.

"He's up there! He can't move! He can't—" She gripped his tunic with both fists. "Thomas, you have to do something!"

He turned toward the fire—then back. "A blanket. Get me a blanket!"

Joan spun toward the hearth and yanked the throw from the back of a chair. "This—here—take this!"

Cranmer sprinted to the kitchen and plunged the blanket into the water barrel, soaking it through.

Then, without a word, he draped it over his head, lowered his body, and charged into the smoke.

The stairs were already hot—wood sagging, softening under his boots. The hallway above was a wind tunnel of flame, breathing in long gulps and spitting out sparks.

He dropped to his knees, crawling low beneath the black ceiling of smoke.

Matthew's room—left side, above the kitchen.

But the door was gone. The room itself was burning. And yet—through the smoke—Cranmer saw him: Matthew, still alive, slumped on his bed. The mattress hadn't yet caught—but the wall behind him blazed like a forge.

Cranmer leapt through a river of fire stretched across the floor.

"Matthew!" he shouted. "Hold on to me!"

But Matthew only shook his head.

"Go!" he bellowed. "Let me be!"

Cranmer reached for him anyway.

"Don't touch me!" Matthew shoved him away, surprisingly strong.

"This is mine!" he roared. "My fire. My ending. Let it come."

Cranmer recoiled, stunned.

But there was no time. The floor behind him groaned and split. The blanket over his head was already smoldering.

He lunged, grabbing Matthew by the shoulders. Matthew fought, cursing, twisting. They fell to the floor as flames surged behind them, walling off the hallway.

Cranmer didn't pause.

He wrapped his arms beneath Matthew's and dragged him backward, through fire, through heat so savage it burned through his soaked blanket.

He couldn't see the stairs—but he remembered where they had been.

Each breath tore through his throat. His skin blistered. Matthew screamed and kicked, still trying to be left behind.

Then the floor gave way beneath them with a crack like thunder. The two of them—locked in struggle—fell through.

Wood shattered. Beams snapped.

They landed hard—Cranmer's ankle wrenching beneath him, sharp pain shooting up his side.

The world turned orange.

Matthew was pinned beneath a burning beam.

Cranmer rolled away, clutching his leg, ripping the last scorched fabric from his chest.

Somehow, Joan was there. She'd been waiting by the kitchen, a pitcher of water in hand. She threw it across his smoldering body, then dropped beside him, helping him crawl—half-dragging him—toward the front door.

Matthew didn't scream anymore.

Cranmer turned once—seeing the flames consuming him.

Joan pulled him out the door.

They stumbled into the street, collapsing across the road, their lungs heaving in the chill evening air.

The Dolphin burned behind them, its windows glowing like open mouths, vomiting fire. The roof collapsed inward with a groan, sparks rushing skyward.

Cranmer lifted his eyes through smoke and tears, but the sun was gone—swallowed by cloud and shadow, as if even heaven turned its face away.

7

The Knife Between

THE CART CAME TO a slow, muddy stop in front of Forde's Inn at Charing Cross, on the western outskirts of London. Emilie leaned forward, peering through the misted veil of the carriage flap.

Master Penington, a neighbor from up Hills Road, climbed down first and extended a hand to help her.

"There we are, Mistress Emilie," he said. "And not a wheel lost, though we nearly had one outside Bishop's Estereferd."

He was a cloth trader by profession, though he confessed the London trips were more for breathing space than business. His wife, Lyla, ruled their home with brisk efficiency and sharp elbows. When Emilie had approached him the day before, asking for passage, he had agreed within the hour. "Three weeks since my last escape," he'd muttered with a wink.

They had traveled most of the night, stopping briefly at an inn in Bishop's Estereferd. Master Penington had wanted to wait out the weather, but Emilie insisted they press on.

Now, under a slate-gray afternoon sky, she stepped down onto the gritty street.

Forde's Inn. The name had stood out in Hugh's stories—half-boasts, half-invitations. It was the only place in the city she could recall him mentioning by name.

Penington glanced up at the painted sign swinging overhead.

"You'll be all right here then?"

Emilie nodded quickly. "Yes. Thank you—truly."

He tipped his hat. "Then I'll leave you to it."

And without another word, he turned, urging his cart forward down the Strand, hat low over his brow.

Emilie stood still for a moment, watching him disappear into the blur of horses and wheels and street chatter. Then she turned to face the door. This was the place. She had made it. Surely now, everything would fall into place.

The bell over the door jingled as Emilie stepped inside. The common room was dim and quiet, the fire down to low coals. From somewhere above, the tread of heavy boots creaked across the floorboards, and soon a man descended the stairs, wiping his hands on a stained apron.

Charley Dulcy, the innkeeper, paused midway down. He squinted at her, his brows pulling together in mild suspicion. A woman alone, carrying her own bag, and not dressed for fine company. He said nothing for a moment.

"If you're lookin' for work," he said finally, "I don't have any for you here."

"Oh no," Emilie replied, lifting her chin and summoning what she imagined were society manners. "Forgive my appearance—I've been traveling. The rest of my luggage will arrive later. I'm looking to inquire about lodging."

Charley gave her another once-over, then shrugged. "You can have the room at the top of the stairs on the right."

"Thank you," Emilie said. She climbed a step, then paused. "You wouldn't by chance know of a Master Hugh Chedsey, would you?"

Charley blinked. Now that was a name he recognized. Chedsey passed through often enough, usually with coin to spare and a taste for boasting. Charley had no great opinion of him, but he did know better than to speak too freely to anyone asking questions—especially a woman who looked both desperate and determined.

"Hugh Chedsey . . ." he repeated, pretending to think.

"Yes," Emilie added, "I believe he mentioned working with Cardinal Wolsey—perhaps as a secretary or advisor of some kind?"

That sealed it. Charley nearly snorted. "Can't say I know the gentleman," he said flatly.

Emilie nodded politely. "Thank you." She turned and made her way up the stairs, her bag bumping softly behind her.

The room was smaller and darker than she'd imagined. The inn Hugh had described in his stories had lords and ladies visiting him here, late-night discussions of court affairs, candlelight waltzes with political intrigue. This place smelled of mildew and last night's ale.

But Emilie waved away the doubt. Perhaps Hugh had exaggerated, or perhaps the inn had fallen on hard times. None of that mattered. This was only temporary. She would find him, and everything would begin.

She had hoped the innkeeper might recognize his name—might even offer a knowing smile or promise to pass along a message. But that didn't happen. No matter. If Hugh wasn't here now, he would be soon. Or perhaps he was elsewhere in the city, busy with court matters.

If she couldn't find him here, she would go to the Cardinal's offices. Surely someone there would know him.

Two weeks passed.

Each morning, Emilie set off with a new lead, a new hope. And each night, she returned empty-handed. At Wolsey's offices at Westminster, she wasn't even allowed through the outer gate. The names Hugh had dropped in his stories—impressive at the time—brought nothing but shrugs or outright scoffs.

But Emilie held her ground. Let them laugh. Let them sneer. Soon enough, she would find Hugh, and he would welcome her—and their child—with open arms.

Still, her purse was thinning. The rooms at Forde's were far beneath the comfort even of The Dolphin, and the weather had turned. Cold seeped in through the floorboards.

Winter was coming. And she had not expected to be here so long.

Late one afternoon, Emilie returned to the inn tired and hollow. She had meant only to sit and rest a moment, but sleep claimed her where she lay, face pressed against the thin blanket.

She awoke with a start. A burst of laughter from below jarred her into blinking. The window had gone dark. From the rising volume beneath her feet, she could tell the common room was now packed—and raucous. Judging by the din, something was being celebrated.

Then she remembered: Hallowmas. Not a traditional time for merriment, but rowdy men needed little excuse.

She washed her face, re-pinned her hair, and straightened her dress as best she could, then stepped downstairs with a fluttering hope: perhaps Hugh had come to celebrate.

But the crowd was not what she'd hoped. These were not students or gentlemen travelers. No quiet conversation or thoughtful drinkers. These men shouted and jeered and clanked their mugs in rhythm to a bawdy song someone had started at a table. The air smelled of spilled ale and unwashed wool.

A Scot cried out, "Look at the lovely lass!" and a wave of invitations followed, each one louder and lewder than the last. She pushed through the bodies, eyes on the front door, dodging groping hands.

Then she stopped short. A memory: Hugh had once joked about this inn's lack of chess players. It had made her laugh. Perhaps someone here had played him?

She turned and pressed toward the counter where the innkeeper stood. "Excuse me," she called above the din.

He glanced up. "Can I get you something?"

"No, thank you. I was wondering—do any of your customers play chess?"

"What was that?"

"Chess! It's a game."

"Chest?"

"No—chess. Like checkers, but—"

"We've got a skittles court in the back."

"No, it has . . . strategy and—oh, never mind."

She turned again, squeezing toward the door. The idea of cutting back through the crowd toward the stairs flickered, but the thought of those hands again—no. The door was closer. Air. Quiet. Something other than this.

Outside, she breathed deeply, fog rising in the streetlamp haze. Without quite meaning to, she crossed the street, her feet taking her farther from the laughter behind her. She looked back.

This was supposed to be the place. Hugh had spoken of it often. But had he meant this exact inn? Maybe she had misremembered the name. Maybe she had come too early. What if a letter had arrived just after she left The Dolphin, asking her to meet him elsewhere?

She felt herself slipping, teetering at the edge of belief. Why was she even here? Why had she thought—

Then she saw him.

Like a spark against the night, a familiar stride—confident, quick—crossing the road toward Forde's Inn.

Her breath caught. She straightened, heart pounding. Hugh. He had come! Her fears vanished. Every ache dissolved into anticipation.

"Hugh!" she called, her voice rising in joy. "Hugh! Over here!"

He stopped and turned his head.

"It's me—Emilie! I've come!"

His shoulders fell. For a moment, he stood motionless. Then, without a word, he turned and entered the inn.

He must not have seen her clearly. It was dark. He hadn't been expecting her. She hurried across the street, hope still clutched in her chest.

Inside, the inn's noise met her like a wall. But she spotted him—tankard in hand, heading toward the back room.

"Hugh!" she cried again, forcing her way through. She reached him just as he opened the door.

"Hugh. I've come, Hugh. Just as we planned."

He turned, looked at her fully—and frowned.

"Go home," he said, flatly.

She blinked. "But . . . I've come."

"I told you to wait until I sent for you."

"I know. But I had to. I'm—Hugh, I'm going to have our baby."

He closed his eyes, sighed. "Emilie, we had a good time. Some laughs. That's all it was. A diversion."

She staggered back half a step. "But . . . the baby . . ."

"Tell you what," he said, half a grin tugging at his mouth. "You can keep it."

She reached toward the necklace at her throat. "But this—your mother's necklace—"

He laughed. A short, pitiless sound. Then he stepped inside and shut the door.

My dearest Emilie,

I do so miss you, my dear, dear sister. I received your note saying you had arrived, but its brevity left me concerned. I hope the city has not overwhelmed you. You'll remember our mother's half-sister, Olivia, lives in London—on Threadneedle. I have written to her to see whether you could pay her a visit. She may be able to assist you during your stay.

So much has occurred here; I hardly know where to begin. Truthfully, where to begin is not the problem. Rather, the difficulty is in how to tell you. A fire destroyed our inn. How it started, I do not know. I was asleep in the common room when the smoke awakened me. It began upstairs, and I could do nothing to stop its spread. Emilie, our dear brother could not be saved. Thomas was there, and despite his brave efforts, the building caved in over Matthew—Thomas barely escaping.

We held a service for Matthew. What could be said of his life? Misery followed him for years. Yet, misery was also his choice— just as it was our parents'—just as it had been becoming mine. Though I have yet to resolve to my mind's satisfaction how, or rather why, our good God allows evil to inflict us, Thomas has at least succeeded in making me realize that choosing to be overwhelmed by the evil is not the fault of God. I fear for you as well, Emilie. Do not allow whatever befalls you there to crush you in spirit. I am here for you and will always be.

I do not know if you have yet found Hugh. If you have and he has welcomed you, you may not accept what I must now tell. Believe me that it is no fabrication to turn you back, nor do I tell it for mere spite. I saw Hugh in Cambridge the day you left. I confronted him for his lack of communication to you, even telling him of his child that you carry. Not only did he dismiss you and your baby out of hand, but in his intoxicated state, he dragged me to the back room of an alehouse and did to me that of which I can hardly force myself to think, much less write.

Emilie, that man is evil. With all the love I have for you, I plead with you—avoid him!

Oh, Emilie, take care! I love you so, and wish you were back with me. One word and I'll come for you. Thomas and I both send our love. Roger is beyond despair.

Until we reunite, hopefully in happy circumstance, I remain forever and always—

Your loving sister
Joan

Emilie placed the letter on the bed beside her, staring at it without focus. After Hugh's rebuff, she had stumbled upstairs in agony. Flinging herself across the thin mattress, she had cried until dawn, her tears carving raw trenches through the last of her fantasies.

Late that morning, a knock at the door stirred her. Still dazed, she had rushed to open it—hoping, praying—but it was only the innkeeper with a letter.

She didn't think her pain could deepen.

But it did.

Reading of Matthew broke something fragile. She paused halfway through to wipe her eyes and press the letter against her chest.

But as she read on, something changed.

The sorrow drained slowly from her limbs—replaced by something colder. Sharper.

She fingered the necklace at her throat, then ripped it off.

No more tears.

No more trembling hopes.

Only venom. And a newborn heart of hate.

While Emilie remained at Forde's Inn, Hugh decided its familiarity was no longer worth the risk. An alehouse closer to the river would serve as well. The closer to the water, the lower the clientele—but even mingling with the dregs of London society was preferable now to crossing paths with Emilie. He found a place on Villiers Street known simply as Stone's—a dim, rough room with cracked beams, a crooked door, and little lighting beyond the hearth's flicker. But it was quiet enough in corners and noisy enough in crowds—perfect for private talk.

He sat there one evening with Richard.

"But are we sure he can be trusted?" Richard asked, lowering his voice though the surrounding clamor made it nearly impossible to be overheard. Despite being the day after Hallowmas, a fair number of regulars still raised tankards in half-hearted celebration.

Hugh narrowed his eyes. He hated being questioned, especially by Richard. He had spent two months traveling, making contact after contact, building layers of trust and deceit. Had Richard not seen that?

"Yes, Stephen Gardiner can be trusted," he said, voice low and edged. "Especially more than those Oxford snobs."

Richard nodded and leaned in again. "So the plan is what, exactly?"

"The same as it was two months ago," said Hugh, annoyed now. "Infiltrate. Separate. Destroy. Gardiner's ties in both canon and civil law will give us access. He'll introduce us to the Archbishop of Canterbury—Warham. Warham's no longer Lord Chancellor, but as archbishop, he still holds the ear of most of the Church."

"And assuming Warham's favorable?"

"Then he gathers bishops—saturates the hierarchy before making the move. The king finds himself surrounded before he can strike back."

Richard hesitated. "But if Warham isn't favorable—what if he exposes us?"

Hugh's grin was cold. "He won't. But if he does, I'll frame the entire thing as Gardiner's overreach. I'll pull back—express horror at the suggestion. At most, we lose Gardiner."

He leaned back, folding his arms, satisfied. "It's a good little plan."

Hugh didn't stay long. He had thinking to do—and socializing with Richard sat low on his list of pleasures. Once outside, he breathed deep and smiled. The Thames air was thick with damp rot, but to Hugh it was ambition filling his lungs. Everything was lining up.

"Hugh," said a voice from the shadows.

He turned. A hood covered her head, but he didn't need the light to know the voice.

"Ah, Emilie. How did you find me here?"

"Richard," she said evenly. "He came to the inn first before seeming to remember you'd changed venues. I followed him."

Hugh tilted his head. "I really must do something about Richard. Not too trustworthy, that one."

She took a step closer. "No. Not too trustworthy," she said. "I suppose you're the expert there."

He began to smirk, lowering his head—just enough so that he happened to catch the flicker of metal.

The knife came fast. But the faint glint gave enough warning for him to jerk sideways just enough. The blade sank under his ribs, not into his heart. Still, he screamed and dropped to the ground, clutching his side as blood spilled through his fingers.

But Emilie was not finished.

She lunged down at him, a blur of fury and tears. Her arm rose again, blade slashing toward him.

"You ruined me!" she shrieked. "You lied to me! You used me!"

He lifted an arm, blocking the strikes. One slashed his forearm, another tore his collar, a shallow cut bleeding down his cheek.

Richard burst from the alehouse and began pulling her away as she twisted and kicked, eyes wild, mouth forming curses.

Hugh staggered to his feet, breath ragged, face slicked in blood. His side throbbed, pain burning hot and deep.

"You bloody whore!" he howled. "I've wondered how to rid myself of you. Now you've made it easy."

Blood ran from his jawline where her blade had caught his face—a red slash from ear to chin.

"I'll see you dead!" Emilie spat, lunging forward before Richard restrained her again.

"You're the one who'll hang," Hugh growled, voice thick.

"I don't care," she shouted back. "I don't care if I hang! All I want is to live one moment longer than you—to hear that you are dead!"

Hugh took a step toward her—then stopped, sneered.

"Well, it seems you've failed in that."

She spat at him.

He slapped her. Hard.

The impact echoed off the stone walls.

He did not return to his rooms that night until the moon was low, and the blood had dried against his side. Emilie, still trembling in rage, sat in a stone cell beneath Newgate, her hands bruised, her face raw with tears. She had lost everything—but not her hatred.

8

When Love Redeems

NEWGATE'S GAOLERS MADE A lucrative trade of human misery. In a city without a formal police force, arrests were often carried out by whoever caught the criminal—neighbors, guardsmen, even common citizens. Once confined, prisoners fell entirely under the gaoler's care—and his price. The filth alone could kill you before your sentence did. And London's law favored the noose over mercy. Most crimes were capital; few awaited trial for long.

Inside Newgate, comfort came at a cost. A coin or two might loosen iron manacles or exchange them for lighter ones. More could buy a straw bed or the privilege of privacy. A silver shilling might summon a washwoman to chase off the lice. For those with means, prison became delay; for the poor, it was death row by starvation or plague.

The gaoler kept no books, owed no account. Money passed hand to hand—sometimes food, sometimes favors. Though Emilie had no friends in the city, she was young and pretty. That had value—until lice and filth stripped it from her. Then she would be of no use to anyone.

Letters could be sent—but only by those who could pay. One prisoner, kinder than most, added Emilie's note to her own. And so, days later, word reached Joan.

Roger had meant to ride out before, but the Dolphin's burning—and Cranmer's lameness from his fall—had left Joan with nothing but ash and fear. He could not abandon them until they were safe. Now, with a roof over her head and Cranmer able to move about, the letter from Emilie left no room for delay.

Roger paced the narrow room.

"Now I must go," he said. "I need a horse."

"You'll need money as well," Cranmer pointed out.

"I'm sure the Peningtons will lend us one," said Joan. "They live on Hills Road—the house with the stable, just north of St. Paul's?"

"Yes, yes. I know the one." Roger nodded. "Then I'm going."

"I want to come too," Joan said.

Roger shook his head. "I have to ride hard, and extracting her from that prison would be better handled by me alone. Besides, Thomas still needs you—he's not entirely mobile. Let me go quickly, and I'll return with her as soon as I can."

Joan relented. "Alright—but please hurry." She stepped into the back room and returned with a small bundle. "Clothes," she said. "Emilie may need them."

As the door shut behind him, Joan stood quiet a moment, then sank slowly into the chair by the window. Silence settled over the room, thick and unsparing. Her eyes stayed on the grain of the table, tracing it without focus.

"You know what passage I always come back to?" she asked suddenly. "It's in Job. Right at the beginning. One servant runs in with bad news. Then another. And another. His animals are gone, his workers, his children—all of it, one after the other. No time to breathe. Just . . . wave after wave.

Cranmer waited.

"That's what this feels like," she said. "Like someone planned it out. Like sorrow has a schedule." She shook her head. "And I still don't understand. I've asked a hundred ways—I still don't."

"You're allowed to ask," Cranmer said. "So did Job."

"But what was God's answer?"

"He showed Job the sky," Cranmer said. "He asked him if he'd set the stars in place. If he knew where the snow was stored. If he could tame a storm."

"So the answer was, 'I'm bigger than you'?" Joan asked.

Cranmer's voice softened. "The answer was, 'I see more than you.'"

Joan was quiet a long time. "And that's supposed to help?"

"No," Cranmer admitted. "Not right away."

She turned toward the window. "If I had the power to stop suffering—and didn't—you'd question me."

"I would," Cranmer said gently. "But . . . if we could see the whole story, Joan . . . maybe we'd judge differently."

She looked down at her hands, fingers clasped tight. "So he just sees more? Watches more? That's it?"

"God sees with purpose," Cranmer said. "A purpose born of pure love. I'm not that. I can't see like that. I'm not pure love. You're not love. God is."

She met his eyes. "But how can his love be different from ours—when he tells us to love like he does? How are we supposed to know how?"

Cranmer took a breath. "I'm not saying his love is different. But he acts from a broader vision. When we say to God, 'Love me now—give me what I think I need,' he sometimes must wait. Not because he's distant. But because he sees what we don't. Still, his love doesn't stand off. It doesn't just watch. His love enters our suffering with us. It stays. He doesn't turn away. He sees."

Joan stared past him toward the door. Her voice dropped to a whisper. "Then I hope he sees Emilie."

Cranmer said nothing. He only reached over and took her hand.

The closer he came to London, the harder Roger pushed his horse. But the beast, lathered and panting, grew numb to the digs of his heels and slowed anytime the urging ceased. Roger had been to London only once before, years ago—but he remembered Newgate Prison. Or he thought he did. Evening pressed in as the city swallowed him, lanterns flickering to life behind grime-streaked glass. He tried to trace his memory—had he come up Cheapside? From the west? No, perhaps he had turned—

He stopped at an intersection, reins slack. The horse tossed its head.

"Can you direct me to Newgate Prison?" he called to a passerby.

The man chuckled, jerking a thumb over his shoulder. "Turn east. Twenty yards. Can't miss it."

Roger looked left—and there it was. Cold stone rising like a blister from the street.

"Ah . . . thank you," he said—but the man had already disappeared into the crowd.

The building stood thick and brooding, like a fortress hunched over the misery it housed. Roger dismounted and spent the better part of a quarter hour banging on its thick door and pacing its perimeter until a bar finally clacked, opening the door, and a rough voice barked, "What is it?"

A squat man with a ring of keys and an air of annoyance stepped into view. "I'm the only one here," the gaoler grunted. "A little patience, please."

"I've come for one of your prisoners," Roger said, stepping closer. "Emilie Ladner. I've come to pay for her release. I need to see her."

A pause. A sniff. Then he pulled the door open a bit more. The gaoler stepped back to let Roger through, eyeing him carefully. "What was her name again? Can't just walk out with someone because you bang on the door after dark."

"Emilie Ladner. I need to see her," Roger pressed.

"All right, all right," the man muttered, eyeing Roger from boots to brow. The gaoler led him a few paces down a narrow corridor toward a table strewn with moldy papers and a sputtering candle. He made a slow show of flipping through them.

"What did you say her name was?"

"Ladner," Roger fairly shouted. "Emilie Ladner."

"Ladner, Ladner . . . woman, is she?"

"Yes, a woman," Roger snapped. "Young. Fair-haired. She's been here only a few days."

"Ah. Yes, I think I remember. Follow me."

The descent into the lower levels brought a sour stench and a crawling damp that soaked Roger's sleeves. They stopped at a heavy door. The gaoler drew a key from his belt, twisting it in the lock.

"Here now," he said, "I think this is the one."

The door swung open.

Roger rushed past him. In the corner, barely visible in the dimness, a crumpled bundle of clothing stirred.

"Emilie?" He knelt beside her. "Emilie, it's me."

She turned slowly, and in the weak light, he saw her face—smudged, hollow, eyes sunken. Her hair was matted against her cheeks. She looked up, and at the sound of his voice, recognition broke through. Her hands trembled as she clutched at him, and her body sagged forward.

"Roger," she gasped, clutching him. "Roger—I want to go home."

"You will, Emilie," he said, wrapping his arms around her. She didn't let go, even as he rose to his feet.

Turning to the gaoler, Roger said, "I'm taking her with me. What's your price?"

The gaoler sniffed. "She's here on a crime—murder or attempted, I think. Her accuser wouldn't be pleased if I just handed her over."

"Name your price."

The man rubbed his chin. "Let's see . . . her keep these past days, the paperwork, the risk . . ." He eyed Roger. "Twenty pounds. And that's a favor."

"Twenty . . . I don't have twenty pounds. I have . . . I have ten."

"You'll need more. Come back tomorrow with more."

"I have . . . I have a horse," Roger said.

The man raised an eyebrow. "And what would I do with a horse?"

"Sell it."

The gaoler rubbed his jaw again. "Don't get out much," he muttered. "Difficult to manage."

"Ten pounds and the horse. That's all I have."

The gaoler narrowed his eyes. He was no fool; he'd read many a desperate man and knew when a bluff had bottomed out.

"Ten and the horse," he said at last, "and that brooch." He pointed at Roger's collar.

Roger swallowed hard as his fingers lingered at his collar. The brooch had been his father's. But Emilie stood beside him, broken. There was no choice. "And the brooch," he said, unclasping it and letting it fall into the gaoler's hand. He also gave the pouch of silver. "The horse you saw outside."

"Done," said the gaoler.

Emilie shifted more securely in his arms, and they headed out.

On the street, she stumbled, dropping to her knees. Roger swept her back up, cradling her like a child. She felt like a husk—light as paper, but all the heavier for what she'd borne.

"Where . . . where will we go?" Emilie murmured. "No money . . . no horse . . . no one here . . ."

"Don't worry," he said, with a trace of a smile. "I still have ten pounds. I only *said* I gave everything. He believed it when I threw in the horse."

Emilie breathed an "Ah," as she relaxed in Roger's arms.

"We'll find an inn. You'll wash, eat, sleep. Then we'll make for Cambridge, tomorrow or the next day—whenever you're ready."

"Roger, I'm sorry," she whispered.

"No. None of that now."

She tilted her head toward him, her voice barely audible. "Joan?"

"She's safe, she's fine," he said. "She misses you. She would've come, but I wanted to get here fast."

Emilie's body sagged against him again. "He . . . what he did to her . . . I wish I'd killed him."

"What?"

"She didn't tell you? Roger . . . he hurt her."

Roger faltered. "Tell me."

And she did—haltingly, weakly, her voice trembling, cracking, tears threading through each broken phrase. It was slow, and hard, and the horror of it grew in him as she went on.

They reached an inn just as Roger's arms began to fail. He paid for two rooms, ordered food and a bath. Emilie washed and dressed in silence, ate just enough to satisfy Roger's insistence, and finally, in the bed's embrace, let herself sink into warmth and stillness.

As she settled in, she looked up at him, eyes wide and shadowed. "Don't leave."

"I won't," he said from the chair, watching over her.

My sweet Joan,

How can I ever thank you? You were so good to me—so good—when I was thinking only of myself. I can't bear to think of what you went through because of me. Every time I close my eyes, I see it all again. But worse than the horror is the ache I feel knowing you suffered because I was blind. Forgive me, Joan.

Roger—dear Roger—he pulled me out of that nightmare. We meant to return to Cambridge, but . . . I can't. The baby—yes, it's true—won't let me. I'm meant to rest, the doctor says, and so I shall. I've barely left the bed.

Roger found a little place we might move to once I'm strong enough. He's fixing it up now—he won't let me lift a finger.

Oh, Joan, I wish I could see you! I miss you terribly. But I know it's far, and I wouldn't ask it. Just—know that I love you, and I swear I'll listen to your wisdom from now on. I've learned too much to do otherwise.

With all my heart,
Emilie

Joan was alone when the letter arrived. Seven torturous days had passed since Roger left—seven days of pacing, of false starts, of waiting for word. She had replayed the imagined timeline over and over: one day to travel, one day to negotiate Emilie's release, one to prepare, two days to return. By now, they should have arrived—yesterday at the latest.

The moment she recognized the London postmark, her hands trembled. She tore open the letter, hardly breathing. Relief flooded her as she scanned the opening lines. Emilie was alive. Safe. Recovering.

But before she reached the end, her resolve took shape. She would go to London.

She rose from the table, mind already racing through preparations. But her body did not follow.

A wave of dizziness overtook her. She blinked, swayed.

And then, before her foot could find its next step, the world tilted, and Joan collapsed—her body limp upon the floor.

Her eyes fluttered open.

In the hush of evening, shadows played across the ceiling, and the pale glow from a single lamp fell upon the still figure seated at her bedside. Thomas Cranmer. His hands gently enclosed one of hers, and as she stirred, he leaned in.

"What . . . what happened?" Her voice was dry, barely above a whisper. "I . . . was reading . . ."

"The letter from Emilie, yes," Cranmer said softly. "You fainted. You've been asleep since midday. The physician came. He said you're resting well."

Joan blinked, slowly remembering. Then, as if startled from a dream, she tried to rise. "I have to go . . . to London . . . to Emilie."

"Joan, wait—listen." He pressed her hand a little more firmly. "Emilie is resting, confined to her bed, recovering from her . . . from the strain of all she's been through. She's safe, and in no immediate danger."

He hesitated, drawing a breath. "But the physician said something else. Something unexpected."

She turned toward him again, her brow furrowed.

"He believes . . . he believes you may be in the same condition."

She stared. "What . . . what do you mean?"

Still holding her hand, he tried to ease the words out gently. "He thinks you may be with child."

"With . . ." Her voice caught. She blinked once, then again, as if the words needed to be shaken into meaning. "With child?" Her hand moved unconsciously to her stomach. "I'm . . . pregnant?"

"It's not certain," he said. "But there's no other explanation he could find for your fainting . . . for your symptoms. And the timing . . . it does seem to fit with . . ." His voice faltered. "With what happened. Weeks ago. With Hugh."

The name burned within her. She turned her face away, pressing her hand to her mouth.

"Joan . . ." Thomas began, but she was already weeping.

"What now?" she whispered. "What now?" The question spilled out with rising panic. "What . . . what am I supposed to do?"

Thomas bowed his head. His grip on her hand did not loosen. The moment was too full, too fragile for anything less than truth.

"Joan," he said, steadying his voice. "We've shared so much these months—talked, argued, laughed, cried. I've seen your courage. I've felt your sorrow. And I've come to know something as true as anything I've ever known."

He looked up and met her eyes. "I love you."

She tried to pull her hand away, shaking her head. "Thomas . . . don't. We haven't . . . we haven't spoken of this. Not like this. Not under these circumstances. Don't let this child—not even yours—force you into anything."

"We are not forced," he said, gently holding her hand fast. "You're not forcing me. This child is not forcing me. I know my heart."

She turned her head to the wall, but he pressed on.

"Life does not wait for tidy timing. It throws storms at us—and we try to stand. Sometimes we stumble forward instead of standing still. But even in the storm, sometimes we get to choose who we take with us." He moved closer. "Joan, I choose you. Not because of what happened. Because I love you. Would you let me give you my name, my life—completely?"

Her eyes brimmed again, but the tears this time were not from grief.

"Your fellowship," she whispered. "You'd lose it."

He smiled faintly. "Perhaps. Perhaps not. But if that's the price for being yours, I'll pay it without regret."

He brought her hand to his chest, holding it there. "So now, with no other concern—forgetting everything but this one truth—will you marry me, Joan Ladner?"

She stared at him, at the quiet fire in his gaze, at the promise behind it.

And something in her—something long buried under ashes and loss—began to breathe again.

She nodded slowly, then spoke aloud the words her heart had long whispered:

"Yes, Thomas. I will marry you."

He smiled, bent forward, and kissed her gently.

And in that moment, with pain behind and hope before, they were complete.

9

Blowing in the Wind?

Several days later, Cranmer sat in the office of William Capon, Master of Jesus College. This was only Capon's first year as Master, but he had been at Cambridge (St. Catharine's Hall) since the 1490s as a student and then professor.

Cranmer had just concluded highlighting the events of the past few weeks and then divulged his intention to marry.

Master Capon stood at his window gazing out for a moment in thought. Then he said, "I had heard about the fire. Very much a shame. I had, in fact, also heard of this Ladner family previously. On more than one occasion I have had to discuss an issue of dedication with Master Cressy. His involvement with Emilie Ladner has put a strain on his work here."

"I have tried to urge him toward his studies in the past."

"Hmm. Yes, well . . ." He turned from the window. "While I must admit your explanation provides a more reasonable point of view for his actions, I am afraid that we are going to be withdrawing Master Cressy's fellowship. The missing of classes, both those of his study and those he teaches, is now too much. *Your* performance, however, has been exemplary . . . to this point." He sat down.

"Now, this other Ladner sister . . . this Joan—is she the one they call 'Black Joan'?"

"Uh, yes, well, that appellation her sister gave her for . . . moodiness."

"I see," said Capon, nodding in thought. "Some would think that the story of this Hugh Chedsey swooping in to seduce one sister and then flying away would, perhaps, provide an easy cover for the other sister's condition as well."

"A cover?" Cranmer asked.

"A cover, yes . . . an innocent excuse for a perhaps not so innocent affair."

Cranmer was astounded. He stood as he replied. "You believe I am inventing this heinous rape as a cover to my own . . ."

"Please, Master Cranmer. I am not accusing you of attempting to delude me. I wish only to ensure that it is not you who is being deluded. You did not see the . . . rape, correct? You heard of it only from this other Ladner sister. . . from . . . this Black Joan. You have known her now four . . . five months?"

Indignant, Cranmer argued, "She would not . . ."

Again, Capon interrupted. "Once more, I do not accuse anyone. Please sit down. But think for a minute how this may look. A woman you did not know existed four months ago, becomes a friend, becomes pregnant, looks to you—a kind, righteous soul—and you . . . you offer marriage, casting aside your fellowship, your studies, your planned life . . . everything. Would an honest woman in love lead her beloved away from all he had held as dear and important in his life? On the other hand, could a woman who would wish to so lead a man from his life possibly be less than honest in the story she told to influence him?"

Cranmer shook his head. "No, Joan would not create this deception. I have known her for only a short time, it is true. But she did not pursue me, nor I her. She is not dishonest in this."

"Very well," said Capon. "It is after all a matter for you alone to decide. I believe it my duty, however, to urge you to consider what others may think concerning the propriety of your actions."

Cranmer remained silent.

After a moment and not receiving a response, Capon continued along a different tack. "Tell me, Master Cranmer, why did you provide me so much detail of the Ladner family misfortunes prior to announcing your coming marriage? Are you marrying because of the tragedies heaped on this Ladner woman or because you truly believe this marriage to be the will of God?"

"I . . . I believe this to be God's will, yes."

"And . . . your schooling here. Did you believe that to be God's will as well?"

Cranmer paused. "My schooling? I . . . yes . . . I believe it to have been God's will."

"But surely you understand that should you marry, you will forfeit your fellowship. How can you believe it God's will for you to be here and at the same time believe it God's will to forfeit your fellowship so that you cannot teach here?"

Again Cranmer paused. He had not prepared for a debate. He had expected only a decision of whether he could continue in his fellowship though married. But Capon was attempting to cast doubt concerning God's blessing of his decision to marry.

"Master Capon," Cranmer began, "we read the Holy Scriptures, we pray to our Lord for guidance, and then we move as we believe God would have us move. I have read God's Word. I have prayed for leading. I believed God wanted me here at this place. And now I believe God would have me marry. I have no other argument."

"Very well, then. Should you decide other than your present course, you will remember that we usually extend a year of grace to those who voluntarily withdraw," said Capon dryly. He would not waste more time. "I am sorry to see you go. But I wish you well."

"Thank you, sir."

"Good day."

Joan could not believe it. Her irritation roiled as Cranmer recounted the interview.

"You should have told him that since it was God's will for you to be at Jesus and God's will for you to marry, that he was obligated to follow God's will to allow you to keep your fellowship! How dare he question your understanding of God's leading in your life!"

Joan was feeling better.

They arranged a very small ceremony—only a priest, the Peningtons, and a couple university friends were in attendance. They planned to marry and depart for London the same day. Joan had written to her aunt explaining that she had need to be in London for a while. Her aunt graciously had invited her to stay at her home. Her second husband was a banker, a profession only recently established in England. They lived close to The Change near the other money handlers.

Cranmer had obtained employment as a lecturer at Buckingham Hall. Though the pay was very little, it would at least provide something. He would take Joan to London and see Emilie and Roger. Then he would leave her at her aunt's residence and return to Cambridge to his employment. Either when Emilie could travel or after she gave birth, they would all return to Cambridge.

As Cranmer helped Joan into the cart, he glanced for the thousandth time at the sky—still as bright a blue as he could wish for. The journey to London would probably take them a full two days, possibly three if the bumpy ride and Joan's on and off again illness happened to coincide. He climbed in beside her on the second bench seat.

Joan squeezed his hand and smiled while the Peningtons waved their goodbyes. One of the Peningtons' horses was tethered behind the cart for Cranmer's journey back. The driver slapped the reins, causing the cart to jerk forward, and the newlywed couple spent the rest of their wedding day bouncing along on the road to London.

They made fairly good time the first day, better able to accept the rough ride with the joys of wedded bliss filling their thoughts. They spent their wedding night at the same inn at which Emilie and Master Penington had stopped on their trip to London several weeks earlier. And although they woke in the morning still very much in love, rising from the bed gave them immediate reminders of the previous day's jolting ride. Bruised and aching muscles challenged their resolve to be in London by late that afternoon. With a quick breakfast, however, they were underway again.

"Thomas?" Joan asked after settling in to the travel as best they could. "I was wondering about after we return to Cambridge. We haven't thought much beyond my visit to Emilie and the birth of her child. But what then?"

"What then?" Cranmer repeated. He half shrugged his shoulders. "Then . . . we continue. We concentrate on our own child."

Joan paused to smile. He amazed her in his goodness. He had already accepted her baby in his heart to be his own.

"Yes, I am in love with our family," she said. "But, I was wondering about . . . other things—where we would live . . . how we would live. You know that what you are paid for lecturing could hardly support yourself alone."

They rode in silence for a few moments. Cranmer had always lived frugally and had expected frugal living would keep them afloat. A place to live? He had assumed they would live at the house Joan was now renting. But, of course, he knew her inheritance money could not last forever—and it was half Emilie's.

"How much is the house you now have?" he asked.

She looked at him and smiled, though her brow furrowed a bit. "It is an interesting coincidence," she said, "that the rent and your monthly pay are almost equal. If we did not need food and a piece of cloth now and then, we could be content."

"I could find other work," said Cranmer.

"*I* could find other work," she replied. "I've done it all my life. I can find a kitchen that will pay me."

"Waltham!" Cranmer said suddenly. "I can get a position in Waltham through Roger's uncle."

"Waltham? Why . . . "

"Roger mentioned this to me before. Of course without a fellowship, he will be leaving Cambridge. He plans to secure some appointment through his uncle in Waltham. And he may likely take Emilie with him, if she'll have him now. That first day I ever met you he had told me that if I should marry you, he would have his uncle find a position for me as well. I cannot believe now how prophetic his words have come to be."

"Waltham," Joan said. "Hmm. I could still work in a kitchen there."

"But you don't know yet whether we will need it. I'm sure we will be able to get along."

"Thomas," Joan said, "more than anything, I want to put aside money so that someday you may return to your studies whether they allow you a fellowship or not. Whatever you earn in a Waltham position can be augmented by what I can earn. And someday, it will be enough."

Now it was Cranmer's turn to be overcome by Joan's heart.

"Joan, I chose you over my fellowship because I wanted you. This is God's way—his will. You can rest in this. I'm going to follow it with all my heart."

"I can't believe my sister is married before me." Emilie laughed as she embraced Joan. The two women clung tightly, the moment filled with the joy of reunion and the hush of sorrow not far behind.

They had arrived in London the night before and found modest lodging in an inn not far from Emilie's house. Now, in the morning light, they sat beside one another—Joan slightly flushed from the bumpy journey, Emilie propped against pillows with her hands resting over her swelling belly.

"How are you feeling?" Joan asked, smoothing Emilie's covers as she settled beside her.

"Halfway there," Emilie said, smiling faintly. "Not worse, not better. But better now—with you here. How long will you stay?"

"Until you come home with us," Joan said. "Thomas leaves tomorrow, but I'll be nearby. Aunt Olivia has offered her house."

"Well, at least for now," Emilie said, with a knowing glance. "She doesn't yet know all the circumstances, does she?"

Joan shook her head. "No. But she will." She took Emilie's hand and squeezed it. "We're not hiding anything."

Emilie nodded and blinked away sudden tears. "You really have forgiven me."

"Oh, Emilie—"

Before Joan could finish, Roger bounded into the room, all grins and arms wide. "Together again at last!" he crowed, kissing Emilie's forehead and hugging Joan. Then he turned to Cranmer, clapping him on the shoulder. "And you, my friend! Married and everything!"

Cranmer smiled, subdued but warm. "Good to see you again, Roger."

"Oh! And news!" Roger's voice dropped, dramatic. "Guess who's rotting just across the way, locked in the Tower?"

They stared.

"Hugh Chedsey," he announced, "arrested for treason. Caught redhanded by none other than Stephen Gardiner."

"What?" Emilie gasped, paling.

"Gardiner set a trap. Lured him in with promises of support—then had him reveal his whole delusional plot to Archbishop Warham. He even had designs on Spain helping him rule! The fool thought he'd start a revolt and come out king."

Joan's face darkened. "So all that talk in Cambridge—none of it was real."

"Oh, it was real," Cranmer said grimly. "Just not the part we thought."

Roger walked to the window and pointed toward Tower Hill. "When they bring him out, we'll hear it from here. The whole execution."

Joan's eyes went distant. "I don't want to see it," she whispered. "But I want to know it's done."

There was silence—the kind shaped by pain now soothed.

Then she spoke again. "He was like smoke. Slipping through every-thing. Until now."

Over the next four months Roger spent most of his time back and forth between Emilie and Joan, who, like her sister, did not handle pregnancies so well. The first month had not been so bad with Joan living at Aunt Olivia's and still well enough to be of some help to Emilie. When Aunt Olivia finally learned the way each of her nieces got pregnant, she politely but firmly thought it best that Joan find other living arrangements. Her husband frequently entertained business clients, and it just wouldn't do for this kind of news to be bandied about. Roger made arrangements at an inn close by where Joan could stay.

Cranmer was able to visit three times in those few months. On one of those visits, Roger and Emilie were quietly married, wishing to welcome their child into a proper home. Joan had become completely bedridden just prior to Cranmer's last stay, from which, therefore, he did not return to Cambridge.

"Tomorrow," Roger said as Cranmer showed him in to their rooms. "Hugh is scheduled for execution tomorrow."

"I now wish I could attend," said Joan weakly from the bed.

"I wish I could swing the axe," said Roger.

"How is Emilie?" Cranmer asked.

"I think okay now. She started labor, and I called the midwife, but it turned out to be too early. I've got to get back. The midwife is there now, but she'll be wanting to go."

It was on the following day that the crowds began to form on Tower Hill. Emilie went into labor again, and Roger sent word to the midwife.

Through her window, Emilie heard the crowd milling about. And so did Cranmer from the living area. Joan was sleeping peacefully, so he had come to keep Roger company while he waited. He had also been drawn by some strange curiosity to the execution preparation across the way of this man whom they had known personally for only a couple of days, yet who had so profound an effect on their lives. This man of de-ception, pride, lust, and violence—surely he deceived even himself. But then Cranmer wondered about the choices all of them made. They all claimed to follow God, and yet. . . . He himself had told Master Capon with sincere conscience that he believed it God's will to marry. Did he also commit the fraud? Did he also, when desiring something so much, justify it to himself by merely labeling it God's will? How did he know what God's will really was? Could he even have been mistaken about his attendance at Jesus College? Yes, he studied theology, but did that automatically make it God's will?

Joan's questions mingled with these in his heart. They also touched on the will of God but taken from the opposite direction. Rather than wonder about God's will in the choices made in life, she wondered at God's will in the happenstance of life. Why was it so hard to understand?! If God cared for them so much as to create, to save, to foster relationship . . . why was understanding his will such a mystery?

The afternoon arrived with a heavy heat. Inside Emilie's house, the air was thick and unmoving. Emilie's labor had begun in earnest by midday.

Joan, resting in her room across the street, lay in fitful sleep.

Cranmer sat with Roger in the front room while the midwife worked in hushed determination behind the closed door. Emilie's cries came in waves—brief, then sharper, then long and strained.

Suddenly, a scream.

They both leapt to their feet. But when Roger took a step, Cranmer's hand to his shoulder advised restraint.

"Perhaps wait," he suggested "The midwife's not calling. Let her finish."

More time passed in fitful pacing.

Then—another sound. Not a scream this time, but the clear, startled cry of a baby.

Moments later, the midwife opened the door fully. She looked tired but smiled. "A boy," she said. "Mother's weak, but she'll recover."

Roger rushed in, and Cranmer followed more slowly.

Emilie, pale and drenched with sweat, turned her head as they entered. Her eyes locked onto Roger.

"You're here," she whispered.

He moved to her side and kissed her forehead. "Of course, I'm here! You did it."

She gave the faintest smile. "He's beautiful."

The baby mewled in the midwife's arms. She handed him gently to Emilie, who cradled him, weary but luminous.

Cranmer stood back, smiling.

"I must tell Joan," he said softly.

He crossed the narrow lane to the inn, feeling a rare buoyancy in his chest. But as he stepped inside, that joy vanished.

He heard it first—a low cry, then a gasp.

He rushed into the room.

Joan lay on the bed, trembling, her face white, her hands clutching her belly.

He ran to her. "Joan?"

Her eyes were wild. "Is it done?" she gasped. "Is he dead?"

"No," Cranmer cried out. "He's fine and well." But then he quickly realized Joan did not mean the child but rather the loathsome villain across the Tower yard.

A long moan ripped from her throat. "It's coming. Thomas, it's happening now."

Confused again, Cranmer dropped to his knees beside the bed, realizing Joan was speaking of her own child now.

"It's too early!" Cranmer tried to reason, but Joan's contortions sent him dashing out and back across the street. "The midwife!" he cried. "Come now!"

"Another birth?" she asked, startled.

"Yes. Hurry."

The midwife looked at Emilie and then to Roger, "She's resting. I'll be quick."

Joan's screams began as the midwife gathered her things.

Outside, across the square, the gates at the Tower clanged open. The murmuring swelled.

Joan moaned again, curling forward.

The midwife burst into the room and took command, sending Cranmer to fetch water, cloths, anything useful. Joan's contractions came fast and hard—too fast.

"No," the midwife whispered. "It's too early . . ."

But there was no stopping it.

Outside, the crowd shifted.

The block waited.

Inside, Joan screamed.

"Push now!" the midwife cried. "I see the head!"

Joan arched, eyes wide, breath seizing in her throat.

From the window, she heard him: "I die today not for sin, but for faithfulness," and knew he lied.

The executioner raised the axe.

A newborn's cry rang out, thin and sudden.

Then—outside—the dull, final thud.

Cranmer turned in hope.

Joan lay motionless now, with a soft struggle in her breath. Her eyes were half closed, but she lifted one hand toward Cranmer who took it in both his.

"For all this," she whispered, barely audible, "I love you more." Her hand went limp as her eyes closed, and her breath faded away.

The midwife leaned close, fingers at her neck. She said nothing—only turned, and gently placed the infant girl beside her mother's still body.

Cranmer collapsed to his knees.

And from outside, the silence closed in.

Cranmer sat in the common room of the inn. They had held the brief funeral that morning. Few attended. Aunt Olivia came, but only for a moment before bustling back to her life. They laid her then in her grave. Joan—his love, his wife. He wept again. Her image was constantly before him. Her dark tresses on the pillow framing her face of so much beauty interwoven with so much misery—layers of joy entwined with layers of grief.

He could not sit still. He moved without conscious direction and found himself across the road and approaching Tower Hill.

The hill that had been filled with so many was empty now. He found himself on top of the mound itself, just below the platform newly stained with Hugh's blood. For some reason again he had been drawn to this man—the man who had destroyed the most important person in his life.

The will of God—what was it? Capon's words came back to him—*how can you believe it God's will for you to be here and at the same time believe it God's will to forfeit your fellowship so that you cannot teach here?* Was it God's will for Joan to die thus laying the path for him to return to Cambridge? Then with a shudder he realized that this was the exact argument he had presented to Joan almost a year ago on their second meeting. He had once told her that his father's death had been part of God's plan—to steer him from Oxford to Cambridge.

Earlier he could not be still from grief. Now he could not move. From deep within, a cry rose up. It burst from his heart and shattered the still air. He had not wanted to sacrifice Joan! But had this draw to Hugh been his subconscious way of escape? Had he recognized in him the only means to alter the path he had chosen away from Cambridge—away from . . . God? No. No! Not Joan! Not love. He would not believe that Joan stood between him and God. It was Joan who had turned his thoughts to deeper relationship even with God through these weeks. But why did the pleasures God created always seem contrary to chosen paths when considering his will?!

Cranmer sat. His eyes fixed on a dandelion, all white with seed, and he remembered a picnic. He remembered Joan wondering about God and purpose, plucking a dandelion and blowing its seeds. He pulled the dandelion and blew. The wispy white floated, meeting the sky above him. He wondered again, as Joan had once asked, why God made such beauty to let it break apart.

Later, the decisions came swiftly. With Emilie still recovering and caring for her newborn son, and Cranmer heading back to Jesus College to resume his fellowship, it was agreed that Joan's newborn daughter would join Roger and Emilie's new family.

They had named Emilie's boy William, for Emilie's (and Joan's) father. The girl, born in shadow yet bright with fierce life, would be called Joanna.

She had dark hair, like her mother's, and a brow that already seemed to furrow in thought. Cranmer had held her once—just once—before giving her into Emilie's arms, afraid that holding her longer might make letting go impossible. She blinked up at him with a stillness he knew too well. She would ask questions one day, he thought. Deep ones. Hard ones. She would carry her mother's spirit forward.

Cranmer accompanied Roger and Emilie to Waltham, where Roger's uncle had arranged a position. But then Cranmer took his leave, promising to write. Roger and Emilie, each cradling a child, stood watching him go. Cranmer paused to take in the scene, waved, and with a deep breath, he nodded once to himself before turning toward the road to Cambridge.

He had chosen for love. And though grief still followed, he would carry it with purpose.

PART 2
Thomas Cromwell

I loved—but those I loved are gone;

Had friends—my early friends are fled:

How cheerless feels the heart alone,

When all its former hopes are dead!

Though gay companions o'er the bowl

Dispel awhile the sense of ill;

Though pleasure stirs the maddening soul,

The heart—the heart—is lonely still.

Lord Byron from *I Would I Were a Careless Child*

10

Summoned

SOME SAY THAT TIME heals all wounds. But time does not deserve the credit. It is not that time heals, but that time buries. The countless events, conversations, and daily urgencies that crowd the mind slowly press the past beneath their weight. Memory becomes layered—shrouded more than erased. But for Thomas Cranmer, Joan remained not a shadow to be covered, but a form beneath the surface that still shaped the terrain above.

Though her voice had softened in his thoughts over the years, though her image sometimes came half-formed at morning light, the impression she had left on his soul was permanent. She had not merely touched his life—she had re-formed its contours for him. Love had introduced him to the questions that no study could silence.

Cranmer had long believed that God—the almighty Creator—was both real and active in the course of human lives, down to the hidden turns of thought and impulse. But Joan's questions, which had become his own, gnawed deeper than mere theology. Why would a God of power allow evil to prosper? Why would a God of love allow those he loves to suffer? These were not challenges to faith; they were provocations to seek. And Cranmer had resolved that his life—whatever shape it took—would be bent toward finding the answers.

Jesus College welcomed him back, reinstating him as fellow without hesitation. He completed his Doctor of Divinity soon after, and at last received Holy Orders. A priest now, sworn to the Catholic Church, whose lifeblood pulsed still from Rome. And yet, that same year—the year of Joan's death—a German monk named Martin Luther nailed his own questions—formalized as theses—to a church door in Wittenberg, and the world began to shift.

In England, the tremors came more quietly. In Cambridge, a "Little Germany" of Augustinian friars began meeting, whispering of reformation. Cranmer sometimes attended. He rarely spoke. He only listened.

His interest was not in protest but in understanding. He found himself drawn increasingly to the Scriptures, to their rhythm and logic and startling clarity. By the time he was appointed University Examiner in Divinity, his knowledge of the Bible surpassed that of many who had taught him. He would pass no candidate who could not reason from the Word.

But Scripture also began to disturb him. Not with contradiction, but with what it left unsaid. The primacy of Rome, so loudly insisted upon in every homily and confession, was startlingly absent from his understanding of the New Testament text. He realized it, quietly. He did not speak of it. He only folded it into his slow, deliberate process of belief. Joan had taught him that truth was not a thing to chase, but a thing to uncover—layer by layer, without fear.

He moved forward, as he always had: carefully. Slowly. But the axis of his heart had tilted. Her voice, long silenced, had never stopped shaping the questions he asked.

The knock came just as Cranmer reached to turn the page of his Psalter. He paused, one hand resting lightly on the open book, wondering who would be calling so late.

He crossed the room slowly and pulled open the door.

"Ha! I knew you'd still look the same—pale, scholarly, and surprised by real people!" Roger Cressy grinned from the threshold, arms open and sweeping Cranmer into embrace.

"Roger!" Cranmer exclaimed once released. "You should have written," he said, half rebuke, half warmth.

Roger stepped back, grinning. "And miss the look on your face? Not a chance."

Cranmer looked him over—older, yes, but not diminished. The old energy was still there, flickering just under the surface. The weight of years had shifted Roger's balance from bounding to grounded, but not changed the man himself.

"Still, I hope we're not a disruption."

"You were never a disruption—are never a disruption," Cranmer said firmly. Then, "'We' you say?" peering around.

Roger shifted aside, revealing the young man behind him.

"Yes! This strapping lad is Will. He's not so tall as me yet, but he's twice as stubborn."

Will bowed. "It's an honor to meet you properly, Master Cranmer."

Cranmer took a moment before speaking. The boy before him was no longer a blur of memory. Will stood with quiet confidence, hands clasped behind his back, eyes alert. His features held something of Emilie's delicacy, but it was Roger's posture he carried—shoulders straight, jaw set just so.

"Ah! Will! Good to see you. You carry yourself like your father," Cranmer said at last.

Will nodded, almost bowing again.

"This is a happy surprise," Cranmer smiled. "What brings you now?"

Will spoke up immediately. "I am interested in schooling on a more advanced level. I wanted to visit Cambridge—Jesus College. My father has spoken of it so much."

"Hm. And you still wanted to come," Cranmer laughed.

"Yes. And also Oxford. We've planned to head there after our visit here. I've been reading about Wolsey. He started in Oxford."

Cranmer's smile deepened. "Yes, he did—Magdalen College. But don't underestimate Cambridge. We have our own notables—Erasmus, Latimer."

Will nodded, visibly pleased.

"Come," Cranmer said, stepping back. "There's warm bread left from dinner. And I'd rather talk in the light than in the doorway."

Will moved ahead, eager, but Cranmer held Roger gently at the arm as he passed.

"Emilie?"

"Well," Roger said. "A bit theatrical, as ever. But content. She sends her greetings."

Cranmer hesitated a moment, glancing toward the door. "And . . . Joanna?"

Roger caught the look. "She stayed at home with Emilie. This trip was more for Will."

Cranmer nodded. "Of course."

But his posture softened—less rigid. The question had been genuine.

Roger watched Will disappear down the hall and exhaled, smiling faintly.

"He wanted to see Cambridge. Wanted to meet you. See what it means to live where decisions are made."

Cranmer's eyes lingered in the direction the boy had gone.

"He'll find the world usually resists shaping," he said.

Roger clapped his shoulder. "I hope he tries anyway."

They'd eaten simply—cheese, bread, a pot of stewed pears leftover from the midday table—but the conversation had lingered long after the plates were cleared. Will had taken to Cranmer's study with a kind of reverence, nearly forgetting to excuse himself in his eagerness to explore.

Now the older men sat by the hearth, the candlelight playing in the lines beside their eyes. Cranmer stretched his legs out toward the fire.

"He's a fine boy," Cranmer said at last, tilting his head toward the other room. "Eager. Polite. And already scanning the world for his place in it."

Roger leaned back in his chair, one leg thrown over the other. "He's always been that way. Eyes ahead. Never liked being told 'later.' Still doesn't."

"You've done well with him."

Roger gave a small laugh. "That's kind of you. But it's mostly Emilie. She keeps the household in motion. I just try not to trip over it."

Cranmer glanced toward the doorway, voice lowering slightly. "There's a discipline in him I didn't expect."

Roger nodded. "He's precise. Orderly. Sometimes too much so. He insists on being called 'Will' now—nothing boyish. Says 'William' sounds self-important, but 'Will' is strong. Has ideas about how grown men should speak. Even calls me Master Cressy when he wants to make a point."

Cranmer raised a brow. "Truly?"

Roger chuckled. "You'll see."

There was a pause—comfortable, but with tension humming beneath.

Cranmer shifted. "And Joanna?"

Roger's face changed with a quiet tenderness.

"She's—remarkable. Actually, we call her 'Jo.' Looks like Joan. Same dark brows, same walk—you'd see it in a heartbeat. But it's the way she thinks that stops me. Quiet, but not passive. Watches everything. She doesn't just ask questions—she lives with them. Carries them around, weighs them, waits. It's not like Emilie or me. She's not like us."

Cranmer listened, gaze low.

"She knows everything," Roger went on. "About Joan. About Hugh. We never kept it hidden. Emilie said we owed her the truth—and Jo's always known what to do with truth once she has it."

Cranmer nodded slowly. "She must ask about her mother."

"Often. But not the kind of things we can answer. She wants to know how Joan thought—why she spoke as she did. That kind of knowing. And that—well, that's more your territory than mine, or even Emilie's, though she's her sister."

Cranmer's voice was quiet. "Yes, she sounds like her mother." Then, "I'd like to see her."

Roger replied without hesitation. "Then come to Walthamstow. I was going to invite you. A few days after this business here is done would be perfect. Emilie would be glad for it. Jo too, I think."

Cranmer offered a faint smile. "I'll see if I'm able. But yes—I'd like to."

Will burst back through the doorway, face alight.

"Master Cressy! You didn't tell me there were this many books!"

Roger blinked, then broke into a grin. Cranmer turned, amused more by the tone than the content.

Roger raised an eyebrow at Cranmer. "See? Told you."

Will stepped further into the room, addressing Cranmer now. "I expected to see this in one of the colleges' libraries—but not in your own home. It's incredible. You have manuscripts in Greek. And volumes I've never even heard of. Erasmus, of course—but also Hilary of Poitiers and . . . someone named Hugh of St. Victor?"

"Hugh's a favorite," Cranmer said, his tone warming. "A master of clarity, even when he's wrong."

Will laughed. "I'd like to read more of him. May I?"

"Of course," Cranmer said, nodding toward the shelves. "They're meant to be read."

Will turned to go again, already vanishing back into the room of leather and vellum and cracked bindings.

Roger leaned over to Cranmer and admitted, "I surely thought he would set his sights on our lords of court. Actually, I still think so. Will is ambitious, and I'm not sure whether his interest in religion is on his compass heading toward God or the king."

"Speaking of court," Cranmer said, "I received a letter just the other day from Thomas Cromwell, saying he was to pay me a visit."

"Cromwell?" Roger repeated. "He rose under Wolsey, didn't he? I know the name—runs things now, or so we hear. Hard to keep track of who's actually in charge these days. Waltham's close enough to Westminster to catch the echoes but far enough that everything's third or fourth hand. Still—if Cromwell ever wants you to call on him, you come stay with us."

Roger stood, stretching. "Well, Will will probably be at those books till the candles burn out."

Cranmer stared down the hallway for a moment.

"I hope they last."

The morning sun struck the chapel roof at a low angle, turning the slate a pale silver. Will kept a half-step ahead, his eyes roving from stone inscription to ironwork to creeping ivy. Cranmer had begun with the sacred—the chapel, then the scholar's hall—and now led them past the student residences, each corner unlocking a memory.

"Students used to haul water from the well here," Cranmer said, pausing by a moss-worn circle near the cloister wall. "No pipes. No stoves. You studied with frozen fingers in winter."

Will grinned. "It builds character, I'm sure."

Cranmer returned the smile. "It built the sort of men who stopped complaining."

Roger lagged a pace behind, casting glances at side paths as if tracking down old ghosts. "I don't suppose we might swing by Hills Road? They've rebuilt an inn where The Dolphin stood—different name now, but same stone."

Cranmer raised an eyebrow. "A pilgrimage to sacred ground?"

"The holiest of places," Roger said. "At least to a student's appetite and wallet."

They turned toward the southern boundary. The lane curved gently, narrowing to a hedge-lined walkway where the outer wall sloped toward the gate. As they neared the corner, a carriage pulled in and halted near the stone post. A man stepped down, brushed the dust from his cloak, and looked about as if expecting someone to appear.

"Excuse me," the man called, striding toward them with purpose. "I've just come from London and was told to find Master Capon. I've also a letter to deliver to a certain Thomas Cranmer. Might either of you direct me?"

Cranmer stepped forward. "You've found him. I am Cranmer."

The man blinked, then let out a sudden laugh. "Well. Either God is efficient—or Cambridge is far smaller than I remember."

He extended his hand. "Thomas Cromwell."

Cranmer accepted it with a courteous nod. "You arrived earlier than I expected."

"Couldn't sit another day behind parchment. Business nearby made the timing right. Thought better to speak in person—with things as they are."

"Would you care to step inside?" Cranmer gestured toward a college side hall just beyond the hedge. "We can speak more privately there."

Cromwell nodded once, then turned to Roger and Will. "And you are?"

Roger stepped forward. "Roger Cressy of Walthamstow. This is my son, Will."

"Cressy," Cromwell repeated, as though making a note of it. "Pleasure. Young man—don't waste your youth being quiet. Ambition fades faster than wisdom."

Will gave a shallow bow, unsure whether it was advice or warning.

"Take Will to The Dolphin's resting place," Cranmer told Roger. "I'll join up with you later."

Cranmer led Cromwell into the stone archway and through a side door into the college hall, quiet and cold even in the sun-warmed morning.

Inside, Cromwell wasted no time.

"I've come to summon you to court. The king has questions only you can answer—or rather, only you can answer without making things worse. Your name is tossed about as that of expert on biblical matters, God's law, and all that. But you are also known for your steady politics—not prone to create a ruckus, so to speak."

"To court?" Cranmer repeated, eyebrows lifted. "Uh, when?"

"Immediately . . . well, soon," Cromwell answered. "Forgive the bluntness, but time is short, and patience is not our monarch's spiritual gift. Prepare for a week there. But it must be soon. If you leave tomorrow, you should arrive with two days' travel—three at the most."

Cranmer folded his hands behind his back, taking a slow breath. "Then I'll need to speak with Master Capon. I cannot leave without his approval."

Cromwell nodded. "Of course. Respect for order. I expected as much."

He turned toward the door. "I'll find a meal while you pay him a visit. There's an inn not far—the one your friend was hoping to visit, I imagine. I passed it earlier. Crooked sign, good smell of stew."

"I know the place."

"Good. I'll be there."

They stepped back into the courtyard. Cromwell returned to his carriage, and Cranmer made his way toward Master Capon's office.

The corridor outside Master Capon's office was dim and cool, thick with the kind of silence that fed hesitation. Cranmer sat on a worn bench beneath a narrow window, fingers interlaced in his lap, eyes on the flagstones.

He had never liked these meetings—not here, not at any stage. The waiting brought out old instincts: to weigh each word, to defer, to weigh again. He had once thought silence a virtue. Now he wondered if it were only habit.

He thought of Joan. Not her face, not even her voice, but the fire in her arguments. The challenge. Joanna—Jo—had it too, according to Roger. And deep down, he longed to hear it for himself. And if Cromwell's summons was what it seemed, there would be no room for such fire at court. No room for lingering doubt. Only the swift, clean precision of action.

The door opened. A clerk leaned out. "Master Capon will see you now."

Cranmer rose, smoothed his sleeves, and stepped into the Master's office.

Master Capon sat behind a broad oaken desk, spectacles low on his nose. He did not rise.

"Doctor Cranmer," he said, "what can I do for you?"

Cranmer bowed slightly. "I've received a summons from a man named Thomas Cromwell, currently serving with the king. He requests

I attend court. I seek your permission to arrange for my students' instruction during my absence. It may require several days—two weeks possibly."

Capon leaned back, sighing through his nose. "Cromwell, is it."

"Yes."

"And what, pray, does this Cromwell want with one of our theologians?"

Cranmer hesitated. "I believe it concerns . . . a matter of Scripture. Possibly one of marriage. But I've not yet been told explicitly."

Capon leaned back in his chair and frowned. "Yes. I've heard rumblings. The king is eager to put away his wife—and now perhaps he's fishing among the colleges for support. He married his brother's widow with papal blessing, and now claims Scripture forbids it. Leviticus versus Deuteronomy, as it suits him. But we both know the real reason: no male heir, and a certain lady with dark eyes whispering promises in the wings."

Cranmer's expression didn't change. "Even so, I would go as a scholar, not a spokesman."

"I'm afraid that's not a distinction anyone at court will honor." Then after a pause, "No, Doctor Cranmer—I must decline. Jesus College does not dispatch its masters at every whistle from Westminster."

Cranmer lifted his chin, not sharply, but enough to make the stillness pause.

"Thank you for your time," Cranmer said.

He turned without argument, walked to the door, and let it close softly behind him.

Outside, the sun was high, casting a soft gold across the grass. Cranmer blinked as he stepped into the light—and saw the carriage.

Cromwell was seated just inside, pen in hand, a folded parchment across one knee.

He looked up. "So you'll leave here tomorrow?"

Cranmer came to the open door. "Master Capon declined. Politely. But firmly."

Cromwell exhaled with a short, sharp puff. He stepped out, already adjusting his sleeves, and walked with a firm pace to the door. Cranmer followed.

As they approached the office, the clerk barely began his practiced line—"Master Capon is indisposed with pressing matters and cannot be disturbed"—before Cromwell strode past him and pushed open the door.

"Wait here," he said over his shoulder.

Cranmer obeyed. The clerk stood beside him, pink with offended propriety but unsure what to say. The five minutes that passed felt much longer.

Then the door opened again.

Cromwell emerged with the same brisk stride and calmly composed expression. His gloves were already in hand.

"I'm off, back to London," he told Cranmer. "We will expect you in the morning four days from now."

And he was gone.

Cranmer didn't know whether to ask him if Capon agreed or to go in to ask Capon himself. But by the time he recovered enough to move, he just left the building. The coach was already down the road on its return.

At that moment, Roger and Will appeared from the far end of the green, walking with slow contentment and the slightly uneven stride of men who had eaten well.

"Was that Cromwell? Is he gone?" Roger asked, gesturing with his thumb toward the retreating coach.

Cranmer nodded absently, still in thought.

Will grinned. "He didn't look the type to linger."

Cranmer smiled faintly, unsure whether he'd just been invited or conscripted.

Back in Cranmer's quarters later that day, the lamps were already lit. The room smelled faintly of ink and pears.

"So," Roger said, easing into a chair. "You're going to London. Good. You'll come with us to Walthamstow. We're only a two- to three-hour horse ride from court. Emilie will be delighted."

"Back to Walthamstow?" Will asked. "But what of our visit to Oxford?"

Roger sighed. "Will, situations change. We must adapt."

Will looked crestfallen. "But I'd been hoping—"

Roger cut him off with a firm but gentle hand to his shoulder. "We'll return. But right now, it's Walthamstow."

Cranmer was deep in his own thoughts: *I look forward to seeing her.*

11

The Fire and the Text

The road from Cambridge to Walthamstow wound through open fields and past the first stirring hints of spring—hedgerows greening, ditches full of thawed water, and crows that watched from fenceposts with solemn patience. The cart jostled with each rut, but no one complained. The air held a promise: of home for Roger and Will, and of uncertain beginnings for Cranmer.

The multiple-day ride gave Cranmer time to think. As they neared Walthamstow, he thought particularly of meeting Jo. Roger, for once, allowed the silence. Only Will occasionally remarked how a roof had been retiled, or a wall re-laid where he once startled a goose. Not memories— an inventory. Just notes, filed in order. The kind of things a boy reports when trying to sound like a man.

Walthamstow appeared not as a village but a tangle of quiet lanes and tidy hedges, with housefronts close to the road. Roger pulled the cart through the final bend with a "Ho there!" and a wave to a neighbor, and moments later they turned into a gated lane leading to a low-roofed home with whitewashed walls and smoke rising from a narrow chimney.

Before the cart even stopped, the front door swung open. Emilie emerged, apron in hand, wiping flour from her fingers. She looked scarcely older than when Cranmer last saw her—but her eyes had a deeper calm, and the apron betrayed a life now shaped by daily rhythm rather than courtly charm.

"Roger Cressy! Back already? And, oh, with company. Is that—that, is!—Thomas!"

Her voice caught mid-sentence as she saw him step down from the cart.

Cranmer smiled. "Emilie."

She came forward quickly, and he opened his arms just in time for her to hug him tight. There was no delicacy in it—just warmth, honest and unexpected.

"You look tired," she said, stepping back. "Are they working you to death already?"

"He looked this way at twenty," Roger offered from behind. "He calls it piety. I call it worry."

"Well, we've both aged," Emilie said, glancing at Roger with mock indignation. "But I think I've gathered more gray hairs than both of you combined." Then turning back to Cranmer, "Come in. You must be hungry."

Will jumped down from the cart and disappeared inside, calling out something about the smell of roasted something.

As Cranmer moved toward the door, Emilie paused.

"We need to call Jo in. She's in the garden. Just a momen—"

But then she appeared.

She stepped out from behind the stone corner of the house, hair still damp from washing, a basket of herbs in her hand. She was tall for her age—taller than Joan had been, or so it seemed to Cranmer. But the resemblance was unmistakable. The angle of her brows, the way her head tilted slightly as she appraised him—he had seen that gaze before, in a field outside Cambridge, when a girl with fire in her voice had asked if God was cruel.

"Jo," Emilie called gently. "Come meet Dr. Cranmer."

Jo approached slowly, not shy, but deliberate. She looked at him the way one might study a figure in a stained-glass window—curious, un-afraid, seeking some deeper truth in the lines.

Cranmer bowed his head slightly. "Joanna. I'm honored."

She nodded. "I've heard about you."

Cranmer smiled faintly. "I've heard about you, too."

Her lips twitched—almost a smile—and she turned, leading the way inside.

Roger leaned toward Cranmer. "Don't expect much at first. She speaks when she's ready."

"She already has," Cranmer said.

The hearth crackled low. Shadows leaned long across the floor, and the scent of rosemary and ash lingered in the corners of the room. Dinner had been simple but filling—roasted lamb and bread, a bit of cheese, a tart Emilie insisted wasn't burned though Roger claimed otherwise with every bite.

Will had gone off to the back room where Roger kept a few books—most theological, a few classical. He said he wanted to see if any of them mentioned the names he'd heard at Jesus College. Cranmer doubted the rustic shelf held anything by Hilary of Poitiers or Hugh of St. Victor, but Will had disappeared with the same focus he gave to every pursuit.

Roger, content and drowsy, had excused himself to bed with a parting yawn and a muttered prayer that tomorrow not arrive too early. Emilie had lingered long enough to touch Jo's shoulder and whisper something before retiring behind the curtained doorway.

That left only Cranmer and Jo, sitting by the fire in mismatched chairs.

He didn't speak at first. He was still watching her. She had Joan's bone structure—that had been clear from the moment she turned her head—but it was more than that. She didn't fidget. She didn't rush to fill silence. She simply *waited,* with that quiet strength he remembered too well.

"You watch people," he said at last.

Jo turned slightly toward him, but didn't answer right away.

"I do."

"Why?"

She shrugged lightly. "Because people say things they don't mean. But they move in ways that are true."

Cranmer studied her a moment longer. "And what have you seen in me?"

Another pause. Then, "You carry grief. But not like someone running from it. More like someone trying to make peace with it."

His breath caught a little—surprised, not wounded.

"You're Joan's daughter," he said, more to himself than to her.

"She's always been my mother," Jo said simply. "Even if I didn't know her."

"You know *of* her," he said. "But do you want to know *her*?"

Jo nodded. "I've asked Mother. And Father. They've told me what they can. But they didn't see her the way you did."

He leaned forward, resting his arms on his knees. "She was fierce. Not loud—but fierce. She asked questions like swords, and she waited for answers like someone ready to judge the soul behind them."

Jo looked into the fire. "They say I ask too many questions."

"Then they don't know how the soul works."

She looked back at him. "Do you?"

"I've spent my life trying."

The fire popped as a log slipped lower, the glow softening along the floorboards.

Jo spoke again, more quietly. "Why did she die?"

He didn't answer for a long time.

When he finally spoke, his voice was low. "Because life here is fragile. Because sometimes the body breaks before the soul does. And because God—though always good—is not always easy to understand."

She didn't look away.

"I don't believe in a cruel God," she said. "But I also don't think he stops the cruelty."

"No," Cranmer said. "He doesn't. Not always."

"So what does that mean?"

"It means," he said slowly, "that love has more enemies than we imagine. And God's not at war with us. He's at war *for* us."

Jo was silent for a long time.

Then, "She would have liked that answer."

"She gave it to me," he said.

The morning came quietly, with a pale light slipping in through the small leaded panes. Cranmer had risen early, more out of habit than necessity. He'd arranged his few belongings—papers, Psalter, a well-worn copy of Gregory's *Pastoral Rule*—and folded his cloak across the bench at the foot of the bed. Outside, a blackbird sang with unearned confidence.

Downstairs, the fire had already been coaxed back to life. Emilie moved about the kitchen with quiet ease, spooning out oat porridge and humming a tune Cranmer didn't know. The room smelled faintly of clove and something just beginning to bake.

Roger entered with a yawn and a groan, hair tousled, boots half-fastened.

"You priests always rise like crows," he muttered, pouring water into a basin to splash his face. "What time is it? Or better yet, why is it?"

Cranmer smiled. "Sun's up. I take that as permission."

Jo appeared next, hair loosely braided, sleeves rolled to her elbows. She offered a quiet nod before helping Emilie with the table. No words yet—but her presence was not withdrawn. If anything, it felt like a continuation of the conversation from the night before, only with breakfast in place of firelight.

Will was last, still buttoning his doublet as he came through the door. "How long will you be there?" he asked.

"I think they want me for a few days," Cranmer replied. "So today, I expect I'll be back before dark."

"Cromwell expects much from a morning's talk," Roger said, sitting down and eyeing the porridge dubiously.

Cranmer gave a faint shrug. "The king wants answers. Cromwell's job is to find men who give the right ones."

Jo looked up. "And you want to be one of those men?"

"I want to speak what's true," Cranmer said. "Whether they trust me will depend on whether they actually want it."

Roger chuckled. "Then speak slowly. Let them think it was their idea."

Cranmer lifted his spoon. "You should have been the court adviser."

"I'd have been hanged within a week."

As the last spoon was scraped and the table cleared, Will slipped out to the barn. By the time Cranmer fastened his cloak, the horse stood at the gate, breath steaming in the morning chill.

Roger followed Cranmer out, brushing crumbs from his front. "You've got weather for it, at least. No excuse to wait another day by claiming the roads are mucked over."

Jo walked over to where Will held the reins and stroked the horse's nose. "Your day will be easier today," she told the animal, loud enough for only Will to hear.

He laughed, "The old nag will be happy someone else—anyone else—hops up on him today."

Jo smirked. "Father pulls the reins like he's trying to raise a drawbridge."

Will smiled and gave her a light nudge with his elbow. She rolled her eyes, but her smile held.

Cranmer mounted with practiced ease. The horse stamped once, eager but steady. He glanced down at the three standing before him—Roger's squinting good cheer, Will's half-amused restlessness, and Jo's stillness, eyes shaded from the sun but watching every detail.

"Give Emilie my thanks again," he said. "And save me a place at the table tonight."

Roger waved a hand. "If I don't eat it all first."

Will grinned. "We'll hold him back."

Cranmer turned the horse toward the road. As he passed the garden wall, he heard Jo's voice—quiet but clear.

"Don't forget what you said."

He called back. "Which part?"

She met his gaze evenly. "That God is at war *for* us."

He nodded once and rode on.

The spires of Westminster rose through the morning mist like questions waiting to be asked. Cranmer pulled his cloak tighter against the river chill as he guided the horse through the early bustle of the city—the clatter of carts, the call of fishmongers, the echo of cathedral bells.

"He passed the Abbey, its towers looming pale in the morning light, and at a stone arch beyond the gate, a liveried attendant stepped forward, clearly watching for someone."

"Dr. Cranmer?" the young man asked, with a glance at the seal-ring on Cranmer's finger.

Cranmer nodded and dismounted, handing the reins to a waiting stable boy.

"You're expected. This way, please."

The man turned without further ceremony and led him through the outer court and into a narrow hall that opened into an inner garden cloister. They passed two guards and a pair of young scribes before reaching a heavy oaken door. The attendant knocked twice and pushed it open.

"Dr. Cranmer, sir."

Cromwell looked up from a desk layered with papers, quills, and an untouched plate of bread. His eyes lit with a glint of calculation.

"Well, the scholar has come." He rose and came forward, extending a firm hand. "I half expected Cambridge to station guards at the gate."

"They considered it," Cranmer said, shaking his hand and offering a wry smile. "But when Cromwell pushes a door, even college masters know better than to bar it."

Cromwell smiled. "I'll have that carved on my tombstone."

He gestured to a chair near the fire. "Sit. We'll not talk here—it's all parchment and ears. But warm yourself while I send for company."

He stepped to the door, opened it partway, and spoke briefly to the attendant still waiting outside. "Find Bishop Baynes. Tell him Dr. Cranmer is here, and we'll need his wisdom within the hour."

The door closed again.

"You'll like Baynes," Cromwell said, returning to pour a measure of wine into two cups. "He's a churchman with a lawyer's brain. He'll ask better questions than I would, if I let him. But for now, I'm more interested in your answers."

Cranmer accepted the cup, watching the flame of the hearth flicker in its red surface.

"I assume you know what I'm about to ask," Cromwell said, sitting.

"That depends," Cranmer replied. "Are we speaking of marriage, or war?"

"Both," Cromwell said with a chuckle. "But we'll start with marriage."

The door opened again, this time more cautiously. A man in clerical black stepped through—neither tall nor old, but composed, his bearing quietly episcopal. His eyes scanned the room, pausing on Cranmer with the kind of interest that measures and weighs.

"Ah! Already," Cromwell said, standing.

"I was on my way," Baynes replied.

"Bishop Edward Baynes," Cromwell said, standing. "Court advisor, Oxford alumnus, and reluctant confessor to more than one noble who fears damnation after diplomacy."

Baynes offered Cranmer, also standing at the introduction, a short bow. "Dr. Cranmer. I've read your work on the Eucharist. Bold. Perhaps too bold for tenure in some quarters—but then, you're not looking for tenure."

Cranmer returned the bow, measured but courteous. "Not bold enough, if the truth is to be known."

Baynes offered a smile with more edge than warmth.

Cromwell stepped between them, clapping his hands lightly. "Well, now that introductions are done and minor jealousies aired—shall we move where no one's scribbling at the walls?"

Cranmer gave a faint smile, amused despite himself.

Baynes's brow twitched, his mouth about to deny, but he held his tongue. *I'm not jealous*, his eyes seemed to protest—*just principled.*

Cromwell turned to the door and waved them both through. "Let's take it to the chamber off the Jericho Cloister. Tapestries and no draught. Better suited for dangerous thinking."

Baynes raised a brow at Cranmer. "Then it's good you came cloaked."

Cranmer gave the faintest smile. "I've brought worse weather with me before."

The chamber Cromwell led them to was smaller than expected, but well-appointed—wood-paneled walls, a hearth already lit, and thick tapestries muffling the outside sounds. A long table stretched near the window, its surface cleared except for a tray of fruit and a pewter jug of water.

Cromwell motioned them in, closing the door behind. "No scribes. No ears. No walls that whisper."

Baynes raised a brow. "So, a rare room in Westminster."

Cromwell ignored the comment and took a seat at the head of the table. "Let's speak plainly. The king is convinced his marriage to Queen Catherine was never lawful. He has appealed to Rome for a dispensation to annul, but Rome is reluctant to issue a second dispensation that would overturn the first—the one that permitted the marriage in the first place. Spain doesn't want a new dispensation either, and right now the pope seems to be listening to Spain more than to us. So we have to do this on our own. Our king seeks a declaration—not a divorce. He doesn't want to end a marriage; he wants to establish that the marriage was never lawful in the first place. We need a theological foundation, firm enough to silence Rome and convince England."

Cranmer took the seat opposite, hands folded. "He wishes the marriage declared invalid?"

"Exactly. And for that," Cromwell said, glancing at Baynes, "we need minds that speak both Latin and Scripture."

Baynes folded his arms. "And tongues that don't tremble at the word 'heresy.'"

Cranmer turned to him. "Is that what this is?"

Baynes didn't answer directly. "That depends on who gets to define the term."

Cromwell leaned forward. "We know what Rome will say. We need to decide what England must say."

A pause.

Cranmer spoke carefully. "The king married his brother's widow, with papal dispensation."

Baynes nodded. "Granted by Julius II."

"And now," Cranmer continued, "he wishes it undone."

Cromwell interjected, "Because he believes the pope erred—that he never had the right to dispense with God's law."

Cranmer looked at Baynes. "Leviticus says such a union is cursed. Deuteronomy allows it to preserve a brother's name."

Baynes didn't flinch. "And the Church has centuries of precedent reconciling both."

"But is reconciliation the same as obedience?" Cranmer asked. "Or have we papered over contradiction to keep power intact?"

Cromwell smiled faintly. "That's why you're here. We have priests to recite canon law. We need someone to explain what the Bible actually says—and what it dares not say."

Another pause.

Cranmer looked between them. "And what would you have me do?"

Baynes answered this time, slowly. "Read. Pray. Write. Then come back with a truth strong enough to steady a throne." He folded his hands. "As Master Cromwell has said, let's speak plainly. The king married his brother Arthur's wife. That's a violation of Leviticus."

Cranmer didn't flinch. "He married her because Arthur died, And Deuteronomy tells us that if a brother dies, 'the wife of the dead shall not be married unto a stranger . . . her husband's brother shall go in unto her.'"

Cromwell glanced from one to the other, letting the exchange play.

Cranmer continued, "Look to Luke 20. The Sadducees present a woman who marries seven brothers. Christ does not question the law itself—only the assumption that marriage continues in the resurrection. And Christ not questioning the law means the law is not at fault."

Cromwell interrupted. "But there you argue from silence. Shall we all be polygamists because God did not correct David?"

Cranmer shook his head. "But the pope issued a dispensation—a dispensation that allowed Henry to marry his dead brother's wife."

"For holiness's sake?" questioned Baynes.

"No," admitted Cranmer. "It was issued under pressure of a treaty, not conviction."

"Then, why should it be honored as holy?"

"Perhaps it shouldn't," Cranmer said. "But a dispensation's origin—however political—does not itself make the marriage unlawful. That must be shown from Scripture."

Cromwell raised an eyebrow. "Ah, yes! You believe the matter rests on Scripture, then, not papal authority."

"I—I do believe Scripture must be the foundation. Or the Church stands on sand."

Baynes looked to Cromwell briefly, then back to Cranmer. "Then how can you ignore Leviticus? It—*Scripture*—states, "If a man takes his brother's wife, it is an unclean thing, he has uncovered his brother's nakedness, they shall be childless.""

"But Deuteronomy . . ." Cranmer began again.

"Deuteronomy's command," Baynes interrupted, "was specific to preserving the brother's name in Israel. We are not Israel. Henry is not king of Israel."

A silence settled. The fire snapped softly.

"I'd like time," Cranmer said. "To think. To pray. To consider more than words on a page."

Baynes inclined his head. "Wise men take counsel before issuing verdicts."

Cromwell stood. "Then you'll return tomorrow."

"Yes," Cranmer said, rising. "Tomorrow."

They nodded their farewells. As Cranmer stepped into the corridor, Cromwell's voice followed.

"The king does not wait well. But I'll give him reason to."

That evening, after clearing away the supper dishes, each nursed some hot broth Emilie had poured into small cups—claiming it aided digestion. Jo had already finished hers and sat curled in the corner of the hearth chair, legs tucked beneath her, flipping through the small, smuggled New Testament she'd uncovered from where Roger kept it hidden. Roger leaned against the wall, a look of concern softening the usual playfulness in his eyes. Will stood near the window.

Cranmer had just finished recounting the discussion with Cromwell and Bishop Baynes. He had not mentioned pressure or power—only passages. But the undertones were clear enough.

"They want you to decide between the Scriptures?" Jo asked, her voice even.

"They want me to make a case," Cranmer replied. "A case that the king's marriage was never lawful."

Will frowned. "But isn't that what the Church is for? To settle these things?"

Roger gave a small chuckle. "The Church hasn't settled anything without a fight since before you were born."

Jo spoke again, slowly. "In Luke—when the Sadducees ask Jesus about the woman who marries seven brothers—he doesn't criticize the law, does he? Just their assumption about marriage continuing in heaven."

Cranmer looked up, startled. It was the very argument he had presented to them but had left out of his summary. "You're correct, he doesn't," he answered.

"So doesn't that suggest Jesus accepted the levirate law?" she continued. "Or at least didn't find fault with it. If he thought the whole thing was wrong, wouldn't he have said so?"

Emilie gave Jo a brief look of admiration.

"You're arguing from what Jesus doesn't say," Will countered.

Jo shrugged. "Sometimes silence is a kind of approval. Isn't it, Father? What was that Latin you've said before? *Qui tacet con . . .* something"

"*Qui tacet consentit,*" Roger finished. "Silence gives consent."

"So Jesus gave consent to the brothers marrying by his silence," Jo concluded.

Cranmer nodded, thoughtful. "A valid observation. The levirate law was upheld for centuries."

Jo sat forward. "Father, do you remember that scholar passing through—Master Bilney?"

"Yes," Roger answered. "He was part of that band in Cambridge they call *Little Germany*—men stirring reform."

Jo nodded. "He spoke of that law in Leviticus 18. And didn't he say the Hebrew word in verse sixteen didn't always mean 'marry'? That it could mean only 'to take'—even to lie with?" She turned back to Cranmer. "Is that true?"

Cranmer blinked. "The Hebrew?" He paused, searching memory. "If I recall, the word is *laqach*. And yes, it can mean either—to take in marriage or simply to lie with. The context decides."

"So then it might not be about marriage at all," Jo pressed. "Only a command not to lie with your brother's wife—nothing about widowhood."

Cranmer leaned back, his gaze steady on her. "Which would mean the verse has no bearing on Arthur dying and Henry marrying his widow. It would apply only if the brother were still living." He gave a slow nod. "An important distinction. And interestingly, when the Septuagint translated *laqach* in the Deuteronomy passage—the one permitting marriage to a brother's widow—they used *lambanō*, not *gameō*. To take, not to marry formally. The ambiguity remains."

Roger glanced at Emilie. "She doesn't miss a step, that one."

"She never does," Emilie murmured.

Will stepped forward. "Then what's the argument for Leviticus? There must be something more than just that line."

Cranmer looked at him. "The Church's tradition leans toward Leviticus treating any union with a brother's wife as improper, regardless of the reason."

"Yet that's not what Deuteronomy says," Jo added.

"No," Cranmer agreed. "And therein lies the difficulty."

"So who decides?" Will asked.

"That is what we are grappling with," Cranmer smiled.

Will would not let it go. "The king should decide. He's the king."

"And ignore the pope?" Roger asked.

Will thought a moment. "Well, yes, ignore the pope. The pope involves himself in politics. Why can't the king involve himself in religion? Luther says the pope . . ."

Cranmer interrupted, "You've read Luther?"

"I've heard of him," Will said a little quieter.

Over his initial wonder, Cranmer said, "Well, Will, whether the pope or the king, we have to be true to Scripture."

The firelight played softly across their faces.

"They want Scripture to speak with one voice," he said. "But it speaks like a chorus, each singer voicing his own part of this complex and layered truth. I have to play the choir master. I have to bring it together."

Jo looked into the flames. "And what if the king wants only to sing a solo?"

Cranmer didn't answer. He just stared into the hearth, the embers cracking beneath the weight of silence.

12

The Listening Chapel

The fields still held a faint frost, but the sky ran clear, the wind gentle. The ride south moved at a steady pace, the horse's breath visible in the morning air. Jo rode beside Cranmer atop a smaller mare Roger had provided. She sat gracefully in the side-saddle, back straight, chin tucked slightly, one hand gripping the reins, the other resting loosely at her side.

Cranmer glanced at her more than once.

She hadn't said much since they set out, though she had insisted on coming. He hadn't intended it at first. But the idea had lodged after their fireside conversation. When she asked the next morning, her words were simple: "You said the king wants Scripture to speak. I'd like to listen."

He had paused, weighing the risks, and then agreed (although allowing her to listen would be Cromwell's call).

She was, in many ways, his truest link to Joan—not just in form or feature, but in fire. And something in him—maybe something cowardly, maybe something noble—wanted her there. Not to fight his battle. But to remind him why battles mattered.

They didn't speak for miles. The hoofbeats and rustling woodland filled the silence well enough. Once, passing a hedgerow, they spooked a trio of pheasants. Jo laughed quietly as they broke into noisy flight.

"Even royalty flees when startled," she said.

Cranmer smiled faintly. "They fly with less dignity, though."

The road curved, rising slightly toward a crest that would soon open onto the northern edge of London. Jo pulled her cloak tighter against the wind.

"When we get there," Cranmer said, finally breaking the quiet, "I'll first leave you with an attendant while I seek permission from Cromwell to allow you to accompany us. But if he won't allow it, and truly he may not, you'll have to wait elsewhere. But I will try to show you all the glamor I can of the buildings and court."

Jo nodded.

"If anyone asks, you're my niece."

"I am," she said, looking at him sideways—more puzzled than defiant.

Cranmer didn't answer, but his grip on the reins tightened.

The towers of Westminster came into view, their stone silhouettes etched against the late morning sun. Another few miles, and they would be there. Jo sat taller in the saddle.

She had come to listen.

He prayed only she would not hear too much.

They reached Westminster's outer gate as the bells tolled mid-morning. The stone walls loomed higher here, closer and more confining than they had seemed from the road. Guards at the entry watched them approach, hands resting on hilts but faces calm.

Cranmer dismounted first and handed the reins to a stable boy already jogging toward them. He turned as Jo slipped down from her mare with practiced grace.

An attendant in the king's livery stepped forward from beneath the archway.

"Dr. Cranmer?" the man asked.

"Yes."

"You are expected. Shall I take the girl to wait?"

Cranmer gave a nod. "She is my niece. Joanna. Please see she's made comfortable."

The man inclined his head. "Of course. Follow me, mistress."

Cranmer hesitated. "I'll seek permission for her to observe our discussions. If I'm granted it, I'll come fetch her."

"Yes, sir."

He looked once more at Jo, who returned his gaze with steady calm.

"I'll wait," she said. "And I'll listen."

He touched her shoulder lightly, then turned to follow another page toward the inner court.

The attendant, meanwhile, guided Jo through a quiet passage that curved past the east wing. He made no effort at conversation, though his steps were brisk and sure. They passed a stairway and two closed chambers before reaching a small vestibule.

He stopped.

"This door opens to the side chapel," he said. "It's empty most mornings. Quiet. Best place for waiting, I'd say."

Jo looked uncertain. "Will someone come for me?"

"I'll check back once his business concludes. But you'll hear them in the hall before then. Don't worry."

He pushed the door open and gestured her inside.

The chapel was dim but not dark, the filtered light from a stained-glass lancet window painting fractured blues and reds onto the flagstones. A simple wooden altar stood at the far end, flanked by worn benches and a few tall candles, unlit.

Jo stepped in slowly.

"This is fine," she said.

The attendant nodded once, pulled the door gently closed, and left.

She stood still a moment, letting her eyes adjust. Then she walked toward the second row of benches, sat, and laid her hands on her lap. There was a book stand near the front. She rose and moved toward it, curiosity tugging at her.

Behind one of the thick stone pillars at the chapel's side, she found an open Psalter resting on the shelf. The Latin slowed her—words half-known from Roger's books, others guessed by cadence or remembered from margin notes. She mouthed them softly, unsure of full meaning but unwilling to stop.

She had come to listen.

And she was now in the very place no one would think to look for her.

Cromwell's office was as it had been—papers layered, bread uneaten, the scent of wax lingering faintly. He motioned for Cranmer to sit but did not join him immediately, choosing instead to stir the fire with a metal rod before speaking.

"Well?" he said at last, without turning. "Has the Scripture spoken?"

Cranmer took a breath. "It speaks. But not always in a single voice."

Cromwell gave a dry chuckle. "That's why it needs a governor."

He turned and sat, hands steepled. "Tell me."

Cranmer hesitated. "Deuteronomy still appears stronger. And my niece—Joanna—brought up something I had mentioned yesterday, which I believe strengthens that passage."

He paused. "She noted, as I did, that in Luke's gospel, when the Sadducees present Jesus with the woman who married seven brothers, he offers no rebuke of the law itself. And—*qui tacet consentit*—silence gives consent."

Cromwell's brow twitched, half amusement, half wariness. "You're bringing me exegesis from your niece? From a girl? How silly of me not to seek her out first."

"She's sharp," Cranmer said quietly.

"No doubt. But sharp girls don't steady kingdoms." Cromwell leaned forward. "Why are you bringing me opposing arguments from a child? The king is not interested in legal acrobatics. He needs clarity. Certainty. A case—*from England's leading theologians*—that silences the bishops and overawes the commons."

"I understand," Cranmer said. "But certainty is not always truth."

"No," Cromwell replied. "But it wins the day."

He stood abruptly.

Cranmer hesitated. "Before we go—Joanna, my niece, is just outside. She's heard these arguments and shown uncommon clarity. I know she's but a girl, but I wondered if—"

Cromwell cut him off with a wave of his hand. "Sharp girls are best left to sharp sewing. We'll not invite more questions by letting a child into court business."

His tone softened slightly. "Keep her sharp, Cranmer. But keep her out of this."

He turned and crossed to the door. "Come with me."

Cranmer rose slowly. "Where?"

"To a better room for this conversation."

He pushed the door open and led the way, his stride brisk.

"We'll speak in the chapel," Cromwell said. "Sometimes God's will is best heard where people expect to find it."

The chapel stood quiet, its shadows long in the midmorning light. The heavy door creaked as Cromwell pushed it open, motioning Cranmer inside before following and letting the latch fall behind them with a soft click.

Cromwell paused near the entrance, scanning the nave. His eyes moved methodically—pews, altar rail, candle stands, the recess behind the lectern. Nothing stirred. Satisfied, he stepped forward.

Behind a stone pillar near the south transept, Jo had ducked low at the sound of the latch. She clutched the open Psalter to her chest, heart suddenly loud in her ears. She had wandered there at the attendant's suggestion, and, finding the space empty, had seated herself in quiet reading. When the door opened, instinct had drawn her behind the column.

She had meant only to listen today. Now, she dared not move.

Cromwell crossed to the front of the chapel and turned to face the door, his voice low and clipped.

"I've always preferred this room for difficult conversations," he said. "Not because it's holy—though it is—but because it reminds us who we're pretending to speak for."

Cranmer stood just behind him, eyes trailing the intricate stonework of the altar. "Is that what we're doing? Pretending?"

Cromwell turned sharply. "No," he snapped. Then checking himself, "But—others are. And I need you to sound more like God's will than Rome's fear."

A silence settled—weightier than before.

"I've heard of how you speak to students and peers," Cromwell said, stepping closer. "You know how to take a murky passage and make it blaze. You convince with calm. That's rare."

Cranmer remained still.

"But we don't need clever. We need committed."

"I am committed," Cranmer said, quiet but firm.

"To what?" Cromwell challenged. "To your conscience? To the text? Or to the man God has placed on the throne of England?"

Jo's breath caught.

Cranmer replied, "To—to—truth. And to the God who authored it."

Cromwell's tone shifted—softer, persuasive. "Truth doesn't float above history, Thomas. It lands in the world. And when it lands, it must pick a side. The king has chosen his. He needs the Church—*our* Church—to stand with him."

"And if Scripture stands against him?" Cranmer asked.

Cromwell moved past him, touching the back of a pew lightly with his fingers. "Scripture has stood against many things. It has also stood *for* many—kings among them."

He turned. "You see contradiction. I see opportunity. You see conflict. I see necessity. The people must believe God is with the king. And you, Thomas, can give them that belief—must—yes, must give them that belief."

Cranmer didn't answer. He looked up toward the carved rafters, as if the silence itself might offer guidance.

Cromwell's voice dropped to almost a whisper. "God does not always thunder. Sometimes he simply opens a door and waits to see who walks through it."

Behind the pillar, Jo pressed her back tighter to the stone.

Cranmer lowered his gaze. His voice, when it came, sounded worn.

"I've walked through doors before. Not all of them were right."

Cromwell's eyes narrowed. "Meaning?"

"Meaning I've mistaken pain for purpose. Assumed silence meant consent. I stood once at a door I thought God opened. I married. I believed. And then, she died."

He hadn't meant to say it—not here, not to Cromwell. But the words spilled, and something in him gave way with them.

Cromwell folded his arms. "So now you fear doors?"

"No. I fear misnaming them. I fear calling them divine when they may be only convenient."

A flash of real irritation crossed Cromwell's face. He took a step forward.

"This isn't about your past. Or your regrets. This is about your king. And your country. And the future of both."

He let the words settle, then added—calmer, more measured—

"Do you know what happens if you fail to give him what he needs? The king will find someone else. Someone less torn. And you'll have taught the realm not that God is faithful—but that his servants are indecisive."

Cranmer's shoulders tensed.

"You'll go back to Cambridge," Cromwell said, voice like pressed iron. "You'll read. You'll try to write, try to lecture. But no one will be listening. They'll recognize you as a failure. You will have failed. And you'll watch from a distance as others shape the soul of England, while yours shrivels." Cromwell paused, then forcefully, "Stand up, man!" His gaze pierced through him. More quietly but just as forcefully, "Stand up for your king. What you decide here—now—will shape this nation. And it will shape you. Your life to come—whether you have a life to come."

Cromwell paused again.

The silence was long.

Cranmer's eyes dropped.

"I—will do what I can," he said, the words dry in his mouth.

Behind the pillar, Jo's hand clenched around the edge of the Psalter.

Cromwell nodded once, satisfied.

"Good. Then England may yet believe that truth walks with the crown."

He turned toward the door.

Cranmer stood still a moment longer. Then followed.

The door opened. Shut.

Jo remained frozen. The hush of the chapel pressed in again—but it was no longer quiet.

Cranmer stepped out into the corridor. The echo of the latch behind him sounded final, like a door closing not just on the chapel, but on something less easily named.

He walked slowly, not toward any destination, but simply to move. His feet echoed on the stone floor, each step too loud, as though he were trespassing into his own future.

He had once believed his mind to be his greatest ally—the tool that clarified, tested, and directed him. Even amid uncertainty, he had trusted thought to carry him, to steady the tremors of emotion. But now, something else was guiding him. Not conviction. Not clarity.

Fear.

It was shaping him.

He had heard it in his own voice—that catch of hesitation, that softening of resistance. He had felt it in his silence, in the way he had stood mute before Cromwell's pressing certainty, his veiled threat. He had not argued. Not truly. He had deferred. And though no vow had passed his lips, he knew that Cromwell had heard consent.

That knowledge settled into his chest like lead.

He did not know how to stand against it. Not the power of the court, nor the storm of kingly will—but his own shrinking soul, his own quiet acquiescence to the path of least resistance. He had always thought he would recognize the moment of testing. That it would come in fire or fury. But it came in a whisper, in a chapel, cloaked in reason.

And then another thought—sharper than fear—pierced him.

Jo.

She would be waiting. She would ask. Not harshly, not rudely. But honestly. And he would have no honest answer to give. Not one that matched what she believed him to be. Not one that matched what *he* had believed himself to be.

His breath came shallow. He could not face her yet.

He paused in an alcove, let the wall steady him.

The weight was not only what Cromwell had said. It was who he feared he was becoming.

Jo didn't move for some time.

The door had closed. Their voices were gone. Only the faint flicker of candlelight and the cold press of stone kept her company now. Slowly, she slid down the base of the pillar, Psalter still in hand, and drew her knees to her chest.

What she had heard felt like a blow—not a betrayal, exactly, but a fracture. A splintering of the image she had carried since before she met him.

Cranmer, the quiet strength. Cranmer, the mind that dared to ask hard things and wait for better answers. Cranmer, who had once loved her mother.

Now—Cranmer, caught in silence. A silence that sounded too much like surrender.

She had come to listen. But she had not expected to hear that.

Her thoughts tangled, tripping over questions she couldn't quite form aloud. She wanted to be angry. A part of her even tried. But something gentler settled in first.

He was afraid.

She saw it now, clear as the carved cross above the altar. Not the fear of men, exactly. But the fear of getting it wrong. Of choosing wrong. Of standing against a tide so strong that even rightness, once spoken, might drown beneath it.

She looked down at her own hands wrapped around the Psalter.

She had always longed to know her mother—not just stories, but substance. And in quiet moments she had caught glimpses: the angle of her thoughts, the sharpness of her questions, the way she leaned toward fire rather than away from it.

But here—here was something more. Her mother had loved this man. Not just admired, not just been admired by. Loved. Not for his perfection, but for his mind and heart, even where both were frayed.

Jo could feel it now—not just in memory or imagination, but in something real, binding her to both of them. And if her mother had chosen him, then maybe love had seen what disappointment could not.

She couldn't un-hear what he had said.

But she could look deeper.

Not all strength was certain. Not all good men spoke loud. And maybe, just maybe, someone needed to remind him of what he once made others believe: that truth—however faint—was still worth following.

She closed her eyes. Just to still herself.

She didn't know yet what she would say.

But she knew she would not let him walk out of this alone.

Cranmer continued down the hall, the echo of his own footsteps swallowed by the hush of Westminster's inner corridors. He had nearly reached the cloister when an attendant in livery stepped briskly into view.

"Dr. Cranmer," the young man said, offering a shallow bow. "Master Cromwell requests your presence again tomorrow. He said to begin charting the next steps."

Cranmer nodded, his face unreadable. "Tell him I'll be here."

The attendant inclined his head again. "Shall I bring your niece to you now?"

"Yes," Cranmer said, after a pause. "Please."

He watched the young man disappear down a hallway and took a long breath. The weight of Cromwell's words still pressed on his chest—threats folded in civility, promises laced with peril. He'd meant to defend the truth. But whose truth had he spoken? And with what conviction?

Jo appeared a few minutes later, walking toward him with measured steps. Her expression was calm, but her eyes were darker than when he had left her that morning. They met in silence.

They walked side by side across the green, where the winter grass whispered underfoot. The stable hands had already brought their horses to the post near the gate. Cranmer glanced at the mare, then at Jo. He searched for a way to speak, but the right words had not returned to him.

Jo, too, was quiet—her thoughts a tangled root of sorrow and resolve. She had seen something in Cranmer that unsettled her. But she had also begun to understand the storm that raged behind his quietness. And the cost of standing—or falling—in a world like this.

Just before reaching the saddle, Cranmer cleared his throat.

"I hope the morning was not too dull," he said, forcing a faint smile. "How did you pass the time?"

Jo looked at him—just long enough for her voice to land with weight.

"I was in the chapel," she said.

13

When the Heart Leans

THEY RODE NORTH AS the shadows lengthened, the late light slanting gold across the fields. Cranmer kept his eyes ahead, the reins loose in his hands, his body swaying easily with the horse's rhythm. Jo rode beside him, quiet. Neither had spoken since leaving Westminster's gate. A quarter hour passed that way, the silence crowded—questions, thoughts, regrets, fear.

Finally, Cranmer spoke.

"You were in the chapel."

Jo didn't answer at first. Then: "Yes."

He nodded slowly. The horse's hooves clopped steadily along the dirt road, soft with spring.

"I didn't expect you to hear what you did," he said at last.

"I didn't expect to hear it either," Jo replied. Her voice wasn't cold—just steady. Watching.

They rode a little farther.

"You think I've betrayed the Scripture," he said. It wasn't a question, but it hung like one.

"I think," she said slowly, "that you're afraid."

He turned slightly toward her, then back to the road. "You're not wrong."

Jo looked ahead. "Fear's not failure."

"No," Cranmer said. "But it is loud. And clever. It speaks in voices I almost believe."

She was quiet a moment, then: "So does truth. Just not as quickly."

A flock of crows burst from a hedgerow as they passed, cutting across the path toward the fields.

Cranmer exhaled. "I wanted to be better than I am. For you, too. I wanted you to see something worthy."

"I did," she said. "I still do."

He glanced at her.

"I heard what you said," she added. "But I also heard how long it took you to say it."

Cranmer didn't reply, but something in his face eased.

They rode on, the road curving gently through a stand of elms. The sky deepened to a pale rose in the west. The worst of the distance was behind them now—but not all.

As they approached the house, a figure darted from the side yard— Will, waving, eager. He reached the gate just as they dismounted.

"Well?" he said, his eyes bouncing between them. "What was it like? Did you see Cromwell? Did anyone shout? Were there guards? What did you eat?"

Jo smiled in spite of herself. "No one shouted. We saw Cromwell. And yes—there were guards."

"And what's he like?" Will asked, his excitement undimmed.

Jo hesitated, her gaze drifting slightly. "Forceful," she said. "And . . . fearsome. Not loud—but like the point of a spear."

Will grinned. "Sounds brilliant." Then he turned to Cranmer. "Will you go again?"

"Yes," Cranmer said.

"Can I come?"

"We'll see."

Inside, the table had already been laid. Emilie fussed at the edge of the table, adjusting spoons and napkins, while Roger filled bowls with the last of a lamb stew. They all gathered, the weariness of the day settling in as the warmth of the home took over.

Once seated, Roger glanced across the table. "So," he said, "Leviticus or Deuteronomy?"

Cranmer caught Jo's eye. He stirred his bowl before answering.

"A bit of both," he said.

Roger blinked. "How's that possible?"

Cranmer exhaled. "They want Leviticus. It's cleaner for the case."

Emilie's brow furrowed. "But they're still married. You can't just . . . undo it. Not because someone's unhappy."

Will leaned forward. "But it's the king. Why shouldn't his will be followed?"

Jo bristled. "Because his will isn't the same as God's."

Will met her eyes. "Who says?"

Jo didn't answer him. She looked at Cranmer.

Roger turned to Cranmer as well. "And you? What do you say?"

Cranmer's hand paused over his spoon. Slowly, without looking up, he said, "I'll defend the king."

Will gave a short, satisfied nod. His eyes slid to Jo.

She said nothing.

In fact, Jo said hardly anything for the rest of the evening. Roger and Emilie drifted off to bed. Will lingered, then finally stood.

"Do you think I may come with you tomorrow?"

Cranmer gave a slow nod. "I suppose so."

Will grinned. "This will be grand." He looked quickly to Jo, who managed a small smile for his sake. Then he left, the floorboards creaking beneath his eager steps.

The fire had burned low by the time Jo spoke again. She was still seated, arms folded, eyes tracing the flickering shadows on the far wall.

"Why will you defend the king?" she asked quietly. "Is that where your heart truly lies?"

Cranmer sat back in his chair, staring at the candlewax at the base of the flame.

"Deuteronomy, Leviticus . . . even Ezra. They don't all sing the same song." His voice was low, heavy. "Ezra condemns foreign wives, fearing spiritual defilement of marriage. Marriage purity is necessary. That's why Rome upholds Leviticus. It's why Henry needed dispensation in the first place. If Scripture divides—if precedent leans one way—how do I stand against it without clarity?"

Jo turned to him, brows drawn. "So it's not fear anymore? You truly think the king is right?"

Cranmer's jaw tightened. "I think . . . I don't know. And if I don't know, how can I oppose him? On what basis?"

He looked at her then, his eyes hollow. "Why can't Scripture be clear?"

Jo studied him, and her voice softened.

"Perhaps," she said, "we read it wrong."

Cranmer frowned slightly, uncertain.

"We read it like a law book," she continued. "Every word weighed, every line a ruling. But what if it's not that kind of book? What if it's God's long conversation with his people—a testimony of love, of struggle, of return? Not rules to obey, but relationship to restore?"

Cranmer was silent.

Jo went on, slowly: "You said once the Bible doesn't speak in a single voice. Maybe that's true. But maybe it sings in harmony. A harmony you hear only if you stop looking for rules and start listening for relationship."

Cranmer blinked. "You sound like your mother."

Jo nodded faintly. "She didn't want answers so she could win arguments. She wanted to know whom she could trust—especially when the world broke around her."

Cranmer looked at her, then looked away—then back again, frowning gently.

"You speak of her as though you knew her."

Jo met his gaze, steady. "Well, you've told me something about her, and I recognize that in me. I believe she lives inside me. Not in memory. In motion. In the way I see. The way I question. She left it there—in the marrow."

Cranmer looked down. His voice, when it came, was hushed. "And did she?—know whom to trust, I mean."

"She did," Jo said. "In time."

She paused. "But it wasn't the certainty of Scripture that convinced her. It was the constancy of love."

The room fell still. Only the fire crackled—a soft breath of warmth between them.

Cranmer leaned forward, resting his elbows on his knees. "I want to believe that."

"Then start there," Jo said gently. "Not with verses. With the God who gave them. Let love be the measure—not fear."

Cranmer looked at her a long moment, his face unreadable. Then, finally, he nodded—just once.

Not in triumph.

But in beginning.

The kitchen at Walthamstow was warm with early light, streaks of gold slanting through the mullioned windows. Emilie moved briskly, setting out bread and a pot of porridge. The air smelled faintly of smoke and spice.

Will had risen early and sat at the table, boots already on, hair hastily combed. He asked questions between bites—how long the ride would be, whether they'd meet other councilors, if Cranmer thought Cromwell would remember him from the week before.

"Slow down, boy—you'll get to London before your breakfast even notices you were here," Roger quipped, pouring himself a cup of small ale.

Jo was quieter. She stirred her porridge absently. Cranmer, seated across from her, watched her once or twice but didn't speak.

The mood wasn't heavy—just gently pulled at the edges, as if the house itself sensed a change in rhythm.

"I expect we'll be home before dusk," Cranmer said at last.

Will nodded. "And if we're not, well—I wouldn't mind staying in Westminster."

Emilie raised a brow. "As long as you don't make a nuisance of yourself."

"I wouldn't," Will said with mock offense. "I'd be the very soul of discretion."

Jo gave a faint smile but didn't look up.

When breakfast was cleared, Will grabbed his cloak, practically bouncing toward the door. Cranmer followed more slowly. Jo stood and walked with them to the outer step.

The horses were already saddled. Roger had given Will the same smaller mare Jo had ridden the day before. She waited quietly, reins flicking at the morning flies.

Will mounted easily and then looked to Cranmer. "Shall we?"

Cranmer gave Jo a final glance. "We'll return before supper."

She nodded. "I'll keep a place warm."

And then they rode out—Cranmer steady, Will eager.

Jo stood in the doorway, watching them disappear down the road. Not a grand farewell, not a marked goodbye. But something passed in that morning's light—a chapter closed quietly, the kind that only later proves to be a turning.

Jo lingered a moment longer in the doorway, then stepped back inside. Emilie was rinsing the porridge pot, sleeves rolled above her elbows, humming something faint and tuneless. Roger was wiping down the table, the last curls of steam from the breakfast mugs rising between them.

"Did you see his face?" Emilie said over her shoulder. "He's nearly grown into that grin. Court won't know what to do with him."

Roger chuckled. "They'll learn. Or they'll send him back." He reached across and plucked a wayward strand of hair from her forehead, brushing it behind her ear.

Emilie paused, then leaned her head briefly against his arm before returning to the basin.

Jo watched them, unnoticed. The ease between them. The love that didn't ask to be admired. Built slow and solid, like the beams above their heads.

She turned, quietly, and began to gather the dishes. The day felt new. Uncertain. But not without comfort.

The road south curled between budding fields and early spring hedges, the morning air cool but not biting. The hooves of their mounts made a steady sound, softened by patches of old rain and new grass.

Will rode half a length ahead, turning often in the saddle. "Do you think we'll see the king today?" he asked, eyes bright. "Or at least some lords? Maybe the Lord Chancellor?"

Cranmer gave a faint smile. "You're more likely to see a clerk's back and a long wait."

Will grinned. "Still better than Waltham's council meetings."

Cranmer didn't answer right away. The city was nearing now—its towers and smoke-blurred spires rising ahead.

"Court is not a stage, Will," he said at last. "It's more like a maze. Every corridor seems to lead somewhere, but most take you in circles."

"But Cromwell—he's the center, isn't he? Doesn't everything come back to him?"

Cranmer glanced over. "In this season, yes. But seasons change."

Will looked forward again, undeterred. "Still. I want to see how it works. All of it. Not just for show. I want to understand it."

Cranmer gave a soft nod. "Then today may teach you more than you expect."

They fell into silence for a while, the city drawing closer with each bend in the road.

Will sat straighter. "Do you think Cromwell will remember me?"

"He may," Cranmer said. "But don't count on it. And don't push. Watch, listen. Let the day speak first."

Will nodded, chastened but still clearly alight with anticipation.

They crested a small rise, and Westminster opened before them—its walls familiar now to Cranmer, its promise entirely new to Will.

Cranmer pulled his cloak tighter. "Whatever comes, remember this: grand halls echo louder. Choose your words accordingly."

Will raised an eyebrow. "Even compliments?"

"Especially compliments."

The guards at the gate stepped aside at Cranmer's name. As they entered the courtyard, Will's eyes widened at the sheer press of movement—pages hurrying, carts being unloaded, a falconer speaking softly to his bird.

It was no throne room. But for a boy from Walthamstow, it was the beginning of everything.

Westminster moved like a living organism—wheels creaked, messengers crossed yards, and bells marked unseen summonses from halls beyond sight.

Will followed close as Cranmer dismounted and handed off the reins to a groom. As they passed through Westminster's central hall, the archways yawned wide, ceilings rose higher than Walthamstow's church, and the bustle had a rhythm all its own.

Cranmer turned to him at the foot of a staircase. "I'll be with Cromwell. Likely some time. Stay out of the way—but not out of sight."

Will nodded, but his eyes were already taking in a row of shields set into the wall above them.

A nearby attendant—young, not much older than Will—caught the exchange and gave a small grin. "First visit?"

Will turned. "No. Second. But I didn't get to see much the first time."

"Well, stay on this floor and don't go through any closed doors, and you'll probably live." The boy winked, then added with mock gravity, "But if you see a black-robed man with a gold chain and no eyebrows, run."

Will blinked. "Who? Where?"

The attendant laughed. "Just an old joke meant to keep every new attendant toeing the line." Then he smiled again and trotted off down a hall, carrying a stack of scrolls.

Will wandered—cautiously—past a sunlit colonnade where guards stood in shadow, past a cluster of men in heated discussion over a dispatch, past a tapestry being mended by two silent women. He took it all in, details lodging in his mind as if they belonged to a story being written around him.

Then came footsteps—quick, purposeful. He turned to see Cranmer walking beside three others, one of whom was unmistakably Cromwell.

Cranmer caught Will's eye. "Master Cromwell," he said, pausing the group, "this is William—my nephew."

Cromwell turned, assessing the boy in a blink. "You've brought him to watch the wheels of government turn, then?"

"If they'll let me," Will said.

Cromwell arched a brow. "And what have you seen so far?"

Will hesitated, caught between awe and wit. "Mostly corridors," he said, then paused. "Though . . . very well-dressed ones."

That earned a surprised chuckle from one of Cromwell's advisors. Even Cromwell's mouth tugged, barely.

"And what would you expect of corridors in a place like this?" Cromwell asked.

Will straightened. "Well, sir—less polish. And more purpose."

Cromwell's eyes narrowed—not critically, but measuring.

"You've got opinions, then."

"My sister says so."

Cromwell smiled.

"It is nice to see you again," Will said at the pause.

"Again?" Cromwell asked.

"Yes, sir. We met briefly—at Jesus College when you came to meet Dr. Cranmer."

"Ah yes!" Cromwell said remembering. "You were with your father—Cressy, is it?"

"Yes, sir," Will said, beaming.

Cromwell eyed Will more closely. "And how long have you been riding with your uncle?"

Will hesitated. "Only today. But I've followed his work. And yours."

"Have you?"

"Yes. And I think what you're doing is . . . brave. Necessary."

Cromwell tilted his head. "Is that so?"

Will pressed on. "It's just—well, people fear change, sir. But fear never made anything better. And maybe what's needed isn't just arguments—but clarity. Something people can grasp. Something they'll remember."

The others in the group shifted slightly, a couple clearing their throats, one of them frowning, but Cromwell's eyes didn't leave Will.

He gave a short nod, then turned to the others. "Bright young men should be introduced to their country's operation." He glanced back at Will. "We're going to discuss some strategy for your uncle, William, no harm in your coming along."

Will tried not to grin too widely. "Thank you, sir. And—it's Will."

Cromwell paused. "Will?"

Will straightened a little. "You said William. But I go by Will."

Cromwell gave a slight smile. "Will it is, then."

He turned back down the hall, and they moved forward together—Cromwell, Cranmer, the advisors, and Will at the edge, stepping into a new room, a new day, and something more than he'd expected.

❖ ❖ ❖

The council chamber was broad and timbered, the windows high-set, filtering pale morning light. A map of the British Isles stretched across one wall; another held bookshelves sparsely filled with legal texts and scrolls.

A long table waited near the front, where chairs had already been drawn and notes laid out in uneven stacks.

Cromwell settled at the head, gesturing the others to sit. Cranmer took a place at his left. Will, hesitating, slipped into a lower seat against the wall, his eyes darting from face to face.

The talk began without fanfare. The Rome issue came up first—new envoys, new documents, another plea.

One advisor, lean and pale, tapped a parchment. "A revised draft—sharper in its appeal to canon precedent."

Cromwell didn't bother to look. "The pope's ear is still Spanish. We send this, we stall, and we're ignored."

"Even so," another said. "there's merit in appearing reasonable—to the emperor and the French, at least."

Cranmer nodded slightly. "Even if fruitless, the gesture could temper perception."

"But perception doesn't annul a marriage," Cromwell snapped. "Or secure loyalty."

He stood, moving behind his chair. "I tire of this cycle—request, rebuff, repeat. Is there nothing new?"

The room was quiet.

One advisor began to speak, but Cromwell waved him off. "If the old answers were working, we'd be through already."

Someone mentioned sending Cranmer across England—to curry favor, engage theologians, strengthen support.

"It's something," Cromwell said, but without conviction. "But it is still only us. Europe follows the pope, and right now the pope is listening to Spain more than us. We're wasting our time petitioning Rome."

And then, from the wall, Will spoke.

"So then, Europe's not following the pope. It's following Spain—Charles V."

Heads turned.

Cromwell blinked. "Yes, apparently."

Will swallowed, but sat straighter. "If Europe and the pope follow Spain . . . shouldn't we be going to Spain? I mean, instead of to the pope?"

A few advisors exchanged amused glances.

One shook his head at Will. "It is annulment we seek, and that strikes at Charles's own kin—Queen Catherine and her daughter Mary. He's loyal there. We've considered it. Best hold your tongue, lad; let us do the strategizing. We can't bypass the pope."

"Not bypass, really. I just thought to shift the conversation," Will said. "To where the influence truly lies—to Charles who governs half the continent. He may not favor Henry, but he might favor theological clarity."

Another advisor spoke. "That was my idea as well. But Catherine reflects Spain's tenuous treaty with England, and Charles wants England as an ally to keep France at bay."

Will's eyes darted to Cranmer, who gave a slight shake of his head.

Yet Will spoke again. "Pardon me, sir, but . . . could we not offer a replacement treaty? If England offered the princess Mary in marriage to Charles, it would secure the same treaty status."

The advisor stroked his beard. "And it would strengthen his own dynasty. If England supported him with France, would he really turn down such an arrangement for the betterment of Spain and his empire on all fronts?"

Silence held a moment.

"And," Cranmer wondered, thinking aloud, "engaging the empire's scholars publicly, then, could shift the debate."

Cromwell, thoughtful, stepped forward.

"It could work," Cromwell said, then glanced again at Will. "If the pope's power rests on fear and formality, then perhaps clarity and conscience will serve us better."

He turned back to the others, already moving. "We'll need a delegation. Dr. Cranmer will lead it. Calais first, then Strasbourg. Possibly Zürich."

The room stirred with renewed energy.

And Will, seated in shadow at the wall, felt something settle in his chest.

Not pride. Not even excitement. *Belonging.*

The room was bustling, but in the motion, Cromwell paused—glanced at Will. A small smile flickered. Then he turned back in earnest.

The table at Walthamstow was loud with clatter and voices—mostly Will's. He leaned forward between bites, describing everything from Cromwell's stride to the shape of the council chamber windows.

"... and then he looked at me—me—and said, 'It just might work.' That's what he said. 'It just might work.'"

Emilie smiled as she passed the bread. "So you've solved England's crisis and returned in time for supper."

Will grinned. "Not just returned. I've been asked back."

Roger raised his brows. "Back?"

Will nodded quickly, swallowing a mouthful. "Tomorrow. To observe. Learn. Help where I can. Master Cromwell said I had a sharp eye."

Jo glanced at Cranmer, who was unusually quiet, slowly spooning his stew.

"So you'll go again?" she asked.

Will looked to Cranmer for confirmation.

Cranmer gave a slow nod. "He's been invited," he said, though a shadow passed behind his eyes. He wondered, just for a moment, what price that invitation might carry.

"And I accepted," Will added.

"Of course you did," Emilie said with a chuckle. "The question is whether you'll sleep tonight at all."

Will sat taller. "I might. But I hope morning comes quick."

Jo watched him, and despite the flurry of talk, she smiled—genuinely. He was becoming. And something in her admired that.

Roger leaned back. "So tell me again—what exactly did you say that so impressed Cromwell?"

Will paused, then shrugged slightly. "I just asked why we were trying to persuade the pope when the pope was listening only to Spain."

Roger gave a low whistle. "And that was your idea?"

"It just came out," Will said, a little surprised still. "I thought—if Charles V is the real influence, then maybe he's the real place to speak. That's all."

Jo tilted her head. "That's not all—that's strategy."

"Well," Will said, humility slipping, "the real strategy was offering Charles Mary to marry—and ships to keep France at bay." He then grinned again.

Cranmer didn't smile, but he looked across at Will with something more enduring: respect.

14

The Shape of Influence

The week that followed moved like ink across vellum—slowly at first, then quickly, spreading farther than expected.

Letters multiplied. Cranmer, Roger, and Jo worked late at the long table in Walthamstow, drafts piled beside clean sheets, each line weighed for tone and clarity. Across the channel, names were being chosen—universities, bishops, theologians with reputations for scholarship and independence. The plan was simple in shape, daunting in scope: convene a meeting in Calais, present the king's case, and gather continental support not just to answer Rome but to influence the empire that seemed to hold Rome's strings.

It was not a mission of war, but of persuasion. A council of ideas. Yet everyone sensed the gravity—this was not just theological inquiry. It was a gamble. And it carried the weight of a kingdom.

Cranmer moved through those days with quiet purpose, but Jo saw the strain around his eyes. He copied arguments with practiced care, but paused often—lost in thought, or in worry. Whether it was the upcoming voyage or what he feared it might require of him, she couldn't tell.

Roger took the planning in stride. He would not be on the journey itself, but his connections and logistical sense kept messengers moving, ink flowing, and timetables steady. Emilie kept the household steady, too—dinners warm, tempers low, the air in the house balanced between ambition and care.

And Will—Will floated on a new current. He rode into Westminster most mornings now—late enough to miss the frost, early enough to be missed when he left. Cromwell hadn't said as much, but the rhythm was unsustainable. Something was bound to change.

He still shared the evening meals, still asked questions of Jo and Cranmer, but something in him had begun to stretch forward—toward court, toward Cromwell, toward the next.

Each night before bed, Jo would linger a moment in the hallway, listening to Cranmer's quill still moving in his study. She didn't interrupt. But she waited for the pause. And when it came, she would speak just loud enough through the door:

"Don't forget who you are when you've nothing to fear."

To which he always answered—sometimes wearily, sometimes wryly, sometimes barely audibly—"I haven't."

By the end of the week, the letters were sealed, the delegation announced, and the time had come.

A journey across the sea to seek truth.

The morning air was crisp, the hedges dusted with silver dew. Birds rustled softly in the hedgerow as Cranmer stepped out into the small front yard. Jo followed him a moment later, drawing her shawl tight across her shoulders.

They didn't speak at first. The silence between them was not strained—just full, like something that had already spoken.

Finally, Jo turned to him. "You'll follow the truth?"

Cranmer looked at her, then down at the cobbles underfoot. "I'll try."

"That's not enough," she said gently. "Try harder."

He smiled faintly, then shook his head. "It's not always about effort. Sometimes . . . it's about knowing what it is you're following."

She tilted her head. "You're not sure?"

"I'm sure I want to be," he said. "But sometimes truth moves just as you reach for it. Like a shadow on water. Before I follow it, I think I need to find it."

Jo nodded, slowly. The words marked her.

Behind them, the door opened. Roger and Emilie stepped out, followed by a younger servant carrying a satchel. Will, already prepared, was leading the horses up the lane.

Emilie stepped forward and wrapped Cranmer in a brief but firm hug. "You'll eat well over there, I hope," she said, her voice lightly teasing. "You're thinner than sense."

Roger gave him a longer look. "Letters," he said. "Even when you've got nothing to say. That's when people want them most."

Cranmer nodded, accepting the charge.

Jo stood just behind Emilie. She didn't speak again—just looked at him, searching for something she could hold onto.

He met her gaze, and for the briefest moment, he wondered if she could see clearer than he ever would.

Then he turned and walked toward Will, who was tightening the last strap.

They mounted and, buoyed by the chorus of wishes and goodbyes from the small cluster by the door, they turned their horses south.

The road toward London lay quiet in the morning light. Trees swayed gently above the hedgerows, and the horses' hooves thudded steadily against the packed dirt. For a while, neither Will nor Cranmer spoke. The silence was not strained—only still, like water before a stone breaks its surface.

It was Cranmer who broke it.

"You've done well, Will," he said, his tone even but sincere. "I hope you know that."

Will turned, a surprised but pleased smile on his face. "Thank you. That means a great deal coming from you."

Cranmer gave a slight nod. "I've watched you—your mind, the way it works. You see connections. Not many your age do."

Will looked ahead, squinting slightly toward the outline of the city in the far distance. "I suppose I just want to be useful. At court, I mean. There's so much happening—so much that could change if the right people think the right things."

Cranmer raised an eyebrow. "The right people?"

Will didn't catch the tone. "Yes—those who influence. Like the scholars you'll meet in Calais. That's the king's real hope, isn't it? That you persuade them. That they, in turn, pressure Charles. While Cromwell secures the political promises here."

Cranmer was quiet a moment. "That's part of it. But I've not set out merely to persuade. I want to hear them. Understand how they think. Let truth be drawn from the discussion."

Will turned again, a faint crease on his brow. "But isn't the goal already clear? The king's position isn't up for debate. It's your task to bring others to it. Not to wander through a dozen views looking for the best tone."

There was no heat in his words—only conviction. But Cranmer felt it keenly.

"Truth doesn't always travel fastest when driven," he said softly.

Will nodded, but added, "Still, it needs a destination. And the Church needs direction. That's what Cromwell's doing, isn't it? He doesn't just let the realm debate itself into confusion."

Cranmer didn't reply at first.

Had it been only a couple of weeks ago that the boy asked if Cromwell would remember him? Now Will spoke like a man who had forgotten he was ever a boy.

He watched the lad's posture—upright, sure, already molded by the cadence of Westminster. An attendant, yes, but one already stepping into a world that wore certainty like a seal.

Cranmer shifted slightly in the saddle.

"Don't mistake clarity for truth, Will," he said. "And don't mistake momentum for rightness."

Will was quiet for a moment, then replied with a half-smile. "And don't mistake hesitation for wisdom."

Cranmer almost smiled. Almost.

London rose before them now—low and wide, wrapped in smoke and promise.

The rest of the ride passed with little more said. Not cold. Not strained. But something had shifted—like a compass needle, slowly realigning.

By the time they reached the gates, Cranmer understood something new: the boy who rode beside him had begun his ascent. How easy it is for reverence to turn to confidence—and confidence to quiet command.

The wind off the Thames carried the scent of salt and tar. Cranmer stood at the quay, watching the ropes hauled and the gangplank secured. The ship was modest, but sturdy—hired for passage, not ceremony. No one waved farewell. Will had disappeared into the weave of Westminster. Jo remained in Walthamstow. Only the sea waited.

The journey—the sail down the Thames and the crossing—wasn't long (about two days), but long enough to feel the leaving. Cranmer kept to himself on the short voyage, leaning against the railing, watching gulls trace circles in the mist behind them. He neither read nor wrote. The wind did all the talking.

Calais rose like a citadel of gray and brown, its battlements softened by distance, its French streets still strangely English. Though no longer in England, Cranmer did not feel abroad. The harbor was thick with English soldiers and merchants, and St. George's Cross flew over every wall.

Lodging had been arranged in advance—rooms above a records office overlooking a narrow square. Modest but sufficient. The larger house next door, newly repurposed for their gatherings, had been readied by order of Cromwell. The tables had been cleared, inkpots filled, extra chairs brought in. A fire was already lit when Cranmer stepped through the door.

Letters had gone out the week before—Paris, Leuven, Strasbourg, Zürich. Not summonses, but invitations. Come. Speak. Be heard. Let Scripture and conscience shape the matter. Let thought, not threat, lead.

By the second day, the first responses arrived. Two affirmatives. One regret. One delay. It was beginning.

Cranmer stood by the window of the study room, watching the square grow quiet with dusk. The mission was in motion. But his mind still echoed with Jo's voice.

"Don't forget who you are when you've nothing to fear."

He closed his eyes. A breath. Then turned back to his work.

When they had taken their leave of each other in London, Will watched as Cranmer disappeared toward the docks, his figure growing smaller in the morning haze. For much of his life, he had admired the man—his scholarship, his poise, the quiet reverence others gave him.

But now, watching him go, Will's thoughts drifted elsewhere—to his father. Not Roger, the man who raised him, but the one who died on Tower Hill. Roger Cressy had always spoken carefully of him, but Will had pieced together what he had wanted history to remember: a man loyal to crown and Church both. A man who had died not as a rebel, but as a Catholic with convictions sharpened by politics.

He had always thought his father's death was a cautionary tale. But perhaps it was a model—proof that loyalty to crown and Church didn't have to be a choice. His father had served both. So could he.

Cranmer, for all his learning, seemed to move in fog—waiting for Scripture to clarify what power had already decided. He was a good man. But slow. And perhaps too willing to let the world turn while he pondered it.

Charles V would not do that.

Will wasn't sure when the admiration began—maybe only this week—but it was there. A ruler who held together empires and faith. A man of structure. Of legacy.

Will gave a little shake of his head and headed into the hall. He had just climbed the stairs when Cromwell strode toward him.

"Ah, there you are—finally," Cromwell said.

"Here," he said thrusting a document into his hands. "This is a draft of our letter to Charles. Baynes and a few others are in the counsel room. Take this to them for review."

"Yes, sir," Will replied quickly. "Uh—may I read it first?"

Cromwell frowned, then—remembering Will's knack for insight—nodded. "You may. It was your idea, after all."

The letter read:

> *Most High and Mighty Prince, our right well-belov'd Cousin and Ally,*
>
> *We write to Your Majesty in the spirit of Christian fellowship and princely concord, praying this letter finds you and your dominions in peace and strength.*
>
> *As Your Majesty well knows, our conscience has long been troubled regarding our marriage to the Lady Catherine, your most noble aunt. Though undertaken with sincerity, we are now, by plain reading of Holy Scripture, persuaded that such a union— she having been the wife of our late brother of blessed memory— stands in contradiction to divine law. We cannot believe that any earthly dispensation may rightly set aside what God himself has forbidden.*
>
> *This is no rejection of the Lady Catherine's dignity, which we have always sought to preserve. Nor is it driven by grievance or novelty, but by sincere obedience to God, to our people, and to the succession of our realm.*

To that end, we propose—should it please her—that she return to Spain, accompanied by her daughter, the Lady Mary, whose person and future we hold in highest esteem.

Further, in pursuit of lasting alliance and Christian unity, we offer with all honor our daughter, the Lady Mary, born within solemn matrimony and declared legitimate by act of Parliament, as a fitting consort to Your Majesty. Wise beyond her years, reared in virtue, she is worthy to stand beside an emperor.

Let this not be seen as rejection, but as a setting right. With it, we uphold conscience, preserve dignity, and offer strength to both our houses. By this union, our realms may stand together against common threats, most notably the ambitions of France, and secure peace for all Christendom.

Such a marriage shall not only bind our families, but extend the reach and influence of the House of Habsburg unto these isles—confirming Your Majesty's place as defender of faith and order across Europe.

England shall not be idle in Your Majesty's defense. We stand ready to offer military support, should any foe threaten your dominions.

We submit this proposal with full confidence in Your Majesty's judgment, and trust that you will see in it the path of concord, dignity, and divine favor.

By the hand of Stephen Gardiner, Secretary to the King, and with our Royal Seal affixed,

Henry R.

Will scanned over it, a crease forming in his brow. Noticing it, Cromwell tilted his head.

"You're not happy with something?" he asked.

"No, sir," Will hurried. "I mean, well, yes. I would think two paragraphs are reversed. Would we offer the return of Queen Catherine and Mary to Spain before suggesting the marriage? If returned, can England truly offer Mary in marriage? She would be no longer ours to give."

Cromwell took the letter back.

"Hm," he muttered. "Yes, we should reverse those ideas. We must offer Lady Mary first to wed, then propose that Queen Catherine accompany her to Spain." He looked up. "Well spotted. Take this to the council and show them the change. Then come back. I have another task for you."

Will hurried off. Cromwell stood watching him go.

That boy's a blade, Cromwell thought. *Sharp. Rare.* Then he turned back toward his office.

One afternoon early the next week, the bells of Westminster struck the half hour as Will fastened his cloak, readying for the late ride home. He had timed it well; if he left now, he could be back in Walthamstow before nightfall.

He had just stepped into the corridor when Cromwell's voice called after him.

"Will. A moment."

Will turned, surprised. Cromwell approached, rolling a parchment between his fingers like a baton.

"This arrangement won't do," Cromwell said briskly. "You coming in midmorning and leaving midafternoon. There's work here. Much of it. I need consistency."

Will frowned faintly. "I didn't mean to disappoint, sir. I thought—"

Cromwell waved a hand, already moving on. "You haven't. But if you mean to stay useful, it must be official."

He handed Will the parchment, which bore a wax seal Will didn't recognize.

"I'm offering you a place. As my clerk. You'll stay at court. Work with me. Learn."

Will blinked. The enormity of it landed all at once. He had hoped, but not dared assume.

"I—I would be honored."

Cromwell's mouth twitched at the stammer. "Good. Stay tonight. Ride early tomorrow to gather what you need from home. Be back by evening."

Will nodded, still trying to keep the grin from overtaking his face. "Yes, sir. I'll not delay."

Cromwell's tone shifted into business as he pulled a bundle of parchment from beneath his robe and stepped back into his office.

"Now. We have other matters. A letter from Dr. Cranmer arrived this morning. His first full report from Calais."

Will leaned slightly forward as Cromwell unrolled the letter and read aloud excerpts:

"... promising engagements with scholars from Leuven, Paris, and Cologne ... cordial discussions regarding the king's case ... evidence of softening positions in certain quarters ... confidence that a formal statement may be achieved within weeks."

Cromwell set the letter down.

"He writes like a man who thinks he's already won," Cromwell murmured, eyes flicking upward.

Will frowned, brow knitting. "What mention of securing Habsburg influence? Or of pulling Charles's counselors into open dialogue?"

Cromwell stopped, genuinely pleased. "None. Exactly why you'll be useful."

Will looked puzzled.

"Cranmer lives in texts," Cromwell said dryly. "He trusts too much in the strength of ideas alone. My concern isn't just what scholars in Strasbourg or Zurich say in letters. It's what gets whispered in Charles's court tomorrow. I want you to keep Cranmer thinking toward the real goal: influencing the Empire. Press him, gently but firmly, if he drifts too far into academic fog."

Will straightened, its significance crystalizing.

"I will."

Cromwell nodded once, sharp and satisfied. "Good." Then he held up the stack of papers. "And this," he said. "I want you to summarize. I don't have time to sift through all this, neither do my advisors. Pull out the essential details for not only this but every letter he sends. "Get this done now," he said already turning for the door. "You can leave at first light to gather your things—but be back quickly. We have work."

Will allowed himself one deep breath, then gathered up the letter. The parchment felt warm in his palm. The path forward had never been clearer.

The next morning, the sky hung low with soft gray clouds, the air still and damp from a night rain.

Will urged his horse into a brisk pace along the now familiar road toward Walthamstow, eager but already restless. His mind raced ahead—of packing, of returning, of belonging to the world he had glimpsed.

Around a bend, he reined in sharply. A lone rider approached from the opposite direction. Roger.

Roger slowed and waved. His face, normally bright and open, was creased with concern.

"We wondered where you'd gone," Roger said as they drew alongside. "When you didn't return last night—Jo was ready to come look for you herself."

Will shifted in the saddle, half sheepish, half proud. "I stayed at Westminster. Cromwell asked me to."

Roger blinked. "Cromwell?"

"I've been offered an apprenticeship. I'll be living at court now. Officially."

The words pressed into the stillness like a seal into wax.

Roger said nothing at first, letting the horse walk quietly beside Will's.

"You're certain?" Roger asked at last.

"I am." Will's tone was light, almost breezy. "It's what I've wanted. To learn, to help shape things. It's not just talk, Father. They listen to me."

Roger gave a small nod but stared ahead, jaw tightening just slightly. *So soon*, he thought. *The boy who had once raced sticks in the brook behind the house is now talking of influence, of shaping kingdoms.*

He forced a smile. "Well. I always knew you wouldn't stay in Walthamstow forever."

They rode the rest of the way in companionable quiet.

When they reached home, Emilie met them at the door, relief plain on her face. Jo stood just behind, her expression unreadable.

As Roger and Emilie stepped away to speak privately, Jo pulled Will aside into the small garden.

"You're staying at court," she said—not asking.

Will smiled faintly. "How did you know? I wanted to tell you myself."

"You did. It's right there on your face."

He laughed. "I had forgotten. My sister sees everything."

Will's face was still alight with the energy of the news. "It's everything we talked about," he told her. "I'll be working with Cromwell. There's so much to be done."

Jo studied him. "So much to be done for whom?"

"For England. For the king," Will answered, as though it were obvious.

Jo's brow furrowed. "And for truth?"

Will hesitated just a breath too long. "They're not at odds."

"Sometimes they are," Jo said quietly.

Will's tone sharpened just slightly. "Jo, I'm not going to play riddles. This is what I've been hoping for. I won't apologize for it."

"I'm not asking you to," Jo said, her voice steady. "I ask only you remember that serving power isn't always the same as serving good."

Will's jaw set. "You think I don't know that?"

"I think you're rushing so fast to catch the world that you haven't stopped to ask what you're chasing."

A flash of frustration crossed Will's face. "And I think you've spent so long watching that you're afraid of what happens when someone finally does something."

The words lingered between them. Neither spoke.

At last, Jo exhaled and shook her head, the soft disappointment more wounding than anger. "You should go pack."

Will held her gaze, then turned sharply back toward the house.

Jo remained, standing alone in the quiet of the garden, listening to the sound of his boots fade across the flagstones. She wasn't angry. Just afraid he was leaving something behind he wouldn't find again.

15

Truth in the Balance

THE SPRING SUN SLANTED thin light across Westminster's stone court-yards. Inside, the rhythm of court life had not changed—clerks scurried with bundles of documents, messengers whispered news behind raised sleeves, and the sharp ring of iron-tipped staffs marked the passage of men in power.

Will sat at the small writing desk assigned to him outside Cromwell's office, a stack of folded reports and dispatches spread before him. He had spent the morning parsing Cranmer's latest letter: a meticulous account of conversations with theologians from Strasbourg and Basel, a near-triumphant tone running through every line.

Will frowned as he read the final page again. It was too soon. Too confident. He could almost hear Cranmer's voice—careful, scholarly, detached from the game unfolding in London.

Cromwell swept in, his heavy robe trailing, his face unreadable beneath its ever-present scowl.

"Well?"

Will stood immediately. "The report is thorough, sir. Too thorough. Dr. Cranmer is making progress, but he's pressing forward without waiting for further guidance."

Cromwell tugged off his gloves and paced. "I know. News arrived this morning from our ambassador in Brussels. Charles is softening, but conditionally."

Will straightened. "Conditionally?"

Cromwell nodded. "He will entertain the proposal. But he insists no declaration—none—from any major voice of the empire undermining the authority of Rome. He cannot be seen as complicit in destroying the Church's order. Charles is maneuvering, as ever. He must look unwilling even as he leans toward us."

Will clenched his jaw. His mind pivoted to his father—the real one, the man whose execution had stained Tower Hill. While Roger had spoken of him only in cautious fragments, Will had assembled those fragments into something steadying for himself: a man loyal to crown and Church both, whose dream had been order through unity. Not rebellion. Not chaos. Not scholars arguing in back rooms while kingdoms drifted. In Will's imagining, it had been a world where England might one day stand not apart, but beside Charles V's dominion.

And now Cranmer threatened it.

"We have to get word to him," Will said, trying to keep his tone measured. "Stop him from securing any further written endorsements from imperial theologians."

Cromwell stopped pacing. "I've already sent a courier. But the roads are slow, the Channel uncertain. He may have moved too soon."

Will swallowed hard, fighting a wave of frustration.

Cromwell studied him. "You feel this deeply."

Will dipped his head. "It matters, sir."

Cromwell's gaze softened ever so slightly. "We do what we can, Will. Even when others . . . complicate it."

Will drew in a breath, steadying himself. "Yes, sir."

The parchments rustled as Cromwell slid them back into a stack.

"Summarize this," Cromwell said briskly. "Include the parts we can still use. The rest we may have to bury. At least for now."

Will nodded again, already reaching for his quill. The urgency had not passed, but the next step—his step—was clear.

The chamber smelled faintly of salt and aged wood. Cranmer leaned back in the high-backed chair, rubbing his eyes as the candle burned low. The sea winds tapped softly against the heavy glass.

A soft knock interrupted his thoughts, but too weary to rise, Cranmer merely called, "Come."

A young courier stepped in and bowed slightly. "For you, Dr. Cranmer." Cranmer took the folded packet, sealed in plain wax, and waved the man off.

Dearest Uncle,

The house feels quieter than it should. I sometimes imagine I hear your step in the hall or your voice from the study. We miss you.

Mother sends her warmest thoughts, and Father (as always) reminds you not to neglect your health or your meals. I most of all hope that the days are treating you kindly.

I pray your work is going well. On the morning you left, you told me that you must first find the truth before you can follow it. I have thought on that, especially now when I imagine you surrounded by learned men who speak loudly and with practiced confidence. But I wonder if truth is not always where we expect it. Sometimes it walks quietly beside us. Sometimes it lingers at the edges while the louder voices pass. Sometimes it feels more like love than law.

I will not pretend to understand the weight of what you carry. I know only that fear has a way of blinding us to what we already know. Sometimes we trust others too easily, as if they alone can tell us what truth must be. Sometimes we even silence ourselves to keep their approval. So I remind you only of this: when the voices grow sharp, and arguments twist into cleverness, remember the simpler way. Truth finds its home not in certainty, but in love.

Write soon, dear uncle. Do not let us wonder too long. We watch and wait—I most of all.

Still and always your niece,
Joanna

Cranmer sat still, the letter open in his lap. He read it twice, then a third time, fingers tracing the familiar loops of her hand.

That line burned in his thoughts.

"Truth finds its home not in certainty, but in love."

It stirred something warm in him, yet the theologian's habit rose immediately in defense. Was it too convenient? It sounded dangerously close to surrender, as though love alone might excuse abandoning the pursuit of what is right. Cranmer rested his chin in his hands. Wasn't that the danger of the age—that divine instruction might be replaced with personal conviction or affection? Cranmer shifted uneasily.

Job had not yielded to what felt easy. Job had not let the unknowable silence of God lead him to assume anything. He had demanded answers, even when answers did not come. Jo's mother had been like that too: Joan had wrestled, had demanded explanations when no one—certainly not Cranmer—had them to give.

He exhaled and rested the letter atop his Psalter. He thought he had built enough of a reply in his mind to answer Jo kindly but firmly when he next wrote.

Yet even as he settled into that resolve, a memory surfaced—quiet, persistent.

It had been only weeks ago when Andreas Osiander had arrived with the delegation from Nuremberg, and with him, his niece. Cranmer had not expected to notice her. Yet he had. Not for beauty, though she was striking in her own way, but for the unusual steadiness of her gaze, the quiet poise with which she watched the room. She had spoken little, only when directly addressed, but even then there had been something— clarity without sharpness. Assurance without pretense.

He had caught himself looking for her in the days that followed. Listening for her thoughts. Wondering.

The surprise of it still unsettled him.

He had not asked for such a stirring. He had believed that part of him sealed—out of reverence, perhaps, or guilt, or simply exhaustion. But there it was. A quiet pull. A shadow of want. Not yet love, and certainly not distraction. But something undeniable. A flicker of the life he thought he had already given away.

He had not spoken of it to anyone. He barely let himself name it.

Still, Jo's words pressed again in his mind: *Truth finds its home not in certainty, but in love.*

Could it be so?

He did not know. But for the first time in many months, he let the question rest beside him without defense.

The drizzle came early that afternoon, soft against the glass as Will sat bent over Cranmer's latest bundle of correspondence. The candles on his desk burned low; the stack of papers remained high.

So far, the reports had been hopeful. Private discussions with Strasbourg, Basel, Zurich, even tentative interest from Leuven. Will read the summaries aloud as Cromwell paced the chamber behind him, fingers laced behind his back, his robe trailing over the worn rushes.

"'Collegium Theologicum of Zurich expresses cautious sympathy. . . .'" Will paused, marking the note. "'Basel willing to consider convening scholars for further deliberation. . . .'"

Cromwell grunted approvingly. "Good. Quiet progress."

Will smiled faintly as he continued. "'Strasbourg magistrates engaged. Master Bucer cordial. Hopes high.'"

He set aside the summaries and reached for the next page from the pile—a fresh letter, not yet annotated. His eyes narrowed as he scanned the first lines. The smile drained from his face. He froze mid-sentence.

Cromwell noticed instantly. "What?"

Will didn't look up. "It's Bucer."

Cromwell halted. "What about him?"

Will swallowed. His voice came quieter, reading: "'A public address delivered yesterday by Martin Bucer before the Strasbourg Council, now posted as an open letter: *It is against divine law for any man—even pope—to bind or loose a matter God has already decided. King Henry must act without papal consent, for his soul and his realm.*'"

Cromwell stood utterly still. Then, slowly: "He published it?"

Will nodded. "Posted at Strasbourg. Widely circulating."

Cromwell's expression darkened. He moved to the window and stared out into the damp courtyard.

"Damn him," Cromwell whispered. "The man means well yet may have just doomed the whole affair."

Will frowned. "Because of Charles."

Cromwell turned, sharp now. "Yes. Charles cannot be seen siding with defiance. He gave us a window. But Bucer's open defiance makes it appear the English are already pulling the empire into rebellion."

The rain struck harder. Will stared down at Bucer's bold words, half in admiration, half in horror.

"He's right though," Will said softly. "It is the truth."

Cromwell's gaze pinned him. "And the truth may have cost us everything."

Silence stretched. Will clenched the letter tightly. The contradiction burned. Bucer had done what Will might have admired in another life—spoken boldly, without regard for consequence. Yet now, all Will could see were the fractures it risked. The truth was no longer the prize—it was a threat. A force that could undo everything they'd carefully built.

Cromwell straightened. His voice became cold and efficient again.

"Draft an urgent dispatch to Dr. Cranmer. No further written endorsements. Verbal discussions only. And if Bucer can be persuaded to soften, he must do it. Now."

Will nodded, already reaching for parchment and quill.

Cromwell's voice softened by the faintest degree. "You've wanted work, Will. Here it is."

Will pulled a fresh sheet from the stack and dipped his quill.

The candle flickered, guttering slightly in the draft. Will exhaled slowly.

He could feel the weight shifting as the fine drizzle picked up against the tall window. Something was turning. And he was right in the middle of it.

Cranmer was just returning from his morning walk. As he reached the stone wall bounding the garden enclosure behind his lodging quarters, he paused for a moment to breathe in the cold, sea tang of the morning air. He would miss that. The delegation's work was nearly finished. Months of work completed. The last letters were copied and sent. He would sail within days.

Gulls wheeled and called above the harbor wall. Cranmer watched them circle and dive. The soon departure gave him time—the first in a long while—to contemplate the broader strokes of his work here. He felt satisfied. The interviews, the discussions, even the sharpest objections— all captured in his reports—had shaped the issue well. The king would have sturdy support to take his step forward. This was truly reformation work—more consequential than anything he had achieved at Jesus College.

As his mind settled on Jesus College, he thought again, as he always did, not of his most recent years there but of the couple when he was happiest—when he and Joan had shared their lives. Tears rose unbidden. He brushed them away and shook his head. He couldn't spend his life looking backward. But Joan had been his true love, and thinking of her led him naturally to Jo. So much alike. So vibrant. So beautiful, especially their souls.

But he also felt an unease and wondered about it. Why did his thoughts of Jo warm him but feel somehow at odds with his work here that also satisfied. Maybe it disturbed him that he was harsher than usual in his last letter responding to hers. She had said, "Truth finds its home not in certainty, but in love," and that was emblazoned now on his mind. But he had written to her of its dangers. Yet even voicing that to himself gave him unease. How could love be dangerous?

He breathed deeply again and turned to go inside.

A folded letter lay waiting on his desk, and the plain wax unbroken. He recognized Jo's hand at once.

He sat heavily and opened it.

> *Dearest Uncle,*
>
> *The garden is full of roses now, though Mother says they stubbornly refuse to bloom without you here to greet them. Father grumbles that the vines have taken his fence hostage. I walk past them each morning and wonder if your sea wind feels as cool as ours.*

Cranmer paused to smile. *Yes, Jo, it does*, he thought. *And it will be good to get back.* He suddenly realized how much he would have enjoyed the country life that Roger had chosen.

> *You said in your last letter that my words about love might risk becoming permission to accept whatever pleases us, to stop pursuing truth when the answers are hard. I understand. But that is not what I believe. Nor, I think, is it what you truly believe either.*
>
> *You taught me that God does not despise questions. Job questioned. My mother questioned. I have questioned. But Job never let go of God even when certainty failed him. That was love—the refusal to let go.*
>
> *Love is not the end of truth-seeking. It is the reason we dare to seek at all.*
>
> *It steadies us when fear tempts us to abandon the search. It holds us in place when certainty slips from our grasp. Without it, the hunger for perfect knowledge turns harsh and cold, driving us into the arms of whatever voice offers quick clarity.*
>
> *You once said you envied how my mother refused to be satisfied with silence. But it was your love for her that taught her not to run from it either.*
>
> *So I ask you, gently: hold fast to the truth you know of God— of his love. Let that truth give you patience for the truths you do not yet see. That is what I meant. Not comfort over conviction, but trust that love does not mock us for waiting.*

*We wait for your return. Even knowing you will soon cross
back to us, your absence feels long. Do not let your letters stop.
With hope and affection,*

As ever, your niece,
Joanna

Her letter, full of warmth and care, still returned that unease he had felt before. He remembered once telling Joan that truth mattered more than tenderness. But he was no longer certain they could be separated.

He stared out toward the shifting gray of the sea. Gulls still scattered and circled where fishermen dragged heavy nets across the quay.

But then, for the first time in days, a soft smile touched his lips.

Not surrender. Not excuse.

A reminder.

To hold.

To keep seeking.

To return.

The soft creak of the door interrupted his thoughts. Margarete leaned into the room, her face framed in the pale early light.

"Breakfast will be ready soon," she said gently in German-accented English. "Shall I tell them to wait?"

He smiled faintly. "No. I'll come."

She gave a small nod and closed the door behind her.

As the door closed quietly behind her, his gaze lingered on the empty space she left.

She had surprised him—first by catching his attention, then by continuing to hold it. He remembered their early conversations, brief but sharp-edged with insight, as she accompanied her uncle to the meetings in Calais. Once at supper, she had asked a question no one else had thought to raise, and he had turned to see the calm confidence in her eyes. Another time, walking in the garden outside the hall, they had spoken—just the two of them—about the nature of peace in uncertain days. Her thoughts had stayed with him longer than he expected. She never insisted on being heard, but when she spoke, he listened.

What began as quiet interest had deepened over the following months, almost unnoticed, into affection. And affection, over time, had asked for something more. There had been no dramatic declaration— just a deepening trust and the shared decision to walk forward together.

Now Margarete was here at his side, his wife, his friend. Unassuming, steady, a comfort amid the swirl of politics and debate.

He had once believed himself bound to Joan's memory forever—and in many ways, he still was. But love, like truth, could endure and still allow room for new seasons. There was no betrayal in this new bond, no forgetting—only the strange grace of finding life still able to give.

Cranmer stood slowly, tucked Jo's letter safely into his Psalter, and followed the warm scent of bread and broth from the kitchen.

The thick gray clouds pressed low over Westminster as Will closed the door of the small chamber Cromwell had given him as a workspace. The writing desk in Cromwell's outer office had proven useless: even the passing breeze sent precariously stacked papers flying, which Cromwell had noticed. The long table in Will's new room solved the problem, and it was already littered with dispatches and drafts of diplomatic correspondence. But atop the pile today lay something else.

A familiar envelope, plain wax intact. Jo's hand unmistakable.

Will smiled faintly and slid a finger under the seal.

He unfolded the letter—several pages, as always—and leaned back in his chair.

Dearest Will,

I do not know if this letter finds you at leisure or in haste. I suspect it is the latter. I sometimes wonder if even in sleep you keep court matters turning in your mind.

Father says you must be learning quickly; Mother says she hopes they are teaching you rightly. I hope only you are remembering to eat something besides bread and cheese. We would love to see you. Could you not spare a Sunday?

I smile with you in your enthusiasm to walk among those who shape the future. Yet I fear the future you hope to shape.

You have always been bold, Will. Even as children, you ran forward while I stood back to watch. But not every door should be rushed through, and not every success seized just because it can be.

You once wrote that working with Cromwell felt like shaping nations. I believe you. But shaping nations is not the same as shaping souls.

One must not come at the cost of the other.

What is a kingdom if the people inside it are hollowed by fear and ambition? What does it profit you to rise, if you lose yourself on the way up?

Will frowned. Did she not understand? He was making a difference. Men at court were listening to him! Jo had always worried too much.

I have heard of this road swallowing men. Good men. Men who began with conviction and ended with only convenience.
Please, Will. Do not forget who you are. Do not forget who we are.

He flicked through more pages. "The saintly Joanna," he muttered. "Always the philosopher."

Remember: strength is not in forcing things into place. It is in knowing when to stand still, to refuse the rush toward victory that sacrifices what matters most.

"Refuse victory?" Will laughed quietly. "She must have forgotten who I am."

He scanned more paragraphs, thumbing through them faster now.

I write not to scold but to remind. Love is not weakness. Relationship is not distraction. Truth without love fractures. Power without relationship corrupts.
You once told me I overthink. Perhaps I do. But I would rather think too long than fall too fast.
Come home soon. Or at least write back. The roses still defy Father's pruning, and Mother says they remind her of you.

As ever, your sister,
Jo

Will let the last sheet drift to the table. He stared at it for a moment, expression unreadable, then he shook his head and gave a small chuckle. "She always was the preacher, shepherding the rest of us."

He tapped a finger lightly on the last page, where it read, *What does it profit a man if he gains the world but loses his soul?*

"Easy for her to say from Walthamstow," he muttered. "The world listens only to those who first seize it."

He flipped through the pages again, scanning again. The careful, looping hand blurred past his eyes as he caught familiar phrases: *remember who you are . . . relationship over power . . . truth and love intertwined . . .*

Will stopped at none of them.

As he was gathering the sheets, a knock sounded.

Cromwell stepped in, glancing at Will's handful of papers.

"Letter from Cranmer?"

Will shook his head. "No, sir. My sister."

Cromwell raised an eyebrow at the thickness. "Long."

Will smiled faintly. "She's a plodder too."

Cromwell grunted in acknowledgement and picked up a rolled scroll. Then, after a pause:

"You're only hours from home, Will. Why letters at all? You could ride there tomorrow."

Will hesitated, then gave a practiced shrug. "There's too much to be done. I serve best here."

Cromwell studied him briefly. "So be it. The next council session is within the hour. Be ready."

Cromwell left.

Will glanced once more at the sheaf of Jo's letter.

He tapped it, once. Then slid it beneath the weight of royal papers.

Not discarded. Not burned. Just buried—where it could no longer interfere.

He did not pick it up again.

16

The Weight of the Seal

THE THAMES LAY SULLEN under a pewter sky as the small ship nudged its way upriver toward London. The mist hung low, softening the outlines of spires and the jagged rooftops of the city. Cranmer stood near the prow, his cloak pulled tight against the damp chill, watching the faint silhouettes come into focus. He left Margarete with friends in Kent, for now. The uncertainties of his position, and the delicacy of returning as a priest who had married abroad, made caution the wiser course. He would settle first. Then, quietly, he would send for her.

The journey from Calais had been uneventful, yet his thoughts had been anything but calm. Letters from Cromwell had awaited him at every stop along the southern coast—hints of unrest, subtle warnings about the shifting climate at court. Now, as London loomed ahead, the weight of what awaited settled fully on him.

The dockhands barely glanced at the lone, quiet traveler as he disembarked near the Customs House. London bustled with its usual noise—vendors shouting, carts clattering, bells tolling the hour—but beneath it all Cranmer sensed an undercurrent of strain. Rumors had clearly outrun him. The king had made his intentions clearer since Cranmer had left for the continent; the word "archbishop-elect" was whispered with either reverence or suspicion in corners of court and church alike.

A single messenger from Cromwell waited at the edge of the quay. The man bowed stiffly and handed Cranmer a sealed note. Cranmer broke it open and read the few spare lines:

Your arrival is known. Do not delay. Court awaits. The archbishopric must be settled. And the Submission bill proceeds. Be cautious.

Cranmer folded the parchment into his sleeve and glanced once more at the restless river. The tide had turned, both literally and figuratively.

He decided to answer Cromwell immediately and made his way up the narrow lanes toward Westminster, the familiar sights brought little comfort. The scholars at Cambridge had been blunt but courteous; the theologians at Calais had been thoughtful if guarded. But here in London, every conversation seemed to carry layered meanings and careful evasions.

Pausing briefly at an intersection, he looked east toward the Tower's jagged outline in the distance. The last time he had stood here, he had been a lesser voice in a larger debate. Now he would be called to lead the clergy at the king's pleasure. The thought left him cold.

Yet he pressed on. The king would summon him soon. The clergy were already divided. And Thomas More, Lord Chancellor still, remained ominously silent.

Cranmer exhaled into the damp wind and continued walking toward Westminster.

The knock at the door came not long after Cranmer had finished unpacking the few belongings he had brought from Calais. Cromwell had provided temporary lodging in a house on the Strand, not far from Westminster. Cranmer opened the door to find Will standing there, cloak dusted with early spring drizzle, a parchment case slung over his shoulder.

For a fleeting moment, Cranmer felt the quiet comfort of familiarity. Will's youthful energy had been something he had grown strangely fond of, even if he now sensed an undercurrent of change in the young man's bearing.

"Will!" Cranmer said warmly. "I wasn't expecting you so soon."

Will grinned. "Work always presses." He stepped inside as Cranmer gestured him through. "Cromwell sent me the moment word came you'd docked."

Cranmer led him toward the hearth, where a small fire crackled against the lingering damp. "You look half-frozen. Sit. We can share a meal."

Will shook his head with an apologetic smile. "I cannot. I must return to Westminster shortly. The council is in session and expecting updates."

Cranmer studied him a beat longer. The boyishness still lingered, but Will stood straighter, spoke faster, and wore court manners like a second skin. He was becoming what the court needed him to be.

"I understand," Cranmer said quietly. "Then tell me what brings you."

Will unslung the case and produced a sealed packet. "The latest directives from Cromwell. Some news." His voice softened slightly. "Archbishop Warham passed last week. You know he had been ill."

"Yes." Cranmer nodded, understanding already dawning. For a breath, his thoughts drifted to how far events had carried him since Joan's death years ago.

Will continued, brisk again. "And the king expects you at Parliament tomorrow. The Submission of the Clergy bill passed Convocation while you were gone. There will be a formal recognition."

Will hesitated just briefly before adding, "They'll want the next Archbishop's presence as a sign the clergy accept."

Cranmer arched an eyebrow.

Will gave a faint smile. "There are . . . rumors."

Cranmer exhaled. *The Submission of the Clergy*—the king's declaration binding the clergy to royal authority rather than papal supremacy. A single act with vast consequences. The Parliament ceremony would be little more than a pageant for what had already been determined behind doors. Warham's death had left a vacancy, and the king's plans had swiftly moved to fill it—with the Submission as the first test of obedience.

"Thank you for coming yourself, Will."

Will smiled again, genuine but brisk. "I wanted to be the one to tell you. You'll do well. The king trusts you."

Cranmer gave a soft, weary nod. "We shall see."

Will backed toward the door, already half-turned as if halfway gone. "I'll see you tomorrow at court. There's much to do."

"Tomorrow, then."

The door shut behind Will with a soft click. Cranmer stood a long moment, staring at the place where he had been. The kettle bubbled faintly on the hook over the fire. Quiet again.

Will paced a tight circuit just beyond the heavy oak doors of Cromwell's chambers. Nicholas leaned against the cold stone wall, arms folded, watching him.

"You're going to wear a groove into the flagstones," Nicholas remarked.

Will shot him a look but half-smiled. "You've never waited for Cromwell before. He makes you sweat on purpose."

Nicholas chuckled. "I thought you thrived on politics."

"Politics, yes. Guesswork, no."

Nicholas tilted his head thoughtfully. "You're different since the business of Calais. Leaner. Sharper."

Will shrugged. "More tired."

Just then footsteps echoed down the hall. Both men turned as Cranmer approached, his traveling cloak still dusted with river mist. His face bore the calm of habit, but faint lines of fatigue traced his eyes.

Will stepped forward immediately. "Dr. Cranmer, good morning."

Cranmer smiled faintly. "Will. And who is your friend?"

Will gestured. "Nicholas Latimer. He's a court clerk—and, yes, a friend of mine."

Nicholas bowed quickly. "An honor, Dr. Cranmer. I've followed your work from afar."

Cranmer nodded politely. "Then perhaps we'll speak further." He looked to Will. "Shall we?"

Will held open the door, and the three entered the warmth of Cromwell's office.

Cromwell stood near the hearth, arms clasped behind his back, staring into the flames as if judging them. On the table lay several sealed packets and a single rolled parchment bound in silk ribbon.

At the sound of the door, Cromwell turned. His sharp eyes softened slightly at the sight of Cranmer.

"Dr. Cranmer. Welcome back. You've done well."

Cranmer bowed. "The credit belongs to the delegation. I trust the reports have reached you."

"They have. And they will serve the king well." Cromwell motioned toward the chairs. "Please."

Cranmer sat. Will and Nicholas remained standing by the door.

Cromwell didn't sit. Instead, he picked up the scroll with deliberate care and walked it over.

"Warham is dead," Cromwell said quietly. "The archbishopric stands vacant."

Cranmer blinked, fingers tightening faintly around the arm of his chair.

"The king intends to name you his successor."

Silence.

Cranmer stared at the scroll. "I did not seek this."

Cromwell smiled thinly. "Few who change the world do."

Cranmer accepted the scroll reluctantly, his shoulders visibly heavier.

"The Submission of the Clergy bill has passed Convocation," Cromwell continued. "Parliament will formally acknowledge it this afternoon. The king expects you present."

"I understand."

Cromwell breathed deeply, satisfied now. The matter had moved along more easily than he expected and was now settled. His tone lightened. He even allowed himself a smile.

Then his eyes flicked briefly to Nicholas. "Oh, yes, one other matter." He waved Nicholas forward. "You'll need a clerk. Nicholas Latimer comes recommended. Able. Discreet. More theologically grounded than most. He will serve as your assistant."

Nicholas bowed again. "I'm honored, Dr. Cranmer."

Cranmer studied him a moment, then nodded. "Then I shall rely on your wisdom."

Nicholas smiled. "If I'm to offer wisdom, I pray it finds me quickly, sir."

A knock sounded sharply at the outer door. A summons. The session would be called to order.

Cromwell moved toward the door. "Time presses. We must go."

As they filed out, Will and Nicholas trailing slightly behind, Cranmer cast a glance at the parchment still heavy in his hand.

The weight of it had only just begun.

The corridors of Westminster Palace echoed with the shuffle of hurried steps and muffled voices. As Cromwell, Cranmer, Will, and Nicholas advanced toward the Queen's Chamber where the Lords were gathered, a figure stepped out from a side chamber ahead of them, flanked by two gentlemen.

Tall, broad-shouldered, cloaked in rich scarlet and sable, Henry VIII walked with the easy swagger of one who expected all to part before him. His eyes, sharp and assessing, immediately lit upon the approaching group.

"Cromwell! And our good Dr. Cranmer!" Henry's voice boomed warmly across the stone hall. The gentlemen of the chamber stepped aside as the king strode forward, a wolfish grin curling beneath his auburn beard.

Cranmer bowed deeply. Cromwell offered a respectful inclination of his head.

Henry clapped Cranmer heartily on the shoulder. "Returned at last, I see! Your work abroad has pleased us well. You will find England eager for your hand."

Cranmer straightened, meeting the king's gaze with measured calm. "Your Majesty is gracious. I hope my efforts have been of service."

"Of service?" Henry laughed. "You've done what none of these plotting bishops could. We move at last, Thomas, at last!"

Henry's eyes flicked to the scroll clutched under Cranmer's arm. "I trust Cromwell has given you the news?"

Cranmer hesitated. "He has, Your Majesty."

"Good, good." Henry's tone softened slightly, almost fatherly. "The realm must have a shepherd. And you are our choice. There shall be no debate."

Cranmer's mouth tightened faintly. "I did not seek this office, Sire."

Henry chuckled, already moving past the objection. "Nonsense! The right man never does. You will be confirmed in due time. Today we settle the matter of the Submission. Tomorrow, England begins anew."

The king gestured broadly down the corridor. "Come, gentlemen. We cannot leave Parliament waiting."

With a nod to Cromwell, Henry swept ahead of them toward the hall. The courtiers scrambled to follow in his wake.

Cromwell leaned slightly toward Cranmer as they resumed walking. "You've been chosen, Thomas. The king will not be denied."

Cranmer followed, but the echo of the king's words rang louder than his own thoughts.

The Parliament chamber hummed with low, expectant conversation. Sunlight filtered weakly through the high, arched windows of the Queen's Chamber, casting pale streaks across the assembled clergy and nobles. Cranmer sat in the rear with Will and Nicholas, the weight of the sealed commission scroll heavy in his lap.

The king's council occupied the front benches, Cromwell at their center, eyes scanning the room like a hawk watching a restless field.

Cranmer had barely taken his seat when the side door opened and Henry VIII himself swept into the room, trailed by guards and attendants. The room stilled.

Henry paused at the center of the chamber and addressed them with practiced ease.

"The Submission of the Clergy stands. You have all heard it debated. You know what loyalty demands. I expect no delays."

He nodded toward Cromwell and retreated to the royal dais.

Cromwell stepped forward, the parchment of the act in hand.

"The Submission, as declared, recognizes the king's majesty as the supreme head of the English Church under Christ. It binds the clergy to seek no papal dispensations nor judgments without royal consent."

A bishop—older, silver-bearded, dressed in crimson robes—rose hesitantly from the left bench.

"Master Secretary," he said with care, "none here questions our sovereign's wisdom. But there is still concern among some of us—will this not alienate us from Christendom? Could it not mark England as rebellious, isolated from the ancient unity of the Church?"

A murmur rippled.

Cromwell's sharp gaze flicked toward Cranmer.

"Dr. Cranmer. You spoke with the empire's finest minds. Perhaps you can speak to this."

All eyes turned.

Cranmer inhaled slowly. His fingers pressed tightly against the scroll in his lap as he stood.

"His Grace is correct. The concern of isolation was raised at every table I sat abroad," Cranmer began, his voice calm but faintly hesitant. "Yet our case was heard. Not universally agreed, no. But respected."

He looked directly at the bishop. "The Scriptures stand unchanged. Divine law does not shift according to Rome's favor. Our loyalty to God remains, even as our king rightly assumes the duty to govern without foreign interference."

The room held its breath.

Cranmer allowed his words to settle, then inclined his head.

"This act is not rebellion. It is the rightful ordering of the king's duty within his own realm, under God. It affirms our obedience to both crown and conscience."

A hush followed. The bishop slowly sat.

Cromwell nodded approvingly. "Well spoken."

The king rose, his voice booming.

"Then let it be so."

The Parliament chamber erupted into formal assent.

Cranmer lowered himself back onto the bench. He stared blankly ahead, jaw tightening faintly.

The session continued around him, the machinery of state grinding forward. He remained silent, his gaze fixed ahead as voices rose and fell in ritual assent.

In his heart, he whispered the truth only he knew: *You speak what they wanted to hear. But at what cost?*

The heavy doors of the Parliament chamber creaked open, and Cranmer stepped into the cool corridor beyond. The noise of the session faded behind him, replaced by the soft shuffle of guards and scattered courtiers along the stone passageways.

He had scarcely gone a dozen paces when a familiar figure approached from the opposite direction—cloak drawn close, gait steady but slow.

Thomas More.

Their eyes met across the narrowing distance. Cranmer slowed, uncertain whether to speak. More inclined his head first, courteous and measured, and Cranmer found himself stepping nearer.

"Good day, Dr. Cranmer," More said, his voice low but clear.

"Lord Chancellor," Cranmer returned, bowing slightly. His gaze fell to the item More carried—a velvet pouch, heavy at the bottom, unmistakably containing the Great Seal of England.

"You are leaving court?" Cranmer asked carefully.

"For a quieter life," More replied, the faintest smile touching his lips. "One where service is judged not by sovereigns, but by conscience."

Cranmer hesitated. "And you are content with such a path?"

More regarded him closely, a look almost of pity, yet not unkind.

"I am content to serve the King where I may, and God where I must."

The words, simple as they were, struck deeper than Cranmer expected. A shadow of unease flickered in his mind—the sense of walking a narrowing path with no clear end.

"You think me wrong," Cranmer said quietly, surprising even himself.

More's eyes sharpened.

"I think you weary of the struggle between fear and faith," he said softly. "And that your heart knows the difference between serving truth and shaping it."

Cranmer said nothing. Around them, the corridor seemed to fall utterly still.

More offered a faint bow.

"I bear you no ill, Dr. Cranmer. I pray only that when the moment demands, you will know which master you truly serve."

Without waiting for reply, he moved past Cranmer toward the inner chambers, the heavy pouch swinging gently at his side.

Cranmer watched him go, the edges of More's cloak disappearing into the shadows.

He stood alone a long while, the words lingering heavier than anything else he had carried that day.

Just over a week later, Roger saw him coming down the lane and raced inside to fetch Emilie. By the time Cranmer dismounted at the gate, Roger and Emilie stood ready. Emilie curtsied with an exaggerated grin while Roger dropped theatrically to his knees, bowing low to the ground.

Emilie called out, "Here he is—His High Holiness!"

Roger joined in at once. "Make way for His Beatified Loftiness, Right Noble Custodian of All Holy Matters, Defender of the Cloth, and Most Gracious Overseer of Penitent Sinners!"

Cranmer stood still, shoulders slumped, staring at them both. Slowly, a smile broke across his face, followed by a chuckle.

"So you heard, then."

"Oh, we've heard!" Roger declared. "We may have known before you did. Will wrote as soon as the news reached him."

Emilie rushed forward to embrace him. "Imagine! The Archbishop of Canterbury dining in my humble home."

"Well, not yet," Cranmer protested, returning the embrace. "There's still the royal nomination, papal confirmation, consecration . . . and the king could always change his mind."

"Change his mind?" Roger huffed. "He couldn't possibly find better."

At that moment Jo appeared from the garden, her sleeves rolled, hair slightly windblown.

"Uncle!" she called, hurrying over to him, "You're back! But what— no parade? How disappointing."

Cranmer opened his arms and drew her into a tight embrace. "Oh, Jo." He then glanced from one beloved face to the next, his eyes bright. "I've missed you all so."

"Come inside," Roger said, with a brisk swipe at his cheek. "The stew's just now simmering, and we've so much to talk about."

The evening meal was exactly what Cranmer had needed. The burdens of court and uncertainty fell away amid the laughter and comforting cadence of familiar voices. They shared news—some small, some surprising—and a few details Cranmer offered that left the others stunned into silence. But it was only after the meal, when plates were cleared and chairs pushed back, that Cranmer revealed the most astonishing news of all.

Roger leaned back with a satisfied sigh. "I suppose, like Will, you'll have to stay near court now. But we expect to see you here as often as you can manage."

Cranmer hesitated, his fingers idly tracing the edge of the tabletop.

"There is something else. While I was in Calais, I . . . married."

The room froze.

No one moved. No one spoke.

Every eye locked on him, every mouth slightly agape.

"She's a fine woman. I'm not—" Cranmer stumbled, searching for the words. "I'm not setting Joan aside in my heart. I just . . . I found that . . ."

"Thomas!" Roger bellowed, slapping the table. "Married! That's wonderful news! We've hoped you would, more than once."

Emilie sprang up and embraced him again. "Where is she? Why didn't you bring her? We must meet her!"

"I left her with friends in Kent on the way back from Calais," Cranmer explained. "I wanted to feel out the court first. If I, a priest, had arrived with a wife in tow, all London would have stared at me just as you three are now. But actually, things are pretty well settled. I've sent for her, and she should be arriving in London by tomorrow."

"Tell us about her," Jo said eagerly.

"Is she as fiery as Joan?" Roger asked.

Cranmer smiled. "Her fire is quieter—more of settled confidence."

"Settled confidence?" Roger raised an eyebrow. "So, fewer questions?"

"I would say she has more answers."

Jo tilted her head, thoughtful. "I definitely want to meet her," she said softly.

The next morning dawned soft and hazy, the early mist clinging low over the hedgerows. Cranmer had risen early, as ever, and was finishing his packing when a quiet knock interrupted his thoughts.

Jo stood at the door, cloak folded over one arm, her dark hair loosely braided.

"Uncle," she began, hesitating only briefly, "I was wondering . . . would you mind if I came with you?"

He turned from his travel bag, surprised.

"I want to see the city again," she added quickly, "but mostly—I want to meet her."

Cranmer smiled and gestured her in. "You would be most welcome."

The morning passed quickly. They rode together along the winding road that led toward London, past greening fields and the distant shapes of laborers bent to their work. The steady beat of hooves on packed earth filled the long pauses between their conversation. Jo, as always, watched everything—the angle of the sun, the tilt of a stone wall, the shifting shadow of a bird overhead.

At last, as they crested a gentle rise and London's sprawling form appeared faintly on the horizon, Jo spoke.

"You said last night that Margarete has 'more answers.' What did you mean?"

Cranmer was silent a moment before replying. "Her uncle, Andreas Osiander, is a reformer in Nuremberg. Margarete was shaped in that world. Her convictions run deep."

Jo waited, watching him.

"I have wrestled for years with questions of authority," Cranmer continued. "Rome insists the pope, traced through St. Peter, holds the keys to truth. Margarete believes, as I have come to believe, that responsibility for faith rests not with Rome, but with the individual soul standing before God."

He shifted the reins, frowning. "It was her confidence—her certainty of that responsibility—that first gave me ground to believe I could break completely from papal authority. And yet I am bound still by the king's desires in the matter of his marriage. There are times I cannot tell whether my conscience leads or follows."

Jo nodded slowly, thinking. "But if belief in individual soul responsibility is what gave you the courage to stand against the pope, why would it not give you that same courage against the king?

Cranmer glanced over, a faint smile tugging at his mouth. "Perhaps it should. With the pope, it showed me I did not have to accept what I could not reconcile. With the king, the struggle is not so much about truth."

Jo's brow furrowed. "If not truth, then what?"

Again Cranmer rode silent for a moment.

Finally, struggling, he began, "You believe . . . " but paused. Then, "Jo, there is something else. And it's that something else with which I struggle, and that too has been a conversation point between Margarete and me. You and she both believe truth cannot be owned by decree. It must find its home in love, or it never finds home at all."

Jo smiled faintly, looking out over the road ahead. "I should like to hear that from her own lips."

"You must ask her," Cranmer said warmly. "I suspect she'll put it better than I ever could."

Rounding a bend along the Strand, they saw the house where Cranmer lodged.

Noticing the carriage out front, Cranmer said, "Wonderful! She's arrived already"

The house door opened before they reached it. Margarete stepped out onto the threshold, wiping her hands on her apron. She was of medium height, her features plain but softened by the warmth of her expression. Her dark eyes sparkled as she caught sight of them.

"Thomas!" she called, then, catching sight of Jo at his side, added with pleased surprise, "And you must be Joanna."

Cranmer dismounted, stepped forward, and took Margarete's hands in his.

"You're here" he said softly.

She smiled at him, her fingers closing gently over his. "The journey was smooth—and quick."

Cranmer turned slightly, gesturing toward Jo. "Margarete, may I present my niece, Joanna Cressy—Jo."

Margarete descended the step and reached for Jo's hand with gentle familiarity. "Welcome, Jo. I've been hoping we would meet."

Jo smiled, her uncertainty melting into ease. "So have I."

"Then let's not waste the chance," Margarete told her, not releasing her hand as she led her inside.

17

When Love Listens

THE SUN HAD BARELY lifted above the rooftops when Cranmer pulled on his cloak and leaned to kiss Margarete's cheek.

"I won't be long," he said, though the way he buckled his satchel said otherwise.

She smiled, smoothing the edge of his collar. "Go. They'll be impatient enough without excuses."

He turned to Jo. "Keep her company," he said with a wink. "And don't let her revise all my sermons."

Jo smiled faintly. "Only the ones that wander."

Cranmer laughed and stepped out into the morning light.

They watched from the doorway as he disappeared into the narrow lane, the echo of his boots quickly absorbed by the bustle of London rising into motion.

The moment he vanished, a quiet settled over the room—not awkward, but unshaped. They had shared warmth and conversation the night before, but with only two voices now, the space felt both more intimate and newly uncertain.

Jo crossed to the hearth and eased into the same low chair she had used the night before. She looked up as Margarete moved to the side table and poured a bit of warm cider into two pewter mugs.

"You said something yesterday," Jo began. "It stayed with me."

Margarete glanced over and brought her one of the mugs, then sat with hers nearby. "What was it?"

Jo wrapped her hands around the cup. "You said God doesn't love from a distance. That real love draws near. I've always believed God loves—but more like a kind of . . . unshakable goodwill. Not something active. Not something that moves."

Margarete gave a soft breath of recognition. "Ah. I understand."

She leaned back. "I used to think of it that way too—like a force, or a banner above us. But love, real love, must act. It's not just a feeling or a promise. It's a bond—a kinship—that gives of itself to draw another closer. Not only to protect or provide, but to share in life."

Jo's brow tightened. "To share in life?"

"Yes," Margarete said. "That's the heart of it. God's love is not an idea. It's not static. It enters our world, walks with us, weeps with us, works alongside us. He desires not just to redeem, but to be with. Always."

Jo looked down into her mug, thinking.

"My mother struggled with that," she said softly. "She couldn't see how love like that could stand by."

Margarete was quiet for a long moment. Then she spoke.

"Because it must. Love doesn't seek control; it seeks relationship. There's a difference. And relationship—true, love relationship—cannot be coerced—not by people, not by God. So love gives—and waits. It waits for love to be answered with love."

Jo gave a resigned smile. "It would be easier if it just controlled."

"But then it wouldn't be love," Margarete said. "Love gives of itself— specifically, it gives for the benefit of relationship. And so it must wait. It waits for the other to love too."

Jo exhaled. "And what kind of theology dares to say that love waits?"

"A theology of kinship," Margarete answered. "A theology that doesn't begin with sin but with relationship. That sees God not as judge above, but as Father, Brother, Spirit—drawing us back not through terror or transaction, but through love that gives itself to restore what was lost."

Jo stared at her. "And if it's true . . . if love is the source and the answer . . . then truth must answer to love, not the other way around."

Margarete smiled, eyes warm. "Yes . . . that's where freedom lives."

The rest of the day passed in quiet flow. Margarete and Jo moved easily into one another's company—walking the narrow garden path, preparing a midday meal, even sharing a laugh over one of Cranmer's more unreadable marginal notes. Their conversation returned often to the theme of love—not as philosophy, but as something lived. By evening, a warmth had settled between them, not unlike kinship itself.

When Cranmer returned, he noticed how at ease Jo seemed, as though something long restless had begun to settle. And when she asked the next morning if she might accompany him to court, he didn't hesitate.

Jo stood near the desk, running her fingers along the edge of an ivory seal press. "It's simpler than I imagined," she said.

Cranmer smiled. "They haven't given me the grand quarters yet. I'm still a scholar, just one with more paper."

He turned to sort a stack of petitions on the corner of the desk. "I thought you might enjoy seeing more of the grounds today—if nothing urgent comes in."

A knock at the door interrupted him.

"Enter," he called.

The door opened, and a young man stepped inside, brown curls slightly tousled, a folder of parchment tucked under one arm.

"Good morning, sir," he began. "I have the amended declaration from Lord Audley's office. The one you requested."

His voice faltered mid-sentence.

Jo had turned to face him, and Nicholas Latimer stopped. His eyes fixed on her—just for a second too long. He blinked, looked away, then back again.

Cranmer glanced up. "Ah, thank you, Nicholas." Then, noticing the silence, he added, "Have you met my niece, Joanna Cressy?"

Nicholas's mouth opened, then closed again. He managed a stiff bow. "An honor, Mistress Cressy."

Jo gave a small, amused curtsy. "And you."

Nicholas turned back to Cranmer and handed over the folder, mumbling something about corrections being enclosed. Then, seemingly unsure what else to do, he backed toward the door and fled.

Once out of the office, Nicholas leaned against the wall, exhaling.

Will Cressy approached from down the corridor, leather folder in hand.

"There you are," Will said. "Cromwell's impatient. He wants this delivered directly—" He paused, catching Nicholas's dazed expression.

"Are you ill?"

Nicholas shook his head. "No. No, I just—she's in there."

Will frowned. "Who?"

Nicholas gestured helplessly. "The most divine creature I've ever seen."

Will blinked. "What are you talking about?"

Nicholas leaned closer, voice hushed as if afraid she'd somehow hear through the walls. "Brown eyes, dark hair, quiet like a question you want to answer. She's—Cranmer's niece, I think?"

Will narrowed his eyes. "Wait. Jo?"

Nicholas nodded, "Joanna." His eyes were still wide.

Will stared at him, incredulous. "That's my sister."

Nicholas froze. "Your—what?"

Will gave a short laugh, shaking his head. "Yes. Joanna. She's just . . . Jo. I mean—we grew up together."

He trailed off, bewildered by the idea that someone could be so thoroughly captivated by the person he'd spent his life half-ignoring. To him, she was just the girl who read too much and turned every statement into a debate at the dinner table. It was odd. Almost ludicrous.

He noticed Nicholas still staring at him, mouth slightly open.

"Will you stop looking like that."

Nicholas, without blinking, said, "You have to introduce me."

Will shook his head—not in refusal, but in sheer disbelief—and turned toward the door.

Will entered the office, the heavy door clicking shut behind him.

"Jo!" he said, genuinely surprised. "You're really here. I only half-believed it when Nicholas told me."

She smiled and came forward to embrace him briefly. "Will, so good to see you. Our uncle has been showing me his kingdom of paper."

Will chuckled. "That sounds about right."

"Dr. Cranmer," he said, striding forward, "Cromwell sent this. He wants you to look it over before midday."

Cranmer took the folder with a sigh. "And I was just promising your sister a tour of Westminster."

Cranmer flipped through the first page of the document, brow furrowing. "This will take some explaining. I'll need to see Cromwell myself."

He stood abruptly and reached for his cloak.

"Will, look after Jo for a bit, would you? Show her the side galleries, the court garden—anything but this office."

"I do have work," Will said. Then glancing at Jo and softening, "But, of course, I will. You'll be busying Cromwell, so he won't think of me for a bit," Will said.

Cranmer gave a parting nod to Jo. "I'll return as soon as I'm able. Enjoy your walk."

With that, he swept out, the door closing behind him.

Will turned back toward his sister. "He wasn't joking about the paper. Some days it feels like we're drowning in it."

Jo gave a small laugh. "I believe it."

Will gestured toward the hallway. "Shall we?"

They stepped into the corridor. Nicholas was still there.

Will gave him a quizzical look. "Still hovering?"

Nicholas straightened abruptly. "I was just—yes, I—wasn't sure if you needed anything further."

Will glanced at Jo, then back at Nicholas. A small, amused twitch played at the corner of his mouth.

"Well, perhaps you can help me escort my sister," he said lightly. "Jo, this is Nicholas Latimer—my fellow sufferer in the court's maze."

Jo inclined her head. "We've met."

Nicholas gave a quick bow, trying not to meet her eyes too directly. "Yes. A pleasure. Again."

Will narrowed his eyes. Nicholas hadn't blinked since she walked out.

Just then a clerk hurried past, calling over his shoulder. "Will! Cromwell's looking for you—he's furious about something."

Will grimaced. "Of course, as always." He turned to Nicholas. "Watch her a moment, will you? I'll be back."

Nicholas nodded, a bit too quickly. "Gladly."

Will gave a last glance between the two of them, then hurried down the hallway.

Nicholas watched the last edge of Will's cloak vanish down the corridor. For a moment, the hallway was quiet.

He turned to Jo, unsure whether to speak or to apologize for existing.

"Have you—have you seen Westminster before?" he asked at last.

"A little," she said. "My uncle showed me the chapel the last time I visited."

He nodded, relieved to have something familiar to land on. "To pray?"

Jo looked at him with soft amusement. "I suppose that's what most do in a chapel."

"I have," he said quickly, then cleared his throat. "Prayed there, I mean. Once or twice. It's a good place for that."

She smiled, not at the confession, but at the way he said it—as if prayer were a fragile thing, easily broken by explanation.

"So . . . uh . . . Joanna, would you like to . . . "

"Most people call me Jo. You can if you'd like," she said, tilting her head slightly. "You don't have to—but if you'd like."

Nicholas stared at her, trying to find a suitable response. The only words he thought of were, *I would like very much,* but he didn't trust his voice to say them.

He nodded instead. "Jo."

Her smile deepened.

Nicholas gestured awkwardly toward the hallway. "Would you . . . like to see the cloisters?"

"I would," Jo said, falling into step beside him.

They walked in silence for a few paces, their footsteps soft against the stone. The corridor curved ahead, narrow windows catching the morning light in angled slivers.

Nicholas stole a glance at her. She wasn't looking at him—she was watching the patterns of light on the floor, the fine threads of lead in the glasswork. He cleared his throat.

"There's a courtyard garden just beyond here. It's not as grand as the king's, but it's quiet."

"Do you go to pray there too?" she asked, teasing just slightly.

Nicholas nearly tripped on the next flagstone. "Sometimes," he said, trying not to sound too eager. "It's . . . a good place to think."

Jo nodded. "Not enough people value that."

They rounded the corner and stepped beneath the arched passage of the cloister. Vines curled along the outer wall, and the faint scent of rosemary drifted from somewhere nearby.

Nicholas slowed his pace, half afraid he might spill something foolish if he spoke again.

Jo broke the silence. "You're different from what I expected."

He looked at her, eyes wide. "What did you expect?"

"I'm not sure. Will's letters mention you sometimes, but only in passing. I assumed anyone in court work would be a bit more . . ." She paused, searching.

"Confident?" Nicholas offered, trying not to wince.

"Contained," she said gently. "More, um, Will-like. But you're not. You're . . . open. Honest. It's refreshing."

Nicholas felt something shift in his chest, as if he were being told something he didn't quite believe but wanted very much to be true.

He gave a small, nervous laugh. "That's kind of you to say. I don't often feel . . . open. Or honest. Or refreshing."

"Perhaps you don't feel it," Jo said, "but it shows."

They stepped into the cloister garden. A narrow path looped through raised beds of herbs and crushed gravel. A bench sat in the shadow of an old yew, its edges worn smooth.

Jo paused to study a lavender plant just beginning to bloom. "May I ask you something?"

Nicholas straightened slightly. "Of course."

"You said you pray in the chapel. Why?"

He blinked. "Why do I pray?"

She nodded, her gaze still on the lavender.

He took a breath. "Because . . . I pray to God. Because I'm aware, almost constantly, of what I can't fix. Or control. Or even understand. But when I pray . . . it just reminds me that I'm not alone with the questions."

Jo looked up at him then, and he saw something shift in her expression—not surprise, but attention.

He continued, more steadily now. "Sometimes it feels like I'm throwing words into the dark. But other times . . ." he breathed deeply, "at other times, it feels like the dark is listening."

She let out a slow breath. "That's not how most people talk about prayer."

"I suppose not." He smiled a little. "But most people don't ask."

They reached the bench, and Jo sat. Nicholas hesitated, then took the far end, careful not to crowd her.

She leaned forward, her eyes on the gravel path winding through the garden. "My mother once voiced a question—she died when I was born, but her sister, the one who raised me, told me about it, and it has never really left me: If God is love, why does love stand by?"

Nicholas was quiet for a long moment. Then, carefully: "Maybe it doesn't stand by. Maybe it waits."

Startled at hearing the phrase she had just learned from Margarete, Jo turned toward him.

"And maybe," he said, now forgetting to be nervous, "it waits not because it's passive, but because it wants to be chosen. Not worshipped out of fear or obeyed by force—but known. Wanted."

He stopped, suddenly aware of what he'd said. "I mean—just as a thought. I haven't sorted it all out."

Jo's expression had softened into something like wonder. "You may not have sorted it—but you've felt it."

Nicholas looked down, a small smile tugging at his mouth. "I suppose I have."

The light was thinning outside, stretching long across the floorboards as Jo dried her hands on a cloth and handed Margarete the last of the washed plates.

They had moved through the evening in gentle rhythm—small tasks, small words, both women content with the kind of quiet that doesn't press for more.

Margarete glanced over. "You enjoyed your walk?"

Jo hesitated, then smiled. "I did. Uncle's clerk, Nicholas, showed me the cloisters and their gardens."

Margarete smiled. "Your Nicholas seems thoughtful."

"My Nicholas?" she questioned with a chuckle a little more aggressive than planned. She paused, startled, realizing she was now acting as nervous as he had when they first met.

"Well, yes, he is thoughtful," Jo said, recovering herself.

She remained in her thoughts a moment. She folded the cloth, laying it precisely along the edge of the table.

"He listens," she said at last. "Most people wait to talk. He doesn't."

Margarete nodded. "That's rarer than it should be."

Jo glanced toward the window. "He said something about prayer. That it's like speaking into the dark . . . and sometimes it feels like the dark is listening."

Margarete was quiet, thoughtful.

"It struck me," Jo added. "Not just what he said, but how much he meant it. He didn't speak like someone defending a belief. He spoke like someone living inside it."

Margarete turned, wiping her hands. "You recognize that because it's what you've started doing, too."

Jo gave a soft smile. "I think I want to."

They sat for a while in quiet, the house gently creaking into evening.

Jo absently continued to move and align her folded cloth along the table's edge. "It's strange to think that moments like today can happen at all in a place like this."

Margarete looked over. "What do you mean?"

"This city," Jo said. "This court. It all seems made of strategy and edges. But Nicholas . . . that conversation . . . it was simple. Clear. Like something that doesn't have to win to be true."

Margarete nodded. "There's more honesty in quiet corners than in all the grand chambers of state."

She paused. "I've found myself thinking about the queen."

Jo looked up. "Catherine?"

Margarete nodded slowly. "I know very little of her, of course. But it's hard not to wonder what pain she carries. To be set aside like that . . . and to remain composed, visible, faithful. Whatever else she is, she must feel more alone than most."

Jo was quiet.

Margarete added, "I don't think truth ever comes cleanly through power. But I do believe it can come through pain."

Neither of them spoke for a long moment. Then Jo said, "I'd like to meet her."

Margarete looked over, surprised.

"I don't mean formally," Jo added. "Only . . . if it ever happened, I think I'd want to."

Margarete smiled faintly. "Then perhaps it will."

Jo returned to court the next day—and the day after that. By week's end, their routine had settled. She would walk the long stone corridors with quiet attentiveness, and somehow, always, Nicholas would find her. Or perhaps she found him. They never said. A word here, a shared observation there—a moment stolen between tasks. It wasn't much. But it became something.

Cranmer noticed, of course. At first, only that Nicholas was often not where he was supposed to be. Then, after a moment of exasperated searching, he caught sight of the two of them from a distance—Jo seated near a window, Nicholas beside her, both of them leaning slightly in, talking as if the rest of the court had vanished. Cranmer said nothing.

But when Will asked later where Nicholas had gone, he simply smiled and returned to his page.

Later that week, Jo arrived a bit earlier than usual. Yet Nicholas was already waiting in the outer hall, unusually nervous.

"I wondered," he said, not meeting her eyes at first, "if you might want to meet my mother. She works nearby. In the royal kitchens, actually."

Jo's brow lifted. "You mean here?"

He nodded. "She's—well, she's the queen's cook. Queen Catherine. But don't let that worry you. She'll adore you instantly."

Jo hesitated, then gave a small smile. "I think I'd like that."

Nicholas lit up—just enough to betray how much it meant to him.

The kitchen was hotter than Jo expected. Not unpleasantly so—just full of the kind of heat that came from real labor. Copper pots gleamed along one wall, and the air smelled of herbs and roasted root vegetables. Somewhere behind a sectioned curtain, someone was singing.

Nicholas stepped inside ahead of her, calling softly, "Mother?"

A woman emerged from behind a broad chopping table, flour smudged across one cheek. Her apron was streaked with broth and flour, her sleeves rolled to the elbow. She was already chuckling before she spoke.

"There he is, creeping in like a cat again. I knew I felt the door." She wiped her hands on her apron and hurried over. "What have you brought me, then? A parchment to sign? A prince in disguise?"

Nicholas looked momentarily stricken. "Mother, this is Jo—Joanna Cressy."

The woman stopped, then beamed. "Mistress Cressy! Forgive me. I don't often see beauty coming through the kitchen door. Not that it doesn't belong—just that it's rare."

Jo smiled, a bit taken aback. "Thank you. It's lovely to meet you."

Nicholas's mother gave a short curtsy, then shook her head. "Oh, none of that here. I'm no lady. Just Latimer's cook. Or Queen Catherine's, depending on who you ask. But to Nicholas"—she elbowed her son gently—"I'm just Mother. But you can call me Bess. Or I suppose 'Mistress Latimer' is the proper way, but everyone else calls me Bess, so that should do."

Nicholas chuckled under his breath.

She turned to Jo again, eyes crinkling with mischief. "He's been walking you about the court, has he?"

"A bit," Jo said. "It's been a kindness."

"I doubt it was hard work," Bess said. "He's always gone soft over things that are quiet and good. Found a bird once when he was eight. Spent two days trying to mend the wing. Cried like a bishop when it flew away."

"Mother."

"Don't worry," she said with a wink. "I'll save the worst stories for your wedding day."

Jo laughed—unexpected and full. Something about the woman made it easy.

Nicholas's mother smiled at the sound, then turned toward the table. "You've time for a taste? The queen's not due for another hour."

"We'd be honored," Nicholas said.

Jo nodded. "Very much."

"Then sit," she said. "And I'll see if I can find something that's not meant for royalty but still worth remembering."

Nicholas and Jo took their seats at a narrow table near the hearth, each with a shallow bowl of pottage and a piece of crusty bread before them.

The kitchen had quieted, and they had just finished their last bites. A few trays had been washed and stacked, and Bess was drying her hands with the same stained cloth she always seemed to have near. Then the back door creaked open.

Bess turned first, eyes brightening. "Your Grace," she said with a small, respectful nod. "You're early today."

Queen Catherine stepped into view, her figure modest in a dark blue gown trimmed with pearl buttons, her face composed and pale. She moved a bit more slowly than usual, one hand pressed lightly just beneath her ribs.

"I thought I might speak with you about this afternoon's meal," she said, her voice low and even. "Something lighter, perhaps. My stomach's unsettled."

"Of course, of course," Bess said, already reaching for her note slate. "I'll bring a bit of broth. With an egg. An egg always settles the stomach."

Catherine gave a faint smile, but her eyes had already shifted—to Nicholas.

"And you," she said softly, a teasing note in her voice. "Avoiding your work?"

Nicholas stood at once. "Just a short visit, Your Grace."

Bess stepped in quickly with her ever-present chuckle. "You know my son, of course. But he brought someone to introduce to me. This is Joanna Cressy—his friend."

Catherine's gaze moved to Jo. She gave a polite nod, her expression unreadable. "A pleasure, Mistress Cressy. Are you visiting court for the day?"

Jo rose and dipped a quiet curtsy. "Yes, Your Grace."

"And what are your thoughts of what you've seen?" the queen asked kindly.

"It's breathtaking—the grandeur, the bustle, the purpose. I told my uncle just this morning it feels like too much for a single day."

"Ah." Catherine tilted her head slightly. "And who is your uncle?"

"Dr. Cranmer, Your Grace."

A shift. Not a chill, but a tightening in the air. Catherine's posture straightened. Her words came slow and measured.

"Then I suppose your thoughts have already been chosen for you," she said resignedly.

Jo met her gaze, calm. "I'm still developing which thoughts are mine."

Catherine studied her a moment longer. The edge in her stance softened, just slightly.

"That would be a rare gift in these halls."

She looked again to Bess. "I'll have that broth when it's ready. No rush."

She turned to leave.

Jo, moved by instinct more than plan, said quietly, "Thank you."

Catherine paused. Just a breath.

Jo added, "For staying kind—when the world's grown sharp."

The queen didn't turn immediately. But after a moment, she did.

"Kindness, child, is not weakness. Though some would like it to be."

She stepped back into the room, her gaze holding Jo's.

"And you carry no sharpness to my door?"

Jo smiled gently. "Sharpness dulls thinking."

Catherine gave a quiet, short breath—almost a laugh, almost a sigh.

Jo added, "I've heard enough to wonder how you've borne what most would collapse under."

Catherine's expression stilled. She looked at Jo now—not as a curiosity, but as a woman.

Nicholas shifted, glancing at the sun's lowering angle through the shuttered window. "Jo—I should return to Dr. Cranmer. He'll be expecting me."

Catherine replied, eyes still on Jo. "Return then. I'll take care of your friend."

Nicholas hesitated—just for a second—then offered a small bow. "Yes, Your Grace. Jo—I'll see you later."

He was gone.

Catherine looked back to Bess. "Bring the broth to the inner room. And something for Mistress Cressy to drink."

Then to Jo: "Come with me."

Jo blinked, unsure what she had stepped into—but followed.

They made their way through a short passage that opened into a small, sun-warmed space—wood-paneled, quiet, with a low table and cushioned chairs beside a hearth gone cold. A place for solitude.

Catherine lowered herself with care into one of the chairs and gestured for Jo to take the other. Her posture was formal, but not rigid. A queen at rest, perhaps, but never off guard.

"Well, Joanna Cressy," she said, voice softer now. "Let's find out what thoughts are yours."

Jo sat slowly, smoothing her skirt. "I have more questions than answers."

Catherine arched a brow. "That's a rare confession. Most arrive with answers to sell—and questions to silence."

Jo smiled faintly. "Then I hope I'm not like most."

Catherine studied her a moment longer, then said, almost to herself, "You're about my daughter's age."

Her tone shifted faintly. "But you carry your thoughts more openly."

Another pause, then: "So more questions than answers. Your uncle doesn't seem to suffer from that affliction."

Jo hesitated, then replied gently, "He carries certainty well. But I've come to see . . . it isn't always peace. Sometimes it's weight."

That softened something. Not much—but enough to shift the air between them.

Catherine gave the smallest nod. "So you're not merely repeating what he's said?"

"No, Your Grace," Jo said. "Though I've listened to him. And to others. But it's what I've been hearing lately that's stayed with me."

Catherine waited.

"Someone close to me said," Jo continued, "that love doesn't control. It waits."

The queen tilted her head slightly, not dismissively, but with curiosity. "And what has that to do with my marriage? Or with God?"

Jo drew a breath. "Only this. Everyone who speaks of your marriage does so in terms of law, or politics, or sin. But I don't think I've heard anyone ask how you understand God in the middle of it."

Catherine's brow tightened—thoughtful, as if measuring something unspoken. "Law and sin belong to God. So do kings. If I speak of them, am I not speaking of him?"

Jo met her gaze, calm. "They may speak *of* God. But I've started to wonder whether they always speak *with* him."

That caught Catherine off guard.

The silence stretched a moment too long. Then a quiet knock came at the door, and Bess entered, balancing a tray.

She set it gently on the table—broth in a delicate porcelain bowl, steam curling from its surface. A second cup for Jo, filled with a lightly spiced cordial.

"Thank you," Catherine said without looking up.

Bess nodded and withdrew.

Catherine lifted the spoon, stirred the broth absently. "And if I told you I feel abandoned?"

Jo's eyes dropped to the cooling bowl between them. Then she looked up again.

"I think I would understand."

She paused.

"My mother died when I was born. But the woman who raised me—her sister—told me something my mother once said, and never stopped asking: If God is love, how could love stand by?"

Catherine looked up, eyes sharpening—not with suspicion, but memory.

"She prayed for help," Jo said. "She believed. And help didn't come. She was . . . mistreated. Hurt. And afterward, she still believed. But not with the same kind of hope."

Catherine was very still.

Jo folded her hands. "I've carried that question with me. And lately, I've started to wonder whether, though the question may never have been wrong, perhaps the kind of love she imagined was."

Catherine set the spoon down carefully. Her voice, when it came, was low. "And what kind of love do you imagine?"

Jo smoothed her skirt absently, as if steadying the words before they came. "One that waits. One that gives. One that . . . doesn't force—but also doesn't walk away."

"And do you believe God loves like that?"

Jo hesitated only briefly. "I'm learning to."

Catherine sat back with a kind of weariness that let her spine soften against the chair. For a queen, it was more than rest. It was permission. Trust. "Then you are braver than most who come here. And far less sure."

Jo met her eyes. "Certainty may make speeches. But love listens."

Catherine gave a quiet breath. It wasn't quite a sigh. More like a release.

"I think," she said, "you may stay a while longer."

They sat in silence for a moment. And then they spoke again—not about law or sin or doctrine, but about faith. About silence. About the difference between being unloved and feeling unheard.

The table was modest but warm—bread just out of the oven, roasted root vegetables, a small dish of stewed apples catching the light in its glaze. Cranmer had poured the wine himself, a gesture Jo found oddly grounding. This man who now carried the fate of a kingdom still took time to notice when someone's cup was low.

Margarete set down a basket of sliced rye and took her seat. "Not court fare," she said with a smile. "But it will do us better."

Cranmer gave a faint, tired laugh. "I've seen enough gilded trenchers this week to last me through next Lent."

They began to eat in easy silence—three people who didn't need to prove anything to each other. The clink of cutlery and the low creak of chairs marked the rhythm of their small reprieve from a world bent on decisions and decrees.

Yet even in the comfort of this table, Jo's thoughts wandered.

She set down her fork. "I spoke with the queen."

Cranmer looked up. He didn't speak, but the lift of his brow asked enough.

"She came to the kitchen," Jo said. "She was tired. And kind. And . . . utterly alone."

Margarete didn't interrupt. She folded her napkin and watched her.

"I didn't plan to say anything," Jo continued. "But she wanted to hear. She listened."

Cranmer set down his knife. "And what did you tell her?"

Jo hesitated. "That no one seemed to ask how she understood God in all of this. Not as a matter of doctrine. But in love. Whether she felt abandoned."

Cranmer's gaze lowered. His hands folded on the table, and for a moment, he didn't breathe.

"She said she did," Jo added quietly. "She did feel abandoned. By king, by court . . . by God."

The words settled like ash over the meal.

Margarete spoke gently. "And you? How did you respond?"

Jo glanced between them. "I told her I understood. That my birth mother once asked that same question. How love could stand by."

Cranmer leaned back in his chair. His eyes weren't wet, but they held something fragile behind them. "She was right to ask."

Margarete reached across the table, not to comfort but to steady. "Love waits," she said. "It does not abandon—but it cannot force. And it does not announce itself through power, but through presence."

Cranmer looked at her, then at Jo. "It's strange. I've spoken of God all my life. But it feels as though I'm only now beginning to meet him."

There was a long pause. Then Margarete said softly, "Then meet him well, Thomas. Even now. Especially now."

18

What Must Be Said

TIME PASSED, NOT MARKED by grand events or feasts, only by days. A few visits. Letters. And the slow settling of roles that once felt temporary.

Cranmer and Margarete made their way to Walthamstow more than once in those intervening weeks. At first, it was only to rest, to eat food not served on silver, to hear laughter unshaped by court. But eventually, it was more.

Roger and Margarete became quick allies—both plainspoken, both loyal, both suspicious of the self-important. Emilie delighted in Margarete's calm wit and strong hands, and Margarete, in turn, seemed warmed by the bright, unguarded goodness that flowed through the Cressy household like sunlight through a clean window.

Through the weeks and months, Jo had spent equal time at Walthamstow and London, her frequent visits a delight to Margarete and Cranmer (and Nicholas). The trio had all been shaped in quiet ways by that supper when they had shared the queen's reflections—shaped in ways that none of them could name, but all of them remembered.

Cranmer had, at last, become more than Archbishop-elect. The formalities had passed, the papal confirmation—ironic though it now seemed—had arrived, and he and Margarete had moved into Lambeth Palace. The old rhythm they had started to build—simple meals, unhurried evenings, long walks in quiet lanes—had given way to barges and couriers and days measured in petitions. The river crossing to Westminster took only minutes by ferry, but the weight it carried made each arrival feel longer.

Still, the season had turned. The quiet was giving way.

The king's court had grown restless. Whispers had solidified into timing. The day was approaching—no one said precisely when, but all knew it was near. The marriage would be addressed. The church—what remained of it—would be summoned. And Cranmer, as ever, would *stand in the breach.*

So it was that one clear morning, Roger and Emilie brought Jo into London once more.

They set out early, horses calm, roads unusually still. Conversation was light—Roger's half-finished joke, Emilie's delight at a market girl's hat, and Jo's usual thoughtful, watchful silence.

They stabled the horses near Westminster, then crossed the river by ferry to Lambeth, the current pushing them downstream as the towers of the palace rose against the midday light. Margarete greeted them in late morning, their arms full of bread and cold meat and a cloth-wrapped wheel of cheese, intending only to visit—but then someone said, "Let's bring it to court. Thomas must be forgetting to eat."

And that was how, not long after midday, Jo found herself again walking the echoing stone corridors of Westminster, flanked by Emilie's cheerful step and Roger's protective stride.

The air inside felt tighter now. Not tense, exactly—but expectant. Like a held breath.

The chapel stood quieter than she remembered, the courtiers' chatter thinner, more practiced. Even the windows, bright with midday light, seemed not to cast as far.

And then Jo saw him.

Cranmer, robed in full formality, was speaking to a clerk at the far end of the gallery. He hadn't noticed them yet. His bearing was upright—commanding even—but something in his shoulders had changed.

He looked taller in his robes.

And smaller inside them.

One of his hands rested on a rolled document, the other gestured toward the chapel doors. His expression was taut—focused, but not at ease.

Then something in the corridor caught his eye. A movement. A sound. A presence not entirely expected.

Margarete.

And beside her—Jo. Roger. Emilie.

Cranmer blinked once, then dismissed the clerk with a nod. His feet were already moving.

"You've come?" he said, more surprised than questioning. He glanced from one face to the next, lingering a moment longer on Jo. "All of you?"

"We didn't plan to intrude," Roger said cheerfully. "Only to feed you."

Margarete lifted the cloth-wrapped bundle in her arms. "They brought half the countryside with them. I helped only to carry it."

Cranmer gave the barest smile. "I should've known. The temptation of Walthamstow's fresh bounty is irresistible."

Emilie leaned forward conspiratorially. "We thought you might be forgetting to eat again."

"I am," he admitted. "So your timing is impeccable. Come. The office is warm and empty for now."

He turned without another word, and they followed—his robes brushing stone as he led them briskly down a narrow side passage.

They said little as they walked. The mood was light, but the walls seemed to hold a different kind of weight today. The deeper they went, the more tightly it settled.

At the door, Cranmer opened it for them. "Quickly now. I have only a moment before I'm summoned again."

They entered quietly, the stone corridor giving way to the closeness of a room too full of papers and too empty of breath. The window was open slightly, the sound of distant bells drifting in on a breeze that didn't cool much.

The office smell of parchment and wax and the faint tang of damp wool soon gave way to country ham, sharp white cheese, pickled onions, and stewed pears newly uncorked from a jar.

Roger laid the bread and cheese on the long side table. Emilie set down a wrapped parcel of meat. Margarete found a pitcher and poured the morning's cider into cups.

Cranmer didn't sit.

Jo noticed it first. He moved as though there wasn't time for a chair—as though a chair might hold him too long.

"You're in full robes," Roger said after a moment, slicing a wedge of cheese but not lifting it. "Is something happening?"

Cranmer glanced at him, then down at the edge of his sleeve. He exhaled.

"Yes," he said. "The annulment is to be declared."

A silence fell.

Roger looked up. "Today?"

"In less than an hour."

Margarete, still standing, set her cup down slowly. "Then it's done."

"Not until I say the words," Cranmer replied, quieter than before.

Emilie's brow furrowed. "But if you must declare it, then it isn't really your choice anymore, is it?"

"No," he said, "but the weight of it is."

Jo looked at him carefully. "You said once that you were only just beginning to meet the God you serve."

Cranmer nodded faintly.

"And today?" she asked.

He didn't answer.

A soft knock came at the door, then it opened partway.

Nicholas.

He stepped in with a bundle of papers and a flushed face. "Sir, they're asking for you. The last details are confirmed."

Cranmer straightened. "Yes."

He looked to the others. "You're welcome to observe—but quietly. The north gallery will be best."

He turned to Nicholas. "Take them. Make sure they're settled."

Nicholas nodded. "Of course."

Cranmer paused at the threshold. His eyes flicked across them—his wife, his niece, the two Cressys. His world, in all its trembling familiarity.

Then he was gone.

The corridors grew quieter as Nicholas led them upward.

Cloaked guards stood at attention. Courtiers murmured in passing. A servant bowed low as he passed, carrying a tray stacked with ink pots and parchment. And all the while, Jo walked just behind him—her footsteps light, her mind thudding.

At the landing before the gallery doors, Nicholas paused.

He opened the door, beckoning them in with a finger to his lips. Roger and Emilie eased in, followed by Margarete. Jo paused, wanting to speak privately to Nicholas. Nicholas, sensing her intent—and wanting that moment with her as well—closed the door for a moment.

He turned toward her—already flushed from the climb, but now visibly struggling to speak. "I didn't know you'd be coming today."

"I didn't either," Jo said. "We only meant to bring lunch. Apparently, history was on the menu."

He gave a tight laugh, then looked down. "I wish it wasn't."

Jo waited a beat. "Nicholas."

He looked up.

"I'm leaving again after today," she said softly. "Back to Walthamstow."

He nodded, but slowly.

She tilted her head, eyes searching his. "I don't want to go not knowing what this is. What we are."

His breath caught slightly. "Jo, I—"

She stopped him gently with her hand on his arm.

"I'm not asking for everything. Just . . . something true. Something you're not afraid to say."

Nicholas swallowed. Then, quieter: "I think of you when I should be working. I pray in the chapel, and your name rises before everything else. When you're here, the world . . . tilts expectantly. And when you're gone, it tilts back, but no longer level."

Jo's lips parted, her breath trembling with a smile too tender to speak. But then her face sobered.

"Do you ever wonder what this will do to the queen?"

Nicholas blinked—caught by the shift. Then he nodded. "Every hour."

Jo looked toward the gallery doors now looming like silent judgment.

"She's not just losing a marriage," she said. "She's losing her name."

Nicholas was quiet. "And the man pronouncing it—your uncle— may carry the blame for what others have already done."

They stood in silence, shoulder to shoulder, not touching but tethered by something quiet and fierce.

A bell sounded in the lower hall.

Nicholas inhaled. "We should go in."

"Thank you," Jo said quietly, "for saying what I needed—and didn't expect. You should know . . . it lives within me now."

Neither moved for one more heartbeat.

Then he turned and led her into the gallery.

The door closed behind him with a softened click. Cranmer stood a moment in the corridor, collecting himself.

He had not yet spoken to the king today—no formal preparatory word. Cromwell had sent word that they would meet just before the pronouncement, and now that moment had come.

The air here smelled of oiled leather and the faint perfume of rosewater. A shadow of incense from morning mass still lingered. Everything around him was ceremonial—but no part of it sacred.

At the far end of the passage, the heavy door opened, and Cromwell emerged, speaking low to an attendant before waving him off.

He saw Cranmer and gave a nod. "He's waiting."

Cranmer approached.

"He's pleased," Cromwell said softly. "The form is settled. The backing firm. You've done well."

"I've done what was asked," Cranmer replied.

Cromwell gave a small, unreadable smile. "And more than that. You've given England clarity."

"To some."

"To the only one who matters," Cromwell said, motioning toward the door.

Cranmer hesitated just a breath too long.

Cromwell turned to him more directly now. "Thomas. This is not about yesterday's loyalties. Or tomorrow's regrets. It's about now. The future will remember this moment with clean lines. Don't blur them by second-guessing what cannot be changed."

Cranmer looked at him—really looked at him.

"I've stopped expecting clean lines," he said.

Before Cromwell could answer, the inner door opened.

Henry VIII stood within, not robed but still resplendent in deep burgundy, gold chain heavy across his chest.

He stepped forward, arms slightly outstretched. "Ah, my archbishop."

Cranmer bowed. "Your Majesty."

Henry took his hand briefly, then turned and gestured toward the chamber. "All is prepared?"

"Yes, sire," Cranmer said.

"Good. Then let it be done."

He said it with the ease of a man ordering wine—or war.

As the king turned back into the chamber, Cromwell gave Cranmer a small nod.

"You were chosen for this," he said.

Cranmer didn't answer. Not to Cromwell. Not to anyone.

Cromwell followed the king inside.

Cranmer turned to pace.

The hall leading to the pronouncement chamber curved just slightly—a slow arc lit by narrow windows. Cranmer walked it alone.

One more step. Then another. The silence felt physical now.

And then he saw her.

Queen Catherine, Her Majesty, stood at the far end, alone, her back to the wall, hands folded in front of her. No attendants, no fanfare. Just presence.

For a moment, Cranmer considered turning about, back to the chamber. But she had already seen him.

He approached slowly.

"Your Grace," he said, bowing low.

Catherine inclined her head, her gaze measured but not cold. "My lord."

He straightened, uncertain how to continue. But she filled the silence.

"So it is today."

Cranmer nodded. "Yes."

She studied him a moment longer. "And you are the one who will speak it."

"I am."

A pause. "Does it cost you?"

He looked down. "Yes."

Her expression didn't soften, but something behind her eyes shifted. "You did not seek this role."

"No," Cranmer said quietly. "But I accepted it."

Catherine was silent. Then, with a voice even and low: "I wonder sometimes how long a heart can remain unbroken simply by calling its fracture obedience."

That stopped him.

He said nothing.

"I spoke with your niece," she added, her tone almost casual.

Cranmer looked up.

"She asked about God," Catherine said. "Not as argument. As long-ing." She tilted her head slightly. "It was the first time in many months I felt seen."

A long silence settled.

"She is . . . thoughtful," Cranmer said.

"She is brave," Catherine replied.

They stood facing each other—two figures carved by power, and bent beneath it.

Cranmer swallowed. "I am sorry, Your Grace."

Catherine gave the faintest nod. "So am I."

He gave a slight bow and slowly turned. Once at the door of the chamber, he paused and looked back.

But she was already gone.

The chamber was quiet. Stone walls, tall windows, light angled across polished floors.

At one end, a raised table stood with three chairs. Only one was occupied.

Cranmer.

The other chairs, meant for counsel or for show, remained empty. Only his decision would matter now.

He sat robed in full formality, his hands resting on the arms of the chair, knuckles pale. Before him, a small stack of parchment lay precisely aligned. Ink. A seal. Nothing more.

Along the side gallery, courtiers and clergy murmured in low voices. The king was not present—by design, not disinterest. What was to hap-pen needed weight, but not witness.

Jo sat with Roger and Emilie on one of the rear benches. Margarete just beside her. Nicholas stood to the right, eyes forward, expression still.

The silence deepened—not hushed, but hollow. The kind of quiet that follows endings no one will name.

Still, faint murmurs lingered—until Cranmer stood.

Then, even they fell away.

He looked across the room—not to meet anyone's gaze, but to *feel* the moment's shape.

Then he spoke.

"In accordance with the sacred laws of Holy Church, by authority granted and recognized in this realm, and by evidence presented and weighed, I—Thomas Cranmer, Archbishop of Canterbury—do declare the marriage between King Henry and Queen Catherine null and void from the beginning. It is, and has ever been, invalid in the eyes of God and this Church."

A rustle—like a breath, like judgment.

Cranmer continued.

"Let no man say otherwise. Let no paper claim otherwise. Let no soul suffer for speaking what conscience now affirms."

He paused, sealing the parchment with the press of his ring.

"The judgment is made. The court is adjourned."

He sat again. Not with relief. With finality.

In the gallery, Jo exhaled—slowly, like something had broken loose but had not yet fallen.

Roger's hand tightened around Emilie's. Margarete's eyes did not leave her husband.

Nicholas looked down.

And from an unseen corner of the chamber a clerk stepped forward and carried the sealed document away. And in that quiet, something unseen began to shift—though no one would know it for some time.

PART 3

Thomas More

My life is like a broken bowl,

A broken bowl that cannot hold

One drop of water for my soul

Or cordial in the searching cold.

Christina Rossetti, from *A Better Resurrection*

19

When Love Is the Guide

THE OCTOBER SUN FILTERED gently through the narrow chapel windows, catching in the soft folds of Jo's veil and the worn gold threads of Cranmer's stole. Lambeth's modest sanctuary, more often used for private devotion than ceremony, had taken on a hush that felt like reverence rather than absence. The kind that comes from meaning held too deeply for sound.

Cranmer stood before them, the book open in his hands, his voice clear though not loud. He read the vows with practiced cadence, each phrase carefully shaped, sacred more than solemn. And yet, as he looked between Jo and Nicholas, his words felt less like pronouncements and more like memories he could no longer touch.

Jo's voice caught as she repeated her lines—not from nerves, but something deeper. Nicholas reached for her hand, a glance passing between them, and she steadied.

"I give myself," she said softly, "not because I know what every tomorrow holds, but because love is the only guide worth following through them."

A few in the room stirred at that—not out of disapproval, but recognition. Emilie dabbed at the corner of her eye. Roger gave a small, proud nod. Will, standing near the rear, straight-backed in a precisely tailored coat, gave the faintest nod—less from sentiment than from something like respect. As if, for once, words had caught him unprepared.

Cranmer's eyes flicked to the side. Margarete stood near the wall, neither tearful nor smiling. Watching him.

He felt it—the unspoken tension that had grown between them. Her presence was never cold. It was worse than that. It was open. Open in a way that invited him to step into the light and risk being known again. And that was what he could not yet do.

He looked back to the couple. Nicholas had taken both of Jo's hands now, his thumbs grazing the backs of her fingers. The final blessing came too soon, too briefly, and Cranmer raised his hand with a benediction that felt thinner than it should have:

"May the Lord who binds hearts in covenant keep you in faith and peace, all the days of your lives."

The "Amen" that followed was small and uneven.

The newlyweds turned to face the room. There was no swell of music, no grand recessional. Just a breath, a pause, and then the rustling of feet as guests shifted and followed them out into the adjoining hall where warmth and wine awaited.

Cranmer closed the book slowly. As the room emptied, Margarete remained where she stood. For a moment, he thought she might approach. Instead, she said simply, without force, "Do you remember saying those words to me?"

He looked at her, startled. "I do."

She held his gaze just a second longer. "I remember meaning them."

Then she walked past him, leaving only the scent of rosemary and the ache of things too long unspoken.

The hall adjoining Lambeth Chapel had been dressed with care—long tables lined in linen, their edges softened by herbs and late autumn ivy. Tall windows stood open to the afternoon air, letting in a breeze just crisp enough to keep the candles flickering, though not enough to cool the warm press of guests. The scent of roast chicken and fresh bread mingled with wine and woodsmoke.

Roger Cressy stood near the head of the table, one hand resting on his goblet, the other raised mid-air like a juggler balancing sincerity and cheer.

"A word," he said, not loudly, but with just enough gravity to quiet the room.

Jo and Nicholas, seated beside one another just beneath the high windows, turned to him with unpracticed grace. Jo's hair had begun to come loose from the ribbon at her temple, and Nicholas's expression held the tentative relief of a man who had crossed a threshold and found himself still intact.

Roger cleared his throat. "To those who married today—may you never regret it. And to those who've been married long enough to doubt that blessing—may you remember that love, at its best, is not a feeling or a wind, but a choice you keep remaking."

A few guests murmured in agreement. Emilie smiled gently. Will gave the faintest eye-roll behind his cup, as if amused by his father's fondness for sudden gravitas.

Roger continued. "To Jo and Nicholas—who are not only good and kind, but stubborn enough to believe that love is still the best rebellion against fear."

He lifted his goblet. "To covenant. May it outlast all kingdoms."

The room echoed with a dozen soft "hear, hears," and the clinking of glasses rose above the music, which had resumed with a quiet flute and a viol.

Cranmer raised his cup but did not drink. His gaze drifted toward the end of the table where Margarete sat beside Emilie, her expression serene but her fingers resting motionless beside her untouched plate.

As the table's hum grew around them, Emilie leaned in and gently brushed a crumb from Margarete's sleeve.

"You've barely touched your chicken," she said, her voice light.

"I've never been much for public meals," Margarete replied.

"Oh, you struck me as someone who'd enjoy a gathering like this," Emilie said with a small smile. "I come from a country atmosphere and always dreamed of galas."

Margarete gave a soft hum of agreement, neither denying nor affirming. Her gaze drifted across the room—toward Cranmer, who was speaking with Will and Cromwell in slow, measured tones.

"I'm watching him," she said.

Emilie followed her glance. "He carries a great deal."

"He does," Margarete said. "But lately, I wonder if he's carrying it— or hiding under it."

There was no bitterness in her voice. Just the tired ache of someone who had waited too long for a conversation that never came.

Emilie lowered her voice. "You don't think it's just the weight of his office?"

"I think it's what he gave away to sit in it."

Emilie frowned slightly, not in disagreement but in concern. "Do you think he regrets the annulment?"

"No," Margarete said. "I think he believes it was necessary. That's the most dangerous kind of regret—the kind that won't speak its name."

Emilie was quiet for a moment. Then, "He still listens to you, I think."

"No," Margarete said again, but this time more gently. "He listens to his conscience. I just happen to sound like it now and then."

She turned to Emilie, eyes clearer than before. "I don't want to rescue him. I want to be near him when he starts telling the truth again—to himself, I mean. But the space between us has grown cold. And it's not because I left it empty."

Emilie's hand rested lightly on hers. "He's still searching."

"I know. But the longer he delays naming what he fears, the more it becomes who he is."

Across the room, Cranmer rose slowly, murmured something to Will, and made his way toward the outer corridor.

Margarete watched him go, then turned back to her plate. "And what I fear," she said, "is that he'll become what he was never meant to be—and believe it was God who asked it of him."

Nicholas had stepped away from Jo for a moment and now stood among a few fellow clerks near one of the side tables, a goblet in hand, half-listening to Will recount something about Erasmus and the Oxford curriculum. He nodded along, but his attention kept drifting—back to Jo across the room, then forward again to the low hum of conversation around Cromwell, who had just moved away from Cranmer and now stood alone, studying the arrangement of wine cups as if they might reveal policy.

Nicholas slipped away from his group and approached Cromwell with that particular form of caution that comes when a man is unsure whether his standing is as secure as the setting implies.

"Master Cromwell," he said, giving a small nod of respect.

Cromwell turned, surprised only for a breath. "Ah. The husband of the hour." He extended a hand, firm and brief. "You wear the day well, Nicholas. A woman like Jo doesn't settle. She chooses."

Nicholas gave a quiet laugh. "That's certainly how it felt."

Cromwell studied him a moment longer, then leaned slightly closer, lowering his voice to match the mood. "Tell me—does the weight of the vow feel heavier or lighter now that it's spoken aloud?"

Nicholas glanced toward Jo before answering. "It doesn't feel heavy. But it does feel . . . real—substantive, even. Tangible in a way it didn't before. Like I've stepped onto something I can't see the end of—but I believe it's solid."

Cromwell's expression didn't change, but his eyes sharpened. "Then you're ahead of most."

There was a pause, comfortable enough, before Cromwell added, "You've gained a wife and, perhaps, a soul to raise. A tidy return on a vow."

Nicholas shook his head lightly. "It doesn't feel tidy at all. It feels like the beginning of everything uncertain—and worth it."

Cromwell offered a faint, sideways smile. "Uncertainty is all the world gives. What matters is choosing your weight before the wind comes."

Nicholas didn't answer right away. He felt the truth of that sentence press against the day's joy—not undermining it, but deepening it. Then he said, "Jo and I have spoken about children. About what kind of life we'd want to give them. We don't know if it will come—but we've decided to live as if it might."

Cromwell nodded. "That is the only wise way to live—*as if it might.*"

He shifted his gaze then, following Nicholas's to Jo.

"She is a woman who sees what others don't. I've known a few like her. They either break—or change the people around them."

Nicholas tilted his head. "And which do you think she'll be?"

Cromwell met his eyes. "That depends on whether the people around her are willing to be changed."

The flute music paused then—just a heartbeat, just enough for the silence to settle. Cromwell clapped Nicholas lightly on the shoulder.

"Enjoy the evening, young master. You won't get many nights this honest."

Then he moved off, leaving Nicholas wondering whether Cromwell's "honesty" was meant to teach or warn.

Jo turned at the sound of laughter near the corner hearth. A short, round woman with a flushed face and hands still slightly chapped from years of work was speaking animatedly with Roger and Emilie. Her accent held the countryside, but her spirit was unmistakably present. Nicholas's mother Bess was getting to know Roger and Emilie.

"And so I told him," Bess was saying, "you can keep your goose if you like, but don't let it near my oven again unless it's plucked proper this time."

Emilie laughed, eyes warm. "You're everything Nicholas said you were."

"And more, I'd wager," Roger added, smiling.

Bess gave an exaggerated curtsey, then took Emilie's hand in hers. "Your daughter is the treasure of England. That's what I've been telling everyone all night."

"She's ours," Roger said with playful pride. "Though I'm still not sure how we earned her."

Bess leaned in. "And my Nicholas—he's rough around the edges, but his heart's been gentled since she came along. You should've seen him as a boy—always trying to fix broken things."

"He still does," Emilie said softly. "Not people—just what pain leaves behind. I'm so glad Jo found him."

Jo, having stepped close enough to hear, reached out and embraced Bess. "I'm so glad to be part of your family."

"Oh, love, I've gained a daughter. Brings tears, it does," Bess said, patting her cheek. "Even Latimer was sniffling at the ceremony."

"I haven't met him yet," said Roger.

"Oh, he's over by the wine. Quiet, as ever. But proud—though he'll deny it."

Jo smiled, then glanced at Roger and Emilie. "We'll introduce him."

The small exchange glowed like a hearth in winter—brief, warm, and full of belonging. It didn't demand notice. But it mattered. They were family now.

The warmth of the hall had deepened as the sun lowered, gold fading into a soft amber. Some of the guests had drifted out onto the small veranda where lanterns had been lit. Others remained at the tables, chatting low over wine and laughter. Jo had stepped out briefly for air and now returned, her expression open, searching. She found Margarete near the corner of the hall, where the candles burned lower and the noise of the room softened.

"You disappeared," Jo said gently, sliding into the chair beside her.

Margarete turned to her with a faint smile. "Just watching. Sometimes that's the only way I hear anything true."

Jo looked across the room. "It's strange. I thought today would feel like the end of something—the end of waiting, maybe. But it doesn't. It feels like I've walked through one door to face a dozen more."

Margarete nodded slowly. "That's how beginnings often feel. Not clean. Just more awake."

Jo turned toward her more fully now. "We've talked about children. Nicholas and I. I want them. I really do. But something in me keeps asking—what if I can't? Or worse, what if I can . . . and I'm not enough?"

Margarete didn't answer at once. She took a breath, watching the flicker of a candle as it leaned in the draft.

"I once thought love would come when I was ready. When I had all my answers sorted and all my fears laid down. But that's not how it works. Love is not a mystical presence that arrives on its own when your soul has ordered itself."

Jo was quiet.

Margarete continued, her voice low. "You said something in your vows—that you chose love because it was the only guide worth following. I heard that. And I think it's true. But I'd add something."

Jo turned her head. "What?"

"That love doesn't promise certainty. People often expect love to come with guarantees, with safety and clarity. But love first and most, is a vulnerability. You open yourself. You offer who you are. And then you invite."

She took a breath, then continued, "And you wait. You wait for that other loving heart to open—to invite as well. And when both of you keep showing up—day after day, with your eyes open and your hearts still willing and inviting—that's when fear begins to lose its voice."

Jo studied her a long moment. "You've lived that, haven't you?"

Margarete's smile was small. "Some of it. Enough to know that fear doesn't vanish. It just gets redefined."

Jo leaned in a little. "What do you mean?"

"I mean . . . most people live thinking fear is something to run from. But sometimes fear is just awe that hasn't been named yet. Sometimes it's the weight of what matters most pressing down on your soul, asking if you're willing to carry it."

Jo's eyes shimmered—not with tears, but with something like realization. "That's . . . what today felt like."

Margarete nodded once. "Then you're walking the right way."

Jo glanced back out at the tables, then to the doorway where Nicholas stood in conversation with Will. "There's so much I don't know. About God. About what this life is becoming."

"You're not alone in that," Margarete said.

Jo's voice dropped. "Do you think God is . . . angry when we're afraid?"

"No," Margarete said without hesitation. "I think God is most present when we bring him our fear instead of hiding it. That's when he starts reshaping it."

Jo sat back, letting that settle. Then: "You make it sound so simple."

Margarete smiled again, just barely. "It's not simple. It's just true."

❖ ❖ ❖

Cranmer stood near the outer edge of the hall, where the light from the windows no longer reached. A servant passed him a fresh cup of wine, which he accepted but did not drink. His gaze had been elsewhere all evening—wandering, inward.

Cromwell approached without ceremony, pausing beside him as if both men had come to the same quiet space by accident.

"An elegant affair," Cromwell said, his eyes scanning the room. "Simple, but sincere."

Cranmer gave a slight nod. "She insisted it not be elaborate."

"Smart," Cromwell said. "It's the hearts you remember, not the drapery."

There was a pause, long enough that either of them could have walked away.

Cromwell stayed. "I watched you during the vows. You looked as though part of you was officiating—and part of you was wondering what it meant to believe any of it."

Cranmer didn't answer. His eyes were on Jo and Nicholas, now standing near the veranda door.

"She spoke clearly," Cromwell added. "Not just well. That line about love as a guide—it didn't sound rehearsed."

"It wasn't," Cranmer said. "She wrote her own vows."

Cromwell nodded. "And meant them, I think. Most vows are theatrical obedience. Hers were more dangerous."

Cranmer turned slightly. "Dangerous?"

Cromwell's voice lowered just a touch. "When people believe in love as a guide, they're harder to control. Because they won't follow fear. And they won't bow to power—not even kindly meant power."

Cranmer was still. "You think she's a threat?"

Cromwell shrugged. "Not today. Not to the king. But maybe to you."

That landed—not hard, but pointed.

"Why speak of it now?" Cranmer asked.

"Because Thomas More received his letter this week."

Cranmer turned to face him fully.

Cromwell continued. "He hasn't answered yet. And his 'answer' will not be what the king hopes. When he refuses—because we both know he will—it won't be Parliament who first responds to him. It will be you."

Cranmer's face didn't move, but his grip tightened slightly on the cup he still hadn't tasted.

Cromwell didn't press. "You should be prepared. The crown wants loyalty, not a debate. But if it comes to debate, you'll need to make More look like the one who moved."

He started to turn, then paused.

"And Thomas . . ." His voice was quiet now, for Cranmer's ears only. "Be sure what you fear. Because fear will shape your tone before it shapes your mind."

Then he moved back toward the heart of the hall, his steps light, his presence already shifting to someone else's circle—leaving Cranmer alone at the edge, the wine still untouched in his hand.

The last of the plates had been cleared, and the music had softened to a low instrumental echo. A few guests still lingered, chatting in half-circles near the hearth or stepping into the cooler air outside. The celebration had dimmed into its second breath—the quiet, reflective end that always follows joy shared honestly.

Jo and Nicholas stood just beyond the doorway, beneath the reach of the lantern light. The garden path beyond was dark, but the stars were beginning to show themselves—soft, tentative lights against the fading blue.

Jo leaned lightly into Nicholas's arm, her head just brushing his shoulder.

"It's quieter now," she said.

"Too quiet?"

"No. Just enough."

Nicholas looked down at her, his voice low. "You seemed far away a few times."

Jo nodded. "I spoke with Margarete."

He waited, patient.

"She said that fear doesn't vanish—it just gets redefined. That sometimes it's just awe, waiting to be named."

Nicholas turned that over. "You agree?"

"I think I do." She glanced up at him. "Today I felt everything. Joy. Wonder. But also something heavy pressing on me—not in warning, just . . . reminding me that what we just did wasn't small."

Nicholas gave a quiet breath of laughter. "No, it wasn't small."

"I'm not afraid of you," Jo said, half-smiling. "But I think I've begun to understand what fear of God really feels like. Not panic. Not punishment. But that sharp breath you take when you realize you've stepped into something much larger than yourself—and it sees you."

Nicholas was silent for a moment. Then he said, "That's how I feel about today too. Not just the vows. The people. Watching all of them—your uncle, Margarete, Cromwell. It feels like we're standing on something that's already shaking."

He paused, then added, "But you're right. I'm not afraid of you either."

Jo laughed, soft and real. "That's something."

They stood that way a moment longer, watching the night gather.

Inside, Cranmer had drifted back to the corner near the hall's arched windows. His goblet sat untouched on a ledge now, forgotten. He saw Jo and Nicholas beyond the glass—still, joined, speaking in low tones too far to hear.

He watched them without envy. Without clarity. Just a kind of ache.

Then, from across the room, his eyes caught Margarete's. She hadn't moved. Hadn't spoken. But she had been watching him watch them.

Their gaze held for only a breath—but it was enough.

He looked away first.

Margarete turned her face back to the window.

20

The Silence before the Storm

PARLIAMENT WAS NOT YET in session, but its shadow already loomed. The Act of Supremacy, though not yet named aloud, had been drafted in spirit months earlier. By October, its passage was a certainty. All that remained was the gathering of votes, the quiet breaking of dissent, and the soft rituals of submission that came before official decree.

The crown moved slowly, but with purpose. Key figures had already been approached—first by letter, then by silence from the crown, letting the weight of delay speak louder than words. Not all responded. Not all needed to. Some, like Thomas More—the former Lord Chancellor—had already made their positions clear not by stepping forward, but by taking a step back. He had refused to swear to the Oath of Succession that spring, speaking no direct treason but withholding the affirmation that mattered most. It was not his words that troubled the king. It was his quiet.

Now he lived in Chelsea, writing by lamplight, walking in gardens too small to distract him, refusing all positions and titles that might bind his conscience. No sermons, no protests. Just stillness. For More, silence was not defiance. It was his last defense. A narrow space between betrayal and martyrdom. He hoped, perhaps, that by saying nothing, neither the Crown could claim his soul nor the Church could release it. But that kind of silence sharpened fear more than any rebellion could.

At court, the waiting was as brittle as it was rehearsed. Nobles passed one another in hallways with warm eyes and guarded words. Servants hurried more quickly, not because there was more to do, but because it looked like loyalty. Anne Boleyn moved through these rooms like a storm briefly calmed—crowned, empowered, and increasingly impatient. She had gained the throne but not the reverence. And reverence, she believed, was her due.

To the men who had secured her rise, she was still somewhat useful. To those who had once loved her wit and defiance, she was now more difficult to love. She tested friendships the way one tests fabric—pulling hard to see what gives first. Some frayed quietly. Others snapped. Henry bore her moods with the weary tolerance of a man who believed he deserved everything he had demanded, including her.

But it was Mary, Catherine's daughter, who best embodied the court's tension. She was neither queen nor heir, neither noble nor free. Too proud to beg, too devout to flatter, and too clever to ignore, she appeared through the outer halls of the court like one standing in exile among her own people. To some she was tragic. To others, dangerous.

Though her official household had been relocated, she was kept close—not among the queen's retinue, but near enough for supervision, far enough for shame. She attended few audiences but could be seen crossing galleries, escorted, her presence tolerated but never invited.

It was from her chamber that the trouble began. A silver cross—simple, old, and not particularly valuable—went missing from a carved wooden box beside her private altar. She said it had belonged to her mother—a keepsake from earlier, steadier days—and no one questioned that. When the topic came up, she did not speak of its monetary worth. Only its meaning. "It was mine," she said. "And someone has treated it like nothing."

Her words were soft. But her tone was not. By the next morning, three servants had been questioned. One was dismissed. One fled. And one—a boy named Jonas—said nothing at all.

He was young. Quiet. Careful. The kind of servant who drew no attention until attention found him. When a steward suggested his name, others nodded—not because they knew him, but because they didn't. He didn't belong to anyone powerful. He didn't speak much. And he was, by unfortunate coincidence, often assigned to the queen's wing, where tensions were higher and forgiveness slower.

No formal charge had been made. Not yet. But rumors moved faster than evidence. By the time Nicholas heard of it, the story had already grown sharp with suspicion.

The corridor near the steward's office carried the muted energy of a court in mid-breath—errands passed quietly but quickly, no one certain where the pressure was coming from, only that it had arrived.

Will Cressy leaned against the stone ledge of a recessed window, turning a half-eaten plum in his hand. "All over a little silver cross," he said, shaking his head. "It's not even worth enough to melt."

Nicholas stood nearby, reviewing a list of assignments on a folded parchment. He didn't look up.

Will went on. "And our 'Princess' Mary. She's royalty—or was—but dreadfully brittle, that one. Carries herself like a martyr and scowls like it's a weapon."

Nicholas glanced over. "She's had reason to be brittle."

Will waved the comment away. "Still. Now they're sniffing around the servants' wing like it's a nest of traitors. Stupid boy probably nicked it for a dare. Or for a girl. Bratty pages are always playing knight with things they don't own."

Nicholas folded the parchment. "What was his name?"

Will shrugged. "Jonas, I think. From the queen's wing. No one I've dealt with. Took it when they were moving Mary out."

Nicholas was quiet. He knew the name. Knew the boy's mother, in fact—a weaver's widow who had once cleaned linens for his aunt. He remembered Jonas at ten, holding his sister's hand like a rope through a storm. Quiet. Watchful. Careful not to get in anyone's way.

He didn't speak again until Will tossed the plum core out the open window.

"Do they know he did it?" Nicholas asked.

Will snorted. "Don't need to know. Just need someone to blame before Mary decides the walls are conspiring against her."

Before Nicholas could reply, a movement down the corridor drew both of their eyes. Cromwell approached with a presence that made even passing stewards straighten unconsciously.

He was holding a folded document.

"Gentlemen," Cromwell said, glancing between them. "Might I borrow your attention?"

Will immediately straightened, brushing his sleeves.

Nicholas tucked the parchment under his arm, following Cromwell's lead as the moment shifted from gossip to something far more grave.

Cromwell approached with his usual blend of quiet and command—like a door swinging open before anyone touched the handle.

"What are we discussing?" he asked, stopping before them.

Will stood straighter. "The theft in the queen's wing. Boy named Jonas, apparently."

Cromwell's brow barely moved. "Ah. Yes. A silver cross."

Will smirked. "The court's atwitter. Pages watching their pockets. Ladies inventing ghosts."

Nicholas said, "I knew the boy once. His mother worked for my aunt. He's careful. Doesn't seem the sort to steal."

Cromwell gave him a look—flat, unreadable. "No one seems the sort, until they are."

Then, without pause, he drew a folded document from beneath his coat. "We've received word back from Chelsea."

He handed it to Nicholas.

Nicholas opened it slowly, skimming the neat, spare lines. Will leaned, but didn't press.

"It's not from More," Nicholas said.

"No," Cromwell replied. "More replies by not replying. The messenger says he declined to sign, speak, or explain. A silence as full as any sentence."

Will gave a short laugh. "He's playing the ghost of conscience."

Cromwell didn't smile. "He's playing for time. But the act will pass. When it does, silence won't protect him."

He turned slightly, surveying the corridor. "Parliament opens in three weeks. Between now and then, every voice must be counted. Every hesitation, closed."

He pointed to Will. "You'll go to Lambeth. Clergy lists need confirming. Those who've signed, those who haven't. Quietly."

Will nodded, half-grinning. "With discretion, of course."

Cromwell turned to Nicholas. "You'll help finalize the record of inquiries. Cross-check with Crompton in archives. Anyone who's delayed response should be noted."

Nicholas gave a short nod, but his eyes were already drifting—down the hall, where a steward had cornered a page against a column, voice rising low and firm.

Cromwell followed his gaze.

After a moment, he said, "First the list. Then see to your boy."

He didn't wait for an answer. By the time Nicholas looked back, Cromwell was already gone.

Nicholas left Will and descended to the lower courtyard. He moved briskly despite the stones underfoot being slick with the thin sheen of an October mist. He carried Cromwell's instructions folded under his arm, his mind already rehearsing names he might need to cross-check, clerks who would stall, scribes who'd misfiled.

As Nicholas passed the kitchens, the door opened with a burst of warm air. A young maid stumbled through, arms full of spoiled greens, chased by the scent of leeks and burned butter.

Behind her, a stable boy leaned in the doorway, muttering toward someone inside. "It's not like Jonas meant anything by it. Liza just panicked, that's all."

Nicholas slowed. "Jonas?"

The boy looked up, startled. "Yes, sir. That's the one they're holding. From the queen's wing."

Nicholas stepped closer. "Do you know where he is?"

The boy nodded toward the back. "Near the laundry. Not locked in—but he's not free, either. And he hasn't said much."

"Anything at all?"

The boy scratched his neck. "Only that he didn't mean for anyone else to get blamed."

Nicholas gave a quiet nod, then stepped back. "Thank you."

He moved on toward Crompton's office. The mist had thickened slightly. Behind him, the kitchen door clicked shut.

Later that evening, Nicholas stood near the small hearth in the outer chamber of their rooms, unbuttoning the cuffs of his sleeves. The fire had burned low, casting soft amber over the wooden floorboards. Jo stood at the small side table, folding linens and humming faintly under her breath, her rhythm steady.

"I heard about the boy today," Nicholas said, eyes on the fire. "Jonas."

Jo paused. "You knew him?"

"His mother worked for my aunt. I remember her—quiet, dignified. She used to bring him to help fold napkins when he was no taller than this table. Always careful. Always watching."

Nicholas settled into the deep-cushioned chair, its high back and curved arms cradling him in the warmth. "He's not one to cause trouble."

Jo returned to her folding. "What are they saying?"

"That he won't deny it. But he hasn't confessed either. Just quiet." Nicholas shook his head. "I don't think he took it. But even if he did . . . I think he needs someone to hear him out. He needs someone to stand beside him."

Jo placed a folded cloth on the growing stack. "Are you going to speak with him?"

"I've thought about it," Nicholas said. "But Cromwell's already warned me once about getting distracted."

Jo came and sat beside him. "Then let this be your distraction."

He gave her a look—part smile, part ache.

She continued, gently: "Justice matters. But if no one will see him— if no one will step forward when it costs something—then all we're doing is measuring guilt and shame. That's not justice. That's survival."

Nicholas exhaled, slowly. "You are always clear and direct."

"Well, it *is* clear," Jo said. "When someone is alone, and you could stand with him—that's the question. Whether you do."

Nicholas was quiet again. Then he said, "I think I will. Even if it's only to listen."

Jo smiled and returned to her folding.

Cranmer stood near the tall window of his chamber at Westminster— a place for work and sometimes sleep. The pale morning light traced thin lines across the floor. He held a folded letter in his hands but wasn't reading it. His eyes were on the garden below—bare branches, trimmed hedges, the slow rustle of leaves that refused to fall.

Cromwell entered without preamble but paused just inside the threshold, as if weighing the air.

"You've seen the reply," he said.

Cranmer turned, not startled. "If silence can be called a reply."

Cromwell moved closer. "It was never More's voice that caused trouble. It's his restraint. He's made a religion of it."

Cranmer set the letter on the table. "He's a lawyer. And a careful one. You'll not win him with threats."

"I have no intention of threatening him," Cromwell said. "That's why I'm asking you to confront him."

Cranmer raised an eyebrow. "I'm not the Lord Chancellor."

"No," Cromwell agreed. "But you're something rarer—his equal, in a different register. He won't answer Parliament, and he won't answer me. But he might answer you."

Cranmer stepped away from the window. "You're overreaching. More's mind was trained in law, not liturgy. You want me to challenge his footing in his own territory?"

Cromwell was quiet for a moment. "No. I want you to invite him to step off that footing. To speak not as lawyer to law, but as man to man—as believer to believer."

Cranmer's eyes narrowed faintly. "So I'm to ask as priest, but carry the king's blade?"

Cromwell paused. "You're not the blade. Not yet. You're the last hand he might trust."

There was a long silence.

Then Cranmer said, "If I speak with him, I won't do so to convince him—but to understand him. I will not press for signatures like a clerk collecting taxes."

Cromwell gave a nod. "Let it be what it must. But it must be soon. The act is coming to vote. Once it passes, delay becomes defiance."

"I'll send the summons today," Cranmer said. "I'll send it by a courier I can trust—one who won't be brash, puffed up with importance as an emissary from court. Nicholas can carry it. He knows how to speak with respect. More may not feel the need to raise his guard with him."

Cromwell took hold of that thought, a plan forming. "Yes, he's trustworthy. Loyal to you. That's not nothing."

"And he listens," Cranmer said.

Cromwell's gaze sharpened slightly. "Listens. Yes. Let him take the summons. Let him be his polite, disarming self. Maybe More's tongue might loosen. And then—Nicholas must *listen*."

The records room was dim and dry, a breath of dust rising every time a page was turned. Nicholas stood at the high desk beside Crompton, the chief archivist, as they cross-checked clergy signatures against Cromwell's original list.

"Southwark is late again," Crompton muttered, squinting at the script. "Always three days behind. I've half a mind to mark them as non-compliant and be done with it."

Nicholas kept his tone neutral. "Might be worth sending a clerk rather than a warning. They'll move faster when they see they're being watched."

Crompton gave a grunt that might have been agreement and turned the page.

When the list was complete and each name marked, Nicholas gathered the papers and stepped back. "I'll send this on to Cromwell."

"Do," Crompton said, already reaching for the next sheaf.

Nicholas stepped into the corridor, folding the report under one arm. The late afternoon light filtered weakly through the stone-framed windows, leaving more shadow than warmth.

As he turned a corner, he saw a young boy seated on a bench near the outer courtyard—hands folded, head bowed, flanked loosely by two older stewards. Not a prison guard's stance. Just watchmen, waiting.

Nicholas hesitated. Then he approached.

"Jonas."

The boy looked up—his eyes clear, not defiant, not afraid. Just tired.

Nicholas sat beside him, careful not to crowd.

"I knew your mother," he said quietly. "She worked for my aunt. She trusted you."

Jonas looked down again. "She wouldn't now."

"Why not?"

A pause.

"They thought it was Matthew," Jonas said. "He works with me in the queen's wing. Said they'd found something in his linen satchel."

Nicholas frowned. "And?"

"I told them it couldn't be him. That he wouldn't do it."

"That was brave," Nicholas said.

Jonas's voice lowered. "Then they asked how I knew. I didn't answer."

Nicholas studied him. "And that's when they turned on you."

Jonas gave a small nod. "I didn't want to say anything more. But saying nothing . . . it was enough."

Nicholas was quiet for a moment. "Sometimes silence is mistaken for guilt. And sometimes it becomes it."

Jonas looked over, finally meeting his eyes. "I know."

Nicholas stood. "If you want someone to speak for you, I need to know what you'd have them say."

Jonas didn't answer.

Nicholas didn't press. "I'll be nearby."

He stepped away, unsure whether the silence he'd left behind was a wall—or a shield.

Later, still at Westminster, Cranmer's study was unusually still, the air thick with the scent of ash and vellum. The windows stood closed against the late autumn wind, and a single taper burned beside the desk, though daylight still hung behind the clouds.

Nicholas stepped through the open door and paused.

"You asked for me?"

Cranmer looked up from a draft he wasn't reading, his eyes tired but focused. He motioned Nicholas in. "Close the door."

Nicholas did so, and stood quietly as Cranmer reached for a folded parchment, pressing its seal flat against the desk with two fingers.

"This is a summons," Cranmer said. "It is for Sir Thomas More."

He continued almost speaking the words to himself. "It is worded carefully. It does not accuse. It requests—yes, requests a conversation."

Nicholas nodded, though Cranmer wasn't looking at him. Then Cranmer did look up.

"I want you to take it to Sir Thomas at Chelsea. You are to deliver it—personally. Leave first thing in the morning. Take the river. I'll assign a skiff. You should make it there, deliver the message, allow Sir Thomas a moment to prepare for a day's trip, and then be back here before dark. Deliver him to the bishop's guest chamber at Lambeth—over the library. We'll talk there at Lambeth in the morning."

Nicholas nodded again. "He still hasn't signed?"

"He hasn't signed. He hasn't explained. He hasn't spoken."

Nicholas hesitated, then spoke gently. "Would it help if he knew you weren't asking as a prelate—but as a friend? That it's not just the crown that wants his soul, but that someone still cares what becomes of it?"

Cranmer flinched—just slightly—as if the word *friend* struck something raw. His face tightened. For days now, he'd been caught between politics and conscience, watching names gather like a tide, feeling the line between persuasion and coercion blur. He had once believed the cause was clean. Lately, he wasn't so sure.

He stood—too quickly—and placed both hands on the desk, his voice sharp:

"No. I will not dress this up as friendship. I will not ask under false terms or cloak this in robes of shared past. This is not confession. And I am not his confessor."

Nicholas blinked, taken aback. "I didn't mean to suggest—" His voice faltered. "I meant only . . . if he knew you came honestly, not as court or crown—"

Cranmer drew a breath, slow and deep. His shoulders lowered. The storm passed as quickly as it rose.

"I know what you meant. Forgive me."

Another breath. "Too many voices pressing. Too many names waiting to sign—or waiting to be punished. I won't manipulate Thomas More. And I won't see him manipulated."

There was a beat of silence before he handed Nicholas the parchment.

"Take this to him. Speak plainly. Listen well."

Nicholas accepted it with both hands.

Cranmer looked down, then added softly, again almost as if to himself:

"Perhaps he will speak before the silence becomes a verdict."

The morning air was cold but dry, the Thames slow and brown under a dull sky. Nicholas stepped down toward the dock where the small skiff waited, a single boatman seated near the oarlocks. The parchment lay sealed inside his satchel, snug between a prayer book and a folded kerchief.

He was adjusting his gloves when Cromwell's voice reached him.

"Nicholas."

Nicholas turned. Cromwell descended the slope with his usual economy—neither hasty nor slow, as though gravity answered to him alone.

"Just before you cast off," Cromwell said, eyes scanning the river. "I want to remind you—this is more than a delivery."

Nicholas straightened. "The archbishop gave me clear instructions. I'm to be courteous, direct—"

"And you will be," Cromwell said, cutting in gently. "But if More speaks—if he lets anything slip about why he won't sign, what he fears, what line he won't cross—I want to know it."

Nicholas hesitated. "He's a careful man."

"Even careful men forget they're speaking when they think they're only thinking aloud."

Cromwell stepped closer.

"You're not there to press him. But you are there. And you're listening. If he speaks, even a thread—pull it."

Nicholas gave a short nod, though his brow creased faintly. "Does the archbishop know you're asking this?"

Cromwell met his eyes, then looked away toward the water.

"The archbishop hopes you'll speak to More's soul. I hope you'll speak to his hesitation."

Nicholas was quiet a moment. Then softly: "So—whichever will break his silence?

Cromwell hesitated. Then: "We're not trying to break him. We're trying to keep him from breaking himself."

Then he stepped back, nodded once, and turned up the slope, as usual, without waiting for a reply.

Nicholas stood still a moment longer, then stepped into the boat, and seated himself in the stern.

The oars cut quietly into the water. Chelsea waited ahead, silent and still.

21

A Matter of Conscience

The Thames moved like thought—slow, brown, and inevitable. It did not race toward the sea. It submitted to it. Morning hung gray above the water, sky and current matching in their refusal to be stirred. Beneath the rhythm of oars, the boat slipped forward in silence.

Nicholas sat in the stern, his hands folded lightly, his satchel against his side. The summons had done its work. What he carried now was the silence that followed it.

Sir Thomas More sat ahead of him, wrapped in a simple cloak, his shoulders stiff against the damp. He had nodded when Nicholas arrived in Chelsea, nodded again when they boarded. He had offered no other words. But Nicholas knew silence was not absence. Not with this man.

They moved a long while without words. The oars dipped, pulled, and rose again, the sound folding into the damp air like breath in prayer.

"I've read your *Utopia*," Nicholas said at last, his voice barely louder than the water's hush. "Not all of it yet. But enough to know you care about more than power."

More didn't turn, but his voice came back plainly. "That's generous of you. Most read it only to ask what I meant. Few ask what I hoped."

Nicholas tilted his head slightly. "What did you hope?"

More was quiet a moment, as if weighing the question rather than evading it.

"That someone might glimpse a better world," he said. "Not to build it, perhaps. But to remember it's possible."

The boat continued forward, the mist loosening its grip on the water. A gull passed overhead, unnoticed by both men.

"Do you believe the Church is that world?" Nicholas asked.

"No," More replied. "But I believe it is the last thing on earth that remembers it."

Nicholas shifted slightly in his seat. "Even when it's wrong?"

There was a pause—measured, thoughtful.

"Even then. Perhaps especially then. Error inside the Church is still error inside a body God refuses to abandon."

"So to leave it—"

"—is to believe one can be holy alone," More finished. This time he turned just enough to let Nicholas see the corner of his mouth, not quite smiling. "And I've never been that brave."

Nicholas studied him. He wasn't sure if the man was defending a position or confessing one. He let the quiet return for a while, then spoke again—gently.

"But what if God is not waiting in the Church," he said, "but calling from outside it?"

More's gaze dropped to the dark water sliding past the hull.

"I've given my life to serve God as I understood him. If I was wrong, I pray he sees the trying." He looked back to Nicholas. "But if I betray what conscience insists is true—then I'm no longer trying. I'm surviving."

Nicholas didn't respond right away. He drew a slow breath and released it through his nose. The oars dipped again, and again.

Then, without accusation—only the curiosity of one who wanted to understand: "Do you fear the Church more than you trust God?"

More didn't answer, not at first. His hand, resting against the gunwale, tightened slightly—no tremor, no show. Just a quiet grip.

"I fear myself," he said, "more than both."

The mist around them had thinned. The water looked wider now, but not clearer.

They said nothing more.

The morning light had begun to break through the overcast, brushing the window panes of Lambeth Palace with the faintest gleam. The corridor outside the Archbishop's study was still—only the muffled steps of servants elsewhere in the building gave shape to the day's beginning.

Margarete stood just inside the doorway, her hands folded before her, watching as Cranmer moved papers from one side of his desk to the other without focus. A fire crackled low in the hearth, unattended.

"I didn't mean to interrupt," she said softly.

"You didn't." Cranmer glanced up briefly, then back to the parchment. "You're always welcome."

She took a few steps inside. "Is he gone?"

"Nicholas? Yes. The boat left just after sunrise."

A pause.

"Will you meet More yourself?"

"That is what I plan."

"And what will you say?"

He hesitated at that, then set the parchment down with care. "Whatever I must."

Margarete studied him a moment, then walked slowly to the window, resting her fingertips lightly on the stone edge.

"It's strange," she said. "I used to think certainty was what made a man strong. But lately I wonder if it's the ones still listening who carry the most weight."

Cranmer didn't answer.

She turned back toward him. "Have you listened to him? To More? Not just for compliance—but for what he fears?"

Cranmer's eyes lifted, shadowed.

"I know what he fears," he said. "But fear doesn't sanctify error."

"No," Margarete said gently. "But sometimes it reveals what love is being asked to carry."

He stood, too quickly, and walked to the side table, pouring water into a goblet though he didn't drink.

"I'm carrying as much as I can," he said shortly. "For the Church. For the king. For the people," he said, voice tightening, "who need peace. Not chaos. Peace." He looked up. "And for you."

He turned, not angry—just worn.

"I don't have room to carry someone else's silence. Or his guilt."

Margarete took a breath, letting it out slowly.

"I'm not asking you to carry him," she said. "Only not to close your heart to what he might be showing you. About yourself."

Cranmer looked away, sighing deeply. His fingers tightened slightly on the rim of the goblet.

"I know you mean well," he said. "But you don't understand what it costs—being between loyalty and conscience. I'm already stretched thin."

"I know," she said quietly. "That's why I've tried not to press."

He looked at her then—really looked. And something in her calm unsettled him more than if she had wept.

"I'm not shutting you out," he said, almost defensively. "I'm . . . doing what needs to be done."

Margarete stepped closer. "I never said you were shutting me out. I said I miss you."

That silenced him.

She held his gaze. "You're doing what needs to be done. But love isn't only action. It's presence. And lately, yours has been hard to find."

Cranmer's throat moved, but he said nothing.

Margarete let the quiet settle before she added, more gently now:

"You've given yourself to many causes. I know they matter. But I'm not a cause. I'm a covenant."

He closed his eyes for just a moment—then opened them, quieter.

"I don't want to lose you," he said.

"You haven't," she replied. "But you're letting something else take the space where we used to be."

She stepped back, just a little.

"I'll be here when you return from your meeting," she said. "No expectations. Just . . . here."

Then she turned, not coldly, and left him alone with the morning light.

Margarete's footsteps faded down the corridor.

Cranmer didn't move at first. He remained standing by the window, goblet in hand, the morning now fully broken over the rooftops. A low wind shifted through the garden below, brushing the bare branches as if trying to find leaves that were no longer there.

He sighed again, slower this time. Not from exhaustion, but something closer to resignation.

He hadn't meant to speak so sharply. Not to her. But the strain was no longer something he could compartmentalize. It lived in his spine, in the back of his throat, in the corners of every conversation. Everyone wanted something—Cromwell wanted strategy, Henry wanted loyalty, the Church wanted clarity, and Margarete wanted presence. And he—he wanted only to be faithful to all of it. But somewhere in trying, he feared he'd become faithful to none.

The summons had gone out. More was coming. And he didn't know what he was hoping for.

Not compliance. Not defiance either. Maybe just . . . understanding. A voice that could make sense of silence. Or justify it.

He looked down at the half-empty goblet in his hand and set it aside. The day was still young. But the weight of it had already begun to press.

He would listen. He would speak. And perhaps—though he could no longer quite name what that meant—he would do what was right.

The library at Lambeth was still, steeped in the long hush of early afternoon. Sunlight slanted through the tall windows, casting narrow patterns across the floor. A single candelabrum on the central table offered only modest contrast to the natural light. A fire crackled gently in the hearth. Two comfortable, high-backed chairs of dark leather and carved oak had been arranged near the center—angled not quite opposite, not quite side by side.

Cranmer stood when the door opened.

More entered with his cloak still draped across his shoulders, as if unwilling to shed the weight of the road—or the meeting ahead. He paused just inside, taking in the room—the seating, the fire, the lack of attendants. His eyes settled on Cranmer last.

"Your Grace," he said with a nod.

"Sir Thomas." Cranmer stepped forward. "I trust the journey was bearable."

"Bearable and dry," More said. "The boatman kept a rhythm even the Thames seemed to respect."

"I regret the short notice," Cranmer added, gesturing toward the hearth. "The need was . . . immediate."

More allowed a flicker of a smile. "That seems to be the tone of the age."

Cranmer motioned gently. "Please—sit. May I offer something? Wine? Or something warm?"

"I thank you, no." More removed his gloves and set them neatly on the table beside him. "I've eaten, and I find I think more clearly without indulgence."

They both sat.

Cranmer settled into his chair with quiet composure, hands resting lightly on the arms. More sat upright, his back straight, hands folded loosely in his lap.

"We've not spoken since . . ." Cranmer began.

"Since I surrendered the Great Seal," More said, finishing it plainly. "Yes. I recall the silence of the corridor more than the words."

Cranmer gave a faint smile.

More looked toward the fire. "Strange, isn't it—how resignation can feel both like retreat and release. I was never one for idleness, but I've come to see the value in days not shaped by summons."

"You've had time with your family, I hope."

More nodded. "My wife tells me I'm easier to live with now that I've ceased living for everyone else."

Cranmer offered another faint smile, but the words touched something sharper. Margarete's voice from that morning returned—quiet, steady, and unmistakably true: *You've let something else take the space where we used to be.*

More glanced back to him. "And you? Have you found any moments of peace between Parliament and pulpits?"

Cranmer's eyes moved to the flame. "Some. But not as many as I should."

More did not press.

After a moment, Cranmer said, "Thank you again for coming."

"I was summoned," More replied. "But your courtesy is noted."

"I haven't called you here to press you."

More gave a dry glance. "Then I must be in the wrong room."

Cranmer allowed the moment to pass. "I've read your reply."

More's mouth tilted slightly. "Silence is harder to misquote."

Cranmer let the quiet stretch a moment longer. Then, gently: "You could have sent a formal refusal. Or a signed objection. Parliament would've read either as dissent, but at least it would be clear."

More's eyes didn't flicker. "Sometimes clarity is used for leverage. And I've no wish to offer myself as a fulcrum."

Cranmer tilted his head slightly. "Is that how you see it? That saying nothing gives you protection?"

"No." More's tone was steady. "I see it as keeping faith. We talked of finding peace earlier. I have. But not because silence spares me. Because it guards what I must not lose."

The fire cracked softly behind them. Neither man moved.

"I won't ask you to betray your conscience," Cranmer said at last.

More offered a single nod. "Then we begin on equal ground."

Cranmer said quietly, "If I do not ask you to betray your conscience—what, then, does your silence guard?"

More replied, "It guards my soul. If the words I speak regarding the Act are not fully aligned with conscience—if they fall short, or speak more than I know—then both God and the Church may judge me as double-minded. I remain silent to avoid that possibility."

Cranmer leaned slightly forward. "But have you not just now revealed your mind? If silence protects your conscience, then speaking—or signing—would violate it. Signing agrees with the king. If your conscience cannot, then you oppose him."

More turned. His voice, still calm, carried steel. "This is precisely what I feared. Not conversation—but the bending of words to shape accusation."

Cranmer blinked, caught off guard. He began to speak, but More continued:

"The choice before me is not simply to sign or not to sign. That is one pair, one axis. Opposite it stands silence. It may be true that my silence protects me from signing something I cannot in good conscience affirm. But it is just as true that silence protects me from refusing to sign—if my conscience were, in truth, in agreement. Do you not see?"

He looked full at Cranmer.

"You may not, Archbishop, claim my conscience by the evidence of my silence. All you may rightly claim—before man or God—is that I have kept silent."

Cranmer sat back, his hands loosening slightly on the arms of the chair. He did not speak at once.

The fire crackled softly, the only sound between them. In the pause, nothing shifted outwardly—but inwardly, something was reshaping. He let the weight of More's words move through him—measured, crafted, but not calculated. This wasn't defiance. It wasn't arrogance. It was the voice of a man who had decided that clarity might cost more than faithfulness.

At last, Cranmer spoke.

"I see now why the king fears you," he said quietly.

More raised an eyebrow—not in triumph, but in wariness.

"Not because you stir crowds or rail in court," Cranmer continued. "But because you make silence louder than loyalty. You force men to hear what you haven't said—and to fear it more than rebellion."

He leaned forward slightly, eyes steady now. "But silence will not hold forever. Not here. Not now. You must know that."

More gave a slow nod. "I do."

"Then why not speak? Even now, here, in this room—not to Parliament. Not to the king. To me."

More's expression softened—something like sadness behind the steel.

"Because even a whisper travels," he said. "And I do not know which wind carries yours."

Cranmer didn't answer. He sat still again, but this time the silence was heavier—no longer reverent, but conflicted.

More had said nothing unlawful. Nothing rebellious. And yet it was rebellion enough to shake the court. His silence was more dangerous than most men's declarations—because everyone thought they knew what he meant. And truthfully, they weren't wrong.

Cranmer saw it now. Not just the logic. The conviction. The impossible clarity of More's dilemma. And he saw, too, that there was nothing more to discover here. Nothing more to uncover.

If he continued pressing, it would not be to understand—but to persuade. To pull a man from the place he had chosen. Not for conscience's sake, but for peace. For politics. For safety.

For the king.

And perhaps, in some unspoken corner of his soul—for himself.

Because it was Cranmer who would carry the failure if More stayed silent. Cranmer who would answer to Cromwell. To Parliament. To Henry. And Cranmer who would live with the knowledge that he had stood in this room, face to face with a man holding fast—and could not move him. He had come thinking he might rescue More, offer him some lifeline of language or logic. But now he saw the truth, stark and unbending. It wasn't More he was trying to rescue. It was himself—from the guilt of complicity, from the grief of powerlessness, from the slow erosion of conscience he no longer knew how to name.

He looked at More again, and asked the question not as a theologian, not as a bishop, not even as a friend—but as a man trying to delay the fall of an ax.

"Is there truly no path for you to sign?"

More held his gaze. There was no anger in his face—only a steadiness that made evasion impossible.

"There may be many paths," he said softly. "But not all lead forward."

Cranmer said nothing.

More waited, but the archbishop's expression had shifted. It was no longer the measured curiosity of a man trying to understand. It was something else—something searching. Cranmer's eyes were moving, not aimlessly, but as if chasing a thread just out of reach.

And More recognized it.

Not the look of a man trying to convict him.

The look of a man trying to rescue him.

More sat back, a breath catching not from emotion, but from recognition. This meeting wasn't about the Act. Not anymore. Not really. It was no longer about doctrine or duty or even defiance. It was about the quiet desperation of a man trying to survive himself.

Cranmer's conflict was laid bare—not in what he said, but in what he couldn't say. Not in what he demanded, but in what he needed to believe: that More might yield, so Cranmer wouldn't have to break.

More looked away, and for the first time that day, his resolve bent—not in weakness, but in sorrow.

He felt pity. Not for the role Cranmer played, but for the cost he was paying to play it.

He waited a beat, then spoke gently. "Is there more you wished to say—or shall I return to Chelsea before the light fails?"

Cranmer didn't answer at first. There had been more—longer debate, more appeals, some final thread to draw taut. But it had frayed. The truth had settled between them, and there was no pulling past it.

He gave the smallest nod. "Yes. I think all has been said."

More stood, bowed politely, and crossed to the door. He paused only once, hand on the latch—as if to say something—but then thought better of it. The pity remained, and Cranmer saw it.

The door clicked shut behind him.

Cranmer remained seated for a moment longer, the fire's soft hiss the only sound in the library. His hands still rested on the chair's arms, but his posture had slackened. The clarity he had come seeking had not been found. Or perhaps it had—and he had not liked the shape of it.

He rose slowly, extinguished the taper on the table, and made his way down the long corridor toward the residence wing. Each footstep landed with the same reluctant weight: one for the king's demand, one for Cromwell's pressure, one for the man who had just left without flinching.

By the time he reached his chambers, late afternoon light had dimmed enough to pass for evening.

He opened the door to find Jo standing beside the hearth, folding a shawl. She looked up at his entrance, surprised but not startled.

"I thought you'd still be with Sir Thomas," she said gently.

"He's returning to Chelsea," Cranmer answered. He crossed to the wall hook, resting his hand there a moment as if forgetting what he meant to hang. "He spoke all he had to say, and I had nothing left to ask."

Jo offered a faint smile. "And what did you hear?"

Cranmer didn't answer immediately. He moved to the chair by the hearth and sat slowly, as if unsure what the chair might ask of him.

"He won't sign," he said at last.

Jo's expression didn't change.

"He says nothing," Cranmer continued. "Says it with such composure, such certainty. Not pride. Not stubbornness. Just . . . resolve. And now I'm left wondering if it's mercy to keep pressing—or cruelty."

Jo crossed the room and sat across from him, folding her hands in her lap.

"You care what becomes of him."

"I do." Cranmer looked at the fire. "I want to protect him. I want to give him something—anything—that might spare his life."

She studied him.

"And do you think that's love?"

Cranmer turned toward her, a little startled. "What else would it be?"

Jo's voice was soft, but steady. "You speak of giving. Of sparing. But love doesn't always mean rescuing."

He frowned. "Then what does it mean?"

She didn't rush.

"Love is the giving of self," she said. "But not just giving to the cause, or the crown, or the conscience of others. It's giving for the sake of relationship. Love doesn't throw itself to pieces to please everyone standing near. It offers itself so that something real might be shared. Between souls."

Cranmer's brow furrowed.

"I've given of myself," he said, not defensive but worn. "To Margarete. To More. To the king. To the church."

Jo met his eyes.

"But have you given *yourself*? Or have you given *what they needed from you*?"

That question didn't land with a sting—but with the sound of something gently breaking open inside him.

He sat back, staring at the fire as if it might shape an answer. He was still staring into the fire when Jo spoke again.

"You've always wanted to do what's right," she said. "Even when the cost was high."

"That's not a fault," he murmured.

"No," she said gently. "But sometimes, when we stop trusting God to define right, we let need define it for us."

He looked at her, quietly struck.

"You've given of yourself, yes," she continued. "But love isn't measured in cost alone. It's measured in the truth behind the gift. In the goodness it seeks. In the beauty it builds."

She paused.

"That's why love must begin with God. Because he is all those things. If we give without him—without his truth, his goodness, his beauty—we might still be kind. Or loyal. Or brave. But it's not love. Not yet."

Cranmer's voice was barely above a whisper. "Then what have I been giving?"

Jo didn't answer immediately.

"Pieces of yourself," she said at last. "To people who needed you. To a world that demanded you. But not to the relationships that could hold you. And not always from the God who made you."

The door opened quietly.

Margarete stepped in, a hint of wind still in her scarf and color in her cheeks. She held a small wrapped parcel in one hand.

"Sorry," she said, closing the door behind her. "I thought I'd be back sooner. The merchant took longer, and I ran into Bess at the market—"

She paused as her eyes adjusted to the quiet. The weight in the room told her something had been said—something still settling. Jo stood, smoothing her skirt.

"I'll leave you two," Jo said softly. "The fire's still warm."

She slipped past Margarete with a reassuring touch on her arm. At the doorway, she paused—just long enough to glance back at Cranmer, still staring into the fire. Then she was gone.

Margarete turned slowly back to Cranmer. She didn't speak. She only watched him—quiet, intent, reading the weight in his shoulders, the distance in his gaze.

Cranmer met her eyes.

"I spoke with More," he said. "It . . . didn't resolve anything."

Margarete gave the smallest nod. Her expression didn't change.

"It's still difficult," he added.

Another pause. He looked down, then back to her.

But this time, he didn't speak as archbishop, or emissary, or the man caught between crown and conscience.

He looked into her eyes and spoke simply, as himself.

"I love you."

It was quiet. Unrushed. Each word placed with care.

Margarete blinked, once—but didn't look away.

Then she stepped forward and laid the small parcel on the table beside the hearth.

"I know," she said.

And she sat beside him.

22

A Door Half Closed

THERE WAS NO BLAZE of light through tall windows, no chorus of birds rising in jubilant welcome. The palace woke slowly—its stone walls taking warmth grudgingly, its corridors still whispering yesterday's shadows.

But in Cranmer's rooms, the change was unmistakable. The fire from the night before still smoldered in the hearth, and a faint amber hue had begun to soften the corners of the room. Not sunlight—just the hint that it was coming.

Cranmer sat near the hearth, a cooling cup in his hands. Across from him, Margarete stirred quietly at the table, folding back a cloth over the bread. Neither of them had said much. But neither needed to.

It was the first morning in weeks that hadn't started with dread.

He didn't feel unburdened—only less alone beneath the weight.

"You slept," she said softly.

He nodded, still gazing at the cup. "Not the whole night. But soundly. That's something."

"It is."

A quiet stretched again. He broke it.

"It's strange how sleep shifts things. The worries haven't left. But I can see them now. A little more clearly. Like fog at sunrise."

She smiled faintly. "Even fog looks different when you know which way the light is coming from."

He glanced at her—eyes tired but kind. "I forgot how much I missed your metaphors."

Margarete tilted her head, teasing gently. "You never liked them."

"No," he admitted. "But I like you. So they've grown on me."

She stood then, crossed to the table, and poured what was left of the posset into a small cup for herself, its hint of spice still lingering though it had cooled. The scent of something citrus drifted faintly into the room.

Cranmer watched her, quietly aware of how much he had tried to carry alone. Of how little he had let her carry with him.

"Margarete," he said, voice lower now. "Whatever comes next—whatever I must say or stand for—I want you to know . . . I don't intend to walk through it alone."

She turned toward him but didn't speak at once.

"I know," she said at last. "And I'm here. But I'll keep asking what road we're on."

He nodded, accepting the grace in her words.

A pause, then:

"I go to Westminster today," he added. "The Act is coming to vote. Cromwell will have it in hand. I . . . I'd like to read it myself before it passes. Carefully."

She studied him. "For More's sake?"

He didn't answer directly. But his gaze held hers.

Margarete stepped closer and brushed her fingers gently along his shoulder.

"Then go with eyes open," she said. "But come back with your heart still whole."

He looked up at her and gave a slow nod. "That's the goal."

And for the first time in weeks, he meant it.

The light had lifted further by the time Cranmer crossed the south corridor. One of the stewards met him near the main stair.

"Did Sir Thomas depart without incident last evening?" he asked the man quietly.

"Yes, my lord. He would have reached Chelsea after dark, but still with hours enough to take his supper and his rest."

Cranmer paused. "Did he say anything?"

The steward hesitated. "Only that he was grateful for the courtesy of the summons. And the civility of the room."

Cranmer gave a slight nod. "Thank you."

He turned, moving toward the chapel before heading to Westminster.

No confrontation. No second conversation. Just the same silence, now wrapped in manners.

It was, Cranmer thought, a farewell without surrender.

The chamber filled slowly but with the practiced rhythm of inevitability. Robes rustled, low voices settled into stillness, and eyes tracked one another with wary acknowledgement. No one expected drama. The Act had already passed in spirit. This was only the seal.

Cranmer stood to one side of the central table, where the final text of the bill lay in its original hand. The parchment was clean, its lines firm and deliberate. As others exchanged quiet words or adjusted their seating, Cranmer leaned slightly closer, reading again a line he already knew:

". . . the king's majesty justly and rightfully is and ought to be the supreme head of the Church of England . . ."

He traced the language with his eyes, not once but twice. *Is and ought to be.*

The king is—the assertion of present authority, backed by Parliament.

Ought to be—not merely repetition, but a word of implication. Was it divine affirmation? Or legal logic? Could a man of conscience— More—sign this and hold his soul intact?

If the act had read only "is," the case was clear. But "ought to be"— there was space there. Not much. But space.

Cranmer heard the opening words from the clerk and the call for order, but they settled around him like wind against windows. He didn't need to follow the vote. There would be no objection.

And there wasn't.

The clerk tapped the table twice with the wooden rod. The Act was passed.

Cromwell stepped beside him. "Looking for a sermon in the parchment, Archbishop?"

Cranmer didn't look away. "The language leaves room."

"For what?"

"For one man's conscience. Perhaps. Look here. The Act says 'ought to be.'"

Cromwell's brow moved slightly, a flicker of patience already wearing thin. "Ought to be," he said, repeating the phrase without warmth. "Legal convention. Not theological ambiguity. Don't read grace into what was meant as velvet over steel."

Cranmer finally turned. "You see a completed claim. But this phrasing—'is and ought to be'—it allows for a distinction."

Cromwell crossed his arms. "Does it."

"The 'is' states the law as it stands—Parliament has declared it so. The 'ought to be' may not press further. It might merely say: if it is the law in England, then it ought to be recognized as such by Englishmen. Not as creed. Not as confession. But as legal reality."

"And you think More will buy that?"

Cranmer shook his head slightly. "Not buy it. But perhaps he'll see it. As a thread. Something that allows him to acknowledge the crown without betraying the Church—or his soul."

Cromwell's mouth turned in something like a smirk, but it wasn't cruel. "You always were better at threading needles than drawing swords."

Cranmer met his eyes. "I hope only I still know which fabric is worth mending."

He returned to Lambeth in silence, the rhythm of the river offering no clarity, only time. Once in his study, he sat at the desk by the north window, lit a taper, and took up his pen.

> *To Sir Thomas More,*
> *at Chelsea,*
> *by trusted hand*
>
> *Sir Thomas,*
>
> *I write not to persuade but to pose a question. The act, now passed, includes the phrase you know well: "The king's majesty justly and rightfully is and ought to be the supreme head of the Church of England."*
>
> *You understand as I do that language does more than state— it binds. But I wonder if, in this case, it leaves space.*
>
> *"Is" reflects what Parliament has enacted. "Ought to be" may be read not as creedal assent, but as legal consistency: if the law has declared him head, then he ought to be regarded as such within this realm.*
>
> *Might that reading allow you to sign—not in betrayal of your conscience, but in submission to the law of the land?*
>
> *I ask in hope, not pressure.*
> *—T. Cranmer*

He sealed the letter, then stepped into the corridor and found a steward heading toward the outer hall.

"This must reach Chelsea by nightfall," he said, handing over the parchment. "Directly to Sir Thomas. No one else. And if he sends reply, return it to me by week's end."

The steward bowed and departed.

Cranmer stood alone in the corridor for a moment longer, the last of the daylight sinking toward shadow.

He had done what he could.

Whether it would be received as hope—or a deeper sorrow—was no longer his to decide.

With the Act now passed, the tide of demands pressing against Cranmer's desk began, at last, to recede. The noise had not ceased entirely—nothing ever did in court life—but it had dulled, thinned into aftershock. What needed saying had been said. What needed signing, signed. And what followed was, for once, the task of others.

The pressure shifted now to Cromwell, whose docket had grown heavier with enforcement, clarifications, and the inevitable sifting of those who complied too slowly. Will remained deeply entangled in those efforts and, loving it, made sure everyone knew. His hands, he claimed, were still inked with unfinished orders.

Cranmer, meanwhile, for the first time in months, felt something like breath.

It was Margarete who first suggested a few days away—nothing extravagant, only time to step beyond the thick air of Lambeth. Walthamstow, she said. They had spoken often enough of visiting Roger and Emilie since the wedding. Now seemed a fitting moment.

Cranmer agreed before she finished asking. The next morning, he mentioned the plan to Jo and Nicholas over breakfast. They both lit up with easy enthusiasm—Nicholas because he had not seen Roger in some time, and Jo because the thought of Walthamstow brought with it the comfort of woods and water—and, more than that, the warmth of her parents.

Soon the visit had grown from a quiet respite to something more like a reunion. Roger and Emilie wrote back with welcome. Roger was delighted. Emilie had questions. So the four began making plans.

Will, when invited, declined. "Too much left to chase down," he said. "Some of these clergy still think silence is clever. Cromwell disagrees. Strongly."

Jo pressed him, gently. But Will waved it off with the same smile he always used when he wanted out of something without giving offense.

So it was settled. The others would leave on Thursday.

The weather had held—cool and bright—and the bags were packed the night before with little drama. Cranmer rose that morning with a strange lightness, a sense of something nearly like relief. He had even smiled over his cup when Jo teased him about forgetting his boots.

But just after breakfast, a knock came at the study door. A steward entered with a sealed parchment—plain, formal, but unmistakable in its hand.

Cranmer broke the seal and read.

By the time he lowered the letter, the brightness had faded from his face.

He did not speak at once.

Margarete, watching from the doorway, stepped quietly into the room.

"Is it from Chelsea?" she asked.

He nodded.

She waited.

He passed her the page, his voice low. "Yet still."

> *To the Most Reverend Thomas Cranmer,*
> *Archbishop of Canterbury,*
> *from Chelsea, this Wednesday past*
>
> *My Lord Archbishop,*
> *I thank you for your letter and for the grace within it. That you would write not with command but with invitation—this I take not lightly.*
> *You ask whether the phrasing of the Act—is and ought to be—might allow a man room to assent in law while guarding his soul in doctrine. It is a subtle question, and one not unworthy of pondering.*
> *But in the end, I must return to this: when I place my name beneath such words, they no longer belong only to Parliament. They become mine. The ink is theirs, but the will is mine—and the conscience, too.*

*You write with hope that a man might distinguish legal obe-
dience from spiritual agreement. Yet even this distinction requires
speech. And I have made none.*

*Silence, though fragile, is my last defense. It neither affirms
nor condemns. It permits no one to bind my soul but God alone—
and those ministers to whom I have submitted in faith.*

*If I speak—even to explain—I risk crossing lines I have held
for long years. And if I sign, I erase them.*

I remain,
Yours in Christ,

Thomas More

Cranmer stood for a long while at the window. Below, the river
glinted as the sun edged higher, indifferent and sure of its path. It moved
forward, unmoved by the choice of one man—or the cost of it. Cranmer
had reached with reason, and More had answered with sorrow. Not to
wound—but to spare them both the illusion of hope.

"He's closing the door," he said at last.

Margarete didn't answer immediately. She had remained still after
reading, her fingers laced before her.

"He's keeping it closed," she said finally. "That's not the same."

Cranmer turned slightly, brow furrowed.

Margarete met his gaze. "He said silence is his last defense. That
doesn't mean he's certain. Only that he's unwilling to risk a word that
might betray more than it reveals."

"He believes signing makes the words his own," Cranmer murmured.
"That the moment his name joins the Act, it becomes a confession."

"And for him," Margarete said, "confession is sacred."

He nodded slowly. "But that isn't the weight the law asks. I tried to
show him—'ought to be' could mean only what is legally required, not
what is inwardly believed."

"I know," she said gently. "And perhaps you were right to try. But
conscience doesn't always bend to logic. Sometimes it lives in the space
between understanding and surrender."

He looked back to the river. "Then there's no more to do."

Margarete crossed the room and rested her hand lightly on his arm.
"There's always more to do. But not always more to say."

Cranmer didn't respond at first. He wanted to save More's life. But maybe more than that, he wanted to save what was left of his own. "He'll die for this," he finally told her.

"Yes," she said quietly.

"And we'll live with it."

A silence passed between them. Not the chill of defeat, but the pause of recognition.

"He's not the only one wrestling conscience," Margarete said at last. "You're shaping a church with your name on every line. Just be sure your soul can still read it."

That struck deeper than he let show. He drew in a weighted breath.

"I don't know if I can save him," he said.

Margarete shook her head. "It isn't about saving. Not now. It's about standing—each in our place, with what we believe."

Cranmer looked down at the letter once more, then folded it carefully.

"I invited Jo and Nicholas to Walthamstow, thinking we all needed the rest," he said quietly. "But perhaps I'm really trying to find a part of myself I fear I've left behind."

Margarete smiled faintly. "Perhaps you do need to remember something."

He placed the letter in the desk drawer and turned toward her. "Then let's go."

And the light through the window, though no brighter than before, seemed to carry them forward.

23

Where Love Waits

THE SHUTTERS WERE ALREADY open in the front room when Roger stepped inside, brushing his hands against his apron. A quiet sun broke gently across the sill. Emilie was laying out linens—her best, though one was faintly singed from an incident neither of them would now admit responsibility for.

"She'll notice," she said, eyeing the corner. "Jo always did have an eye."

Roger gave a quiet grunt that might've been a chuckle. "Then we'll call it a design choice."

Emilie gave him a look, but her mouth twitched all the same. She folded the edge neatly under. "They'll be hungry when they arrive. I'm thinking roast fowl and warm bread. Maybe some of the plum jam, if we've got enough left."

Roger nodded. "And some beer—Thomas never did learn to like your elderflower cordial."

"I've noticed," Emilie said. "But beer?" She made a face. "It tastes like a hedgerow. Why not ale?"

"They drink beer at court," Roger said. "We must keep up."

For a moment, silence settled. It wasn't heavy. Just familiar.

Then Emilie said, "Do you think he's well? Thomas."

Roger leaned against the post. "I think he's been through enough not to be. But I also think we'll know more when he steps off the cart."

Emilie was quiet again. Then: "I saw something in Jo's last letter. Not written, exactly, but in the spaces around what she wrote. She's worried."

"She always is."

"No." Emilie turned to face him. "This isn't her usual. This isn't Jo fearing for others. It's Jo uncertain in herself."

Roger considered. "She was always more like you."

Emilie gave a small smile. "Not in the way you mean. I've always watched the horizon. Jo's always searched what's underfoot. And if what's underfoot feels shaky to her, then I say we pay attention."

Roger rubbed his jaw. "What do you think's shaken?"

"I don't know," Emilie said. "But I'd wager it has something to do with that man who once had a settled conviction behind his eyes. A calling that made him sure in the best of ways. Now—"

"Now he's archbishop," Roger finished.

"And more than that," she added. "He's caught between his calling and his survival. And I know what it is to weigh both."

Roger turned to the window. "The Church is changing. Fast. Maybe faster than any of them mean it to."

"I never thought I'd say it," Emilie said quietly, "but I'm glad you didn't end up in the middle of it."

He looked at her, surprised.

"You would've been good," she said. "But not cunning. Not enough for court. You think it's just about right doctrine and kind hands. But there's blood in the mortar, Roger. And Thomas's elbows are redder than he ever wanted."

Roger exhaled slowly. "It's not easy, bearing that weight."

"No," Emilie said. "But it's worse pretending you're not."

She hesitated, then added, "I still believe there's a holy fire in us. It may be buried in ash and wet wood and old soot—but it's still burning. Still good."

Roger turned toward her.

"Enough for the two of us," she said softly, "and maybe for our children too, through us."

They stood there a moment longer—smiling at each other, content in what they had together.

Then Emilie clapped her hands lightly.

"Well. Best get the jam. If I leave it to you, you'll eat it straight from the jar and serve none."

Roger smiled. "I have to feed that fire!"

She swatted his shoulder as she passed, but he caught her hand and kissed it. "We'll be ready," he said.

"I hope so," Emilie replied. "Because I don't think they are."

The coach eased into the familiar ruts of Roger's lane and came to a gentle stop just past the hedgerow. The sun had risen full and clean, casting a gold veil over the garden gate, where the scent of rosemary and damp earth met them first.

Jo was the first to climb down. She paused, drawing in a breath that caught more memory than air. The thatched roof rose just as she remembered, the hedgerow curving with the same gentle lean, the worn path still bearing the faintest center groove where carts had passed since her childhood. It was, by all appearances, unchanged.

But she had changed.

She stood still, breathing it in—this place that had once been her whole world. It welcomed her still, but not as a girl. That girl had listened more than she spoke, folded her thoughts away like pressed flowers. She'd studied faces for meaning, often quiet at first—but never given to small talk.

Now she lived in a palace. She had sat across from a queen—not in ceremony, but in conversation. She had watched laws born in the hush of Parliament, seen how power bent and twisted, and how truth still held its shape.

And she had loved—and learned what it meant to give, to question, to stay.

Jo turned toward the house. The old wooden gate creaked softly as the others climbed down behind her. She noticed the door latch—still catching, still not repaired.

She was home, but not who she had been.

From the doorway, Roger emerged, drying his hands on the front of his apron, a grin already formed. Emilie followed close behind, brushing flour from her sleeves.

"You've grown no thinner, Thomas," Roger called as Cranmer and then Margarete climbed down, "so either you've learned moderation or your cooks are too afraid of you to deny seconds."

Cranmer gave a wry smile. "The latter. Without question."

Roger offered his hand, but then pulled him in for a brief, firm embrace.

Nicholas stepped down last, taking Jo's bag with an easy swing of the shoulder.

"Joanna," Emilie said warmly, crossing the garden path and wrapping her daughter in a hug that held more than one season's worth of waiting. Then she drew back, placing a hand gently on her cheek. "You look tired. But better."

"I'm both," Jo replied, glancing toward Margarete. "The air helps."

"It always does," Emilie said. "And Roger thinks his bread helps more."

Roger harrumphed. "It's not just bread. There's roast fowl inside—and none of it burned."

Nicholas gave an exaggerated sniff toward the open window. "I can confirm."

Margarete smiled, stepping forward. Emilie embraced her as well, then met Thomas's eyes and smiled into them with quiet warmth.

"It's good to see you, brother," she said.

He hesitated. "It's good to be seen."

"Come in, then," Roger said, waving them all toward the door. "Shoes off if they're muddy. And if you didn't bring wine, say something clever so we don't notice."

Jo laughed, and Nicholas looked at Cranmer. "Shall I be clever?"

"Save your wit. I think Margarete brought wine." Cranmer murmured, and the whole company followed Roger inside, the door swinging shut behind them with a satisfying wooden thud.

The house at Walthamstow hadn't changed—low beams, smooth hearthstones, the same slight groan in the back stair—but Cranmer paused as he crossed the threshold, as if his shoulders needed a moment to register it. Not relief, not exactly. But the weight he carried loosened here.

Roger took his coat with a warmth that asked nothing, and Emilie—finishing table preparations—glanced up with the quiet authority of someone who would not speak of court unless spoken to.

Jo, sensing his stillness, said nothing either. She knew better than most when to let silence stand.

He stood a moment longer, then exhaled and stepped fully into the room.

The table was set with Emilie's best linens and mismatched pottery arranged with a kind of care that felt more like affection than display. The air was fragrant with roast fowl, with the quiet richness of plum jam and a hint of woodsmoke from the hearth.

They gathered easily, the six of them, finding places as if they had always sat at this table. Roger carved with mock solemnity, presenting each portion with a nod and a quip. Emilie passed bread still warm from the oven. Jo poured cider. For a time, the room was filled with the soft clatter of plates and the warmth of laughter that needed no prompt.

Cranmer leaned back in his chair, the wooden arms solid under his elbows. His face, though still marked by weariness, had begun to soften around the eyes.

"Don't think I've had food this honest in weeks," Nicholas said, reaching for another slice of bread.

"You mean food not designed to look like a swan and taste like a turnip?" Roger asked.

"Precisely," Cranmer said.

"You ought to move here permanently," Emilie added. "We'll put you to work in the garden, though. No title exempts you from weeds."

"I should think it might," he replied. "But I've been wrong before."

Jo smiled. "Only once or twice."

The laughter came gently, naturally.

"I believe many more times than that. I often mistrust—even fear myself—on many occasions."

"Fear yourself?" asked Nicholas. "Funny, that's what Sir Thomas—More—said when we were discussing whether he feared the Church more than he trusted God."

There was a moment's pause.

"He . . . he said he feared himself," Nicholas finished.

"Yes," Cranmer said finally. "Fearing the rightness of your action is always a heavy concern."

"Is he still silent?" Emilie asked, her tone less curious than concerned.

Cranmer hesitated, then took a slow sip of cider. "He remains silent."

"Silence," Roger mused, "can be its own kind of sermon."

"Or its own kind of defiance," Nicholas said.

"If More truly believes the crown's claim is false," Roger said, "then surely God will protect him from the axe."

Emilie's eyes narrowed slightly. "That's not how it works. You know what happened to my brother."

Roger turned toward her, surprised.

"He burned in that inn," she said. "God didn't stop the fire."

"That's not the same," Roger said. "Matthew wasn't a martyr. He had turned bitter. He quit his pursuit of God. More still seeks him."

"But others have died," Jo added gently. "Good people. Faithful ones. I used to ask why—why God would sit back. Your sister," she said turning to Emilie, "my birth mother, asked the same thing. You knew that was her question."

"And have you found an answer?" Emilie asked.

Jo glanced at Marguerite, who smiled strength at her.

"I'm not sure I know each crevice, but I think I'm growing into one," Jo said. "I've seen enough to know it's not always silence. Sometimes . . . it's waiting."

A quiet fell.

Roger pushed back from the table. "Well. If we're waiting for dessert, we'll need more firewood or this room will freeze over."

"I'll help," Nicholas said, rising.

Emilie stood and began clearing a few of the plates. "Jo, would you check the jam? I left it too close to the hearth, and I'd rather not find it bubbling."

Jo nodded and followed her mother into the kitchen.

Cranmer remained seated, his eyes on the fire. Margarete laid a hand gently over his. He slowly curled his fingers over hers.

The evening had shifted—but it had not broken. And that, he thought, was something.

Nicholas had to quicken his pace to match Roger, who, despite the added years and added girth, still moved with the energy of a man who'd never accepted the idea of slowing down.

"The pile's not far," Roger said, glancing sideways. "Though if the ground's still soft, we may come back taller than we left, boots and all."

Nicholas smiled politely. "So long as I don't sink in and vanish entirely."

Roger chuckled. "You're too sharp to vanish, lad. Jo wouldn't allow it."

A beat passed.

"She's well, I hope?"

"Too well for me," Nicholas said with a soft grin. "She's brilliant, of course—but it means I'm always chasing her. I think she sits still, and then she's halfway to the pantry, or the study, or God knows where—with a dozen thoughts in flight. Half the time, I'm just hoping to catch one before it gets away."

Roger gave a low, appreciative laugh. "That's Jo. You marry her and think you've caught a breeze—only to find yourself in a windstorm."

"She surprises me," Nicholas admitted. "Not just her pace, but the depth. It's all still waters—until suddenly it's the deep end."

Roger slowed a little, boots squelching faintly in the damp soil. "She wasn't always like that. When she was small, she'd go days barely saying a word. Thought everything through twice before speaking. Still does, maybe, but now she dares more." He paused. "That old question of hers, though—the one about why God sits back when good people suffer— that one never let go."

Nicholas nodded. "She still wonders. But it's been a while since she said it out loud."

"Maybe because the answer doesn't come," Roger said. "Maybe because there isn't one." He shook his head. "I've always thought—we try too hard to unravel things that are meant to stay tangled. There's a verse—Isaiah, I think—'my thoughts are not your thoughts.' Sometimes you just have to let that be enough."

"Isaiah 55," Nicholas said. "But it's not about resignation. It's a call to seek him. The contrast is there to draw us in, not shut us out."

Roger raised an eyebrow. "Well, aren't you a tidy theologian."

Nicholas laughed lightly. "I live with one. It rubs off."

They reached the woodpile, and Roger stooped to pull a few lengths free from the stack. Nicholas joined him.

"Still, I get your point," Nicholas added. "There's comfort in mystery. But Jo—she doesn't let mystery turn to silence. She asks."

Roger straightened with an armful of logs. "She gets that from her mother. Emilie never let the dark sit undisturbed either." He paused, then said with less bravado, "Truth is, I envy you. I missed that season of Jo's life—the one where she started asking not just because she wanted to know, but because she wanted someone to answer."

Nicholas glanced over, then smiled. "She thinks you'd still have something worth saying."

Roger gave a small, almost wry smile—one that tried to hide the emotion beneath and only half succeeded. "Tell her I'm always happy to try."

They loaded the logs into a battered barrow—barely holding to-gether—and turned back toward the house.

"Any word from Will?" Roger asked after a while. "I was hoping he'd come."

Nicholas shook his head. "Jo sent me after him. I cornered him in Cromwell's chambers. He looked up, listened to my invitation, and laughed—like I'd just asked him to move to France for a fortnight."

Roger grunted. "That boy's fire burns too hot. He'll wear himself to the wick."

"I'll drag him here one day," Nicholas promised. "Even if it's just for your bread and Emilie's, uh, Mum's—jam."

Roger clapped him on the shoulder. "It's a start."

The room had quieted. Dishes sat half-cleared, the hearth dimming to a soft pulse. Margarete refolded her napkin with unhurried care. Cranmer leaned back slightly, his gaze distant.

"You said nothing," he said at last. "When Jo brought up her question. About God's silence. You're rarely one to hold your tongue when it's a matter of theology."

Margarete glanced over, her face soft with thought. "Some answers aren't meant to be handed over like bread at table."

"You mean they can't be?" he asked. "Or they shouldn't?"

She tilted her head. "Sometimes both."

"But if there *is* an answer, and you *know* it—why not say it?"

"Because the truth of it doesn't take root by hearing. Not at first. You have to circle it—wear it like a question for a while. Let it scrape against your assumptions. Let it cost you something."

He looked at her sharply. "How much time do you think we need? Jo's been asking it since childhood. And Joan before her. You've sat beside us while we tried to make sense of it—tried to find some shape for what God doesn't stop." He paused, brow furrowed, voice tightening at the edges. "And now you say you *know*—but still can't tell us?" He exhaled, a low sound that wasn't quite a laugh. "I don't know. . . . It seems that in this, you're as confusing as God is."

Margarete's expression didn't flinch, but a quiet sorrow passed through her eyes.

"I know it seems that way," she said. "But it's not about you suffering more. It's about being ready to recognize the answer when it comes. We have been talking about it. And you and Jo both know more of the answer than you did before. But if I'd said it outright—especially to you—you might've heard it as judgment. As if I were critiquing your choices, your role, your restraint."

He didn't answer, but his jaw shifted slightly.

She touched her fingertips to the table, voice quieter now. "I had to wait. You weren't ready to hear that *love*—real love—doesn't force its way in. It waits to be chosen. And so does God."

Cranmer stared at her, something catching in his throat that didn't become a word.

Margarete folded her hands. "God allows what he hates. Not because he is powerless. But because the only way to redeem it is from *within* it—through love that costs, and trusts, and refuses to coerce."

The silence that followed wasn't heavy. It breathed.

Cranmer looked back toward the fire. His voice, when it came, was nearly lost in its flicker. "Some answers ask to be received, not given."

Margarete nodded once. "And some are already being lived."

Jo had followed her mother into the kitchen, the light from the hearth flickering across the shelves of jars and crocks. Emilie lifted a cloth to cover the bread, then reached for a stack of plates. Jo joined her, wordlessly collecting the utensils and wiping them clean.

"Did Will receive the invitation?" Emilie asked as she eased a dish into the washbasin.

"Yes," Jo said, drying a knife, "but like everything, it was in a rush. I asked Nicholas to track him down, but even that proved difficult. Cromwell keeps him spinning, I think."

Emilie looked up with mild concern. "He would have come if he could, surely."

"I believe he would," Jo said. "But that's part of what frightens me. I'm afraid he won't always know when he can't. That he'll wake one day and realize he's let the better things pass by. Not out of cruelty, just . . . speed."

"Court has a way of swallowing time," Emilie said, wiping her hands. "Swallowing people, too."

Jo nodded, folding the towel slowly. "He wants to do good. But there's so much around him that isn't."

Emilie studied her daughter for a moment, then leaned against the counter, arms folded. "I've heard you speak of love waiting. Twice now, maybe three times. It's stayed with me. What do you mean by it?"

Jo paused, setting down the towel. "I think I used to think love just . . . endured. That it bore things because it had to. But lately—watching people I care for, loving people who don't always know how to fully love in return—I've started to think waiting is the fuller word."

"How so?" Emilie asked gently.

"Enduring can be passive," Jo said. "Like a stone under rain. It doesn't move, but it weathers. Waiting still bears the weight—but with hope. With expectation. It keeps the door open, not just the body present."

Emilie's lips curved slightly. "You've learned a great deal since you left this kitchen."

Jo smiled. "Mostly how much I didn't know."

They worked quietly for a moment, rinsing and drying.

"But it's hard," Jo added. "Waiting. Especially when you don't know if the one you're waiting for even notices the door."

Emilie stepped close, brushed a damp lock from her daughter's brow. "Doors have a way of being remembered. Even by those who pretend to forget them."

Jo looked at her. "Do you believe that?"

"I have to," Emilie said. "It's how I raised you."

Jo gave a soft laugh, and they went on finishing the dishes—two women in the quiet hum of the kitchen, letting the weight of love sit there between them, steady and strong and still open.

The last crumbs of tart had been cleared, the final sips of cider poured. Candles burned low, casting a soft flicker across the table. No one moved to rise just yet. The evening had found its rhythm, slow and unhurried, like the winding down of an old clock content to tick in company.

Jo leaned her chin into her hand, a lazy smile tugging at her lips. "I think I'd forgotten what it felt like to sit this long at table without having to impress anyone."

"Speak for yourself," Roger said with mock offense. "I've been dazzling you all with my wit for hours."

Emilie chuckled. "You've been telling stories about turnips."

"Which is wit," he insisted.

Even Cranmer allowed himself a quiet smile. "Well, then it's been a nourishing evening in every sense."

A gentle quiet settled in again, not heavy, just comfortable. It was Nicholas who broke it this time, his voice thoughtful.

"It's strange," he said, "how laughter like this can exist in the same world as everything else."

"What else?" Jo asked, though she already knew.

He looked down at his cup. "The things we've seen. The trials coming. The ones we know are yet to come."

No one rushed to fill the space. Then Margarete said softly, "Suffering has always shared the table with joy. Since Eden."

Roger folded his arms across his chest. "Still hard to make sense of it. Seems like if God cared, he'd do more to stop it."

Emilie looked at him—more gently than before. "Even with your stories about turnips, I've never doubted you care. And yet you've let our children go through hard things."

He frowned but didn't answer right away.

"It's not the same," he said eventually.

"No," Jo agreed, "but maybe it's not entirely different either."

Cranmer leaned forward, elbows on the table now, voice low. "Do you think that's what the cross was? God allowing his own Son to suffer for something greater?"

"Not allowing," Margarete said quietly, "but choosing. Jesus embraced it."

Nicholas looked between them. "Then when we suffer—when things feel like they're falling apart—it isn't because God is far away."

"No," Jo said. "It's because he's close enough to trust us with it."

A hush fell again, but it wasn't silence. It was something deeper. A kind of agreement not yet spoken aloud. The candlelight danced across their faces—tired, searching, honest.

They didn't speak much after that.

But no one left the table too quickly.

Roger rose at last, stretching slightly as he crossed to the hearth. He took up the poker and stirred the fire with quiet care, the embers shifting, glowing deeper red. The room crackled softly in response.

Yet no one moved to follow him.

There was no unspoken cue to retire, no rustle of chairs or clearing of plates. Only the shared stillness of people who knew they were held—in the warmth of the room, in the bonds between them, in something greater still.

They didn't need to name it. Not yet.

But each one, in his and her own way, leaned into the peace of it.

And the fire burned steady.

24

Into the Flame

WILL STEPPED LIGHTLY ACROSS the stone threshold, the papers still folded and useless in his hand. Cromwell was not alone, which made the timing worse, though Will suspected his master already knew what had delayed him.

Cromwell dismissed the last of three clerks with a flick of his fingers and turned toward Will, his mouth already tight.

"Well?"

Will held out the message. "I couldn't obtain the confirmation. He's preoccupied with the boy—the Jonas matter."

"The Jonas matter," Cromwell repeated, as if testing whether the words themselves might sound more valid when spoken slowly. "And how precisely does a missing trinket and one half-witted footboy require the full attention of my senior administrator?"

Will chose his reply carefully. "He said Lady Mary demanded his immediate presence. He was unwilling to risk further delay."

Cromwell leaned back in his chair, drumming his fingers against the ink-stained blotter. "So the court must pause while Lady Mary seeks justice for a bauble?"

Will didn't answer. He had learned that sometimes silence moved things faster than speech.

Cromwell's hand stopped. "Fine," he said shortly. "Then we give her what she wants. If she must rule on the affair, she will settle it within the week—or abandon the crusade."

Will raised an eyebrow.

"You will go to her," Cromwell continued. "Make it clear, with all appropriate diplomacy, that the matter is to be resolved. And if it cannot be resolved, it is to be forgotten."

He stood, brushing past Will to collect a pile of petitions from the edge of the desk. "I want no more letters. No more gossip. And certainly no more interruptions to my court's function over one servant boy's thieving fingers."

"Yes, my lord," Will said. But Cromwell had already turned.

Will hesitated only a second. "They say the boy was last seen near the queen's old rooms—when the household was moving quarters."

Cromwell gave a dry snort. "Of course he was. Opportunity breeds boldness in even the dullest minds."

He turned, striding a slow circuit behind his desk. "But what troubles me more is not that a trinket has gone missing or that some dolt with opportunity can't keep his hands to himself. It's that my secretary—your superior—cannot spare a minute for a policy matter because of it. We have real work to do, Will. Not nursemaid these petty flare-ups."

He stopped, facing Will again. "Go to Mary. Tell her to settle this within the week or drop it. The court is not her personal theater for vengeance."

Will blinked. "Me?"

Cromwell's brow lifted. "You're nimble with people when you choose to be. And the girl likes games. Perhaps you'll speak her language."

He turned back to his desk, already done with the conversation. "Make it go away, Will. Bring me a signed dismissal—or a conviction. I don't care which."

Will gave a shallow nod and withdrew, pulling the door shut behind him.

The corridor was cool and quiet. He stood a moment, adjusting to the sudden hush. This wasn't a mission he relished. He'd met Lady Mary only once in passing—and what he recalled of her wasn't charm.

Still, Cromwell had given his charge. And if Will wanted to stay useful, he'd carry it out.

He headed toward the royal wing, planning to see if Jonas was still in service there. If he could confirm the boy's movements or hear how others were speaking of the incident, it might help with the awkward task Cromwell had assigned him. The name of Mary Tudor still carried weight—enough, at least, to pull a young man's future into its orbit.

As Will passed through the long corridor, he caught the low chatter of a cluster of stewards. One, gesturing over his shoulder, said, " Lady Mary's in the chapel again this morning. Still furious about that silver cross."

Will stopped. "She's here?"

The steward turned, a little surprised. "Aye. Came late last night, I heard."

Will thanked him, turned, and made his way toward the chapel. The space was modest compared to the grand halls nearby, but it opened wide with stained glass and soft morning light. Mary stood near the altar, speaking in low tones to a woman Will didn't recognize. She turned just then, and the sunlight caught her face.

Will paused.

He remembered her, of course—they'd been in the same room once, briefly—but that had been a girl with a title. This was a woman. The flame-red hair she shared with her father framed a face more striking than beautiful, but in that light, the sharp edges softened. Her poise had a kind of danger to it, but something about her caught him. And that was before she spoke.

"Are you here to ask questions too?" she said as she spotted him.

Will bowed slightly. "Lady Mary. I come at Lord Cromwell's instruction. He hopes we might bring finality to this matter with Jonas."

"Then I hope we can settle it," she said coldly. "Bring the boy to be punished."

Will blinked. "We have no hard evidence yet, my lady. Just whispers. The keepsake hasn't even been found."

Mary narrowed her eyes. "I know he did it."

"That may be," Will said gently, "but unless he confesses or we recover the piece, justice would demand—"

"Justice?" she cut in. "They annulled my mother's marriage. They didn't need evidence to cast her aside."

Will hesitated.

Mary continued, "No one followed the rules then. So why must I now? Why must I wait?"

"Love waits," Will muttered without meaning to.

She turned to him sharply. "What?"

He cleared his throat. "Nothing. Just something my sister says. 'Love waits.'"

Mary's face twisted with recognition. "Love waits? That stupid girl—your sister—she told that to my mother, didn't she?"

Will said nothing.

"'Love waits.' What does that even mean? Wait for what may never come? No. I won't wait. I want Jonas brought forward. Make him confess. Then he'll be punished. That's all."

Will straightened. "Then I'll see it done."

Mary said nothing, only turned back toward the altar.

Will left the chapel without looking back. His stride was brisk, but his mind tangled. Jonas would confess—he had to. And yet Will's task no longer felt like politics. It felt personal.

Jonas was scrubbing a stone threshold outside the lower corridor when Will found him. His sleeves were soaked to the elbows, knuckles reddened, shoulders hunched like he was trying to vanish into his work.

Will leaned against the opposite wall, arms folded, watching until Jonas finally looked up.

"Lady Mary has a task for you," Will said casually.

Jonas blinked, the color draining from his face. "No. I—I can't go to her. She hates me."

Will raised a brow. "Hates you? Jonas, you've been in her service how long? Four years? I've never known her to keep someone she truly hated."

"But I've heard—people say she wants me punished."

"People say all sorts of things," Will said, stepping away from the wall. "All I know is, she hasn't dismissed you. And to me, that says she's more eager to put this away than you are."

Jonas stared, unconvinced.

Will knelt beside him, lowering his voice. "Look, I'm not saying it never happened. I'm saying it doesn't have to matter anymore. Just make a quiet apology, return the trinket, and we all move on. No scene. No shame. I can speak a word for you."

Jonas still hesitated.

Will softened further. "I've seen worse. Far worse. And they walked away with nothing more than a change of post. I'm almost certain this will go the same. You've been good before. You can be good again."

"I didn't mean to keep it," Jonas said, voice barely audible. "I just wanted someone to take it back. Quietly. I didn't know what to do after."

"You've been carrying that weight for weeks," Will said. "It's time you let it go. It's time—"

"But I can't," Jonas interrupted.

"You can," Will reassured him. "You can stop being miserable. I know what you're feeling. I've been in the same place you are now, and I know it's no fun. It tore at me every minute of every day. I couldn't sleep. I felt I couldn't trust anyone. I didn't know what to do.

"But then—I realized there was a way. Just one way to make it all stop. That's what's in front of you now, Jonas. You can stop the misery. You can get your life back. Are you ready to get out from under that weight? You ready to let it go?"

Jonas drew a trembling breath. "But I'm scared. I don't want to get flogged."

"Flogged?" Will scoffed. "I doubt that's even in Lady Mary's mind."

"You'll speak for me?"

"I'll do what I can," Will said gently. "You have my word."

The boy looked at him for a long moment, then slowly reached into the seam of his tunic and produced a small bundle.

"I kept it safe," he said.

Will stood, dusted off his hands. "Then let's put this behind us."

They met in one of the smaller audience rooms, its high windows casting morning light across the floor in angled slats. Mary stood already waiting, arms folded, her dark gown severe, her bearing regal despite the absence of courtly title. A steward lingered near the wall, eyes lowered.

Will entered first, motioning behind him.

When Jonas stepped in, shoulders drawn and eyes downcast, Mary's eyes flashed.

Will noticed. And in that brief fire, he forgot everything else. The indignation in her gaze made her radiant—beautiful in the way a storm might be, beautiful in its force and conviction. He swallowed.

"I've brought him," Will said quietly. "Jonas has repented. He very much wants to be forgiven."

Mary's stare didn't shift. "Forgiven?" she repeated. "As if that's his to request."

Jonas made a half-step forward. "I—I never meant—"

She raised a hand. "Quiet."

Jonas stopped, trembling.

Mary looked to Will. "Do you know what he took?"

Will nodded. "I do. But he returned it. Of his own will."

"And that changes everything, does it?" she asked, eyes narrowing.

"I meant only," Will said carefully, "that his heart is penitent. That he wishes to make things right."

Mary's voice grew icy. "You think returning a stolen gift wipes the slate clean? He dishonored me. Mocked me. Shamed my household. He made me look weak."

Will opened his mouth, but she was already continuing.

"And now—now I'm meant to smile and say thank you for my keepsake, my relic—what was mine and should never have been taken?" She turned to Jonas. "Ten lashes. Tomorrow morning. Let him learn what apology earns."

Jonas gasped, going pale. "No—please, no! You said—" He turned frantically to Will. "You promised you'd speak for me!"

Will's jaw tightened. He stepped beside Jonas, lowering his voice. "I did speak for you. I told her of your heart—a good heart that wants to be forgiven. What else would you have me say?"

Jonas's face crumpled in disbelief.

Will added, turning back to Mary, "Lady Mary is within her right. I think she is being kind in limiting it to ten."

He smiled. Too warmly, too quickly.

Mary caught the oddness in it. A flicker of confusion crossed her face—then calculation. This one was useful. Slippery, yes. But useful.

"Very well," she said coldly. "Ten. And not a stripe more. Let the matter be closed after that."

She turned to the steward by the door. "See that he's locked up until morning. I'd not have him vanish in the night."

The steward bowed and stepped forward.

Jonas didn't move.

Will rested a hand on the boy's shoulder. "Come on, then. Best get ready to move on."

Cromwell was already at his desk when Will arrived, sleeves rolled and ink smudging his fingers. A small fire burned in the grate behind him. He didn't look up at once, which gave Will a moment to glance around the room, noting how little disorder could survive here.

Finally, Cromwell sat back and flexed his hand. "Well?"

"It's done," Will said simply. "He confessed. The cross is returned."

Cromwell raised his eyes then, a flicker of surprise crossing his face. "Already?"

"Lady Mary ordered the matter closed last evening. The punishment is scheduled for this morning."

Cromwell's brow arched as he leaned back. "That was faster than I expected. I send you to settle a weeks-long nuisance, and you manage it overnight." He gestured at Will with his quill. "Well done."

A knock interrupted them, and a clerk opened the door just far enough to admit Nicholas. He stepped inside, a sealed letter in hand.

"From Lambeth," Nicholas said, offering the letter to Cromwell with a slight nod to Will. "I was told to bring it personally."

"Ah," Cromwell murmured, breaking the seal. "And how was your retreat to Walthamstow?"

"Restorative." Nicholas gave a faint smile.

"Then I'll share some glad tidings. Your brother-in-law here has resolved the Jonas affair."

Will turned, smiling faintly.

Nicholas froze. "Resolved how?"

Will hesitated, then said, "He confessed. The trinket was recovered."

Nicholas blinked. "And?"

Cromwell answered, almost proudly, "Lady Mary is having him flogged this morning. Ten lashes. A fair punishment."

Nicholas's jaw set. "He confessed, and you're still flogging him?"

Cromwell glanced up from the letter. "Justice requires conclusion. He confessed, not recanted."

But Nicholas had already stepped back. "Excuse me."

He turned and was gone.

Will hesitated a beat before nodding politely to Cromwell. "If you'll excuse me—"

Cromwell waved him off, attention already shifting back to the page.

Will followed Nicholas down the corridor, catching up near the stairwell.

"Nicholas—Look, it was the cleanest way," Will said, though he felt dirty. "No further scandal, no lasting disgrace—"

"Ten lashes?" Nicholas shot back. "For a boy who returned what he took?"

"That was mercy. Now it is over."

"I think," Nicholas said sharply, "that if someone had spoken for him, it wouldn't have come to this."

They rounded the corner just as the final lash cracked across Jonas's back. The boy collapsed in a heap, trembling, blood running from the welts striping his back. The onlookers began to drift away.

Mary stood nearby, composed, her arms crossed.

Nicholas approached her, fury in his eyes. "This was beyond punishment."

Mary didn't blink. "It was justice."

"He's a child."

"He's a thief."

"Who returned what he took."

"Because he was caught."

Will stepped forward. "Lady Mary acted within her right. It's over now."

Nicholas turned to Jonas, kneeling beside him. "I'm sorry. I didn't know—"

Jonas turned his face away. "Leave me alone."

"I tried to—"

"You weren't there," Jonas whispered between sobs.

Nicholas swallowed hard but didn't argue. He turned back to Mary. "He is a boy. Frightened. Ashamed. There were other ways."

"There *are* other ways," she said coldly. "But I chose this one."

Will felt a pang of regret—but Mary was watching him. He stepped in again. "Nicholas, that's enough."

Nicholas stared at him.

Mary's eyes narrowed slightly, studying Will's face.

Then she turned to one of her stewards. "See that he's removed from my service. Let him be gone by midday."

"Yes, my lady."

Mary strode to the door.

Will took a step toward Nicholas, "Nicholas, look . . ."

But Mary paused for a moment and turned slightly.

"William," she said softly, "I'd like a word about something."

Will looked from Nicholas to Jonas, then back to her. Her gaze was direct, unreadable—yet it pulled at him harder than he expected.

He took a breath, then followed her from the room.

She said nothing as she led him down the corridor. Her stride was measured, her back straight, her hands loosely clasped behind her as if she were strolling through a garden rather than from the aftermath of a whipping.

Will followed, unsure whether she was still angry or merely satisfied.

At last, she turned into a small chamber—one of the sitting rooms set aside for occasional guests or visiting royals. Sunlight filtered through narrow windows, casting long beams across the patterned rug. She moved to the center of the room and turned.

He waited, hands loosely folded, the door still ajar behind him.

"You are loyal," she said at last. "Loyal and unflinching."

Will bowed his head slightly, unsure if the words were praise or prelude.

"I find," she went on, "that most men want something—title, coin, favor. But you?" Her gaze held his. "You want *me* pleased."

He nodded once, guarded.

She stepped toward him. "Why is that?"

"I—" Will hesitated. "You deserve it."

A faint smile touched her lips. "You're clever, William. But clever men can be dangerous if not . . . anchored."

He said nothing.

She raised her hand—not tenderly, not seductively, but with quiet command—and brushed her fingers just once along his collarbone. "Do you know what I need?"

He didn't speak.

"I need someone who can see through things. Who will not flinch when blood is required. Who knows how to be silent. Who knows how to win." Her eyes narrowed. "I have been set aside all my life. Now, most of all, I need someone who chooses *me*."

"I do," he said, throat tight.

She studied him a moment longer. Then, turning, she walked past him to the door, closed it softly, and slid the bolt into place.

The sound echoed.

When she turned back, there was no invitation in her eyes—only certainty.

Will's breath caught. He sensed the danger, but the fire stirred his blood.

He thought of nothing then—not Cromwell, not Jonas, not Nicholas or Jo or any life beyond the threshold of this room.

He thought only of her.

And when she reached for him again, he stepped into the flame.

25

When Love Costs

CROMWELL LOOKED UP FROM his desk the moment Will entered.

"There you are." His tone wasn't biting, but it wasn't warm either. "I was looking for you yesterday afternoon."

Will hesitated at the door, brushing a hand along the frame as though debating whether to enter. "I was finishing up the Jonas matter."

Cromwell leaned back. "I thought the Jonas matter was finished."

Will stepped in, eyes lowered. "It was. Lady Mary—she asked for help with . . . with a few final details."

Cromwell narrowed his gaze just slightly. "Did she."

Will offered no further explanation. He simply adjusted the papers he'd brought with him, waiting for Cromwell to move on.

A few seconds passed before Cromwell spoke again. "No matter. Sit. We've got to go over these requisitions from Calais—they're already late."

Will moved to the side table where fresh ink and quills waited, but just as he pulled his chair, a soft rap came at the door.

Cromwell exhaled. "What now?"

A young page stepped in, breathless. "Pardon, Master Secretary. Lady Mary has asked for Master Cressy. She says it's urgent."

Will instinctively took a step forward. "I'll go at once."

But Cromwell raised a hand. "Will you."

Will paused.

"Remind me," Cromwell said, not unkindly, "who you work for."

Will flushed, caught. "Of course. I didn't mean—"

"No doubt you didn't." Cromwell turned to his desk, scanned a brief parchment, and held it out. "Take this to the stables. Then Lady Mary may have you."

Will nodded, took the page, and started toward the door.

"But come back," Cromwell added, his voice level. "I need you today."

Will glanced back. "I'll return."

He slipped into the hallway, footsteps quickening as he passed the steward's desk, then the south corridor windows. The spring light caught his profile—a gleam in the eye, a tug of smile at the corner of his lips.

He did not look back.

Nicholas leaned against the window frame, watching the square below as servants hurried through the morning chill. The sky was already light, but the air still carried the edge of night. Behind him, Jo cleared the breakfast tray.

"You're thinking about him again," she said.

Nicholas didn't answer at first. He shifted his weight, arms crossed, jaw tight.

Jo didn't push. She carried the tray to the sideboard and returned, folding her hands. "Did he say anything else? Afterward?"

Nicholas shook his head. "No. He wouldn't even look at me. I knelt beside him, Jo. I tried to speak, to say—I don't even know what. But he turned his face away like I was part of it. Like I'd helped it happen."

Jo stepped closer. "You didn't know."

"That doesn't matter. It felt like betrayal to him. And I suppose it was."

She touched his arm gently. "It wasn't your doing. You didn't give the order."

"But Will did. Or at least helped carry it out. And I—I said nothing to stop it."

"But you said you arrived only after the flogging finished."

He nodded slowly. "I did. But I should have spoken earlier. I should have actually been his advocate—not just in my own thoughts."

A quiet beat passed between them. Outside, a cart rumbled over the stones.

Jo glanced down. "Do you think Will regrets it?"

Nicholas was quiet. Then, "I don't know. He seemed . . . proud. As though he thought he'd handled it well."

Jo's brow furrowed. "That's not the brother I know."

Nicholas shook his head. "He isn't. Not the one we know and don't want to lose."

Another pause, heavier now.

"Then talk to him," Jo said at last. "Or invite him. Let's have him here tonight."

Nicholas turned to her. "Here?"

"Why not? I haven't seen him in weeks. He didn't come to Walthamstow. And our parents asked after him, remember?"

"Yes."

"I can give him their greetings. And more than that—we can talk. About Jonas. About what happened. About what's happening to Will."

Nicholas considered. "Do you think he'll come?"

"I think if I ask, he will."

Nicholas looked again to the square, but his shoulders eased just slightly. "All right. Ask him."

Jo gave a small nod, already thinking through how she might phrase the invitation, and what words she would use to make her brother feel welcomed—if not yet understood.

"Let's invite him for tomorrow," she added after a moment. "Tonight would be too soon."

Nicholas agreed. "Actually, I'll see him at court. I can deliver the message."

She looked at him gratefully. "Tell him it's nothing formal. Just supper with us. I'd like to see him. And talk."

Nicholas gave a small smile. "So would I."

Nicholas spotted Will just as he emerged from a side chamber near the steward's court. The younger man was adjusting his cuffs, a trace of amusement on his face as though someone had just said something clever behind the door.

"Nicholas," Will greeted him smoothly, noticing his approach.

"Have you a moment?"

Will glanced back, then gave a small shrug. "Just a moment. I'm on my way to the kitchens—someone hinted at venison."

"It's about supper. Jo hoped you might join us tomorrow evening."

Will lifted an eyebrow. "Jo hoped?"

Nicholas's mouth twitched. "We both did. Your parents asked after you while we were at Walthamstow. And Jo wanted to catch you up on how they're doing."

Will gave a soft snort. "That's kind of them. I suppose they heard I've been making myself useful."

"Yes, a bit."

Will nodded, then added with a dry smile, "Is this about Jonas?"

Nicholas held his gaze. "Partly. But it's supper. Not an ambush."

Will's smile sharpened just slightly. "Good to know."

"Then tomorrow, at the supper hour?"

"I'll be there."

He gave a half-bow and turned down the corridor, his steps unhurried, a flicker of satisfaction in his eyes as he disappeared from view.

The knock came precisely on time.

Nicholas rose and opened the door to find Will standing there, composed, cloak neatly arranged, a trace of cool confidence in his posture.

"Right on time," Nicholas said, stepping aside and reaching for his cloak.

"You said the supper hour," Will replied, stepping in. "I take supper invitations as seriously as summons from Cromwell."

Jo emerged from the small side room, drying her hands on a cloth. "Will."

He smiled broadly and stepped forward. "Dear sister! You're looking well." He gave her a warm hug, then pulled back with a grin. "And still thin. No baby brewing yet?"

Jo blinked. "Well! Still as blunt as ever. But no, it's still just us."

She was, in truth, pleased by his easy closeness. Maybe their talk would be easier than she'd expected.

"It's good to see you," she said, returning a bright smile. "You've not been to Lambeth in weeks."

"Court doesn't easily release its grip," Will said, glancing around the modest but well-appointed room. "But it's good to be here. And that smell! Wait, is that venison? If I'd known you ate like this every night, I'd have moved in."

Nicholas nodded and gestured toward the table. "We kept it simple. Venison, braised red cabbage, mushroom and chestnut pottage—nothing fancy."

Will smiled and moved toward the table, eyeing the plates with approval.

"Ha! Oh, yes. I may never leave. You didn't cook like this in Walthamstow, Jo."

Jo smiled. "I have more choice now than just what bloomed in our garden there."

"And our parents? Are they still blooming as well?"

"Oh, yes. They asked after you," Jo said, as she took her seat. "Sent their greetings."

"Kind of them," Will murmured, reaching for his cup. "I really must get back there one day to see them." Then, "Ah, some ale! Seems I drown in wine at court."

For a few minutes, the conversation stayed light—weather, travel delays, some blunders by newly appointed pages. Will offered a few sly observations that made Jo laugh and Nicholas shake his head.

Then, as the dishes were cleared and Nicholas brought out an after-dinner wine, Jo took Will's arm and led him to some comfortable chairs by the fire.

"I wanted to ask about Jonas," she said gently.

Will smiled yet again. He patted her hand as she released him to sit. "Well," he leaned back slightly, folding his hands. "I wondered how long until that came up."

"As I said," Nicholas interjected quickly, "It's not an ambush."

Will gave a faint chuckle. "No, no. Didn't think it was. But I knew the invitation came with . . . other intentions."

Jo held his gaze. "We were surprised. By the outcome."

Will nodded. "Yes, it was quick," he said, intentionally misunderstanding her comment. "He confessed. The trinket returned. Minimal punishment. All in all, a rather satisfactory settlement to the whole affair. I thought it went well."

Nicholas furrowed his brow. "Ten lashes is hardly nothing," he said, his voice low but intense.

"It's not," Will agreed, accepting the wine from Nicholas. "But consider what it might have been: dismissal in disgrace, charges, even more public spectacle, even more lashes. Lady Mary let it end there."

Jo hesitated. "But—did you speak for him?"

Will looked at her for a moment, weighing how he'd answer. "I spoke of his heart. That he wanted forgiveness. I believed that. I still do. And that is why, I think, Mary stopped at ten."

Nicholas frowned. "But why let it go forward at all? The boy was heartbroken. He returned the cross. Why torture him."

Again Will chuckled. "Hardly torture. He exercised poor judgment. He was caught. The matter needed closing. Mercy isn't necessarily removing the consequence. More often it's limiting it. "

Jo looked down, running her finger along the rim of her cup. "He's just a boy."

"So was I," Will said. "Remember when I left the gate unlatched and our milk cow wandered down the road? I believe it was you who insisted on telling Father. I took my lashes. The difference is—I learned where the lines are. Jonas will too."

"Oh, Will," Jo said, shaking her head. "A couple of Father's swipes at you with a switch are not the same as leather lashes cutting across the back."

"Well, I believe the lashes will work. He'll be careful not to take on impulse what's not his."

There was a pause.

"And that's enough for you?" Nicholas asked quietly. "Knowing he'll learn to be more careful, not better?"

Will gave a small smile. "Careful is better."

Jo and Nicholas exchanged a glance.

"Will," Jo said slowly, "do you think that's the point? Learning to navigate without getting caught?"

"I think," Will said evenly, "that we live among powers who are not concerned with our inner virtues. They reward results, loyalty, adaptability. We do better to understand that than pretend otherwise."

Nicholas sat forward. "But isn't it our calling to live by something higher? Not just adjust to the corruption but stand apart from it?"

Will tilted his head. "And what has standing apart won most men? Poverty? Martyrdom? Anonymity?"

Jo answered quietly, "It won Jesus a cross. And the world its hope."

Will studied her. "This world's full of traps. God gave us our wits to avoid them. Those who rise have the chance to help—and that requires surviving. Jonas learned that. And now, being more careful will help him rise, achieve, influence too."

"But what if influence isn't the goal?" she asked.

Will's smile was not unkind. "Then I envy your clarity. But I prefer to use what's available. Rise first. Then maybe help others."

"That's not love," Nicholas said. "That's strategy."

Will raised his cup. "Then here's to strategy."

No one clinked glasses.

"But mercy isn't just a tool for influence. It's a way of seeing. Of remembering that people aren't just assets—they're souls."

The firelight danced, shadows flickering against the hearth. Jo's eyes lingered on the flames before she spoke again.

"And what about Sir Thomas?"

Will leaned back, unsurprised. "Ah. There it is."

"You knew it would come?" Nicholas asked.

Will shrugged. "Everything leads back to Sir Thomas More these days. A kind of courtly obsession. He's become a symbol, depending on who you ask. Integrity. Defiance. Foolishness."

Jo raised an eyebrow. "And which do you call it?"

"None. Or all." Will swirled the wine in his cup, studying its rim. "He's a man who refused to bend. Who held to his convictions knowing where they'd take him. Admirable, in a way. But also impractical."

"Impractical?" Nicholas leaned forward. "He's preparing to die for what he believes."

"Exactly," Will said calmly. "And it won't change a thing. The Act remains. The crown moves on. Cromwell drafts new orders. The court doesn't pause to weep over martyrs, Nicholas. It steps over them."

"But isn't that the point?" Jo asked. "That he knows it won't change the crown—but it speaks to something deeper? That truth is worth suffering for even if it gains nothing in this life?"

Will studied her, then gave a slight nod. "I don't deny the poetry of it. But poetry is not policy. Conviction may be noble, but in governance it is flexibility that keeps one breathing."

Nicholas frowned. "So nothing is worth standing for?"

"I didn't say that. I said More chose his stand—and he'll pay for it. But let's not dress it in sainthood just because he doesn't flinch. A man may refuse to bow out of pride just as easily as out of principle."

Jo's voice softened. "And yet, you said it yourself—admirable in a way."

Will tapped a finger against his cup. "Yes. Because he plays the part well. He believes it. He's sincere. But sincerity is not sanctity. Nor is it strategy. If he had waited—found the right moment—he might have still lived, still served, still shaped things."

"To shape things," Nicholas said, "you have to be *formed* by something more than survival. That's what he's doing. Living for something higher."

Will gave a slight smile. "And dying for it. Let's not forget the end of the tale."

Jo looked into the fire. "Some stories are meant to end that way. Because they leave behind something the rest of us need to remember."

Again Will studied his sister. "You admire him—Sir Thomas. You said 'truth is worth suffering for even if it gains nothing in this life.' Tell me, Jo—do you believe what he believes?"

She hesitated. "No. But—"

"Then you admire a man willing to die for what you believe is false. That's noble, is it? Dying for error?"

"It's not the error I admire. It's the conviction."

Will's expression sharpened slightly. "But conviction alone is dangerous. You think so long as it's conviction, it's heroic? Even if it's for the wrong cause? More dies not for God's truth, in your view, but for a twisted loyalty to a church you reject. So why praise his death? Wouldn't it be better if he recanted the falsehood and lived to serve a truer cause?"

"It's not that simple."

"Oh, but it is. You laud a man's suffering while quietly dismissing the foundation it rests on. That's like praising an actor's resolve while claiming the play itself is foolish."

Nicholas interjected, "It's not the doctrine—it's the integrity. That a man stands for what he believes, even when it costs him."

Will gave a small nod. "And yet here I sit, accused of lacking that very thing, because I helped secure the cost for someone else's failure."

Jo looked at him, eyes soft but searching. "We don't accuse, Will. We just wonder."

He smiled faintly. "And I wonder, too. About all the saints we revere for dying instead of bending. I think—what if they had lived? What might they have built?"

No one answered. The fire crackled between them.

Outside, a bell rang somewhere in the city, muffled by distance and stone.

Jo rose slowly. "More wine? Or ale?"

Will stood as well to stretch. "Please. And next time, let's talk of easier things. Farming, perhaps. Or cows."

Jo managed a smile. Nicholas didn't.

But as Will turned back to the fire, something in his eyes had hardened—content, settled. And far beyond reach.

Jo poured the wine without a word.

Will remained a few minutes longer, trading small courtesies to soften the edge of things. But the warmth never quite returned. When he left, it was with a composed farewell, his footsteps echoing down the stone hall.

The door shut quietly behind him.

They listened as his steps faded toward the stairwell, down to the lower corridors. Somewhere in the distance below, a carriage rumbled along the cobbled street beside the wall—its wheels briefly audible, then gone.

Jo sat again, wrapping her fingers around her cup. "He has no idea what he's lost."

Nicholas looked into the fire. "Or maybe he does. And that's why he never stops moving."

She nodded, slowly. "It's not just that he doesn't believe as More believes. It's that he can't understand why anyone would suffer for something beyond themselves."

Nicholas's voice was quiet. "Because love, to Will, is still a transaction. He sees strategy where More sees sacrifice."

"And yet—he called More admirable." She glanced at Nicholas. "Do you think that part of him really meant it?"

"I think he recognizes the cost," Nicholas said. "But not the love that makes the cost bearable."

Jo's gaze drifted toward the window, where torchlight flickered against the evening haze. "That's the part that stays with me. Not that More dies for what he believes is truth. But that he does it with such peace. As if he's not afraid."

Nicholas nodded. "Love casts out fear."

A silence settled again, not heavy but reverent.

Jo set down her cup. "Then maybe that's what I admire. Not just his conviction. Not just his courage. But that he loves something—*someone*—so completely, there's no room left to flinch."

Nicholas looked at her. "Do you think that kind of love can survive? In a world like this?"

She smiled faintly. "If it can't, then none of this is worth it."

The fire hissed, then stilled. And the stone walls held the quiet.

26

The Final Plea

CRANMER STOOD AT THE small window of the Lambeth chamber, the stone sill cool beneath his fingers. Morning light brushed the leaded panes, soft and gray. Behind him, Margarete poured warm water into a basin to tend his bandaged hand—though both knew it no longer required tending. He had burned it the week prior reaching into the hearth to adjust a shifting log—something he knew he should not have done.

"I keep thinking of him," Cranmer said.

Margarete glanced up. "Sir Thomas?"

He nodded. "There's a strength in him I can't dismiss. He holds to convictions I do not share, and yet—he unsettles me."

She brought the basin to the table and set it down. "Then go. See him again."

Cranmer turned. "I intend to. But it's not obligation drawing me. It's something more difficult to name."

Margarete met his eyes. "Love?"

He hesitated. "Perhaps. Not affection, certainly. But a desire that he live. That he not waste his life when there may be a way to keep it."

Margarete began unwinding the wrap on his hand. "You think you can offer him something?"

"I've wondered—what if we've framed truth too narrowly? Do we owe the truth to every man? Or only to God? If one signs with the hand but believes differently in the heart, and God sees the heart, has anything been lost?"

She looked at him. "And if he believes signing would sever that very connection with God?"

"He might be wrong," Cranmer said softly. "He might think God's love weaker than it is."

She said nothing, pressing the cloth gently into his palm.

"I suppose," he continued, "I want to give him something that would let him stay. And feel he could still keep his soul."

Margarete nodded slowly. "Then give it, Thomas. Speak to him. Not for England, or the king, or the court. But for him."

Cranmer looked down at his hand—faintly red now, but healing. "I will."

The corridor to Cromwell's chambers was unusually quiet. Cranmer paused just outside, hearing the sound of raised voices from within.

"You rush to judgment like a butcher to market!" came the unmistakable bark of the Duke of Norfolk.

Cromwell's voice followed, clipped and cold. "And you drag your feet like a priest hoping for Rome's return."

"I'm saying he deserves more time."

"He's had time. Time enough to recant, to reason. He chooses silence. That, too, is a choice."

A chair scraped. Then the door flung open. Norfolk stormed out, eyes blazing. He stopped briefly when he saw Cranmer. "If you're here to plead for More, you're already too late." Then, pushing past, he disappeared down the corridor.

Inside, Cromwell stood behind his writing table, sleeves rolled, brow furrowed. He was seething.

"I loathe that man," he muttered.

Cranmer stepped in cautiously. "I take it he was advocating for delay?"

"He calls it prudence. I call it sabotage. He plays the loyal peer, but make no mistake—Thomas Howard remains Catholic to his marrow."

Cranmer blinked. "Yet he's to preside at the trial?"

"Oh, he'll do his job. He wants to keep his head. He just makes it difficult for everyone else to do theirs."

There was a pause.

"Well then," Cromwell said, trying to refocus, "what brings you, my lord?"

Cranmer hesitated. "I'd like to speak to him—again, one final time."

Cromwell looked at him sharply. "Not you too."

Cranmer held his ground. "I think . . . I don't know. But I must try."

Cromwell set his pen aside. "My lord, I know your heart in this. But I must be blunt. The king's patience is worn thin. If More does anything—anything—that embarrasses His Majesty after being shown leniency, heads will roll. Perhaps yours. Perhaps mine."

"I make no promises," Cranmer said. "Only that I feel compelled to try."

"And that compulsion may be your undoing," Cromwell muttered, rubbing his temples. "You're too innocent in matters like this. You'll offer him too much, or show too much softness, and we'll all regret it."

Cranmer waited.

Cromwell sighed. "Take someone with you. Someone who can see clearly when your heart clouds your judgment."

"Whom did you have in mind?"

"Will Cressy. He's proved himself capable of reading men, and perhaps More won't expect it."

Cranmer almost laughed. "Will doesn't even care about the matters at stake."

"Which is precisely why he'll be effective."

"Will?" Cranmer stammered.

"You haven't been paying attention. He has a quick, sharp mind—and he cares about order. And protecting the peace and plans of our king. He's matched men twice his age and come away the stronger."

Cromwell paused. Cranmer looked down, still unconvinced. Cromwell's face darkened.

"The king does not forget the names of those who vouch for failures."

Cranmer looked up at that. "All right," he said, though shaking his head. "But he'll be told to remain silent. It is a delicate matter I'm hoping Sir Thomas will see. I would not want any bluster from Will to spoil his reflection."

Cromwell offered only a faint, unreadable smile. Cranmer waited a moment, then turned with a sigh and left.

The Tower was dim and cool, candlelight flickering over damp stone. They had been ushered into a meeting room of sorts, a rectangular table filling the space with chairs set on either side. The jailer had shuffled off to retrieve the prisoner.

Will wrinkled his nose. "There's something foul in these stones."

Cranmer ignored him. "I fear Sir Thomas may be too set in his ways to change position now."

"On the contrary, I should think," Will said, seating himself at the table, sniffing. "Had I been breathing in this acrid air as long as he, I would swear to anything."

"Oh no," Sir Thomas said entering the room, with the chains clinking in their drag across the stone floor. "I can assure you it's the air out there that's not fit to breathe. In here, I keep company with no one who stabs, slashes, or bites."

Cranmer gave a bitter smile. "Surely you can't say that you prefer the company of rats and lice to that of family and friends?"

"No, not to family, but friends?" More seated himself across the table from where Cranmer had taken his seat next to Will. "Tell me, my lord, are you my friend?"

"I . . . well, yes, I would like to think of myself as your friend." Cranmer looked at him sincerely.

"Then," More asked innocently, "why are you here?"

Cranmer adjusted himself in his seat. "To see whether I can offer you a way to sign the oath, escape this dungeon, and return to your family in Chelsea."

"Ah," replied More, "so as a friend you are concerned for my body's welfare?

"Yes!" Cranmer insisted.

"And what of my soul's?" More shot back.

"Your soul's?"

More kept his eyes locked on Cranmer's. "My soul's welfare. What of that? Are you concerned for that?"

More's eyes seemed to pour into Cranmer's soul. Cranmer felt his heart laid bare before that gaze.

"I am . . . concerned for your soul. Yes."

"Then what would you have me do? Forget my conscience? Consider a vow to a king more necessary—more sacred—than a vow to God? Forfeit my soul?" More leaned back. "Is that how you'd care for my soul?"

Cranmer bowed his head.

Will remained quiet, seated beside Cranmer but leaning back slightly, arms crossed, his expression unreadable.

"Archbishop?" More said softly.

"What if . . ." Cranmer began, then changed tack in his thoughts. He met More's eyes. "Keep your soul before God, Sir Thomas. Keep your vow to him. He is worthy of your vow, your heart, your very soul. But this oath on parchment? A document formed by Parliament? You owe Parliament neither your heart nor soul, so how does signing its document change that? The apostle St. Paul tells us we are declared righteous by faith, not by ink on parchment. Your heart, your soul—they belong to God regardless."

For a moment, no one spoke. Will sat up straight. He had not anticipated Cranmer would argue in this manner. Cranmer urging More to sign under false pretense could backfire disastrously. If More were freed and then denounced the king, heads would roll, including possibly their own.

"My lord," Will began, directing his comment to Cranmer, "to sign an oath to the king falsely is treason."

Cranmer turned to Will. "Sir Thomas is accused of treason already. He will go to the block for treason if he does not sign." He turned back to More. "So signing is not speaking to God, it is satisfying Parliament."

More gave a thin smile. "Save breath though it loses soul?"

Cranmer looked down. "But if one dies but for a mistaken cause?"

"If it is mistaken to obey one's conscience before God, then we are all damned."

Will's voice cut in. "And what if your conscience, Sir Thomas, is just pride with a halo?"

More turned. "Who are you?"

"A man without titles or holy robes. But with enough clarity to see this: you call it conscience, but to me it sounds like you're bargaining. Hoping your death will earn you heaven."

More's gaze hardened. "You think I fear hell more than I love truth?"

"I think," Will said coolly, "you fear being wrong in the end."

Silence. For the first time, More looked uncertain.

Cranmer said nothing. He only watched, heart pounding, as the man who had seemed immovable shifted his eyes to the stone floor.

At last turning back to Cranmer, More said quietly, "If your head were on the block, would you cling to comfort, or to Christ?"

Cranmer opened his mouth, then closed it. The silence lengthened.

It was Will who spoke. "And what if the Christ you cling to is not Christ at all? What if the foundation you're dying for—this conscience you claim—is built on something untrue?"

More's head turned, sharply. "You question my faith?"

Will didn't flinch. "No, I question your certainty. You say you die for truth. But Jo—my sister—she says you're dying for a lie. A beautiful lie, perhaps. But one that creates martyrs before they're even convinced."

More's gaze narrowed. "So she pities me."

"She does," Will said, "because she admires what she thinks she sees in you—a love despite the doctrinal falseness you cling to. And it confuses her. Because it feels true even when your doctrine doesn't."

More turned back to Cranmer. "All I have is my conscience set on God. I won't sacrifice that."

Cranmer felt he had to push. "But the king . . . "

More cut him off. "The king is a man, not God. You seem to appeal more to the king than to God. Whom do you serve?"

Cranmer was shaken. "I . . . I serve God!"

"Then it must be something else. It must be that you fear the king more than God. You fear the loss of your life if you should oppose him."

"Not true!" Cranmer replied wide-eyed. "I agree with the king, because I believe his authority in line with Holy Scripture. I do not find the Pope there."

"Really," More replied studying Cranmer. Then he stood and began to pace but stopped. "Suppose the king had been content with his wife," he proposed. "Suppose she had given birth to a healthy male heir to the throne."

Cranmer answered immediately, "I would welcome it!"

More lifted his hand to stop him. "The king has a male heir, the royal family is all happy and well—and still Catholic, still giving allegiance to the Pope, still burning heretics. You now stand before me in court. I ask you if you believe the Pope is the vicar of Christ to whom all Christendom owes allegiance. I ask you this, warning you that the stake awaits you if you answer no. Now, what is your answer?"

Cranmer hesitated. "I—Scripture doesn't . . ."

More slammed his hand on the table. "Is the Pope the vicar of Christ on earth? Upon your life, answer yes or no!"

Cranmer was visibly shaken. He stumbled over his reply. "He . . . no, he is not."

More held Cranmer's eyes for a moment. "See how difficult that was for you? And it was all hypothetical. If it had been real, if you had spent months in this prison prior to that question, if the executioner were standing there waiting to drag you to your death, I dare say your answer would not be the same." More shook his head slowly. "Your fear is greater than your conviction. What is it God said to the church in Laodicea? 'I would that you were cold or hot, so because you are lukewarm I will spit you out of my mouth.'" Again More paused. He breathed out slowly. "You come to preach religion to me. I have no more stomach for you than does God." And with that, More turned and left, the guard leading him away.

Cranmer was stunned. And ashamed.

Will was silent as well.

They sat a few moments, in their minds, replaying the questions, rehearsing the feelings. Finally, still without saying a word, they left as well.

The day of the trial dawned gray, heavy with anticipation. The hall at Westminster was crowded, solemn. Cranmer and Will stood toward the rear, near one of the side entrances, trying not to draw attention. Margarete was not far from them, her expression unreadable. And at the far edge of the hall, Lady Mary had come, flanked by two of her household women. Her face was tight, and her eyes locked forward.

At the front of the hall sat the presiding peers—at their head, the Duke of Norfolk, robes immaculate, expression stony. He said little, but his presence dominated the bench. Cromwell, seated nearby, kept stealing glances at him, jaw clenched. Norfolk returned not a one.

Sir Thomas More was brought in, weak and lean—bearing the marks of long imprisonment. But his posture was upright. He bowed slightly to the assembly, his gaze scanning the room. When it passed over Will, there was no change in expression. When it passed over Cranmer, there was a faint tightening. But when it found Lady Mary, it paused.

She nodded once, almost imperceptibly.

Will noticed it. And then noticed her eyes shift—past More, past Cranmer—to him. The look she gave was icy. Not shocked. Not angry. Just set. Something had changed. And he knew it.

The charges were read—treason, for denying the supremacy of the king as head of the Church of England. More stood silently as the accusations poured forth. Then he was asked for a response.

"I have not spoken against His Majesty, nor stirred rebellion. I have simply remained silent. And silence, under law, is not treason."

A flicker of irritation crossed Cromwell's face. Norfolk leaned forward.

"You consider yourself above Parliament, then?" Norfolk's voice was cold, ceremonial.

"I consider myself answerable to God first, my lord."

Norfolk exchanged a look with Cromwell—whether resentful or resigned, it was unclear. Then he sat back.

The judges conferred. But the result had been long decided. Witnesses, coached and bribed, came forward. One swore he had heard More deny the king's title. Another claimed More had called Parliament's act unlawful. There was no defense. The verdict came swiftly: guilty of treason.

A murmur swept the hall. Cranmer closed his eyes. Will looked over to Mary. Her gaze was fixed on More, but then shifted—just briefly—back to Will. Her jaw clenched.

Norfolk rose, his voice formal and composed. "Sir Thomas More, having been found guilty of high treason, you are hereby sentenced to death by beheading, to take place at the King's pleasure."

Even as he spoke, his voice was devoid of triumph. It sounded like a man performing a duty he wished were someone else's.

As the hall stirred with whispers, Norfolk's eyes flicked—just briefly—to Lady Mary. She met his gaze, jaw still set. Then both looked away as if nothing had passed between them.

The hall emptied slowly. Will tried to catch up to Mary, but she slipped past a column and into one of the private corridors. He hurried to follow.

"Lady Mary," he called.

She stopped but did not turn. He approached more slowly now, more cautiously.

"I swear to you," he said quietly, "I had no part in what was said. I didn't testify. I came only to observe."

Mary turned at last. Her eyes shimmered, but they were not soft. "You walked into his cell with Cranmer."

"Yes. But I said nothing he didn't provoke. I wanted to understand. I still do."

"You wanted to understand how a man dies slowly—" she said—"by reason, by parchment, by silence."

Will faltered. "I came because I thought . . ." He paused. "Because I wanted to see the man you admire. To see if your conviction was anchored in something real."

Her eyes blazed fresh. "Something real?! That man stood against the king for his belief, for my mother's marriage, for my own legitimacy. And he is going to his death for it! He is the only one in this whole circus who is real! Did you see that?"

Will took a step closer. "Yes. I did. And I saw you, too. And I still—"

"Don't," she cut him off. "Don't confuse loyalty with longing."

He hesitated. "Then let me prove it."

Her eyes narrowed. "You'll have your chance. Soon enough."

And with that, she turned and was gone.

27

Not by Force

They had arrived the night before. Roger and Emilie, summoned not by command but by concern, had come at Jo's request—or rather, because of her letters. The strain in her hand had been obvious. The depth of grief, the helpless fury, the confusion she was trying to make sense of—it had spilled onto the page like blood from a wound. And so, without pomp or pronouncement, they had come.

Jo had been waiting by the gate when they arrived. She didn't speak right away—just ran into her father's arms, burying her face in his coat. Roger held her tightly, his hand cradling the back of her head, his eyes already wet. Emilie reached them and brushed Jo's hair with her fingers, then kissed her cheek.

"We came as soon as we read your words," Emilie whispered.

"I didn't know where I needed to turn—until I realized it was to you," Jo said.

"You turned right," Roger answered. "We're here."

Now morning hung thick in the air, heavy with silence and shadow. The group had gathered in one of the quieter rooms of Lambeth Palace— more sanctuary than lodging in these recent weeks. The light from the window was pale, barely enough to cut the dim.

Cranmer sat near the hearth, head bowed, fingers interlaced. Nicholas stood by the window, tense, arms crossed. Margarete was in a chair, hands folded in her lap, a stillness about her that was not calm but control. Roger and Emilie sat nearby, quietly taking it all in.

Jo stood. Her movement startled no one—they had felt it coming.

"I won't go," she said. "I won't watch them kill him."

No one responded immediately. The words, simple as they were, held weight.

Nicholas spoke first. "You don't have to. None of us must."

"I know," she said. "But I need to say why."

Cranmer looked up, eyes already heavy.

"I've been thinking," Jo continued, voice sharpening, "about how it all happens. Not just this execution—but all of them. All the burnings and the beheadings. All the declarations that someone is unfit, unworthy, a threat to peace, to doctrine, to order. And then they kill them. With words. With rope. With blade. And they do it in the name of God."

She paused. No one moved.

"That's the rot—when people sanctify control and violence, and call it the will of God.

Margarete bowed her head.

"Sir Thomas More," Jo went on, "stands for what he believes. So did others before him. So will others after. But the evil isn't just in those who swing the axe. It's in the silence. In the neat robes. In the nods of approval. In the way we all say it was unfortunate but necessary."

Emilie touched Roger's hand. Cranmer closed his eyes.

"I won't go," Jo repeated, firmer now. "Not because I'm fragile. Not because I'm a woman. But because I'm a follower of Jesus. And Jesus never took up a sword."

A long silence followed. Finally, Margarete spoke, voice low. "Nor will I go. My spirit grieves enough."

Roger cleared his throat. "We didn't come for spectacle. We came for you. For whatever this morning would require."

Jo turned to him, eyes brimming.

Cranmer stood slowly. "I must go. I gave my word. But your protest, Jo—it's holy. Don't doubt that."

Nicholas hesitated, then said, "I'll go too. But only to be witness—not to the execution, but to the man."

Jo stepped toward him. "Then see him rightly. And come back ready to speak truth."

He nodded, and she held him tightly for a long moment.

Then Cranmer turned to Margarete. "I don't go because I believe in the blade," he said quietly. "I go because I must still believe that some part of this world can be redeemed."

Her eyes searched his, and for a moment she said nothing. Then she rose, stepped close, and placed her hand gently against his chest.

"I know. Redemption starts with giving of ourselves. Even as I give to you, and you give to me. So go. Let your presence be grace, not judgment. Give of yourself."

He held her gaze, then covered her hand with his.

That was all.

The sun was beginning to rise. Soon, the Tower Green would be full. And the blade would fall.

The walk from Lambeth to the Tower was solemn, unspoken. Cranmer and Nicholas crossed the cobbled expanse of Tower Hill and entered the gates. The guards offered them quiet deference; everyone knew the moment at hand.

As they stepped onto the green, the air felt brittle. The scaffold stood stark against the pale sky, its timbers dark from weather and use. A small crowd had begun to gather—nobles in silence, guards at attention, commoners at the edges, hushed.

Cranmer's feet slowed. The sight of the platform struck him like a blow. In his mind, it was no longer Thomas More he was approaching. It was Hugh Chedsey. The clang of the axe. The blood on the block, all mixing with Joan's screams in delivery of her child. The flood of memories broke open.

He staggered once and caught himself.

The memory of Joan surged anyway—her anguished cries from the inn window, the way her body wrenched in pain as Hugh was led to die. She had not watched, but she had known. And Cranmer had watched. Coldly. Certain of righteousness.

He blinked hard, but the tears came anyway. Not soft, not subtle. A storm rising behind the eyes. He turned slightly, pretending to study the green.

Had he changed? Had he softened with time? Or was it only that he had come to love Thomas More and had never loved Hugh? God loved both. Cranmer knew that. But he had loved his own certainty more than Hugh's life.

He had once welcomed the axe as justice.

Now he could barely stand in the shadow of the scaffold.

Beside him, Nicholas stood unmoving, gaze fixed on the rising figure of More, who had now emerged from the Tower. The man walked slowly, but upright. A hush fell.

Nicholas's thoughts churned. He saw Jonas again—bloodied, humiliated, forced into confession not by truth, but by pressure. More would not be broken like that. But still he would die.

Why must it be this way? Nicholas thought. *Even when the judgment is unjust, it is accepted. Not because it is right—but because it is the price of belief.*

He wanted to scream. Or cry. Or pray. But nothing came.

He just watched. And tried not to look away.

As More reached the scaffold, he turned to address those gathered.

"I die the king's good servant," he said, voice clear in the morning air, "but God's first."

Then he began to ascend the steps.

Cranmer moved as if to follow him—not as archbishop, but as a man burdened with sorrow. But More paused and turned. His face was solemn but kind.

"Please, my lord," he said softly, "don't follow."

Cranmer froze. The words were not cruel, but they carried finality. More had not accepted Cranmer's efforts. Not in the Tower, and not here. It was not anger—it was conscience. Even in death, he could not be comforted by a man who, in his eyes, had compromised truth.

Cranmer bowed his head and stepped back.

Another priest—anonymous, unassuming—stepped forward in his place.

More turned again and continued to the top.

Cranmer did not watch the fall of the blade. He turned before it dropped, the weight of More's words crushing down. The Tower Green blurred through his tears. All his years of striving, of silence, of rationalizing power for the sake of peace—what had they yielded? He had once prayed for Hugh's death, thinking it justice. Now he mourned a better man, condemned for conscience. And he knew—this was not redemption. This was the world losing its way again. He had not drawn nearer to God. He had taken only a longer road around.

That evening, the shadows inside Lambeth stretched long across the room. No one had lit the lamps yet. The light of the day—such as it was—had begun to fade.

They sat quietly. No words had come for some time, only breath. The kind of silence that settled not because nothing needed saying—but because too much did.

Jo sat near the fire. She had not cried at the news. Not when Nicholas returned with the word. Not when Cranmer entered last and said nothing at all. But her shoulders were tense, and her hands, folded in her lap, were tight and still.

At last, she said, "She asked you how not to, didn't she?"

Cranmer looked up. "Who?"

"My mother," Jo said. "When you asked her if she doubted God's goodness."

Cranmer gave the smallest nod.

Jo's eyes stayed on the hearth. "She asked, 'Tell me how not to.'"

A stillness followed that sentence, as if even the air needed a moment to absorb it.

"She never meant it as defiance," Jo continued. "She just needed something solid to hold—something to make the pain make sense."

Cranmer's voice was low. "And I couldn't give it to her."

"No," Jo said gently. "Because you hadn't found it either."

He turned toward the others. Nicholas, seated beside Margarete. Roger and Emilie, across from them. No one spoke. They were waiting—for each other, perhaps—for the conversation that had always been circling them.

"She died without the answer," Jo said. "And so did More. And so might we. But I want to believe there is one."

Nicholas spoke, his voice rough. "Not an answer that makes evil go away. But maybe one that makes love possible even in the middle of it."

Roger nodded. "Then maybe we begin there."

"Begin there . . ." Cranmer repeated thoughtfully. "I think you're right, Roger. We always begin at the other end—with the pain. Even when we're catching insight—when we seem to be finding. It somehow turns and we settle on the wrong end."

He paused, frowning as if something were forming just out of reach.

Margarete looked up, hope shining in her eyes.

"And . . . and that's the mistake," he said. "It's backwards. We've been starting in the wrong place. We see the evil. We see the suffering. And we start there—asking how a good God could let it be so. We let the grief define our picture of him."

Roger nodded slowly. "That's what I've done. You see the world's cruelty, and you measure God by it."

"But, no," Cranmer said, more urgently now, "that *is* backwards. What if we're meant to start with love—not the evil, not the pain, but love itself? Of course, that's it!" His voice rose with conviction. "We say God is love—do we even know what that means? What it does? What it requires? First, we settle that. And only then do we ask what kind of God must exist if that kind of love is real."

There was a pause. The words had surprised even him.

Across the room, Margarete released a breath she had been holding. Her head tilted back, eyes brimming. A tear slipped down her cheek, not sorrow, but relief.

Jo turned toward her. "You knew. You've known this all along. You've been trying to tell us all along."

Margarete smiled faintly, blinking the tear away. "I've known. I've known for a while."

Nicholas frowned. "Why didn't you say it before?"

She looked at Cranmer. "I did say it before. But it can't be said in doctrinal discourse. You had to say it. And not just say it—but *see* it. You had to discover it. You had to see its light burst open from your own perspective, from your heart. Letting someone give you the answer is not the same as finding it. You'll carry it only if it's yours."

Cranmer's gaze didn't shift. "I could have been spared years of wandering."

"You could have," she said gently. "But you weren't ready yet. The words weren't yet yours. It would have been an argument to protect, not a truth to live from. And arguments break. Truths endure—if they're rooted in love."

Jo whispered, "So then, let's go on. If it's the place to start, what *is* love?"

Emilie said, "We always say it's kindness or loyalty. Or feeling. But those aren't enough, are they?"

Nicholas shook his head. "Not when the world's on fire."

"How do you see it?" Emilie asked Margarete.

Margarete leaned forward now. "Love," she said slowly, "has to be specific enough to move beyond kindness and care, but broad enough to take in the whole soul. It is the giving away of *me* in the embrace of *us.* It's not just a sacrifice of my abundance. It is, first and deep down, a vulnerability—one that says, 'My heart, my soul, is no longer mine alone. I offer it. I share it. With you.'"

She paused.

"That giving of self for the benefit of relationship—that's love."

Cranmer breathed out. "Giving. For the benefit of relationship . . ." He chuckled to himself. "You've said this to me before. More than once."

They sat with that. The truth of it didn't need to be argued.

It was already known.

Jo's voice broke the silence, quiet but clear. "If that's how we're to love each other . . ." She hesitated, then turned to the others. "And if God wants us to love as he does . . ."

Her voice dropped to a whisper. "Then God must love this way, too. He wouldn't ask it of us—unless it was already in him."

No one moved. The idea settled into the room like dawn light—soft at first, but unstoppable.

Nicholas leaned forward. "You mean . . . he gives of himself?"

Jo nodded slowly. "Not just gives—opens. Offers. Becomes vulnerable. Not to show strength but to form kinship. To say: I am not holding myself apart from you. I'm sharing myself—my truth, my goodness, my beauty—with you. For relationship."

Cranmer's breath caught.

Roger spoke, barely above a whisper. "The God of all creation—vulnerable. Willing to give . . . for us?"

Margarete smiled. "Yes."

Emilie's hand went to her mouth. "But he's God."

"Yes, . . . God . . . *the* God of love," Margarete said. "Love is not beneath him. It is the very purpose he exists."

Nicholas looked up, eyes wide. "Then he never wanted a people to rule over. He wanted a people to love."

"To be loved by," Jo added.

Roger sat back, stunned. "Not a kingdom of subjects, but a kinship of souls."

Cranmer stood. Slowly. "Then every act of God—all of it—creation, covenant, cross . . . all of it was for love."

"And not just love in the abstract," Margarete said, rising with him. "Love like this. The kind that gives. The kind that risks. The kind that waits for the other to respond freely—because to force it would destroy it."

Jo looked at her. "That's why it has to start with love. Because if you start anywhere else—judgment, fear, even power—you end up with a God who doesn't look like Jesus."

Nicholas shook his head slowly, still stunned. "And we've been trying to fit Jesus into an all-powerful image, instead of letting Jesus show us who God is."

Cranmer's voice was hushed now. "And he did show us. He is all powerful. But we confuse things when we settle on violence or control as the height of power. Love is the height. Jesus became Lord of all at the cross, because it was there he gave himself fully."

There was no need to name the moment. The Cross was already in their minds.

God, nailed to splintered wood. Not because he had to prove anything—but because love gives. Because love invites. Because love does not coerce.

Because love wants relationship.

And relationship always requires vulnerability.

Roger sighed, "But then why doesn't he stop the evil? If he loves like this . . . why not end the cruelty?"

"Don't go back to viewing it backwards," Margarete said quickly. "Think from God's love—a love that gives of himself and *invites* us to give of ourselves. Love means giving of ourselves for the benefit of relationship. And you're asking, 'Why doesn't God interrupt that when things go wrong?' But to stop us by force would take away our ability to give. And without the ability to give, we couldn't love at all."

Catching on, Jo added, "So he shows himself. He says, 'Look at me. Here is truth. Here is goodness. I show you beauty. He encourages us to choose for that, but he can't make us choose it. If he did, it would not, could not be love anymore because we wouldn't be giving. Is that right?"

Nicholas said, "Then it can't be forced. Not even by God."

Cranmer looked at them each in turn. "He cannot deny himself. Not even to stop the pain."

"And that," Margarete said, "is why love is stronger than any other power. Because it never breaks itself to win."

Roger asked quietly, "Even in the end? I mean, doesn't God win in the end by destroying all who won't have relationship with him?"

Margarete didn't look up right away. Her voice, when it came, was soft. "No. That's not how love wins."

She paused, letting the weight of her words settle.

"God doesn't destroy anyone," she said. "But where God is not—there is no truth, no goodness, no beauty. No life. Those who reject him are choosing absence. And absence undoes everything."

Emilie murmured, "So it isn't punishment. It's collapse."

Nicholas added, "Like a branch with no root. Or breath with no air."

Cranmer said, "God doesn't win by conquering them. He wins by offering himself. Again and again. Even to the end."

A hush settled again, deeper than before. Not empty—full.

Cranmer rose slowly. He walked to the far window, where the light had almost gone. Outside, the shadows of the courtyard stretched long, like the memory of voices still speaking.

He touched the sill, fingers tracing the worn stone. And then, as if to someone not present, he spoke.

"Joan," he said, quietly. "You asked me once how not to doubt God's goodness."

The others looked toward him, but no one interrupted.

"I didn't know then," he continued. "And I still don't know everything. But I believe this now—"

He turned back to them, eyes full, voice steady.

"Love does not coerce. It gives. It waits. It suffers. It bears all things. And in the end, it still stands."

A pause.

"Love which gives and never coerces—that is the goodness of God."

PART 4

Mary Tudor

I live to show His power, who once did bring

My joys to weep, and now my griefs to sing.

28

A Crown Too Heavy

THE DOOR SLAMMED OPEN with such force that the latch cracked against the paneling.

Cromwell rose slowly, his pen still poised above the parchment. The knock had never come. There was only the king—broad, flushed, his eyes alight with fury and something less definable, something bordering on desperation.

"Your Majesty," Cromwell said evenly, folding the paper with deliberate care. "You honor my office."

Henry didn't sit. He strode in and closed the door himself, his heavy frame filling the chamber with tension.

"Don't flatter yourself, Thomas," he snapped. "I come because this cannot be heard by the walls of court."

Cromwell inclined his head—half deference, half calculation. Henry's voice was frayed. That meant he'd been pacing, rehearsing. Dangerous.

"She is not the woman I married," Henry hissed. "She is sour, Thomas—sour and sharp and sneering. Her voice is a lash. Her presence curdles the room."

Cromwell nodded slowly. "The queen is . . . passionate."

"She is poison!" Henry roared, then caught himself and lowered his voice. "And worse—she dares side with that insufferable brother of hers in matters of policy. As if my judgment needs correction from George Boleyn!"

Cromwell said nothing.

Henry paced to the fire, stabbing at the flames with his cane. "I am king, Thomas. *King.* And yet I find myself under scrutiny in my own marriage bed, weighed and judged as though I were some boy beneath her station."

A pause. The fire cracked.

"And no heir. No living son. Only a string of blood-soaked sheets and endless tears."

He turned sharply, eyes boring into Cromwell's. "You're supposed to guard the peace of my reign. Then guard it. Find the cause. And remove it."

The heavy door clicked shut behind the king, and Cromwell stood motionless for a moment—gazing not at the fire, but through it. His face gave nothing. Only his fingers moved, curling once into a fist before relaxing again.

He did not sit.

Instead, he moved to the side door and opened it.

"Find Cressy," he said to the steward waiting outside. "Now. Tell him to bring parchment."

The steward disappeared. Cromwell returned to the fire, speaking aloud though no one heard him.

"He wants the house clean, but doesn't care what burns in the process."

Moments later, Will stepped in—neat, alert, the tension in the air not lost on him.

"You sent for me?"

"Close the door."

Will obeyed. His brow remained creased. He had sensed the tension as he passed the guards outside—something sour in the air, something scorched.

"Bad news?" he asked lightly, pulling a writing board from the shelf.

Cromwell didn't look at him. "The worst kind. Discontent wrapped in silence. The kind that needs an answer before the question is asked aloud."

Will set the board down and dipped the quill.

Cromwell finally turned. "How closely have you observed the queen's friends?"

Will hesitated. "Friends, my lord?"

"Those who still smile when she enters the room. Those who haven't adjusted their affections to match the king's new inclinations."

A pause. Then: "Norris. Brereton. Maybe . . . Weston. And—yes—Smeaton."

Will nodded slowly, eyes narrowing. "They're frequent in her company. Loyal."

"Exactly," Cromwell murmured, moving now, pacing behind the writing desk. "Too loyal. And too few. They isolate her—and in isolation, fondness begins to look like secrecy."

Will said nothing. The weight of the moment sharpened his posture.

"I want movements, conversations, habits," Cromwell continued. "Who met where, when. What doors were shut too long. What glances lingered. What servants lingered nearby. I don't need proof, Will. I need possibility."

Will lifted his eyes from his writing. "You mean to suggest—?"

"I mean to prepare the soil. The king wants relief. We will plant what grows it."

Will leaned back slightly, struck. "But if none of it's true—"

"Then no man shall hang by accident," Cromwell said coldly. "Only by loyalty."

There was a silence. Not disapproval—just awe at the efficiency of it.

Cromwell stepped closer. "You said once you wanted to serve something bigger than yourself. Well, here's your chance. Justice isn't always about truth. It's about keeping the crown upright."

Will tilted his head slightly. "There are others who might supply . . . deeper rumors. Ones not bound to the queen's circle."

That drew Cromwell's full gaze—a glance that lingered, unreadable.

Will met it evenly, his face composed.

Cromwell turned back to the fire and murmured, "Then listen well. And bring only what matters."

Anne moved like a storm clothed in velvet. Her steps were swift, too swift for ease, and the hem of her gown whispered furiously across the stones. She didn't glance at the guards she passed or the courtiers who bowed too late—her gaze was fixed ahead, but her fury radiated outward like heat. The torchlight caught the sharp plane of her cheek, the tight line of her mouth. She had once walked these halls as if they belonged to her. Now, each echo of her heels sounded like a challenge. She held herself tall, unyielding, but there was a crackling beneath it—a speed to her movement, a sharpness to her breath—that suggested something breaking behind her eyes. "He's ignoring me," Anne snapped, her pace quickening across the polished stone. "He doesn't summon me, doesn't dine with me, doesn't even speak unless it's to ask whether I've bled or not. As if I'm a broodmare to be inspected."

Norfolk, hands clasped calmly behind his back, offered a slight incline of the head. "The king is under strain, madam. Parliament, the monasteries, the council—"

"Spare me Parliament," she said sharply. "He shattered it to have me. Broke Rome, broke Catherine. And now? Now he averts his gaze like I'm some foolish mistake he can't admit."

Norfolk's gaze slid to a nearby guard, and he spoke more softly. "These halls are thin-walled."

"They're thick with cowards," Anne muttered. "And liars. And flatterers. I married for love—and he married for spite."

They turned a corner.

And stopped.

Mary stood ahead, half-shadowed near an arched window. A book in hand, though she was not reading it.

She did not bow.

Anne stiffened. Her voice, when it came, was quiet—but icy.

"What is *she* doing here?"

Norfolk stepped forward quickly. "Her presence is temporary, madam. The guest chambers were vacant, and her health—"

"Her health?" Anne cut in. "Is illegitimacy a disease now?"

Mary's eyes met hers. "It lingers, I've found."

Anne took a step closer. "These are royal halls, girl. Not your mother's chapel."

"I've never been confused on that point," Mary said evenly.

Anne's lips curled. "Then perhaps you'll be kind enough to walk elsewhere and remember your place."

Mary closed the book. "My place is where I'm permitted. Which, it seems, is no longer beneath your heel."

Norfolk placed a hand lightly on Anne's arm. "Majesty—"

Anne pulled away. "You insult the throne by housing its traitor's spawn. Don't think I won't raise it."

"And I will remind the king," Norfolk said gently, "that it was he who placed her there."

That stilled Anne. For a beat, she said nothing.

Then she turned, skirts snapping like banners behind her.

"Keep your ghost in its cage, my lord," she hissed.

Norfolk said nothing, but followed her. She did not look back.

As Anne's skirts vanished around the far corner, Mary stood unmoving. The echoes of the queen's parting fury still stirred the corridor's hush. A moment passed, then another. Then Mary turned—precisely, with no wasted motion—and made her way in the opposite direction, the book still gripped in her hand like a blade.

By the time she reached the guest chambers, her breath was steady again, though her pulse was not. She opened the door.

Will rose at once from where he had been sitting near the hearth. "You're late."

Mary didn't answer right away. She placed the book down with deliberate care and removed her gloves one finger at a time. "I was stopped," she said finally. "By a ghost who still believes herself queen."

Will frowned. "Anne?"

"She mistook me for someone who needed reminding," Mary said coolly. "She thought she could put me in my place. She failed."

Will watched her a moment longer, then said, "I came from Westminster Hall. Cromwell pulled me aside." He hesitated. "He wants names."

Mary raised a brow.

"Men. Gentlemen at court who seem . . . too fond of the queen." He paused. "Fond in ways a husband wouldn't like."

Something flickered in Mary's eyes. "He means to trap her?"

Will nodded. "He means to accuse her."

Mary sat. Her movements were slow, precise. "And you have names?"

"A few. I'm to track movements"

She looked into the fire. "Add the Viscount of Rochford, George Boleyn."

Will blinked. "Her brother?"

Mary's voice didn't rise. "You want to shatter her, don't you? George on the list will do it. They are close—*too* close. Even the king has doubted it. Let the court believe what it's already whispered."

Will hesitated. "Cromwell didn't say—"

"Cromwell wants her gone," Mary said, standing. "Give him something so complete, so rotted at the root, that even if she lives, she won't be able to stand."

Will watched her. "You've thought about this."

"I've lived every cost of her crown."

Late afternoon light slanted through the tall windows of Lambeth, catching the dust motes in golden dance. In the kitchen, Jo moved quietly, arranging a simple tray of bread, stewed apples, and smoked fish. Margarete was folding linen napkins with her usual care, humming faintly under her breath.

"No pomp tonight," Jo said, smiling at the smallness of the table. "Just peace."

"Peace," Margarete echoed, smoothing the last napkin. "And company that listens without needing to speak."

In the corner, a kettle hissed.

The door opened with a quiet creak, and Nicholas stepped in, unbuttoning his coat. "Apologies—slower journey back than expected."

Jo looked up quickly. "Is everything well?"

Nicholas hesitated only a second. "Smeaton's been summoned. Not to music, either. To questions."

Margarete's brow lifted. "By whom?"

"I don't know for certain. But it wasn't casual. They say he didn't leave by the usual doors."

Jo set down the tray. "Why Smeaton? He's harmless. Loyal to the queen."

Nicholas nodded. "Exactly. Loyal to the queen. That's the problem."

Jo stiffened. "That's how it starts," she said softly.

They turned as another figure entered—Cranmer, already dressed down for the evening, hands still slightly ink-stained from the day's scribbling.

"I heard," he said simply. "And more."

He moved toward the table and accepted a cup from Jo. "The king is at Whitehall again, but not alone. Jane Seymour keeps close company now."

Margarete's hands paused. "So it's true."

Cranmer nodded once. "She's modest. Quiet. Unassuming. Everything Anne never really was."

Jo frowned. "You don't think he would—again?"

"He's already halfway gone," Cranmer said. "The rest is ceremony."

Nicholas leaned against the hearth. "But surely not like this. Anne has given everything to be queen."

Cranmer glanced at him sideways. "Not everything," he said. "Not the one thing Henry wanted most—a living son."

Jo exhaled. "It's cruel."

"It's court," Margarete said gently.

The room settled into silence. Outside, bells rang from across the river.

Cranmer looked toward the window, then back to them. "Let's enjoy the meal. We'll speak no more of queens tonight."

But the shadow of one remained, drifting across the small table as the candles were lit.

The coals in Cromwell's study had burned low. Shadows curled like smoke along the paneled walls, broken only by the flicker of lamplight and the occasional scratch of quill on parchment.

Will stood near the hearth, waiting.

Cromwell did not look up. "You said you had more."

"I do," Will said, stepping forward. "The names you asked for. Norris. Brereton. Weston. And Smeaton."

"Mm." Cromwell made a mark on the paper before him. "Yes, we mentioned those. Reasonable choices. Loyal to the queen. Visible. Handsome enough to draw whispers." He finally looked up. "But not sufficient."

Will hesitated. "Then perhaps this will be."

He reached inside his coat and unfolded a smaller sheet. "New rumor. One more name. George Boleyn."

Cromwell's quill paused mid-air.

Will continued, steady. "There's talk—uncertain talk—of closeness between brother and sister that could be . . . interpreted otherwise. If necessary."

Cromwell laid down the quill and leaned back. "Who gave you this?"

Will met his eyes. "It came to me in the way such things do. From someone close enough to know. And clever enough to offer it freely."

The silence stretched.

Then: "The king has long found George too fond of power. Too fond of her counsel. This—" he tapped the page lightly "—would break both."

Will said nothing.

Cromwell rose and moved to the window. Beyond the curtain, the court still hummed with loyalty and lies. He parted the fabric with two fingers—just enough to see the world he was about to remake. "This will not be easy. A brother. The queen's own blood."

"No," Will agreed. "But it will be final."

A long breath. Then Cromwell turned.

"Draft it," he said. "Everything we know. All of it. If there's nothing solid, we'll make the air feel thick enough to choke."

Will nodded once.

"And Will—" Cromwell paused at the doorway. "The king cannot ask for this. He must only receive it. With a sigh and a crown that weighs too much."

Will's expression was unreadable. "Of course."

The door closed behind Cromwell, leaving Will alone with the ink and silence.

Westminster Hall had long since emptied of clerks and courtiers, but one stone corridor still echoed with hushed voices.

Will turned the corner and slowed. Ahead, just beyond the reach of torchlight, Mary stood beside the Duke of Norfolk, her hands clasped loosely at her waist, her face a portrait of careful attentiveness.

Norfolk was speaking low—measured, courtly. Mary, by contrast, looked carved from stillness.

Will started to turn, meaning to slip away, but Mary glanced over and stilled him with a flicker of her fingers.

Norfolk, noticing, turned as well. "Master Cressy," he said with a polite nod. "Out late."

"As are you, my lord," Will replied evenly. "But I'd not interrupt."

"You're not," Mary said, her voice smooth. "We'd reached the part of the conversation where nothing more could be safely said aloud."

"Perhaps just one more thing," Norfolk murmured, mostly to her. "You'll have heard about George. His outburst in council two days past."

Mary's brow tilted. "I heard there was . . . discussion."

"Discussion?" Norfolk scoffed softly. "He nearly lectured the king—chastised him for delaying reform. Quoted Tyndale, if you can believe it. Said God's favor depended on a full severing from Rome, not this halfway hedging."

Will blinked. "To the king's face?"

"To the whole chamber. As if he were leading it." Norfolk shook his head. "Henry's jaw tightened like a trap. But he said nothing. Not then."

Mary's voice was cool. "He never says much when he's weighing how to strike."

"Exactly. And George, poor fool, keeps pushing. He may love Anne more than is wise, but he does not understand Henry. Few of them do."

She turned to Will now, eyes steady. "That's why Anne is not merely falling. She's digging."

Norfolk nodded once, then with a faint smile, added, "Now I shall truly take my leave."

He bowed to her with the faintest trace of courtesy, to Will with even less, and disappeared down the corridor.

Silence hovered between them until the sound of his steps was gone.

Will raised an eyebrow. "A private meeting with Norfolk?" He let the name hang. "Anne's uncle?"

Mary did not blink. "Even Anne's uncle cannot manage Anne. That was the subject."

"And your role in this unmanageable affair?"

She looked out the arched window. "Anne believes herself invincible. She confuses my father's favor with permanence. That mistake has always had a short season. I know that better than most."

Will stepped closer. "You're certain it's ending."

"I've seen the signs." A pause. "And I've heard yours."

That gave Will pause—but only for a moment. "Then you've heard that Jane Seymour is favored."

"I have. And I've considered it." She turned to him now, fully. "She's quiet. Docile. Catholic." Her eyes searched his. "Would Cromwell back her?"

Will's gaze held steady. "He already does."

Mary considered this. "Interesting. So you serve two masters?"

"I serve England," Will said, carefully. "Though which vision of it wins . . . is still under discussion."

Mary smiled faintly. "Tell your other vision this: I do not oppose Jane. She could be a bridge. Not a queen of power, but of pause. She, at least, would not dismiss me as Anne does."

Will's jaw tightened just slightly. "Cromwell sees the same thing. He doesn't mind a pause, as long as it doesn't turn into a reversal."

Mary's tone turned lighter—but no less sharp. "Then for once, you may find us aligned—but for only the short term."

"How long?"

"We'll know when we're not," she said simply. "But for now—use your access well, Will. You may not always have two doors open to you."

Will bowed slightly, more in acknowledgment than agreement. "Then I'll keep one foot in each. For now."

Mary stepped away. "Just don't forget which direction you're walking."

She vanished into the shadows, leaving Will alone in the corridor, where the light no longer seemed to know which way to fall.

29

The Breaking of Crowns

THE CHAMBER WAS SMALL, square, and airless. Not the Tower—not yet—but close enough in purpose. Stone walls, barred windows, and a table at the center. Mark Smeaton sat alone on one side, his hands flat, his face pale but composed. A clerk scribbled in the corner. A minor functionary from the Privy Council—Master Raye, thin and nervous—paced before him.

"You were seen, Smeaton. Seen slipping through the queen's private doors more than once."

Smeaton's eyes flicked toward the window. "I tune the virginals in the queen's chamber. It is not uncommon."

"Alone?"

A pause. "When summoned."

Raye's voice sharpened. "You presume much closeness for a mere musician."

Smeaton folded his hands. "I go where I am told."

From the rear wall, Cromwell watched with his arms crossed. Beside him stood Will, still, unreadable.

Raye pressed on. "And what would you say if it were claimed that you had grown . . . fond of Her Majesty?"

Smeaton blinked, then actually smiled. "I would say it was not unusual to admire one's sovereign."

A flicker of amusement touched Cromwell's mouth. Will didn't move.

Raye stiffened. "You mock the seriousness of these charges."

"You have not named them," Smeaton replied. "So far, I hear only suspicion."

The silence that followed was long enough to fray the edge of Raye's composure.

He shifted. Coughed lightly.

"You—uh—you tuned the virginals. Frequently. Yes. And why so often?"

Smeaton blinked at him.

"To keep them in tune," he said slowly.

Raye opened his mouth again, then closed it. The edge of his notes fluttered in his hand. He searched them, but they no longer seemed to order themselves. He glanced Cromwell's way—once.

That was enough.

Will straightened. "Tell me, Master Smeaton . . ."

"Yes?" Smeaton replied quietly as he squinted into the shadows to see who spoke.

Will stepped forward, voice calm, almost thoughtful. "You tune the virginals, yes. But you also know how to play the court. You've seen how one look lingers longer than it should. How one whispered comment grows teeth by the next day."

He stepped closer. "You've heard your name paired with hers, haven't you? Not from me. Not from him. But whispered."

Smeaton swallowed. He didn't answer.

Will leaned in slightly. "That sort of rumor . . . it clings. Especially so," he almost whispered, "if it's true." Will moved behind Smeaton who twisted in his seat. "But even," Will went on, "if it isn't—true—well, you know the stakes."

"I've done nothing," Smeaton said. But now his voice cracked. "Nothing."

Will's tone stayed smooth though he frowned slightly. "You've done nothing? Are you saying she isn't attractive?"

"No . . . I mean, yes, she's attractive, very attractive."

Will smiled, nodding. "Yes, 'very attractive.' A haunting beauty, wouldn't you say? Well, of course! Our king chose her for his wife, man! Surely you admire her as a haunting beauty?"

"I do," Smeaton told him, sincerity plainly voiced.

Will's smile deepened. "Yes, of course. She haunts you. You want her."

"I . . ." Smeaton stumbled. "But no, I've never done . . ."

"Never?" Will asked. "Then why the pale face? Why the trembling hands? You know how this works, Mark. If you stay silent, others will speak louder. If you stay stubborn, others will accuse first. And their words—their words being first—will weigh more."

Smeaton's voice faltered. "What would you have me say? Accuse someone else?"

Will held his gaze. "We want the truth. The whole truth. While there's still time for it to matter."

Smeaton sagged in his chair. A long breath. Then, quietly: "They said I was often there. That the queen favored me. I never thought—"

"But you let them say it."

"Norris," Smeaton fairly shouted. "Norris, he . . . he spent more time with her than I. He was always there—even sometimes when I was tuning, he was there."

Cromwell stirred at last. "Enough for now."

He moved to the table and placed a hand on Smeaton's shoulder. "We'll write what's necessary. Master Cressy, see to it."

Will nodded.

Cromwell turned to Raye. "Your presence is no longer needed."

Raye's jaw tightened, but he bowed and withdrew.

When the chamber emptied leaving only Will and himself, Cromwell spoke once more.

"The king will want names, opportunities, and witnesses. You produced all that just now. Continue. Next with Norris. Then Brereton. Weston. George last."

He held Will's eye.

"Make it convincing. But leave just enough doubt. We want panic to do the rest."

Will gave a single nod, and Cromwell nodded back. The gesture was slight, but it meant everything to Will.

The first crack had opened. The interrogations had begun.

The light in the chapel was soft—no candles lit, only the filtered blue of morning through the stained glass. Jane Seymour knelt alone at the rail, lips moving soundlessly, hands folded without tension. She did not turn when Mary entered, though the rustle of fabric on stone was unmistakable.

Mary stood in the rear alcove a moment before approaching. When Jane finally looked up, her face was calm, unguarded.

"Lady Mary," she said gently. "I did not expect company."

"I know," Mary replied. "Nor, I think, did you expect to be so often at court."

A faint smile, not evasive but not inviting. "His Majesty's kindness exceeds my place."

Mary walked forward slowly, letting her fingertips brush the carved wood of a pew. "Or perhaps your place is changing."

Jane said nothing. Her hands returned to her lap.

Mary sat beside her. "I'll not press. I wonder only if you've considered what that change might mean."

"For me?"

"For England."

Jane's eyes shifted. "My loyalty is to God. To my family. And of course, to the king, should he ask it."

Mary studied her. "Not to the church?"

"I worship in the only one I've known."

Mary tilted her head. "And if that church finds its strength again—under a queen who shares its heart?"

Jane met her gaze. "Then I will thank God for it. But not because I moved the pieces."

Mary almost smiled. It wasn't much. But it was something.

She rose. "Our Bishop Gardiner believes the church still has a future. You would be in good company."

Jane hesitated. "He is a wise man."

Mary's voice softened. "And you are not unwise."

She stepped back into the aisle.

"I'm glad we spoke."

Jane looked after her. "So am I."

As Mary left, she counted in silence: *Norfolk. Jane. Gardiner. Will.*

A pause.

Enough to turn the wheel.

As Mary stepped out of the chapel, the air struck her with a sharper chill than expected. Morning had not yet shaken off the damp. But she moved briskly, her mind lit with possibilities. Jane's quiet resolve had not been a no. And that was enough.

She rounded the corner near the cloistered walk and nearly collided with the Duke of Norfolk.

He bowed stiffly, his face unusually grave. "Lady Mary."

"My lord Norfolk," she replied with poise. "Out pacing the stones so early?"

"Trying to cool my temper," he muttered.

She fell into step beside him. "What's the source this time? Cromwell again?"

"Who else?" Norfolk glanced sideways. "Another edict—meant to strip more gold from the churches, more loyalty from the abbots. And now I hear whisper of an English Bible to be forced on every parish."

Mary's brow rose. "He moves fast."

"He moves unchecked," Norfolk snapped. "And the king—God save us—thinks every one of his ideas is heaven's breath."

Mary folded her hands before her. "Perhaps the king needs new voices in his ear."

He grunted. "And who would provide them? You?"

She met his eye without flinching. "Not me alone. But I see alliances forming—Jane, for instance. And Stephen Gardiner for another. He may not posture as much as Cromwell, but he holds to the old faith. You've always had your ways. And Will—he has no real influence, but he is . . . useful."

Norfolk sighed, brushing a hand along the stone wall as they walked. "Yes, yes, pieces on the board. But while Cromwell holds the king's gaze, none of it matters. We're shadow players until he falls."

Mary nodded slowly. "Then we wait?"

"For now." Norfolk's voice lowered. "But the moment will come. And when it does—"

She finished for him. "We'll need to act."

They stopped beneath an archway. Rain began to spit from the low clouds.

Norfolk looked out over the inner courtyard. "The girl is sweet. And useful. But she's not strong."

Mary's jaw tightened. "Then we'll carry her long enough to see the crown placed."

Norfolk glanced at her, something like admiration flickering. "And after?"

She looked into the rising wind. "After, we take back the soul of England."

The chamber was colder now, though the fire still burned in the grate. Its light cast long shadows across the stone floor—shadows that flickered over George Boleyn as he entered, chin high, eyes defiant but sharp. He didn't sit until Will, standing at the edge of the chamber, motioned him to.

Cromwell remained silent in the rear shadows, but his presence filled the room.

"Lord Rochford," Will began calmly, no notes in hand. "You've heard of these proceedings. You've heard of me."

George met his gaze coolly. "I've heard rumor enough. And seen the effects of your . . . talent."

"Rumor, then. Let's speak of that."

Will began to pace slowly. "You are the queen's brother. Her confidant. You've defended her often. But also—years ago—when she was first noticed by the king, you spoke of her differently."

George did not answer.

Will stopped. "Do you recall referring to your sister as . . . promiscuous?"

"I will not speak against my blood."

Cromwell's voice came from the shadows. "Truth is not necessarily treason, my lord. Answer."

A long pause. Then: "Yes. I said so. Years ago."

Will nodded slightly. "And later? When she was crowned? You wrote a poem."

He pulled a folded parchment from his coat and began to read:

"A maid unspoiled by time or tongue,

In virtue robed and honor sung."

George's jaw twitched.

"I wrote that in celebration."

"For England's sake?" Will asked.

George nodded. "Of course."

Will folded the paper again. "So. When England needed a pure queen, you called her pure. When England needed a king's mistress, you called her . . . accessible."

George's eyes narrowed. "Do you accuse me of lying?"

"Of serving England—even with lies," Will said softly.

Silence hung. Then Will pressed forward.

"You have been seen in private with the queen. Doors closed. Conversations hushed."

"She is my sister."

"And yet," Will said, "some suggest more."

George sat back sharply. "That's vile. I would never—"

"No? And yet you've already shown a capacity to shape truth as needed. You spoke lies to elevate her. Would you not stoop lower to protect what remains?"

"You suggest incest? It's repugnant."

Will didn't flinch. "Then help me understand this. At the celebration following the marriage, you approached your sister—one arm around her, a drink in the other—and kissed her. On the lips. In full view."

George hesitated, thrown. "It was a brother's kiss. Nothing more."

Will leaned in. "Then tell me, if it meant nothing, why were you the only man in the entire realm who did it?"

George stared at him, nostrils flared. "Because I loved her. As a brother."

"And because you knew no one else could. Not the king. Not a courtier. Only you."

Cromwell stirred. "That will be all for now."

Will nodded and left the table, leaving George staring into the dark corners of the chamber, his breath coming faster than before.

Cranmer closed the door more softly than usual. The hush of Lambeth's inner halls felt sharper than silence—thin, watchful, as if the stone itself had heard what had just been done.

He walked to the hearth but did not stir the fire. May sunlight cut through the narrow windows, though it did little to warm the room. He reached for the back of his chair—

And paused.

Jo was seated near the book table. She rose when he entered but said nothing. Her eyes, watchful and calm, seemed to weigh him the way only she could.

"I didn't expect you," he said.

"I hoped I might be welcome."

"You are."

He gestured gently, and she sat again.

He did not. He remained standing, one hand on the chair's carved back, gaze resting somewhere beyond the window.

"It is done," he said after a moment. "The court has ruled."

Jo waited.

"Nullified," he added. "The marriage—Anne and the king. Voided from the beginning—they were never truly wed."

She still said nothing. Her presence alone was patient invitation.

Cranmer finally sat. "I signed the declaration in my own hand. On paper. As if it could be so easily unwritten."

Jo's voice came softly. "And yet it was required."

He looked at her then. "By whom?"

She didn't answer.

Cranmer leaned forward slightly, fingers tented. "They've executed them. Norris. Brereton. Weston. Smeaton. George."

"Today?"

He nodded once. "Just after midday."

"And Anne?"

"Tomorrow."

Jo shook her head, her voice low. "So there is no turning."

Cranmer leaned forward slightly. "The court has ruled. The judgment stands. And I . . . have made it righteous."

She looked up. "Have you?"

He drew back as if struck—not sharply, but with slow, gathering weight. For a long moment, he said nothing.

Then Jo spoke again, more quietly. "She has a daughter. Three years old."

Cranmer's hands tensed on the edge of his desk. "Elizabeth."

"You declared her mother never married. That the marriage never existed. Then what is Elizabeth?"

"A child of the king," he said, too quickly.

Jo's voice held steady. "Not by law."

A silence stretched between them. Outside, a faint bell rang across the river.

"She has no mother now," Jo said. "And no claim. Not even legitimacy."

"She has a father," Cranmer said, though it sounded more like a wish.

Jo watched him. "And what kind of father buries a crown with its queen and leaves a daughter in the dirt?"

Cranmer's jaw tightened. "You think I don't grieve for her? You think I don't pray—every night—that he will remember her?"

Jo didn't flinch. "Do you think prayer is enough?"

"She is his blood," he said, quieter now. "She will not be cast off entirely. She may be . . . set aside. But not unloved."

Jo stood slowly. "Set aside is how a book lies forgotten on a shelf. Set aside is not how you treat a child."

"She is a Tudor," he said, reaching for ground that sounded firm. "She has strength. And Seymour—Jane Seymour may yet take pity—"

"That's the hope?" Jo interrupted. "That the next queen is kinder than the last?"

He didn't answer.

She stepped forward, voice rising. "You undid her mother's name. And the crown with it. You let your pen blot out a child's future—and now you beg the wind to blow her a gentler stepmother?"

Cranmer sank into the chair behind his desk, suddenly older than he'd seemed. "You don't understand the weight."

Jo stood unmoving. "You mean the weight of the crown? Or the weight of truth?"

He looked up sharply, but said nothing.

Jo pressed on, softer now. "What were you meant to do in that chamber? Only say what was asked?"

"I was asked to judge whether the marriage was lawful."

"And if you had said yes?" Her eyes searched his. "If you had said that it was lawful—that Anne was queen, that Elizabeth was heir—what then?"

"There would have been consequences," he said. "Grave ones."

"For you?"

He hesitated.

She stepped closer. "So say it. Say it plainly. If you had spoken what you believed—if you believe it still—the king would have cast you aside."

"I serve the realm," Cranmer said.

"You serve the king," Jo replied. "Even now. You bowed your head, you gave him what he needed, and in doing so—" she faltered, then steadied—"in doing so, you took a crown from the head of a child."

Cranmer didn't answer. His eyes were fixed on the space between them, as if truth might appear there if he stared long enough.

Jo's voice was quieter now, but firmer. "You said yes to the king once before. You gave him what he wanted when he needed to be rid of his first wife. You told yourself it was right—that it would lead to something good. A true marriage. A stronger realm. A better future."

She took another step forward.

"But it didn't, Uncle. It led here."

His brow furrowed, but still he didn't speak.

She pressed on. "Another wife cast off. A child left in the dirt. A trail of bodies—some you knew, some you named. And now you say yes again. Because you think this time, perhaps, it will lead to righteousness?"

At last, Cranmer looked up. His voice was hoarse. "What would you have had me do?"

Jo didn't flinch. "Judge the marriage true."

He stared at her.

"You were asked for a ruling," she said quietly. "Not for permission. Not for strategy. You were asked if Anne was ever his wife in the eyes of God. And if she was . . . you should have said so."

"And watch it all collapse?" he asked, the frustration surfacing now. "Watch him rage and tear down everything we've begun to build?"

She shook her head. "Watch him rage, yes. But let the truth stand. Let it be known someone would not bend."

A silence fell—heavier than before.

Then she added, more gently, "Because one day, he or someone will ask more. Not just for your judgment. For your faith. Your soul. And if you say yes again . . . what part of you will be left?"

Cranmer remained at the desk long after Jo was gone. Not moving. Not praying. Just watching the ink dry.

Mary stood at the narrow window of the old stone chamber, high enough to see across the Tower yard. The scaffold still stood where it had two days before—its timbers darkened now, its boards newly swept.

Anne Boleyn stepped into view. Small, composed, clothed in black. The guards at her side moved with studied formality. The crowd pressed forward but did not cheer. Even the curious had gone quiet.

Mary said nothing.

She had not come to gloat. Not even to grieve. Only to see.

Catherine had died in exile, alone. Anne would die in sight of all.

One discarded in silence. The other in spectacle.

But both discarded.

Mary's fingers tightened on the windowsill.

Anne knelt. Her headdress was gone now. Her hands folded. The French swordsman stood ready—his blade hidden behind his back.

A breath.

Then the stroke. Fast. Precise.

No cry. No second blow. Just a sharp motion—and stillness.

For a long moment, nothing moved.

Then Mary turned from the window. She did not pray. She did not smile.

She thought only: *He leaves them broken. And we—*

She stopped the thought.

But it stayed.

30

The Cost of Promise

The wedding was barely a week past. The court shimmered again with pageantry, but beneath the silks and garlands, something else stirred—quieter, colder, and less easily swept aside.

In a shaded corner of the great gallery, Norfolk stood with Bishop Gardiner. Their voices were low, but the sharpness in their eyes betrayed more than courtesy.

"Jane is queen now," Gardiner said. "The court has shifted."

"And still the Secretary gives orders like a prince," Norfolk muttered. "He acts as if the throne owes him thanks."

Gardiner gave a slight nod. "And yet he delivered it. Anne is gone. Jane sits in her place. That was his doing."

"Perhaps," Norfolk allowed. "But power makes men careless. He forgets what it is to bend."

"Or he never learned it," Gardiner said. "But that, too, may be corrected."

A quiet moment passed.

"I want to be clear," Norfolk said at last. "My loyalty is to England—not to either Luther or Rome. But I won't see the country remade by a tradesman in robes."

Gardiner's eyes narrowed. "Nor I. Let the useful reforms remain, but not the rule of a secretary."

They turned as footsteps approached. Mary joined them, her face calm, her hands folded.

"My lords," she said smoothly. Not a greeting. A claim. "I trust you've both exchanged your congratulations."

"But we have no time to rest on those laurels," Norfolk replied.

Mary looked toward the hall where Jane sat surrounded by courtiers, her face composed, her eyes distant.

"She does not know it yet," Mary said, "but she has made herself the key."

"To what?" Gardiner asked.

"To the king's affections," Mary said. "And through them, to the balance of power."

Norfolk's brow rose. "And you think she will use that power?"

"I think she won't," Mary replied. "Which makes her all the more useful."

There was no cruelty in her voice—only strategy.

Mary's gaze swept across the crowd. "He listens to Cromwell still. But his grief will rise when Jane falls—"

"Falls?" Gardiner asked.

Mary shook her head. "Not by treachery. By fate. She is too gentle for this court. Her rise will cost her."

Norfolk looked uneasy. "You speak as if it's written."

"I speak as if I know the rhythm of my father and his court," Mary said. "He gains a queen. Then he loses one. But what he fears more than loss is failure."

She looked from one man to the other.

"That is what we give him. A glimpse of failure—in Cromwell."

Norfolk's expression darkened. "And you're sure he'll see it?"

Mary's gaze didn't waver. "He always does—too late. But late is still time enough . . . when you know the rhythm of his heart."

The court settled into its new arrangement with practiced ease. Ambitions quieted, though they did not sleep. Cromwell remained at the king's side, issuing directives with the efficiency of a man who still held the center. But outside the hallways of power, the rhythm of seasons turned unnoticed.

Fall and winter passed without scandal. Lent came and went, its solemnity observed with outward grace. And as the frost loosened its grip, the first signs of spring coaxed life from the soil.

By early April, the news broke: Queen Jane was with child.

Hope swept the court like incense before a procession—sweet, heavy, half-believed. The king walked taller. Courtiers bowed lower. Even the most cynical allowed themselves a private smile. This child, if male, would change everything.

Jo had arrived early for a planned outing with Margarete, and now the two sat with Cranmer over the remains of breakfast when the message came.

It was a small thing—a note from one of the court physicians, passed quietly through a servant's hand. But Cranmer's eyes lit as he read.

"She is with child," he said, almost under his breath. Then, louder: "Jane. The queen."

Margarete smiled softly. "Then the rumors were true."

"The court will rejoice," Jo said, though her tone was careful.

Cranmer stood, folding the note. "More than rejoice. This—this is what we've long prayed for. If it's a son . . ."

He didn't finish. But the air around him shifted. Hope bloomed, buoyed by something close to certainty.

Margarete exchanged a glance with Jo.

"You believe this confirms the path," Jo said, not unkindly.

Cranmer looked at her. "Wouldn't it?"

Jo did not answer.

The great hall gleamed in gold and crimson, banners fluttering softly above as music trailed through the candlelit air. It was a feast of celebration—not for a specific event, but for what the court understood without naming. Spring had come. The queen was with child. And joy, the king declared, had returned to England.

Henry sat at the head of the table, broader now in both frame and presence. Jane, serene beside him, glowed with a quiet grace that the court had come to associate with peace. She was not Anne—no fire, no fierce tilt of the head or sharpened wit—but she was constant, composed. And, as more than one courtier whispered, finally fruitful.

Across the table, Mary sat poised. Her gown was modest but rich, her bearing unmistakably royal. The breach that had once yawned wide between her and her father now lay behind them—at least in public view. She had signed the necessary acknowledgments: the king's supremacy, the invalidity of her mother's marriage. But she had done so with carefully measured humility, never apology.

Jane's hand rested lightly on the table. It had been her urging, gently and persistently, that softened Henry's stance. She had spoken of mercy, of healing, of the image it would give to the realm. A reconciled family. A stable kingdom. A hopeful heir. And so Mary had returned—still watched, still wary, but present.

Henry rose, goblet in hand. Conversation stilled.

"To the queen," he began, voice booming through the hall, "who brings springtime in more ways than one. The gentlest of wives, the most obedient, the most beloved. May England receive from her the blessing we have long awaited."

He turned to Jane, pride lighting his features.

"My true and gracious wife."

A murmur of assent swept the hall. Jane inclined her head, but her eyes moved briefly to Mary, who met her gaze without flinching. A nod passed between them—small, unreadable.

Mary lifted her own goblet, speaking softly, only to herself. "To peace restored." Yet, a faint chill rose behind her ribs. Jane had shown grace, yes—but what if Mary had misjudged her? What if, behind that quiet smile, lay not simplicity, but influence?

Henry's toast was taken up in layers, some more enthusiastic than others. But none dared remain silent.

In the shadows beyond the table's end, Gardiner watched it all. He had no toast to offer—only thought. Jane had healed the breach. But not the wound. That would fester beneath, until the time came to lance it.

The lively meal lingered long, and the celebration after lingered longer still. Music played gently now, and courtiers moved in small clusters—some drifting toward the gallery, others with goblets in hand near the edge of the hall. The king remained seated, deep in talk with Jane and a few favored nobles, his laughter rising now and then above the hum.

In the shadow of a carved archway, Gardiner joined Mary and Norfolk.

"You left early from table," Norfolk murmured.

"I left at the right time," Gardiner replied. "While the king was still pleased and the wine not yet working mischief."

Mary's gaze moved across the room. "He is pleased," she said. "But contentment breeds carelessness. Cromwell thrives in moments like this."

Norfolk's mouth thinned. "The Secretary has begun whispers of new treaties. A Protestant alliance."

Gardiner nodded. "The Schmalkaldic League. He courts them openly now. Lutheran princes. Reformers all."

Mary took a sip from her goblet, watching the musicians shift to a softer strain. "He seeks to bind England to the Lutherans—and thus bind the king to him. If a match or treaty is made, he gains a stranglehold."

Gardiner tilted his head. "A match? With whom?"

Mary didn't answer immediately. Instead, she turned her gaze slowly toward him, eyes steady.

Gardiner blinked. "Oh." The realization hit. "They could try with you. Especially now that you are 'in the fold.'"

Mary's smile was dry. "Cromwell would do it just to spite me. But no—that isn't what he truly wants. He wants control. And he'll use any alliance that grants it."

Gardiner's brow furrowed. "The League is proud. They may be Protestant, but not England's version. They won't yield their doctrines easily."

"Nor should they," Norfolk said, stepping closer. "But if Cromwell presses for union without agreement on the Mass or the sacraments—"

"—they may balk," Gardiner finished. "And if they do, the alliance breaks before it begins."

Mary nodded. "Then perhaps we help them see that clearly. England has not surrendered its soul—not yet."

Gardiner's lips curved into a small, calculating smile. "A firm statement of doctrine might do it."

"Just firm enough," Norfolk said.

Mary glanced toward the king and queen, seated still in golden light. "Let Cromwell chase his German dreams. We'll see what remains when they fall through his fingers."

By early October, the leaves at Hampton Court had begun to curl in gold and rust, and the court moved with a breathless expectancy. The queen was confined. The stars, some whispered, aligned. And at last, on the morning of the twelfth, England exhaled.

A son.

Word leapt from corridor to corridor like fire across parchment. Bells rang before the sun had fully risen. Horses thundered to London with news, and town criers shouted themselves hoarse before noon. A prince—at last a prince—was born to King Henry and Queen Jane.

In Lambeth, Cranmer stood at the window of his study, listening to the distant peel of celebration echoing across the Thames. Margarete stood just behind him, her hands folded, her face unreadable.

"It is done," he said, not turning. "A son. Born in rightful marriage. A Tudor heir without question."

Margarete said nothing.

He turned, eyes wet but steady. "Do you not see it? God has answered. He has blessed this course. Blessed England through this child."

Margarete glanced at the floor. "A child is a blessing, yes. But I do not know that God's voice is so easy to interpret."

Jo stepped into the room then, cloak still drawn from her brisk walk over. She had heard the news in the street when out early, as if from the very stones of the city.

"You've heard?" Cranmer asked.

Jo nodded. "They say he is strong. Loud from the first breath."

Cranmer smiled. "Good. Good. England needs a voice that cannot be silenced."

"But will it speak for God?" she asked softly.

Cranmer looked at her, and for a moment the cheer in his eyes dimmed. Then he looked again to the window.

"The king will summon me soon," he said. "I will baptize him myself."

At Hampton Court, the king was radiant. He strode through the long gallery with renewed vigor, nodding, speaking, even laughing with courtiers who'd not heard such sound from him in weeks. Every chamber echoed with life.

On the third day, the baptism was held in the Chapel Royal, lavish and solemn. Cranmer held the infant prince in his arms—small and drowsy, swaddled in silk embroidered with gold thread—and spoke the words with a reverence that trembled near awe. As Cranmer dipped his head over the prince, he felt a surge of hope rise unbidden. Perhaps this child—this boy—was the sign. Perhaps God had smiled upon the path chosen after all. And yet, even in that warmth, a shadow flickered—how thin the line between favor and presumption.

"Edward, child of England, may you be raised not only in strength but in truth. And may your days bring peace to the realm, and favor before God."

Henry stood proudly at the font, his expression a careful mask of satisfaction and strain. Jane, still confined and weakening by the hour, remained unseen behind the palace walls—her absence noted but unspoken.

Henry said little, but his posture was triumph enough. His son—his heir—was christened Edward, after the ancient Confessor. A Tudor boy at last. The king's eyes swept the chapel not in joy, but in warning: this child was the future, and all must honor him.

And yet, beneath the steel of his gaze, something flickered. Not joy—not fully. Not as he had imagined it across the long years of waiting.

He had waited since 1509—nearly three decades—for this moment. For a living son to carry the Tudor name. For proof that his prayers, his struggles, his marriages, his ruptures with Rome had not all been in vain. It should have been a day of triumph without restraint.

But Jane was not here.

She lay in her chambers, pale and wan, still weakened by the long labor. The birth had taken its toll. He had visited her that morning and held her hand in silence. She had smiled, faintly. Promised she was getting stronger. But even then, he had seen the shadow in her eyes—and worse, in the faces of her ladies.

He wanted to cheer. To laugh and boast and claim God's favor aloud.

Instead, he stood unmoving, pride chained to worry. His son was safe in the arms of a nurse. But his queen—the gentlest of wives, the most obedient, the most beloved—was not yet beyond danger.

For all he had gained, the crown he had longed to place on his own brow was now shadowed again by the specter of loss.

Mary stood among the silent watchers, her hands clasped loosely before her. She did not speak, but her gaze missed nothing—the joy, the tension, the queen's absence. She had seen this court rise and fall on smaller omens.

By the next morning, the court knew: the queen had taken a turn.

There had been hope—brief and golden—that the weakness following labor was merely exhaustion. But now fevers rose and fell with alarming irregularity. Physicians were summoned, mixtures brewed. Prayers offered. Curtains drawn. Still, Jane grew paler by the hour.

Those who had once whispered of divine favor now said little. Some murmured that God's blessings were never unalloyed. Others—more boldly—hinted that no blessing secured by blood could long endure.

Cranmer sat in his study nights later, the lamp low beside him. The baptismal gown lay folded neatly on the table—he had asked to keep it a while. Not for sentiment, he told himself, but reflection. He ran a finger along the stitching of Edward's name, and tried to still the tremor in his chest.

She had been kind, he thought. Devout. Humble in ways Anne never was. Why her?

Across the room, Margarete moved quietly with a basin, setting it down without sound. "She may recover," she said, not looking at him.

"And if she doesn't?" he asked.

Margarete paused. Then: "Will God's favor vanish with her breath?"

Cranmer didn't answer. Jo, who had spent the day with Margarete, who had wondered with her and exchanged thoughts and heaviness and hope, entered just behind. She set a wrapped parcel near the window. "Nicholas brought this from court," she said. "Word is—she's worse. The king has canceled all meetings."

"He's devastated," Margarete murmured. "He waited so long."

"And so did everyone," Jo added. "But waiting doesn't mean we asked rightly."

Cranmer looked up.

Jo dropped her head. "I don't mean condemnation," she said quickly. "Only that . . . we've all longed for the heir. And now that he's here, we each see what we want to see."

"You think we're wrong to hope?"

"No," she answered, eyes wide, though voice soft. "But maybe hope shouldn't come with certainty." She paused, struggling for words. "God is not so easily proven."

Cranmer stood and crossed to the window. Beyond, the lamps of London flickered beneath a clouded sky.

For a moment, no one spoke. Then Jo said, more gently, "You remember what my mother used to ask you?"

He nodded without turning. "Why God allows what he could stop."

Margarete spoke next, quiet but clear. "And we've discussed this. We've held it close in wonder and in awe and in hope. God said that love doesn't force. That love allows—for the sake of what it hopes still might be."

Cranmer's hands tightened on the windowsill. "It was enough then."

"It still is," Jo said.

He whispered, almost to himself: "Let her live. Let her live, and let this not be in vain."

A knock came at the outer door—sharp, urgent, but not frantic.

Cranmer turned. Jo rose before he could move, stepping into the hall. A moment later, she returned with a young man, breathless and pale, his cap clutched in trembling fingers.

He bowed low. "My lord. I was told to bring word—directly."

Cranmer gave a single nod. "Speak."

The messenger looked from one face to the next. "The queen . . . she . . . the queen has died."

The silence that followed was complete. Even the air seemed to hold its breath.

Cranmer closed his eyes. Just for a moment. Then he moved to the table and set his hand gently atop the baptismal gown. "Thank you," he said to the messenger. "You may go."

The man bowed again and withdrew.

Jo sat slowly on the bench near the fire. "Then it wasn't granted," she said—not as accusation, but as lament.

Across the room, Margarete crossed herself and whispered a prayer. Then she looked up. "God does not always give signs."

Cranmer remained still, staring at the folded silk, his face unreadable.

Jo spoke again, softer now. "We all asked. All of us. Some with pure hearts. Some with pride. Some with both."

"We saw the child and called it blessing," Margarete said. "Perhaps it still is."

"Perhaps," Jo echoed. "But perhaps we wanted the sign more than the substance."

Cranmer's voice was quiet but firm. "We do not serve because we see. We serve because we know him to be good."

He held to the words, repeating them silently—trying to believe they still rose from faith, not desperation.

Jo looked up, her eyes wet but steady. "And when we forget—"

"—we return again," Margarete finished.

The three sat in the stillness that followed—not defeated, but sobered. Outside, the wind brushed faintly against the panes. Inside, the lamp flickered, catching the gold thread in the baptismal cloth.

Jo reached out and took Margarete's hand.

Cranmer did not move. His eyes remained on the gown. His prayer, if he offered one, was silent now. But the tremor in his hand had steadied.

Henry sat alone in the queen's withdrawing room. The fire had burned low, and no one dared stir the coals.

He had sent them all away—nobles, servants, even Edward's nursemaid who had only come to say the child slept soundly. He wanted silence. Or rather, he wanted something to answer the silence.

Jane was dead.

She had slipped from him in the early night, her breath thin, her voice already distant when he had reached her side. She had looked at him—looked through him—with a strange calm, and whispered something he could not understand. Then she was gone.

What had she said? He thought he heard Edward's name, perhaps the word *love*—but was she speaking of herself, or to him?

He had not wept. He would not.

But now, in the hollow hush of the room that still held her warmth, Henry felt his world tilt.

She had been obedient. Gracious. A peacemaker. And she had given him what no other woman had: a son.

A son.

He whispered the word aloud, as if speaking it might steady him. But it echoed strangely in the chamber, as if not yet at home.

He rose, walking slowly to the window. The morning was gray. He clenched his jaw.

This was not how it was meant to be.

If ever there had been a sign of divine favor—surely it was Edward. Surely Jane's quiet virtue, his own rightness in the break with Rome, the tireless reform of church and state—surely these had found approval in heaven.

But now the queen was dead. The rejoicing soured. The prayers unanswered. Or worse—answered and revoked.

Henry gripped the windowsill.

What did it mean?

That Edward lived still meant something. It had to. God would not bless rebellion and then strike down the one who bore the blessing. Unless—unless there was something still to be set right.

He turned away from the window, suddenly cold. Too many had pushed him forward. Too many with eager creeds and hungry eyes. Cromwell. Cranmer. The Germans. And all the time, the Catholics watched—smug, patient, praying for the tide to turn.

He would not let them win—none of them.

But neither would he pretend this death meant nothing.

There would be no remarriage—not soon at least. There would be mourning. Solemnity. Reflection. And perhaps—a reckoning.

He walked to the cradle where Edward had been laid earlier that morning, though the child now slept elsewhere. Henry looked down at the empty bed and placed a hand on the soft blankets.

"You will live," he said aloud. "You must."

He stood there a long time, unmoving, as the silence deepened around him once again.

31

The Unraveling Thread

THE LETTER FROM WITTENBERG lay open on the table, its final lines still stinging.

Cromwell stood motionless, hands braced on either side of the parchment. The windows were closed against the April breeze, but the chamber felt cold. Cromwell had sat on the League's reply for a day, maybe two. Hoping perhaps for a reversal, or a softer message to follow. None came. Now his patience had thinned to threads,

"They've changed their tone," he said.

Will, seated just across, leaned forward slightly. "You mean the League?"

Cromwell's eyes didn't move. "Yes. A fortnight ago, they pressed for mutual defense and shared resistance to Rome. Now—" He tapped the page. "Now they say unity in doctrine must precede unity in alliance."

Will's brow furrowed. "Why the change?"

Silence hovered for a moment. Cromwell finally looked up, his expression tight. "I don't like being maneuvered, Will. And this—this smells of someone else's ink."

Will said nothing.

Cromwell turned abruptly toward a cabinet and yanked open a drawer. "Get Cranmer to respond, if you can. And check with the envoy—was there anyone new at the last meeting? Anyone from Strasbourg? Zürich?"

Will hesitated. "I believe Bishop Fox mentioned a Dr. Schütze—"

"That's not what I asked." Cromwell's voice flared, sharper than the words warranted. "I don't need your beliefs. I need answers."

Will blinked but didn't flinch. "I'll find them."

Cromwell paused, jaw working, then gave a curt nod. "Good."

A beat passed. "And—" he added, his voice quieter, "I shouldn't have barked. The fault's not yours."

Will looked up. "Understood."

Cromwell turned back to the letter, muttering, "Still, I need better than guesses."

He tapped the page again, harder this time. "This language didn't grow in Wittenberg soil. Someone planted it."

He moved to the hearth, picked up a poker, and jabbed at the cold ash as if it still held resistance. "If Gardiner had a hand in this, we'll know it soon enough. He leaks doctrine like a sieve, but only when it suits his game."

Will stepped toward the door. "I'll speak with Cranmer and the envoy."

"Do that," Cromwell said absently. Then, as Will reached for the latch, he added with fresh irritation, "And don't take half the day doing it. We don't have the luxury of your usual pace."

Will didn't reply. He merely opened the door and slipped out, leaving Cromwell alone with the cold grate and his scattered thoughts.

Will stepped into the corridor, letting the door fall shut behind him. He drew a breath and exhaled slowly, steadying his pace as his boots echoed down the stone floor. He had learned not to carry Cromwell's moods on his face—but they still settled deep in his shoulders.

He's unraveling, Will thought. Not in collapse, not yet. But something inside the man was fraying—threads pulled too tightly for too long. He had built a kingdom on precision and momentum. Now, the wheels slipped.

Will turned toward the outer hall, his path set for the riverside dock—then across to Lambeth. He would find Cranmer, or at least send a page ahead. The archbishop had met with the envoys the day before— perhaps he had heard a whisper that would clarify Cromwell's suspicions.

He adjusted his cloak, thoughts already assembling into questions—when a familiar figure turned into the passage ahead. Gardiner.

Head bowed slightly, a hand tucked behind his back, his steps unhurried but deliberate.

Will hesitated. The bishop looked up at that same moment and stopped.

"Master Cressy," Gardiner said smoothly, his voice mild. "You move with purpose."

Will bowed. "A message for the archbishop."

"Ah," Gardiner said, tilting his head. "Not from Secretary Cromwell, I hope?"

Will gave a tight smile. "He's . . . perturbed."

"A common weather these days." Gardiner studied him a moment longer, then took a step closer. "Is this about the League's latest communique?"

Will hesitated, uncertain whether to speak. But the slight narrowing of Gardiner's eyes told him the man already knew.

"They've suggested a binding of doctrine before diplomacy," Will said.

Gardiner's brow lifted faintly. "Have they? Imagine that."

Will said nothing.

Gardiner turned as if considering, then gestured with a single graceful motion. "Walk with me. I was just on my way to speak with the Lady Mary. We may as well compare notes."

Will glanced down the hallway—toward Lambeth, toward his original path—but then nodded and fell into step beside the bishop.

Gardiner's pace quickened as they entered the quiet antechamber beside the chapel. With a flick of his hand, the attendant withdrew. Mary rose from her seat near the fire, her expression sharpening at the sight of them.

"Well?" she asked, gaze shifting quickly between them.

Gardiner spoke low. "The Germans have made reply. They ask for theological alignment before moving forward."

Mary's eyes narrowed in satisfaction. "They bit."

Gardiner gave a slow nod but then glanced sidelong at Will, hesitation clear.

Mary noticed. "You needn't worry," she said smoothly. "Will is with us."

She turned to him then—her smile soft, her eyes anything but. Will understood her look and nodded.

"It seems," Will added, "they want England to affirm certain confessional points—particularly on the Eucharist. The League denies any real presence of Christ in the bread and wine, and they want that rejection made explicit. England still holds to the mystery of presence—even if we don't call it transubstantiation anymore."

"As we expected," Mary said. "And the Secretary will never grant those points."

"Not at first," Gardiner said. "He'll try to wrangle their terms, or delay, or bluff. But the League is proud. They won't bend. And Cromwell wants this alliance."

"The Secretary will never grant it," Mary repeated, turning back to the fire, "because the king will never allow it."

She paused a beat.

"And that is our advantage. When Cromwell realizes he can't press the League any longer, he'll try to press the king. And pressing my father never ends well."

Will stepped out from the antechamber into the sharp October air, the doors shutting behind him with a weight that matched his chest. He took the stone steps two at a time, then slowed, breathing deep as he crossed to the riverside quay.

He couldn't tell Cromwell. That was clear. Gardiner had baited the Germans with precision—an invitation wrapped in theological silk. And they'd taken it, just as Mary had predicted. Now Cromwell stood cornered, the very path he'd paved redirecting under his feet.

But the Secretary didn't know that.

And he mustn't.

Cromwell needed something to chase—something that shifted the question from why to how. Will needed some pivot to catch Cromwell's interest.

He boarded the small ferry to Lambeth, the water cold and restless beneath him. Cromwell's anger earlier still throbbed faintly in his mind, but it was more signal than wound now. The man was unraveling, or close to it, and no one unwinds Cromwell without consequence. Will would offer him something—something real enough to be useful but harmless enough to steer his fury in a new direction.

By the time the boat nudged against Lambeth's dock, the shape of a plan had begun to form.

He needed Cranmer. Or at least Cranmer's speculation—anything that could sound credible when relayed to the Secretary.

The palace doors were ajar. A footman nodded him in and gestured toward the west hall, where light spilled beneath the archway. Will passed under it and nearly collided with Nicholas, arms full of stacked parchment.

"Ah—Nicholas." Will steadied the top scroll. "Is the archbishop in?"

"Gone to the chapel for prayer," Nicholas replied, shifting the papers. "I expect him back shortly. Shall I fetch him?"

Will shook his head. "No need. I'll wait."

Nicholas hesitated, then added, "He's been in low spirits all morning. Spent half the night poring over correspondence. One of the letters was from Strasbourg."

Will perked up. "Bucer?"

Nicholas nodded. "Not directly, but from someone close to him. It mentioned—rather obliquely—that a softened version of the Augsburg Confession might be coming. Bucer and Capito have been working on it, apparently. Some sort of theological middle ground. We're not sure why."

Will's mind clicked sharply into gear. "Did Cranmer say anything about it?"

"Only that it might ease tensions with England, which would then slow England's own reformation."

Will smiled faintly. A candle in a dark room.

"Thank you, Nicholas. That may be the bit of brightness I needed."

Nicholas looked puzzled. "For what? What brightness?"

But Will was already moving. "Thanks for the thing I can say when the truth is something I cannot."

The king's chamber was warm, stifling despite the morning chill outside. Cromwell stood near the hearth, one hand gripping the back of a chair, the other holding the folded parchment from Strasbourg. Henry paced slowly across the tiled floor, his hands clasped behind his back.

Cromwell cleared his throat. "Your Majesty, there's word from Strasbourg. Bucer and Capito are working to soften the Augsburg

Confession—terms that might allow us to find common ground with the League."

Henry stopped, his eyes narrowing. "Softening how?"

"They're beginning to speak more vaguely—less insistence on clear repudiation. Particularly on. . . . the Eucharist. No direct denial of the real presence. Only talk of 'spiritual union' and 'shared mystery.'"

Henry's brow twitched. "Shared mystery? I know what that means. It means they deny the miracle."

Cromwell pressed forward. "Your Grace, they're trying to bridge the gap. If we let the wording stay open, we could move forward on alliance. And once alliance is secured, we hold the stronger hand."

Henry's mouth tightened.

Cromwell drew a slow breath. "They may also yield, in time, on—on other matters. Perhaps even on the cup."

Henry spun around, his face reddening. "The cup?"

Cromwell steadied himself. "They suggest that laity receiving both elements might be a symbol of fuller communion—but I propose we phrase the response diplomatically. No public concession. No change in rite."

Henry's voice rose like a storm. "You want me to give common men the blood of Christ in their ale-warmed mouths? And to deny what the Church has taught since Augustine—that the body of our Lord becomes present, truly and fully, upon the altar?"

"Sire, I—"

"Enough!" Henry roared, his hand slamming down on the table. "Is this how you win your alliance? By letting foreign priests dictate my Church? I broke with Rome to be rid of meddling bishops, not to invite new ones in from the Rhine!"

Cromwell opened his mouth but said nothing.

Henry stepped closer, jabbing a finger. "You tell Bucer and every soft-tongued reformer in Strasbourg that England kneels to no creed but its own. I'll have no cloaked heresies passed off as common sense."

A tense silence stretched. Near the chamber door, Norfolk had paused, still half-shadowed in the corridor, drawn by the noise. His eyes narrowed at the king's words.

Henry turned again. "This alliance was supposed to humble Rome. And you—my Secretary—cannot even manage a treaty with those who claim to hate Rome as much as I do!"

Cromwell bowed stiffly, jaw clenched. "As your Majesty commands."

Henry waved him off, pacing anew. "We'll not be ruled by German syllables and vague phrases. This is England, Cromwell. England—and I am its head."

Cromwell turned, retreating through the hall with silent fury. As he passed, Norfolk stepped away from the door, lingering just a moment longer. A glimmer of opportunity sparked behind his eyes.

Gardiner was hunched over a map of the empire in Mary's receiving room when Norfolk entered, boots echoing on the polished stone. He didn't wait for a greeting.

"I've heard the king," Norfolk said grimly. "He near tore Cromwell's head off."

Gardiner looked up. "Over the League?"

"Aye. The secretary tried to smooth over the Eucharist—speak of mysteries and meanings—but Henry will have none of it. He called the Germans altar-slanderers and near spat at sharing the cup." Norfolk leaned in. "Cromwell's stuck. Which means now's our moment."

Mary closed her book and gave him her full attention. "What are you thinking?"

"A legislative blow. A clear line in the sand, so public and so permanent that no one—here or in Strasbourg—can mistake our position."

Gardiner's brow furrowed. "A royal decree?"

"Parliament," Norfolk said. "Let's not whisper theology behind walls. Let's codify it. Just a few tenets. The king's tenets. Transubstantiation, the cup withheld from the laity, clerical celibacy—the old truths, framed as eternal ones."

"Add three more," Mary said, her voice even as her gaze turned inward. "Vows of chastity, private masses, and confession to a priest. Those six. That will do. But they must be introduced and passed quickly, before Cromwell can maneuver."

Gardiner leaned forward slightly, the firelight casting sharp shadows across his cheek. "If we pass those six as law, there will be no alliance. No need to block it—it will die on its own."

"And the Secretary?" Norfolk asked.

Mary allowed herself the thinnest smile. "Let him squirm. Let him run to the king and try to explain how an alliance might still be possible.

Let him make his case—soften doctrines, hide language, plead necessity. My father will not yield."

Norfolk's brow lifted in satisfaction. "And with the alliance buried, he'll see Cromwell for what he is."

"Let the Act speak," Mary said, though a flicker of tension crossed her brow. "Let it be louder than the Secretary's plans."

She turned back to the fire. "If it is not, then we must find another way."

The door burst open without warning.

Cromwell looked up from his cluttered desk, quill paused in mid-air. Rain flecked the shoulders of the man now striding into the room, breath short, expression taut.

"Your Grace," Cromwell said flatly. "I assume you've heard."

Cranmer pulled off his gloves, fingers trembling slightly. "It passed? All six?"

Cromwell nodded. "With hardly a murmur. The Act of Six Articles—sealed and spoken. A doctrine for the realm. Or rather, a trap."

Cranmer dropped into the chair across from him. "Clerical celibacy. They mean to use it."

"They mean to silence you," Cromwell replied. "Or bait you into silence."

"And Margarete?" Cranmer's voice cracked at the edge. "What do I do with her? Hide her? Send her away? Must I pretend she doesn't exist?"

Cromwell leaned back, rubbing his brow. "The king won't arrest you. Not yet. He may not like the heat around you, but he likes the loyalty more. I'll speak to him."

Cranmer looked down, his jaw clenched. The very idea of sending her away—of pretending she didn't exist—cut something deeper than fear. He had loved her openly for years, and now he must love her as a secret.

"But I need direction now," Cranmer complained. "They'll come for others first, I know that. But it won't stop there. I need—"

Cromwell's hand lifted. "Stop."

He stood slowly, walked to the small window, and watched the gray swirl of clouds gathering over the river. For a moment, nothing.

Then: "You said Margarete came from Nuremberg, yes? A daughter of Saxon stock?"

Cranmer's brow furrowed. "Her family has ties in the region, yes."

Cromwell turned back, something sharper now in his gaze. "When you journeyed through the German provinces years ago—working to untie the knot of Catherine—you brought back more than reports. You brought back a wife. Not through treaty or proclamation, but through alliance all the same. The right match, at the right time."

Cranmer's eyes narrowed. "You're not speaking of me anymore."

"No," Cromwell said. "I'm not."

He crossed back to the desk and flattened a scrap of parchment beneath his palm. "If the League cannot be won by argument—then let them be joined by marriage."

"A German wife for the king?" Cranmer said slowly.

Cromwell didn't answer at first. Then: "Anne of Cleves. Protestant. Sister to the Duke of Cleves—who's no fool and would welcome the security of an English tie. It would not demand confessional unity. It would not enshrine Lutheran doctrine. It would be . . . quieter than what I attempted before."

"And yet more lasting," Cranmer said.

"If it works," Cromwell muttered. "And if the king agrees."

The king sat slouched on the great oak chair, elbows on the armrests, fingers drumming. His face was half in shadow, half in scowl.

Cromwell stood still, waiting. He knew better than to press too quickly.

At last, Henry's voice rumbled low. "So. You've failed with the League."

Cromwell inclined his head. "They were unwilling to separate theology from alliance. Their pride outpaced their interest."

Henry grunted. "And you promised me a union."

"I still can," Cromwell said. "A different kind. One that does not ask your majesty to debate eucharistic formulas or priestly vows."

Henry looked up, eyes narrowing. "What are you proposing?"

"A marriage, sire. With Anne of Cleves—sister to the Duke. Protestant, yes, but moderate. The match would signal alignment with reformers abroad, but without doctrinal entanglement. It would unify two enemies of Rome without forcing either to submit."

Henry tilted his head. "A wife."

Cromwell gave the barest smile. "One with purpose."

"And you think," Henry said slowly, "that rutting with a Saxon girl makes me Lutheran?"

"Never, majesty," Cromwell said. "I would not insult your convictions. This is alliance by kinship, not creed."

Henry was silent again, eyes narrowed. "I've no mind to wed a ghost. What does she look like?"

Anticipating the question, Cromwell reached for a slim parcel resting on the nearby table. He unwrapped it and held it up—a portrait, painted in soft hues, the face framed by gentle curls, the figure noble, demure.

"By Holbein," he said. "Your majesty's own artist."

Henry leaned forward, taking it in. "Hmph." He studied it a moment longer, then sat back. "She's not unpleasing."

Cromwell suppressed his relief. "I can begin negotiations immediately."

"Do it," Henry said. "But understand—if she arrives and looks nothing like this . . ." He tapped the portrait sharply. "You'll answer for it."

Cromwell inclined his head, but a shiver of unease passed down his spine. He had placed every stone with care, but the weight was growing. If the foundation cracked—if the king turned—no scaffolding could save him.

Even as Cromwell set plans in motion, the court hummed with new energy. Rumor traveled faster than ink: the king was to marry again. And not just any woman, but a German.

Norfolk was the first to react.

"A German wife?" he said with a sneer, pacing before Gardiner and Mary. "And to think—we'd nearly pinned him to the old faith, and now Cromwell lures him back to German bedchambers."

Gardiner's fingers pressed together. "Then we find a reason for him to rethink."

Mary stood near the window, eyes distant. "Not a reason. A temptation."

Norfolk turned, understanding dawning.

"Who then . . . wait. Catherine, my niece, yes!" he said proudly. "Young, English, and far more charming than any Saxon matron."

Mary nodded once. "Let her sparkle. Let her be seen. The king is not married yet."

The autumn sun spilled gold across the gravel paths, and the king walked slowly, arms clasped behind his back. His steps were labored, his leg stiff, but his eyes were alight.

Catherine Howard walked beside him, her pale green gown dancing with the breeze. She was not beautiful in the manner of portraits, but she moved as though joy were stitched into her hem.

"You mustn't laugh," she said, hand brushing his sleeve, "but I truly thought the bishop meant *goose* when he said *genuflect*. I pictured the whole congregation honking and flapping."

Henry chuckled, then burst into real laughter—loud, full, the kind that startled the guards nearby.

Catherine grinned. "There! That's the sound I wanted."

He stopped, looking at her. "You're impertinent."

"I'm delightful," she corrected.

He studied her a moment longer, then offered his arm. She took it without hesitation.

They walked on.

"Do you think me old?" he asked suddenly.

She tilted her head. "Do you think yourself unloved?"

He blinked.

"I see your eyes when you speak of music," she went on. "Of chivalry. Of victories. You do not carry years, your majesty. You carry stories. And I could listen to them all day."

Henry's jaw shifted slightly, but he said nothing.

Catherine added, softly, "You are not done yet."

Her words sank deeper than he expected. He had spent months haunted by the silence of a cold bed, by the emptiness Jane left behind. But now, for one breathless second, he wondered—

Was he still worth loving?

Not hope.

Desire.

The Cleves entourage arrived in due course, the Thames bustling with movement and fanfare. Henry had begun to waver days earlier—Catherine's light laugh echoing in his halls, her hand brushing his arm. She was everything Anne seemed, from her portrait, not to be: slight, lively, English.

And then Anne stepped forward, unveiled at last.

Older than the portrait. Sturdier. Her smile tight, her eyes darting. She curtsied deeply and, rising, offered a line rehearsed too carefully: "It is joy to meet your most gracious majesty."

Her accent was thick, her tone unsure.

Henry stared. Silent. His eyes flicked to Cromwell, then back to her.

It was not hatred that filled him.

It was disappointment. Vast. Absolute.

And growing.

32

The Fall of the Builder

THE HEARTH BURNED TOO hot. Henry paced the chamber anyway, sweat darkening his collar. Cromwell stood at a cautious distance, hands folded, saying nothing yet. The king had not spoken in nearly three minutes. When he finally did, it came with a snarl.

"A mare," Henry said. "That's what they've sent me—a Flanders mare."

Cromwell's throat worked. "Your majesty—"

"She is not what was promised." Henry turned, jabbing a finger. "You gave me that portrait—fair, soft-featured, agreeable. Lies painted in oil. Did you think I would not notice the difference once she stood before me?"

"I believed the likeness honest," Cromwell replied, voice measured. "As did Hans himself. You saw what the artist saw."

Henry scoffed. "Then the artist should be whipped for poor judgment." He turned again, fists balled. "I am trapped, Thomas. Married to a woman I cannot abide, because you promised me a queen who would sweeten the sour taste left by Jane's grave."

Cromwell stepped forward, cautious. "It is not permanent."

The king whirled. "Say that again."

"I mean only," Cromwell said quickly, "that your majesty is not without recourse. The marriage was unconsummated. Grounds may be found—"

Henry's glare held him.

"But until such time," Cromwell pressed on, "the alliance holds. Her presence here serves purpose. Even if . . . even if affection does not."

"I will not be turned Lutheran," Henry snapped.

"I would never ask it." Cromwell bowed his head. "Only that this marriage achieves what the politics could not—a show of unity with the German states. A shared enemy in Rome, even if we do not share a Mass."

Henry moved to the window, pulling back the curtain with a grunt. "She tried to kiss me," he muttered. "The first night. She smelled of vinegar and starch. I turned away."

"I understand," Cromwell said quietly.

"No, you don't." Henry's voice cracked like a split beam. "You're not the one lying beside a woman who makes your skin crawl. You didn't lose a queen who gave you a son. And you didn't—" He stopped himself. A deep breath. "I will not remain with her."

Cromwell hesitated. Then: "Would you allow me to begin the necessary preparations?"

Henry nodded stiffly.

"Thank you, Majesty."

"But don't mistake this for favor," the king growled. "This was your idea. And it has failed. If this German insult unravels what little unity I've built, it will not be your enemies who bring you down, Cromwell. It will be me."

Cromwell bowed, deeply. "Understood, your grace."

Weeks passed, and the silence from the German states grew louder than their diplomacy. Cromwell, once the engine of the king's foreign strategy, found doors slower to open and letters slower to arrive. Henry no longer asked his opinion in council—he issued orders. And still Anne remained queen, in name only, while court rumors spread like rot beneath a polished floor.

The fire in Cromwell's chamber at Whitehall had burned down to embers. He hadn't noticed. A half-written letter curled on the desk, ink drying at the nib. His eyes scanned the day's ledgers of foreign correspondence—dates, replies, silences. So many silences.

He had sent two envoys. Neither had returned with what he needed.

A quiet knock. Then the door creaked open. A wiry young man stepped inside, face uncertain.

"Master Secretary," he said, "forgive the hour."

Cromwell looked up. "Rafe." Not Will—of course not. Will had been away for two days, delivering sealed documents to Oxford.

Rafe Sadler stepped forward, holding out a folded page. He was one of Cromwell's junior aides—clever, dependable, if unpolished.

"There's something you should see," he said.

Cromwell took the paper. The seal was foreign—imperial, but not German. French courier. Inside, a transcript of intercepted correspondence. Cromwell read it once, then again more slowly, each word tightening across his chest.

A reference to Gardiner. An oblique mention of Strasbourg. And near the end:

"The Lady, whose loyalty lies not with the realm but with Rome, sowed the notion that doctrinal unity be prerequisite. Her hand is unseen, but her signature is plain."

He sat back, folding the page with careful fingers.

"Mary," he said.

Rafe gave a slight nod. "Two other reports name her. One from Calais, one from Lyon. Both suggest Gardiner wasn't acting alone."

Cromwell exhaled through his nose. "So the fractures I thought foreign were born at home."

He stood, crossing slowly to the cold hearth. "If this is true, I'll need more than whispers. I want confirmation. Names. Patterns. Her full hand."

He turned. "And I want her at court. Not summoned—but present. Public."

"She's often at Richmond," Rafe said. "She'll need time to return."

"Then give her time." He strode to the desk and dipped a quill. "Tell her I request her presence tomorrow at dusk. Not before. And not here."

Rafe frowned. "Where, then?"

Cromwell sealed the note with his ring. "The gallery at Whitehall. Let her walk beneath the painted kings."

Mary had received Cromwell's message late the night before. Rather than reply, she had risen early and made for Whitehall—not to present herself, but to wait. Let him come to her.

The chamber was warm, the fire steady. A book lay open on the side table, though her eyes had not touched it for some time. She stood at the window instead, looking down on the inner court where the horses waited, stamping in the cold.

Will arrived mid-morning, breath showing as he stepped through the gate. She turned from the window and moved to the chair by the hearth, smoothing her skirts.

A knock.

"Come."

Will entered, hesitating only briefly at the threshold.

He wasn't sure what this visit was meant to be. The hour, the silence, the firelight—none of it suggested politics. He had been here before, sometimes welcomed fully, sometimes held back at the last moment. She let him close, then pushed him away, like a flame luring a moth only to pause just before the burn.

Tonight might be different. Or it might be the same. He didn't know which he preferred.

"You wished to see me?"

Mary studied him, then gestured to the seat opposite. "Just for a moment."

Will sat.

"Cromwell has sent word," she said, "asking to meet with me. Not in the chapel or the council chamber or the gardens—in private."

Will's brow creased. "Here?"

She nodded. "He wants to talk. But he doesn't want to be seen talking."

Will shifted. "Why would he not—"

"Because he's uncertain. And when men like Cromwell grow uncertain, they look for levers. And if those fail . . ." Her voice trailed off, but her eyes stayed on him. "He will come. He must."

She stood and crossed to him, laying a hand gently on his shoulder. "When he arrives, I will admit him. You will wait outside. Give us a moment—then come in. Unannounced."

Will blinked. "You want me to interrupt?"

Mary nodded once. "Yes. And see whatever you see."

"What am I to be seeing?"

Her hand withdrew. "Whatever he chooses to reveal."

Will looked down, then back up. "Mary . . ."

She tilted her head. "You said you would help me."

He nodded, slowly. "I did."

"Then be ready."

She turned back to the window as he rose. He paused at the door, but she gave no further word. Only the fire made sound as he slipped back into the corridor.

Alone, Mary let the silence stretch, then crossed to the side table. She picked up the book, unread, and placed it beneath a folded shawl. Then she moved to the mirror, examined her bodice, and with a quick flick, loosened the top lacing just enough to suggest ease, not carelessness. Not yet.

Cromwell would come.

And the moment would be hers to shape.

Cromwell stood at the tall windows of his chamber, watching the last sweep of daylight vanish behind the city's roofs. He had waited long enough.

She was here. He knew it. Word from the inner court said Mary had arrived at Whitehall midmorning, taking up rooms on the east wing. But she had not replied. Not with a note. Not with a visit. Not with a word. For hours, Cromwell had told himself she was merely measuring her reply. Then that she was preparing it. Then that she was delayed.

Now, he knew better.

He turned from the window. "Rafe."

The younger man looked up from the small desk near the hearth, quill frozen above a page.

"I'm going to her," Cromwell said.

"Now, my lord?"

"I've waited twelve hours." His jaw flexed. "That's eleven too many."

He moved for the door, but Rafe spoke again. "Shall I send someone ahead? Inform her?"

Cromwell paused only a breath. "No. If she's already dressed for the court, she can receive a guest."

He strode through the corridors of Whitehall, heat rising with every step. Failure stacked upon failure—the League, the Act, the king's glowering silence—and Mary's name was never far from any of it.

He pushed into her rooms without knocking. The guards let him pass—his name still carried weight, if not warmth. Inside, a pair of maids stood just within the threshold of her privy chamber. They dropped shallow curtsies and vanished through a side door.

Mary sat near the hearth, a book closed on her lap. She didn't rise.

"You sent for me," she said.

"And you did not come." Cromwell's voice was taut, clipped.

"I did. I'm here." She gestured faintly at the room.

"This isn't the same."

"No," she said, "it's better. I can control the doors."

He took a step forward, fists clenched behind his back. "You've been busy. The League collapses, the Act passes, and every whisper in the king's ear wears your perfume."

Mary's eyes flicked up. "You sound like a man looking for someone to blame."

"I am," Cromwell snapped. "Because someone will hang for this."

"And you think it's me?"

"I think you've tried to make it me."

She rose slowly, smoothing her skirt with maddening calm. "And has it worked?"

Cromwell's jaw tightened. "You're tampering with the king's patience. You've turned Parliament against me, you've poisoned his ear, and you've left me chasing shadows."

Mary stepped toward the curtain that separated the rooms. Her voice was low, but not soft. "You don't need shadows, Thomas. You just need to ask the right questions."

She slipped behind the curtain.

Cromwell stood seething. This was not courtly jest. This was treason in pearls. One breath. Two.

He moved.

The curtain yielded to his hand. Firelight flickered low in the adjoining chamber, casting the bedposts in gold and shadow. Mary stood across the room, one hand on the bedframe, her back to him.

He stepped through, no longer caring for protocol—only for control. He had lost too much already.

"Mary," he said, voice rough, "you think you're clever. You think if you outlast me, the king will come running to you. But you don't understand what's coming."

She turned slowly, her eyes level and unreadable. "Don't I?"

"You've made yourself indispensable to no one," Cromwell snarled. "And if you think the crown protects you, you've misunderstood how kingdoms burn."

She took a step forward. "Then strike the match."

Cromwell stood rigid. "I came here to end this."

"No," Mary said, her voice like a thread of silk laced with steel. "You came because you've already lost."

She held his gaze for a beat—then she reached for her bodice. Slow, deliberate. The fabric parted with a rip that startled the air.

"What are you—?"

She grabbed his arm and pulled—just enough to throw them both slightly off balance—and fell backward onto the edge of the bed.

Her scream split the room.

In the corridor, Will flinched at the cry. He had been pacing, uncertain how long to wait. But that sound—urgent, sharp, rehearsed—snapped him into motion.

The footfalls of the guards thundered behind him as he threw open the outer door, stormed through the privy chamber, and tore back the curtain to the bedchamber.

Cromwell stood frozen, disoriented, near the bed. Mary lay sprawled across it, her bodice torn, one shoulder bare. Her breathing came shallow and fast, eyes brimming—not with fear, but something more cunningly composed.

Will stared at her. Then at Cromwell, whose face was taut with shock.

"She cried out," Will said hoarsely.

"She *planned* this," Cromwell answered, voice fraying.

Will's heart pounded. He knew. He knew then what this was.

Cromwell's voice came again—low . . . pained. "No . . . Will. She—this isn't—it didn't happen. Will, please—you know I wouldn't—"

Will didn't answer. His gaze moved between them—Cromwell, disheveled and desperate . . . Mary, eyes wide, the picture of violated innocence.

For one long breath, he stood at the threshold between loyalty and survival.

And then he chose.

"Guards," he said quietly, "hold him. Say nothing. This must be reported."

Cromwell stepped forward, eyes desperate. "Will, no. You know me."

Will pulled away. "I *knew* you."

Will turned and left.
He did not look back.
Not at the man who had built him.
Not at the man he had just buried.

Within hours, the court was humming. A rumor at first, slippery and soft: that Cromwell had been discovered in the chambers of the Lady Mary—alone, uninvited. That she had cried out, and guards had come, and the scene had not been as it should.

By morning, it had hardened into talk of overreach—a man who had risen from nothing now daring to touch the daughter of a king, to court her, perhaps marry her, perhaps ascend by her blood to something unthinkable. Norfolk and Gardiner poured oil on the fire. *He would have made himself heir,* they whispered. *What else could explain his interest in German alliances, in Lutheran theology, in a queen Henry would not touch?*

The charge, when it came, was not for assault. It didn't need to be. The implication was enough: Cromwell had ambitions beyond his station, ambitions that twisted policy into obsession, marriage into a mechanism. And if he would dare pursue Mary, what would he not dare?

Heresy and treason. The words rang out across the council chamber like iron dropped on stone.

Cranmer, desperate, begged an audience with the king. He pleaded for clemency, spoke of loyalty, of years of faithful service.

Henry listened. Then, without expression, said, "He gave me Anne of Cleves." And nothing more.

Cromwell was executed at Tower Hill in July. The morning was gray and spitting rain. He spoke no final defiance, only a prayer, and a quiet hope that those who knew him would remember him honestly.

Will did not attend.

The lamps had long since guttered, leaving only the fire's slow breath to warm the study. Cranmer sat forward in his chair, elbows on knees, hands clasped—his white sleeves dimmed to ash in the flicker.

Jo poured a small measure of wine into three cups and passed one to Will without a word.

No one had spoken in several minutes.

At last, Cranmer exhaled. "He was not a gentle man. But he understood what was at stake."

Will nodded once, then again. "He did."

"I never trusted his temper," Jo said softly. "But I trusted his aim."

"And now?" Cranmer looked at Will—not accusing, but open. "What do you believe his aim was, in the end?"

Will waited to answer. He stared into the fire, his jaw tense. "I believe he saw too much, too far ahead. And didn't see what was nearest."

Jo's eyes flicked to him, reading the double meaning.

Cranmer sat back, the fire tracing lines across his face. "With him gone, the winds change. Quickly. Already they speak of new alliances. New eyes on the throne. And I . . ." He stopped. Then smiled faintly, bitterly. "I suspect my name is being rewritten as we speak."

"You're not alone," Jo said.

But the words, kind as they were, hung too lightly in the air.

Will cleared his throat. "The king's annulment will be next. Anne of Cleves. Quietly swept aside. Then—Catherine Howard."

Cranmer raised a brow. "Norfolk's niece?"

Will gave a short nod.

Jo sat back, folding her hands. "And so we begin again."

They fell quiet once more. Outside, the wind stirred in the courtyard trees, their bare limbs brushing against stone like fingers searching for hold.

The annulment was swift. Cranmer presided, solemn but composed, ruling that the marriage to Anne of Cleves had never been consummated and was thus invalid. Anne was gracious in retreat, accepting the title of "King's Beloved Sister" and a generous settlement. She had never loved Henry. Perhaps she had never hoped to.

The court moved quickly. Catherine Howard, young, vibrant, impossibly slight, became queen within weeks. Henry's appetite for joy—after so much disappointment—found in her the glitter of youth and the echo of something long lost.

But it would not last.

Old indiscretions came to light—letters, liaisons, whispers from her past that bloomed into scandal. Henry raged, then grieved, then signed the warrant. Catherine Howard was executed in February.

He had buried one queen in grief, discarded two, and ordered two to their deaths. The crown sat heavier with each passing year, and his body—bloated, ulcered, and angry—reflected the turmoil within. What he craved now was not passion, not alliance, not even heirs. He needed calm. Wisdom. Someone to soothe the storm that had become his soul.

Catherine Parr was no girl. No naïve courtier dazzled by jewels or titles. She was twice widowed, deeply learned, and quietly devout. She had known grief and borne it with dignity. She had learned when to speak and when to remain silent. And unlike any who had come before, she neither feared the king nor worshipped him. She respected him—and that steadied him.

She did not arrive because no one else remained.

She arrived because she was precisely what he needed.

She brought not passion, but peace. She read to him, soothed him, helped mend the frayed ties between Henry and his daughters. She was, at last, not a mirror of his desire, but a balm for his pain.

But even peace has its price, and her place by the king's side was carved from the ruin of another. Behind it all—forgotten in court but not in consequence—was Thomas Cromwell.

His rise had been meteoric. His fall, swift and complete.

He had brokered the marriage. He had chased the alliance. He had threatened the balance.

And the king had ended him.

Thus closed the chapter of ambition disguised as reform.

Thus ended the long, dark arc of Henry's desperate search—for alliance, for comfort, for control.

He had lost a queen, and then another, and then another still. And with each loss, England grew a little more brittle.

But the crown still gleamed. The throne still stood. And somewhere in the stone corridors of Whitehall, Cromwell's footsteps had only just faded.

33

Before the Storm

THE FIRE CRACKLED LOW in the hearth at Walthamstow. Outside, frost silvered the trees, but inside, warmth clung to wool and wood and years of shared memory. The four of them—Cranmer, Margarete, Jo, and Nicholas—had come here often in recent years. What began as refuge had grown into habit. Walthamstow had become a kind of home.

Roger knelt now stoking the fire. Cranmer sat angled toward it, his hands steepled in his lap, the lines at his mouth more drawn than before. Emilie and Jo prepared supper in the adjoining room, voices soft, movements measured. Nicholas and Margarete sat nearby—Margarete darning a stocking, Nicholas absently smoothing the spine of a closed book with his thumb.

And Will was there.

He had come unannounced that morning, carrying no official dispatch—only a tired look in his eyes and a lingering silence at the corners of his mouth. Now Secretary to the Duke of Norfolk, he was no longer merely the bright-eyed youth they'd once known. His role carried weight, his name was known, and his allegiance, increasingly, was expected.

He had not explained what brought him—only that he'd heard the news.

The king was dead.

Cranmer finally spoke. "His body lies in state at Whitehall. They say the chamber reeks of sweet oils, but still cannot mask the stench beneath." His voice was low, as though the words themselves should be muffled by reverence—or perhaps caution.

Will shifted in his chair. "I heard an ulcer burst before they could lift him to change the linens. That seemed to hasten the end."

Nicholas looked up. "And so the reign ends as it lived—bloated and broken."

Cranmer shot him a quiet look but said nothing.

Jo entered, drying her hands on a cloth. "Do they name Edward king already?"

Will nodded. "Ten years old, crowned in a fortnight. The council rules for him, but Somerset—Jane Seymour's own brother—has the reins, and he leans hard Protestant."

Cranmer's gaze did not lift. "Then the boy will be shaped before he has time to stand."

Will glanced over at Jo, then at the fire. "They've moved Elizabeth to court to be near him. Said her presence steadies him."

Jo didn't reply. But Margarete did. "A realm's future held in the hands of a boy and girl," she murmured. "One with power, the other with eyes sharp as glass. Heaven help us if they shatter."

Cranmer shifted in his seat.

"There's steel in her," Margarete added.

"There is," he agreed. "And steel cuts both ways."

Silence settled again, and with it the weight of the moment. A king buried. A boy raised. A kingdom tilting toward a new horizon.

And Will, caught in the flicker between firelight and shadow, felt something he hadn't expected to feel. He was not one of them—not truly, not anymore. But something in the stillness, in the shared grief that held no ambition, no scheme, tugged at the parts of him not yet calcified.

Home. It was not where he lived. But perhaps it was still where he could be known.

Gardiner leaned forward, eyes narrowing slightly. "The council will fracture. Already there are whispers that Somerset governs more for pride than prudence."

Norfolk nodded. "He makes war on France with a boy on the throne and no coin in the coffers. That is not leadership—it is indulgence."

Mary, seated across from them, stirred her steaming cup of mint-infused water with measured calm but manipulative prompting. "So we merely hope for a change in leadership?"

"No," said Norfolk. "We make it."

Mary smiled to herself for her little success. "And with whom?"

A brief silence passed.

Then Gardiner said slowly, "There are men on that council who wear no Seymour crest and like the smell of power better than loyalty."

Mary raised an eyebrow, almost idly. "Would John Dudley entertain such a move, do you think?"

"Dudley, yes," Gardiner confirmed. "He's clever. Ambitious. Less doctrinaire than Somerset—and more inclined to reason if it advances his place."

"But reason cuts both ways," Mary said. "We elevate him, we may replace one tyrant with another."

"Unless," said Norfolk, "we offer not elevation—but partnership. A chance to correct England's course without preaching either Rome or Wittenberg. Not religion, but realm."

Gardiner leaned back. "He may be open to such language. At the very least, he might enjoy seeing Somerset brought down by his own arrogance."

Mary considered. "And who tells him this? You?"

Gardiner shook his head. "Not directly. That would reek of desperation."

Mary nodded. "Yes. Not every weapon needs a title. Sometimes the quiet ones strike truest. We need someone . . . familiar, yet unaffiliated. Intelligent. Persuasive. Someone he wouldn't suspect."

Norfolk turned to Mary, then slowly to Gardiner. "Will."

Gardiner nodded once. "Will."

Mary didn't smile, but there was something close to it in her eyes. "Then summon him."

They stood in the side chamber off the gallery—Norfolk at the hearth, Will by the window, and Mary seated at a small writing desk.

Norfolk's voice was brisk. "He will not leap at this. His first instinct will be to count the cost. Your task is to tilt the scales."

Will folded his arms. "And what, precisely, am I offering him?"

"Nothing," Norfolk said. "You're offering an absence. No sermons. No Seymour. Just England. He'll supply the rest."

Will's jaw tightened. "And if he suspects where this came from?"

"Then he'll have only ghosts to confront," Norfolk said with a smirk. "Because none of us will stand where the arrows land."

Will said nothing. But his silence lingered longer than usual.

Mary looked up. She had been watching him, weighing more than his words. "You've reservations."

Will turned slightly, just enough to glance at her. "I have caution. You want Dudley as your blade—but if he draws blood, I'll be holding the hilt."

"Which makes you vital," Mary said evenly. "And valuable. And not alone."

Norfolk clapped Will's shoulder. "You're the best suited. We've said all that needs saying."

He excused himself with a nod and stepped into the corridor, the door clicking shut behind him.

Mary rose.

She crossed the room without haste, stopping just close enough that Will could feel the warmth of her presence. Her voice dropped—low, quiet, measured.

"When it's done," she said, "I want to hear it from your own lips."

She leaned in just slightly—not seductive, but sovereign. "Come to my rooms. This evening. Late."

Then she turned and left him there—alone with the echo of her breath and the burden of the task. She had once been an ally to power. Now, somehow, she was becoming its center.

The chamber in which they met was narrow but finely appointed—tapestries of naval victories, a carved sideboard laden with untouched wine. John Dudley, Earl of Warwick, tall and hawk-eyed, stood at the window with his hands clasped behind his back.

"You requested the meeting," he said without turning. "And yet you've said nothing."

Will stepped forward, posture relaxed. "I was gauging the room."

"Gilded with false loyalty," Dudley said. "You'll find it not so different from court."

"I find most things are," Will replied, "once they're cut open."

Dudley turned. "Then speak plainly."

"All right," Will said. "You see the same rot we do. Somerset governs like a prince, not a steward. He wars like a monarch, but his face graces no coin. He bludgeons Parliament, then calls it obedience. He is not England. He is a man pretending to be England."

Dudley watched him. "And who is 'we'?"

Will smiled faintly. "We who still think England worth saving."

The silence that followed was not long, but deep. Dudley poured a glass of wine—just one—and offered it to Will, who declined. Dudley took a sip, then set the glass down untouched again.

"So?" he said. "You come with a warning? A threat?"

Will shook his head. "A gift."

Dudley arched a brow.

"You're not Somerset," Will said. "And you've no use for the kind of reforms that make England unrecognizable. You want strength, order, legacy. You want England to last. I'm here to say—so do others."

"Others," Dudley repeated. "But none who speak openly."

"They speak now," Will said. "Through me."

Dudley crossed to the hearth. "You speak like a man who serves more than one master."

"I speak like a man who remembers what happened when Cromwell forgot which direction the wind was blowing."

That stilled him.

Will stepped forward, slow and careful. "Somerset has no anchor but pride. When the tide shifts, he'll sink—and you can either be the man who throws him a rope, or the one who builds the dock."

Dudley studied him—no movement, no breath wasted. Then, quietly: "You want him gone."

"We want England back," Will said.

Dudley's eyes narrowed. "And what is it *you* seek?"

Will didn't answer.

Dudley studied him. "You're not Somerset. Not Gardiner. Not Norfolk. You're no peer. So tell me—why are you here?"

Will gave the smallest of shrugs. "Because someone knew you wouldn't trust anyone but yourself. And I am, above all things, forgettable."

That earned the faintest curl of the mouth. Not a smile—just the memory of one.

Dudley said, "I'll consider."

Will turned to go, and Dudley asked, "And if I find myself persuaded?"

Will paused at the door. "You'll know where to find me. Secretary to the Duke of Norfolk."

A flicker of a smirk.

"Ah, of course."

Will allowed another pause. "Somerset will make another move soon. A new edict. A new show of force. If you wait too long, it'll be his stage again. And his applause."

Then he left, footsteps echoing down the stone corridor, the scent of woodsmoke and politics lingering in the air behind him.

The corridor was dim, lit by only a torch or two guttering against the stone. Will walked slowly. Not from fatigue—though the day had drained him—but from thought.

He had done what they asked. No—what *she* asked. Played the role. Measured the words. Planted the doubt. And Dudley had listened.

That should have satisfied him.

But it didn't.

What if he hadn't just moved the pieces—what if *he* were a piece himself, being moved?

There was too much in motion now. He had once thought himself clever enough to ride the swell of any tide. But Cromwell had always been there to right his course.

Now he wondered if he was just being swept.

Ahead, the final turn. Mary's chambers.

She had said to come alone. Late.

Not Norfolk. Not Gardiner.

Just him.

He paused, one hand on the heavy latch. He had never feared her—admired her, yes, been drawn to her strength and poise—but had not feared.

Until now.

He squared his shoulders.

And knocked.

Somerset fell not with a crash but a quiet crack—like ice giving way beneath unsuspecting feet. His missteps had multiplied: the French campaign drained the coffers, rebellions in the west and midlands exposed the thinness of his reach, and his tolerance for reform outpaced the people's appetite. But it was not failure alone that undid him. It was trust.

He had trusted too much in his own vision—and too little in the ambition of others.

Dudley moved carefully. He did not storm the gates but shifted alliances with a statesman's poise, letting the council turn inward before he gave them someone to blame. By 1550, Somerset had been stripped of authority. By 1552, he was dead. Officially—executed for felony. Unofficially—because power, once tasted, is rarely shared.

With Somerset undone, the king—guided by the Council, and pressed by Norfolk and Gardiner—raised Dudley to the dukedom of Northumberland.

Will stood once with Northumberland on a wind-swept terrace above the Thames, watching barges move beneath a pale sun.

"You surprised me," Will said.

Northumberland didn't look away from the river. "You hoped I would fail."

"I feared you'd succeed too well."

A pause, just long enough to mean something.

"I have no wish to play priest," Northumberland said. "Nor pope. I govern where God is *silent*—not where others pretend he speaks."

"And where God actually speaks?"

Another pause. "Then I listen. But not to every voice that claims to speak for him."

That was all. Northumberland returned inside, the air around him cold but steady. Will remained alone a while longer, uncertain whether he had helped tame a beast or simply traded one mask for another.

For the realm, the years that followed seemed peaceful. The Book of Common Prayer, revised under Cranmer's careful hand, became standard in churches across the land. Altars were replaced with tables, vestments exchanged for plain robes. The treason laws softened. Indulgences faded.

Parliament moved more briskly, and Edward was growing.

By his teen years, the boy king was no longer merely the image on a coin. He spoke with precision, debated with fluency, and questioned with unnerving sharpness. His tutors—Protestants all—had done their work well. He was not his father's son, but he would not be a shadow either.

Cranmer, though relieved to see reform hold, watched with increasing caution. It was no longer the boy's youth that concerned him—it was his certainty. When the young have power, they often confuse it with truth.

And the Catholic trio—Mary, Gardiner, and Norfolk—watched too.

Mary said little, but her eyes told them she had seen this coming all along. Norfolk, older now and more wary, paced more than he spoke. Gardiner wrote letters—so many letters—and burned the ones that felt too bold.

They had removed one Lord Protector only to see another rise, no less ambitious, no more aligned. The trio had steered the wheel once—but now found themselves passengers again.

"We gave him the wheel," Norfolk said once, "and he thanks us by sailing past our harbor."

"Then we will build a new harbor," Mary replied. "One he cannot ignore."

The king no longer needed whisperers at his side. He was still lean, still pale with youth, but his eyes no longer wandered. He spoke with the precision of a ruler, not the hesitance of a ward. His tutors, long gone. His advisors were still present but stepping back. Edward had begun signing orders in his own hand, reading intelligence reports, and revising proclamations with a red-tipped quill. He asked questions that startled the Privy Council—ones they could not answer with mere platitudes.

He sat now in the long solar at Whitehall, eyes on the frost-rimmed garden below. Elizabeth entered without announcement.

"Sister," he said, not turning.

"You're alone," she said.

"For the moment."

She approached slowly, her gown whispering across the rushes. "That makes some uneasy."

He smiled faintly. "Then they should ask better questions."

Elizabeth studied him a moment. "You look tired."

"I am tired," he said. "But not unwell."

She nodded, but said nothing.

He glanced at her sideways. "They think me too young to rule."

"They think themselves too important to be ruled," she countered.

He gave a soft laugh. "And you? Do you think I'm too young?"

Elizabeth tilted her head. "You are young. But that is not the same."

His gaze held hers. "Would you rule differently?"

"Yes," she said. "But not necessarily better."

"And what would you do first, if the throne were yours?"

She stepped to the window, looking out where the frost clung to every branch. "I would survive."

He said nothing. Only watched her—the careful turn of phrase, the distance wrapped in civility. There was more steel in her than most of his councilors. And none of their vanity.

At last, he said, "I'll name a successor soon. If the coughing worsens."

She turned back sharply. "Don't."

"Why not?"

"Because naming a successor kills you faster."

Their eyes locked again—brother and sister, king and heir, Protestant and survivor. So alike in some ways. So utterly different in others.

Northumberland arrived at Whitehall near dusk, the corridors dim with lamplight and hushed by evening routine. A servant led him without delay to the long solar. Edward sat framed by the heavy tapestry behind him, embroidered with a royal hunt—figures in motion, life in pursuit. It hung like irony above the stillness of a boy who would never ride.

He coughed into a linen handkerchief. The boy—no, the young man—looked thin but alert, his eyes too bright in the shadows.

"Your Majesty," Northumberland said, bowing low.

Edward gestured him forward. "Sit. I need a mind sharper than mine tonight."

"Few would claim that," Northumberland said as he settled across from him.

Edward's lips curled faintly. "They should. Especially now."

He folded the handkerchief and placed it beside him with care. The blood on it had darkened.

"I will not recover," he said. "Not truly. Perhaps not at all."

Northumberland did not protest. They had moved past that.

"I have no son," Edward continued. "And I will not name Mary."

He paused, as if waiting for a reaction.

Northumberland gave none. "Then whom?"

"I had thought Elizabeth. She is Protestant. She is of the blood. And she is capable—perhaps more than most think."

"Yes," Northumberland said, slow and cautious. "But she is also cautious herself. Careful. Measured. She holds her faith like a courtier, not a reformer."

Edward nodded grimly. "Exactly. She bends. She watches. She keeps Rome close enough to pull back when it suits her. What will she do with the reformation when I am gone?"

Northumberland leaned forward. "Then perhaps the question is not who follows Mary—but whether Mary and Elizabeth both can be passed over."

Edward looked at him sharply. "Can they?"

"With resolve," Northumberland said, "and law." He let the pause linger. "And a clear, godly alternative."

Edward exhaled, a dry rasp in his chest. "Whom do you have in mind?"

Northumberland said nothing at first. Then: "Lady Jane Grey. My niece by marriage. Granddaughter of your father's sister—so Tudor blood, but pure in faith. No hint of Rome in her upbringing."

Edward considered him, fingers tapping lightly against the chair arm. "Jane. She is young."

"But learned. Unshakably Protestant. And—if I may—more inclined to be shaped by those who have England's good in view."

"Inclined to be shaped," Edward repeated, his gaze narrowing just slightly. "By you."

"By your council," Northumberland corrected. "By your vision. One you may yet secure, even in absence."

Edward was quiet.

Then: "Write the lineage—line by line. I'll consider it. But it will be *my* hand that signs."

The fire burned lower now at Walthamstow, the room dimming into the kind of quiet that asked no questions. Emilie set cups along the sideboard, humming softly. Roger poured hot cider into them one by one, his movements steady, familiar. Cranmer sat in his usual chair by the hearth, hands open in his lap. Jo rested on the floor nearby, knees drawn up, her head leaned gently against Margarete's side. Nicholas was cross-legged near the far wall, eyes tracing the spines of books but not reading any of them.

Will stood just inside the threshold, coat still on, as though he hadn't decided whether he was staying or simply passing through. The firelight caught the edge of his cheekbone, casting one side of his face in gold and the other in shadow.

Outside, the wind stirred the bare limbs of the orchard. Roger crossed to the door and opened it halfway.

"Walk with me," he said, not looking at Will but not needing to.

They stepped into the chill together, boots crunching softly against the gravel path. Roger didn't speak at first, and Will didn't rush him. The silence between them was old, worn in like leather.

"You don't write," Roger said at last.

"No," Will agreed. "I don't."

"You don't visit."

Will offered a ghost of a smile. "And yet, here I am."

Roger stopped near the edge of the trees. "It's not too late, Will."

"For what?"

"To remember where you're known."

Will looked out across the orchard, the moonlight laying soft silver over the branches. "I remember. More than you think."

Roger nodded. He did not press further.

They turned back toward the house, where the glow from the windows spilled out like welcome.

Inside, Margarete was reading aloud now. A psalm, soft but clear. Cranmer's head was bowed, and Jo's eyes were closed. Nicholas sat with his chin in his hands, listening. Emilie caught Will's gaze as he returned and smiled—tired, warm, knowing.

He took the cup Roger offered and sat near the fire, not in his old place but near enough to feel its warmth.

No one spoke for a while.

Then Jo broke the silence. "Do you think Mary's path is certain now?"

Cranmer stirred but said nothing. It was Nicholas who answered, his voice low. "Edward is fading. And Jane is young. I think the realm will follow the strongest voice."

Margarete folded her hands around her cup. "And if that voice sings Rome's liturgy again?"

Jo looked up at Cranmer. "What will they ask of you?"

His fingers tightened slightly in his lap. He had known the question was coming. He had answered it in dreams, in prayers, in dread. But never aloud.

"What they've always asked," he said. "Only now, the price may be steeper."

Will said nothing. He stared into the fire.

Emilie crossed the room and placed a hand gently on his shoulder. "Then we do what we've always done."

"What's that?" Nicholas asked.

"We stay. We speak truth. And we love." She smiled at Jo, then at Margarete. "Even if we tremble while we do it."

Cranmer glanced toward the window. The firelight caught the lines at his eyes, the weight of years—and of dread.

"Storm's coming," he said quietly.

Jo didn't flinch. "Let it come."

He turned toward her.

She smiled—not bravely, but knowingly. "The storm isn't what we fear, is it? It can rage and tear and howl. But we are already sheltered. We weren't promised calm. We were promised Christ."

Nicholas looked from one to the other. "And he doesn't leave."

"No," said Margarete, reaching across to lay her hand over Cranmer's. "He doesn't."

They fell quiet again, not from fear but from a deeper stillness—the kind that rests in something already won.

34

The Crown Reclaimed

THE ROOM WAS QUIET—TOO quiet for a place that held a king.

Edward lay beneath heavy linens, each breath a labor. The pallor of his skin turned the white sheets gray by contrast, and the shallow rise and fall of his chest slowed with every hour. He had not spoken in some time. Only the wet rasp in his throat offered proof of life.

Elizabeth sat at his side, her hands folded in her lap. She did not cry. She had done that already—in private. Now her gaze was steady, composed. But her lips were pressed too tightly, and her fingers curled against one another in the stillness.

Across the room, Northumberland stood near the hearth, arms folded. The fire had burned low. Its heat was nothing to the chill in the air.

Edward stirred. His head turned slightly, eyes flickering open. He saw her.

"Bess," he said. Barely a whisper.

She leaned forward. "I'm here."

He tried to smile, but only the corners of his mouth twitched. "You look . . . fierce."

Elizabeth gave the faintest breath of a laugh. "I am fierce. You know that."

"I do."

A pause. Edward sighed. "I'm sorry."

"For what?"

"That it . . . could not be you."

Her jaw set, but her voice was gentle. "You did what you thought was right."

He tried to nod but winced instead.

"It will not hold," she said quietly. "You know that."

"It may." A beat. "For a time, at least. Maybe long enough."

"To keep Mary away?"

"To give the people . . . a chance to see another way. A better way."

She swallowed hard. "I hope so."

He reached for her hand. She gave it.

"Don't . . . don't be angry with Northumberland."

Elizabeth glanced toward the man by the hearth, then back. "I'm not."

"He's done what I asked."

"I know."

The silence stretched.

"I was never meant to last," Edward said, his voice now nearly lost. "God lent me this body for a time. I hope I used it well."

"You did."

He closed his eyes. "Tell Cranmer . . . thank you."

Elizabeth blinked, unsure whether the thanks stirred guilt, resentment—or grief.

She squeezed his hand.

A breath. A pause.

And then no more.

Elizabeth sat still, her face unmoving. Only her hand trembled slightly where it held his. She leaned forward, gently placed his hand across his chest, and stood.

Northumberland stepped forward, uncertain.

Elizabeth turned. Her voice was soft, but the steel in it returned.

"I understand why it must be Jane. But do not think it will last."

He hesitated. "You will support it?"

"I will not fight it. But neither will I dance for it."

Northumberland nodded.

"God help us all," she said, stepping past him toward the door. "This storm will not pass quickly."

The courtyard was thick with morning fog and the scrape of hooves on stone. Saddlebags swung into place. Guards tightened bridles. The sky above held the pale threat of sun, but not yet its warmth.

Mary stood near the steps, wrapped in a dark traveling cloak. She turned as Will approached, mud still on his boots from the road.

"So," she said, eyes narrowing. "You were not dead—merely absent."

Will stopped, inclining his head with just enough irony to be dangerous. "I wasn't told the queen-in-waiting had urgent need of me."

Her lips drew tight. "You were told. Weeks ago."

"I was told you were watching," he said. "Not that you were moving."

"And I suppose the trip to Walthamstow was vital to the cause?"

Will said nothing. Her eyes flicked over him, searching.

"You've grown comfortable," she said at last. "Too much time in silk-paneled rooms. Too many conversations with men who burn churches and call it reform."

"Then it's a wonder you've summoned me at all."

"I need more than loyalists," Mary said. "I need clarity. Cranmer plays the humble bishop. Northumberland plays the dutiful counselor. Jane—God help her—plays at being queen. But someone must see what roles they truly intend to play."

"You want a spy."

"I want eyes that see and ears that understand. Someone who knows how to listen and when to speak. Someone who still remembers the old England, even if he's grown used to the new one."

Will shifted, folding his hands behind his back. "You trust me with this?"

She stepped forward, slow and deliberate, her voice lower now. "I trust that you are still English. That somewhere beneath all your cleverness and compromise, there is a man who knows when the storm has changed direction."

Will gave a faint nod. Not agreement—just acknowledgment.

Mary tilted her head. "Framlingham will be my holdfast. When the court begins to shift, send word."

He turned to go.

"And Will—" Her voice stopped him.

He faced her.

She stepped close enough that he could feel her breath in the morning chill. "You chose to miss my rising. I won't forget that. But if you prove useful now . . . I may choose to forget."

A flicker of something passed between them—neither threat nor promise, but something sharp and unsettled.

She mounted her horse. With a curt gesture, she was gone, her company disappearing into fog and future.

Will stood alone in the quiet that followed, the gates of Whitehall just visible ahead.

Eyes and ears, she'd said.

He looked toward the walls.

But whose heart?

The Tower loomed gray beneath the late afternoon sky, its ancient stones made older still by the hush of gathered courtiers. Inside, the council chamber had been swept clean and hung with tapestries, but it could not conceal the chill.

Lady Jane Grey, only 14 years of age, stood near the center, pale and unmoving. Her hands were folded at her waist, white-knuckled against the folds of her gown. Northumberland stood at her right, broad and unreadable, one hand resting on the table beside her.

"The king is dead," he said. "And England requires a ruler."

Jane did not look at him. Her gaze was fixed on the embroidered lions rampant behind the throne, stitched centuries before she was born.

"I do not seek this," she said quietly. "I never have."

"No one is asking what you seek," Northumberland replied. "Only what you will do for your country. For God's cause."

She blinked. "Elizabeth—"

"Is silent," he said. "She will not contest it now. And Mary is abroad in the east, gathering old names and older swords."

Jane glanced toward the far windows. "Then let them crown her."

Northumberland's voice dropped. "And watch England crawl backward? Unmake the reformation? Reinstate Rome?"

Jane said nothing.

"You are of Tudor blood," he went on. "Of Edward's will. Of God's providence. All stand ready to acclaim you. They believe because they see in you a hand raised by God. Now stand—lead them as he would have you lead."

She closed her eyes briefly, then turned—not to the throne, but to the Bible laid upon the table.

"If I accept," she said, her voice barely above a whisper, "I do so trembling. Not for power, but for duty. Not to lead, but to preserve."

Northumberland gave a slight bow, satisfied enough.

"Then, our Lady Jane," he said, "by right of lineage, by our late king's decree, by order of the king's council, and by the will of Almighty God—England names you queen."

Jane didn't move. Her eyes—wide but dry—flicked to the sky beyond the Tower's slit window. She lowered her head, one hand curling around the fabric at her waist. "Then may God help me," she whispered. "For I do not seek this crown."

Cranmer stood in the Tower chapel, thumbing his prayer book with restless fingers. The pages, worn soft from use, fluttered slightly in the summer air.

"Your Grace."

He turned. Jane stood in the doorway, her gown too ornate for one so grave. She curtsied, and he bowed his head.

"Your Majesty," he said, quietly.

She winced. "Don't call me that."

"You are queen."

"I am named queen," she replied. "Whether God acknowledges it . . . that I do not know."

Cranmer studied her a moment, then set down the book. "If your heart seeks him, he will not refuse you light."

Jane stepped closer. "Do you believe this is his will?"

"Which part?"

"That I should wear the crown."

He hesitated. "It is not my place to question providence."

"That is not an answer," she said.

Cranmer half-smiled. "No. It's not."

Jane lowered herself onto a wooden bench near the altar. "I prayed last night for peace. Instead, I felt . . . watched."

He tilted his head.

"As if heaven were waiting to see whether I meant it," she whispered. "Whether I believed the words I said aloud. I did not sleep."

Cranmer sat beside her, careful not to touch.

"The throne," he said slowly, "exposes what the soul prefers to keep hidden. You will find no safety there. But perhaps—" He paused. "Perhaps clarity."

Jane looked at him then. "Have you found it?"

He held her gaze a moment too long. Then: "Not always."

Her voice softened. "Then may I ask something strange?"

"Of course."

"If you could walk away from all of it—court, counsel, crown—if you could simply follow God in quietness, would you?"

A long silence followed.

Then he stood, gently inclined his head, and left without a word.

Jane remained alone in the quiet chapel, the flicker of a candle throwing her shadow long across the floor.

The corridors of Lambeth were quiet. No guards loitered. No staff bustled. The walls, once noisy with clerks and copyists, seemed to lean inward now—watching.

Will moved lightly, as always, unnoticed by most. He was still Secretary to the Duke of Norfolk—on paper. In practice, he answered to no one but the queen-in-waiting. At least for now.

He had come to observe—to *listen*. And there, through the half-cracked chapel door, he heard the faintest breath of Latin.

Will stepped to the edge of the doorway, silent as ash.

Cranmer knelt alone before the altar. The candles burned low. The archbishop's shoulders were hunched, his robes loose, his frame thinner than Will remembered.

He was whispering—first the Lord's Prayer, then some petition in his own tongue, then silence again. Then:

"If I speak, will you forgive me? If I remain silent, will you forsake me?"

His voice broke; he bowed lower. A long moment passed.

Will swallowed. The man was unraveling—or fighting to hold something that kept slipping through.

A sudden gust from the outer door stirred the flame. Cranmer looked up, startled. Will stepped back into the shadow, unseen.

Cranmer crossed himself. And then, oddly—began again.

"Lord, I believe; help my unbelief."

Mary stood by the hearth, firelight playing across her hands as she un-laced a velvet sleeve.

Will waited for her to speak.

"So," she said at last, "what does the godly archbishop say in these last days?"

Will paused. Then: "He says very little aloud."

She turned, sharp. "But you heard something."

He nodded. "He prays. Repeats old creeds. But it isn't strength I saw, Your Majesty. It was *fear*—raw, living fear. He bends, but not out of cunning. He bends because he's breaking."

Mary studied him.

"And what would you have me do?" she asked.

"Nothing," Will said. "Only . . . know it."

She turned back to the fire. "That man burned my mother in effigy. Burned our faith in Parliament. Burned our saints from the churches. And now he prays."

A beat.

"Would you have me spare him?"

Will didn't answer.

Mary looked back once more. Her voice softened—not gentle, but dangerous for its calm.

"I asked for your eyes, not your heart."

Then she dismissed him.

The council chamber was colder than usual.

No fire crackled in the hearth. No servant poured wine. The great window that overlooked the Thames showed only a bleached sky and the far-off glint of banners—too many banners—rising beyond the walls.

Northumberland stood alone at the table, hands flat on the polished oak, a sheaf of dispatches fanned out before him like a confession. The latest was still in his hand: Cambridge had declared for Mary. So had Norfolk. So had most of the shires. Even members of the council had begun to waver.

A door opened. Will entered, silent as ever.

"Well?" Northumberland asked without turning.

Will came forward, a folded parchment in his hand. "The council has met. Without you."

Northumberland's head turned slightly. "And?"

Will placed the document on the table. "They've declared for Mary."

The silence that followed was not one of surprise, but inevitability.

Northumberland didn't reach for the parchment. "So they think to save themselves."

Will said nothing.

Northumberland straightened, his voice clipped now. "Tell me—how long have you known?"

Will didn't blink. "Long enough to know you've lost the realm."

That landed. Not as insult, but as sentence.

"I led for England," Northumberland said. "I stood between Mary and her crown"

"You stood for your own name," Will replied, more gently than the words deserved. "And now it is your name that must fall."

Northumberland laughed, bitter and short. "Then I suppose it is done."

There was a pause. Then he asked, almost curiously, "Do they call Mary queen?"

Will tilted his head. "They never stopped."

Northumberland gave a slow nod, as though receiving a judgment he'd written himself. He moved to the window, watched the distant movement of troops—civilians, really—streaming toward London. Mary's army. Mary's moment.

He placed a hand against the stone wall. "I tried only to give England a future."

"And now," Will said, "you must let her have one."

Northumberland turned back, eyes hollow but resolved. "You'll witness the transfer?"

Will nodded once.

"Then tell her this," Northumberland said. "I surrender. But I do not confess sin."

Will met his eyes. "She'll understand the difference. But the consequence won't change"

The bells of London rang louder than Will had ever heard.

From the windows of the Tower, their echoes seemed to tumble in waves across the Thames, colliding with cheers that rose like a tide from the streets below. Banners bearing the Tudor rose unfurled from spires and balconies. Crowds jammed the lanes, pressing forward, necks craned, as if to witness history breaking like dawn.

And it was.

Inside the great hall, those who had once whispered loyalties to Jane now stood with heads bowed low to Mary. Members of the council—some reluctant, most relieved—offered formal acknowledgment. Even Suffolk knelt—his hands trembling—as if to offer the crown in his daughter's place. The girl herself had been escorted from her apartments with dignity, her crown removed not by force, but by a command that bore no resistance.

Mary entered with measured steps, crimson hem brushing the stones, the imperial mantle of her mother's claim fully upon her.

"I come not in anger," she said, her voice steady, her eyes sweeping across faces she knew had wavered. "But England will not be ruled by deceit. Nor by fear. I take the crown not for vengeance—but for justice. And for God."

They knelt.

One by one, titles shifted. Roles realigned. And the crown—set moments later upon her brow by Gardiner himself—signaled more than a transfer of power. It was an announcement. England, for the first time in centuries, had a reigning queen. Her eyes were fixed on heaven—or on judgment. It was hard to tell.

Will watched from the edge of the chamber, heart clenched. He felt no triumph. No joy. Only a shifting weight—heavy and cold.

She was queen.

And nothing would stop her now.

The air in the chamber was heavy with the scent of beeswax and rosewater—an attempt at civility in a season of collapse.

Northumberland had been sentenced first. His execution, though not yet carried out, was assured. Jane had followed—not in court, but by proclamation. Her fate was sealed with fewer words and no defense, the girl queen who had never wanted a crown now its most pitiful casualty.

Will stood near the tall windows, hands clasped behind his back, as Mary read through a parchment.

"The realm is fragile," she said without looking up. "And treason bruises the root, not just the branch."

Will gave a slight bow. "Your majesty, the council has followed your lead. The people have as well. No one questions your right."

She set the parchment down and met his eyes. "But they may yet question my rule."

He said nothing.

She rose, walked slowly toward the hearth, eyes catching on the tapestry above it—St. George in mid-charge. "They call me the savior of England. Some call me that, at least. But what must be saved must also be cleansed."

Will spoke with care. "And who determines what is impurity?"

Mary turned to him. "Those who serve the true church."

There was silence.

Then Will took one step forward. "I come not to argue theology."

"Then why do you come?"

"For Cranmer."

Mary's face remained still.

Will continued. "He crowned your brother. He anointed your father's will. He was faithful—to the throne, if not to Rome."

"He burned what Rome built," she said coldly. "And built in its place a house of ash and error."

"He has served England," Will said. "And if he erred—let him repent. Spare him, and it will not be seen as weakness but as wisdom."

Mary studied him. "And do you think he would repent?"

"I don't know," Will admitted. "But I would ask for the chance to try."

She walked back toward her chair, slowly. Her voice, when it came, was softer.

"If he were to recant," she said, almost idly, "fully, publicly, undeniably—then yes, there might be a place for mercy. But what is mercy if the soul still rots?"

Will's heart quickened, but he kept his tone measured. "Then I will speak to him."

She sat again, hands folding in her lap. "Speak, then. Persuade him. Let him see the truth."

He nodded once, sharply.

But Mary's gaze lingered on the flame dancing in the hearth.

"He is to be sent to the Tower tomorrow," she said. "You may see him before then."

She did not say *he will live*. She did not need to. Hope, offered without guarantee, was more useful.

Will bowed low. "Thank you, Majesty."

As he turned to go, she called after him.

"Do not mistake the hand of Rome for cruelty, Master Cressy. We do not seek blood. We seek healing. But infection must be cut away before health can return."

He paused. "Even so," he said, without turning, "sometimes the cure can do more harm than the wound."

He left with the weight of purpose, the flicker of hope, and the faint scent of incense trailing behind him.

The stillness at Lambeth broke not with the sound of boots but the sudden rush of footsteps—one man only, urgent, unannounced.

Margarete looked up from her stitching. Jo froze on the stairwell, herbs in hand, her eyes locking with Nicholas's as he stepped from the study. All three turned as Will burst through the entry, breath short, eyes sharp.

"Where is he?" he asked.

"In the library," Nicholas said, already moving.

Will didn't wait for escort. He found Cranmer at his desk, a half-written letter before him, the quill still resting in the ink.

Will stopped in the doorway, composed himself, then entered.

"She's sending you to the Tower," he said plainly. "Today."

Cranmer did not lift his head. "I thought as much."

Will stepped closer. "But there's still a way. She told me—if you confess in your own hand, fully, without condition, she'll consider clemency."

"I've heard as much before."

"I believe her this time."

Cranmer looked up, the lines around his eyes carved deeper than Will remembered. "Then you don't know her as I do."

Will kept his tone measured, diplomatic. "Then write what she wants. Recant the words—not the heart. It's a concession, not a covenant. You live, you wait, and when the tide shifts—"

Cranmer stood, not with anger, but with quiet resolve. "No, Will. Not because it is her way. Because it is not mine."

Will stared at him, jaw tight. "Then you'll die. And whatever you still believe will die with you."

"Perhaps," Cranmer said. "But it will be mine."

Footsteps now—multiple, unhurried but heavy—echoed through the corridor.

Jo appeared at the doorway, Nicholas just behind her. Margarete came quickly after, eyes darting between Will and her husband.

Then a palace page arrived, breathless. "The queen's men are here. Armed."

Cranmer nodded once. "Then we are done."

By the time he stepped into the entry corridor, three royal guards had already been admitted—escorted by Lambeth's own steward, whose face bore the strain of helplessness.

The captain of the queen's men bowed, but only slightly. "Archbishop Thomas Cranmer. By order of Her Majesty Queen Mary, you are placed under arrest. You are to be conveyed at once to the Tower."

The words rang flat and final.

Margarete moved to his side, clutching his sleeve. "No. No, Thomas—you don't have to go. Not yet. Not now."

He placed a steady hand over hers. "It was always going to be now."

Jo stepped forward, voice unsteady. "She gave no word. No sentence. No hearing."

"She gave none," Cranmer said. "And I presumed mercy. That was my mistake."

Nicholas addressed the captain. "He will be treated as befits his office?"

The man gave a practiced reply. "The queen's orders will be followed."

Which meant nothing at all.

Cranmer looked at them—Margarete, pale but upright; Jo, swallowing tears; Nicholas, stolid and quiet; and Will, whose hands were clenched.

"Thrones rise and fall. But God's love stands," he said. "Hold to that."

He embraced Margarete, then Jo, who clung to him until he whispered, "You must be brave, even if I am not."

"You will be," she said fiercely.

He clasped Nicholas's hand. "Watch over them."

"I will."

At last, he turned to Will.

"I would have bought you more time," Will said.

Cranmer offered the faintest of smiles. "You gave me what mattered more."

Then he turned to the guards and nodded.

No chains. No bindings. But he was not free.

The guards fell into step around him, their boots echoing through the halls of Lambeth as they led him away.

The silence he left behind pressed into every stone.

35

The Submission

THE AIR IN THE audience chamber was warm, but Mary stood near the window, her arms folded. From the east, morning light reached across the floor like a slow tide, illuminating the red sleeves of her gown, the subtle stiffness in her shoulders.

Will waited in silence until she turned.

"I am sending him to Oxford," she said. "Where scholars may reach what pity and persuasion could not."

Will didn't ask who. There was only one prisoner whose soul she still seemed determined to win.

"Cranmer," he said.

Mary nodded. "He has written much. He must now unwrite it. Publicly. Thoughtfully. In his own hand. The flames will take his flesh, but the people must see that it was I who reclaimed his soul."

Will shifted. "You will take his life even if he repents?"

Mary's gaze was unreadable. "England will see him humbled. The man who crowned a bastard and defiled our altars will kneel before the true church. That will be mercy enough."

"Spare his life!" Will pleaded.

"Would he spare mine? Or my people's?" Her voice didn't rise. It was colder for its calm. "He fed England lies in God's name. I will not let the lie stand as his legacy. Not before God. Not before my mother's memory."

A pause.

Mary turned fully toward him now. "You think me cruel."

"I think you calculated."

"I must be." She walked closer. "Your place, Will, is not with Cranmer's memory. It is with England's future. Help him see that. Help him choose dignity—my way."

She paused just long enough. "I want him to confess his heresies: the breaking of the mass, the rejection of purgatory, the blasphemy of a married priesthood. Let him write it all in his own hand. And sign it."

Will held her gaze. "Why would he sign? Why would he repent if you promise him only death?"

A beat passed.

Mary shifted her gaze. Her voice softened, almost kindly. "Perhaps there will be room for clemency."

Will's eyes widened in hope. "Then you would consider sparing him?"

Mary did not answer directly. She turned away, her tone now distant. "A true confession can do much. It can mend what pride has torn. It can open doors once shut."

Will nodded slowly. "That's all he's ever wanted. A way back to truth."

Mary moved past him toward the doorway. "Then give it to him."

But Will's heart seized on those few words—*perhaps, clemency, open doors*—and heard what she never promised.

She turned back.

"No family. No visitors. He will find comfort only where I permit it. And I permit you."

Will turned, stiff. "That's hardly comfort."

"It may be the only kind left." She looked back. "I will have him taken today. You may follow within the week."

The sky over Oxford was gray when Will arrived. Smoke drifted along the wind like a veil drawn across the spires. Bells tolled—not the clear peal of worship but the slow groan of ceremony, echoing over the rooftops.

In the square below the university gates, a crowd had gathered.

Will dismounted and pushed forward.

There, tied to a stake, was Hugh Latimer. Thin, trembling, resolute. The flames had already begun to climb.

Cranmer stood under guard, set apart but visible. A broken man—older somehow than weeks ago, shoulders hunched, face unreadable. He did not weep. He did not look away.

Will's stomach turned.

The queen had said nothing of this.

He looked again at Cranmer—this once-prince of the church—now forced to watch the burning of his brother.

And Will knew: if Cranmer signed, it would be from ashes, not reason. And from hope—hope Will was meant to dangle like a crown just out of reach.

The room smelled of cold stone and candle soot. Three scholars from the university circled the central table with measured steps, murmuring among themselves about heresies, inconsistencies, and hopes for clarity. The archbishop said nothing.

Cranmer sat hunched forward, his hands pressed together, the ends of his sleeves chewed from hours of wringing. His eyes followed nothing. The men had spoken all morning, raising questions, citing fathers, dissecting Luther and Zwingli and the Book of Common Prayer. He had offered little in return—only now and then a flicker: an eyebrow raised, a breath drawn—as if he might answer. But nothing came.

The door opened.

Will entered, and with him swept in the court.

Silk replaced wool. Political scent replaced theological heat.

One of the theologians turned, brow creasing. "This is a closed discussion."

"Then open it," Will said coolly, stepping forward. "You've had days—and no doubt more hours of cleverness than he has had hours of sleep. The queen believes it time for a different approach."

Cranmer blinked. Then blinked again.

"Will?" His voice broke into a whisper.

"Are they safe? Margarete—is Jo?"

"Leave us," Will commanded the others.

One bristled. "We've made progress."

Will arched an eyebrow. "Then he's nearly ready. And you won't mind letting me test your work."

The pause was stiff, but the dismissal was final.

When the door closed behind them, Cranmer half rose, asking again with urgency, "How are they all?"

Will sat across from Cranmer. He extended a hand and nodded slowly. "They're well. All of them." A pause. "They miss you. They pray for you. Every day."

Cranmer closed his eyes. "Are they . . . still at Lambeth?"

"For now. But it isn't safe—not like it was. Things have changed."

Cranmer squeezed his eyes shut as if in prayer.

"There's no shame in weariness," Will continued. "They've drained you dry with debate and let no light in this place. But what matters now . . . is not winning arguments. It's living."

Cranmer's voice returned, quiet. "It's not that simple."

"No. But it can be made simple. You know what they want. Not blood—not yet. Just a statement. Your own hand. Words you've already parsed a hundred times."

Cranmer gave a soft, sardonic laugh. "That is not what they want. They want submission. A trophy."

"Call it what you will. But if it keeps you from the flames—" Will leaned closer. "Isn't that what Jo would ask? What Margarete would beg? Nicholas? The child that's coming?"

Cranmer looked up, startled.

"Yes." Will nodded. "Jo told me. The day you were taken."

The older man turned away sharply, his eyes glistening, his thoughts on their hearts. "They should not suffer for my failure."

"Then come back to them. Let this be survival, not surrender. Let this be the way through."

Cranmer pressed a hand to his face, overcome for a moment.

"They're asking for it in your own words," Will said. "It's not much. Just enough to show you're ready to rejoin the fold." His tone softened. "Mary is merciful when she wishes to be. And she's waiting to see."

Cranmer was still.

Will laid a sheet of parchment and a pen before him. "You don't have to mean every word. You just have to write them."

There was no reply. But Cranmer's eyes lingered on the page.

Will stood. "I'll carry it back with me—to the queen. And I'll let the others know. They'll be waiting for you."

He left without pressing further.

The paper was folded with care, the seal already broken, the script familiar. It had been slipped beneath the cell door sometime in the early morning. Cranmer sat on the cot, hunched against the chill, as his eyes traced the curves of Jo's hand.

> *My dear Uncle,*
>
> *The days have settled oddly without you. Lambeth feels like a place waiting for its heartbeat to return. But I write with hope today—real hope.*
>
> *Margarete has taken to humming again, usually while kneading bread or brushing the stair rails. Nicholas has begun carving a cradle. And as for me . . . I suppose I'm knitting when I should be resting.*
>
> *Because we're expecting.*
>
> *I wanted you to hear it from me—because it matters most to say it to you. There is a child, Uncle. A child already loved. A child who will one day ask stories of the man who taught his mother how to think and how to love.*
>
> *We are not afraid. Not truly. I miss you—we miss you—more than I can say. But I do not write to pull you down into our ache. I write to lift your eyes for a moment above these walls.*
>
> *You are not the sum of their accusations, nor the silence they demand. The truth you stood for still lives—in us, and in what is eternal.*
>
> *Remember who you are.*
>
> *And when the shadows press close, remember that even they are touched by morning light.*
>
> *With all my love,*
> *Jo*

He sat long after the letter had gone still in his hands.

Jo's words lingered—not only the joy of her news, though that had struck his chest like a bell—but something quieter beneath the parchment, something harder to shake.

She believed in him. Still. Not because he was a leader or a scholar or an archbishop, but because he had once stood for truth. And she called him—without demand, without shame—back toward it.

He looked down at the ink-stained copy of his own confession—a cautious one. Nothing heretical, not explicitly. He had not named the pope as head of the Church. He had not denied justification by faith. He had not betrayed the Eucharist.

No, it was a submission. A bowing of the head to Rome, to Mary, to survival.

He had told himself it was a temporary yielding, a door left ajar to let him return to the ones he loved.

But Jo's letter had cracked something in that logic.

She had not called him a coward. Had not even questioned his choice. But her hope—her confidence that truth endures, that he still bore it—had made the ink on the confession feel colder somehow.

He folded her letter gently and slid it beneath his pillow. Then he returned to his chair and stared again at the single flickering candle.

They wanted more. They would ask for more. But he was no longer sure where submission ended and betrayal began.

"This is nothing!" Mary exclaimed after reading what Will had handed her.

She flung the parchment onto the table, its edges curling as if embarrassed to be seen. "This is not repentance. This is not recantation. It's a sigh dressed up in ink."

Will stood motionless. "It was the best he would give. For now."

Mary rose from her chair, pacing. "I asked for his theology to be overturned, not obscured. He says he regrets confusion, regrets dissension. That is not denial—it's evasion."

"He wrote it in his own hand," Will offered, keeping his voice steady. "You said you wanted something from him. This is a beginning."

Mary turned sharply. "I wanted a spectacle. Not a footnote."

A pause.

She stepped closer, eyes narrowing. "Do you know what they whispered when they heard he was taken? That he would stand firm. That he would die for his heresies and become a martyr. I will not give him that crown."

Will nodded slowly. "Then let me return. Let me press him further."

Mary studied him for a long moment, weighing something behind her eyes. "You still think him redeemable?"

"I think him persuadable," Will said carefully. "Especially if he believes it will save his life."

She turned from him, gazing toward the fire, her voice low. "I want his pride to bend. His pen to stain. I want him to deny, not merely regret."

She faced him again. "Let the next letter come with Scripture. With doctrine. Let him call the Mass holy, the pope a true shepherd, and the English Church—his Church—a rebellion. And make him write it plainly."

A breath. "Or bring nothing at all."

Will gave the slightest bow. "He will write again."

"And soon," Mary added, reclaiming her seat. "The flames wait for no one."

The room was dimmer than before. The morning fog had never fully lifted, and the narrow mullioned windows blurred the outside world into a smear of grey. A single taper guttered near the table's edge, and Cranmer sat beside it, thinner than Will remembered—more shadow than man.

He didn't rise when Will entered. Just a glance. Just a breath that might've been recognition.

Will crossed the room slowly. "They tell me you've written something."

Cranmer looked down at the parchment before him. Ink smudged at the corner. His fingers bore the stain. "Yes."

Will took the seat across from him again. "Is it better than the last?"

Cranmer didn't answer.

Will picked up the parchment and read. It was more specific this time—some doctrinal reversals, vague yet traceable. He gave a small nod. "You're learning to play the game."

Cranmer raised his eyes. "Is that what this is?"

Will leaned forward. "Let's not pretend. You know how this began. The English reformation wasn't born of divine vision. It was born of a king who wanted a different wife. And you—" he tilted his head—"you gave him the keys."

Cranmer's lips moved. "I gave him . . . permission. But not truth."

Will's tone sharpened. "Exactly. You bent the truth to fit a royal will. That's not reformation, Uncle. That's convenience."

Cranmer's hands clenched together on the table.

Will continued, lower now. "The Church has stood fifteen hundred years. That's not nothing. And you—driven by conscience or favor or fear—thought you could stand against it. And yet here you are. Alone. Diminished. Fading."

Cranmer stared at the candle flame. "Maybe it was ambition. Maybe I mistook certainty for calling." His voice cracked. "But I believed. I still believe."

Will paused but then shook his head to clear it.

"In what?" Will asked gently. "In truth? Or in being right?"

The silence lingered.

Will nodded to the page. "You've begun. Good. Now finish. Name what you've defied. Name who you've defied. And name the truth."

He stood, adjusted his coat, and walked to the door. "I'll return in two days."

Cranmer didn't look up as Will exited. But after a long moment, he reached again for the ink.

As he bent to write, the door creaked once more. A guard stepped in, holding a small folded letter. "From London," he said simply, and placed it beside the growing confession.

Cranmer stared at it. Didn't touch it.

Not yet.

Two days passed.

Cranmer had written the confession—more thorough, more yielding. He'd labored over every phrase, every citation, until the words no longer felt like words at all, only the chisel edge of compromise carving deeper into his chest.

When Will returned, Cranmer handed it over without ceremony. He didn't rise. Didn't speak.

Will scanned it quickly, lips pressed thin. "This may do," he said. He gave no praise, only nodded once, then turned and left, parchment in hand.

The door closed behind him.

And only then—when all else was taken from him—did Cranmer reach for Jo's letter.

> *My dearest Uncle,*
>
> *There are days when I feel you beside me still.*
>
> *I walk the gardens and half expect your voice behind me, asking what I see in the petals. I read the Scriptures aloud, and sometimes imagine you'll step in to explain what I've misunderstood. I know it's foolish. But it's a comfort, too.*

Your letter reached us. Will brought it himself, and I could see in his face how much he longs for your safety. We all do. I pray every night that your mind is at peace, even if your body is not.

The child stirs now—barely more than a flutter, like the rustle of a sleeve. I've begun to rest my hand there, half in prayer, half in wonder. Margarete says the same. She kneels beside me sometimes and prays aloud for the child to know its godfather. I tell her it already does.

Uncle, you once taught me that truth must be lived more than spoken. I've never forgotten it. Nor do I believe you have. You've always been a man who sought Christ more than acclaim, clarity more than comfort. That has not changed.

So whatever is asked of you in that place, know this: no signature, no oath, no line of ink can undo the love you have shown, the truth you have carried, or the Spirit that has guided your steps.

We are still with you. Still praying. Still hoping.

With all love,
Jo

As with the last letter, he read this one twice.

The first time, he swallowed hard—her hand in prayer, the child in motion, Margarete still whispering hope. It all struck like a kindness he could no longer afford. By the second reading, his hand had grown tight around the parchment.

You've always been a man who sought Christ more than acclaim.

What did she know of seeking Christ in this place?

The scholars returned daily with their traps of doctrine, their re-lit arguments. Will pressed him with polished lies about mercy and peace. And he—he had caved. First a brief concession. Then a full recantation. Not just silence now, but signatures.

And Jo . . . Jo still spoke of him as if he were whole.

But he wasn't.

Her words stung—not for what they accused, but for what they assumed. They assumed he still believed, still hoped, still stood. She didn't know how broken he was. How the fear lingered. How the walls, the guards, the smell of soot—how they carved away certainty day by day.

He set the letter aside. Not gently.

She had meant to comfort him. But it only hollowed him further. Because he no longer knew whether her belief in him was faith—or fantasy.

And he had already written more. Said more. Given more.

Too much to undo.
Not yet regret.
But not peace either.

Weeks later, another letter arrived early that morning, placed on the writing desk in his cell.

Jo's hand. Her seal.

Cranmer stared at it but didn't move. He feared to look. He feared that the struggle that had already defeated him would start anew.

There were too many voices already in his head.

Will entered. He brought no preamble, no calculated rhetoric. He had rehearsed new arguments along the road—questions of apostolic succession, papal authority, the ancient seat of Peter. But as the heavy door closed behind him, all those plans fell away.

Cranmer didn't lift his head. He had been told Will was coming. He already had been scribbling on parchment, his body sunken so far into itself he barely seemed to breathe.

Will paused, seeing the lines already written.

Entire paragraphs.

"I expected more resistance," Will said quietly.

No reply.

Will stepped closer, reading upside down. A chill formed at the base of his neck.

Cranmer was not merely revising doctrine. He was razing it.

The Pope named the true head of the Church. The sacraments rightly numbered and administered only by Rome. Transubstantiation affirmed without reserve. The English liturgy denounced. The very reforms Cranmer had crafted with care and conviction—undone in a matter of sentences.

Will watched him scratch the final period. The quill hung for a moment in his hand. Then it fell.

Cranmer did not meet Will's eyes.

"It's done," he whispered.

Will reached for the parchment but didn't lift it right away.

This had been the goal. Complete submission. A confession so thorough it could be read from every pulpit in England. A statement not just of recantation—but of defeat.

It was all here.

Will took the parchment slowly, folding it with more care than it needed.

"Is this what you believe?" he asked, not because he needed an answer but because he needed to hear the lie.

Cranmer gave no reply. His shoulders sagged like broken architecture. His hands trembled, stained with ink and indecision. His voice had no weight. The man who had once faced down kings could barely finish a sentence.

This wasn't victory. It was the absence of even defiance.

Will looked down at the man he had just dismantled.

And for the first time, he felt no satisfaction at all.

He had won—so why did he feel . . . shame?

He turned quickly and left.

Cranmer sat back. It was finished.

Then he saw Jo's letter.

> *My dearest Uncle,*
>
> *This is not a letter of debate, nor of pleading, nor even of sorrow. I have none of those left in me tonight.*
>
> *I have only this: love.*
>
> *Yours was the voice that first taught me that God is not waiting to catch us in a wrong thought but leaning toward us—always leaning—in love. You showed me that God is not a lawgiver with scales, but a Father who runs, a Son who stoops, a Spirit who stays.*
>
> *Did you forget?*
>
> *Or did they steal it from you, inch by inch?*
>
> *Let them take your robes, your titles, your books. Let them take what they think matters.*
>
> *But not this. Not what is most true.*
>
> *You are still God's. That has not changed.*
>
> *You are still ours. We wait for you.*
>
> *Live in God's fear, Uncle—not the fear they wield. Not the fear they whisper through fire and chain. I mean the fear that sings in the heart when love is so great, so holy, you tremble just to receive it.*
>
> *You once called that holy trembling "home."*
>
> *Come home.*
>
> *With all my love,*
> *Jo*

The letter slipped from his hands.

He stared at the floor, breath shallow, hands idle, as if the world had stopped and left only silence behind. But the silence was not empty. It pulsed with something deeper—like the echo of music long buried beneath stone.

Jo's words lingered: *Let them take what they think matters.*

But in their taking, he had nearly given them more.

He had almost given them the very marrow of his soul.

God was not in the storm—not in the noise of trials, the cleverness of arguments, or the fury of fire.

He did not require words that strive to win.

Only the grace to breathe.

To be aware.

To know.

God was in the nearness—in the hush that came when love was no longer doubted.

And Cranmer, at last, remembered.

Margarete's voice—*He does not demand; he gives.*

Will's early fire—*You taught me love does not run from the cross.*

Jo's face—full of belief, even now.

God had not abandoned him.

God was here.

Here in the cell. Here in the ruin. Here in the body of a broken man, not breaking him down—but breaking him open.

He would not let their script be the final word.

Cranmer rose slowly, as if shedding a weight he had long thought welded to his spine.

He stood not in shame but in peace.

Not in despair but in strength.

Not alone.

God was with him.

And he would speak again.

36

The Quiet Hope

"Yes! This is it! This is what I wanted."

Mary held the parchment aloft, the ink still looked fresh—smudged at one corner, as if folded too soon. She read it again—aloud this time—pacing before the hearth like a queen rehearsing a coronation.

"He names the pope, affirms the mass, denounces every heresy he once preached. It is not mere regret—it is confession. Full. Unqualified. And in his own hand." She turned to Will, eyes bright. "This will be read in pulpits across England. Copied and kept. And most . . . proclaimed by the man himself, before the pyre is lit."

Will said nothing.

She stepped closer. "Do you see it? This is not just a man undone. This is Protestantism undone. This is the death knell of every false gospel whispered in my father's court."

Will's jaw tightened. "And then you'll kill him anyway."

She didn't flinch. "Of course. A recantation is not a pardon. It is a correction—a cleansing. And the flame, Will, is not vengeance. It is penance."

A beat passed in the quiet.

"Have it prepared," she said. "The platform. The crowd. The friar to read his words. And Cranmer to confirm them with his own voice." She smiled slightly. "Let England watch the archbishop become Catholic again—just in time to die."

Will bowed stiffly and turned to go.

But at the door, he paused.

"He had wondered if you'd spare him," he said, a flicker of hope shining in his own eyes.

Mary did not look up. "Then let that hope be the first thing to burn."

Lambeth had been unusually still that morning. The air, though warm, clung like a mist, and the corridors of the palace echoed with the hushed movements of a household trying not to wake grief.

Margarete stood by the long window in the west corridor, hands clasped, her face turned toward the garden though she saw nothing. Jo sat nearby, one hand on her belly, the other resting on the arm of the carved chair. Emilie moved between them with quiet purpose, fluffing a pillow here, adjusting a window latch there. She and Roger had arrived the night before, hoping to be a help for Jo and encouragement for Margarete.

The door burst open.

Nicholas.

His eyes met Margarete's first, then darted toward Jo. He had come quickly—his boots were stained, his coat damp with river frost.

"It's come," he said, barely above a whisper. "The sentence has come. They'll burn him. In Oxford."

Jo's breath caught.

Margarete didn't move.

Roger was the first to speak. "When?"

"Four days," Nicholas said. "They're making arrangements already. Will is there—Mary sent him ahead. Everything is to be made public. They'll read the recantations first. Then . . ."

He couldn't finish it.

"They mean it to be a spectacle," Roger said bitterly. "To crush the last flicker of reform."

"No," Jo said, rising slowly with Emilie's help. "They will not crush us. We must go. He must see us."

Margarete turned to her. Though she was not her daughter, she had become as dear to her. "But can you travel?"

"I won't stay here," Jo replied, hand pressed gently over her womb. "He shouldn't die without us near."

"We'll go," Roger said. "All of us."

Emilie nodded. "We'll ready what's needed."

Nicholas stepped forward. "I'll arrange the carts. The road to Oxford isn't easy, but we'll take it slow."

Margarete exhaled shakily, pressing her hand to her lips. Then she nodded. "We go."

And in that still palace, movement returned.

Not hurried, but resolute.

They would go to Oxford—not to witness the fire, but to carry love to its edge.

And to stand in its light.

The cart creaked softly as it rolled over the rutted path. Early spring clung to the hedgerows—buds still tight, blossoms hesitant—and the fields, though waking, wore more brown than green. The sun broke through mist with little warmth, casting long shadows over the frosted lane. A soft wind blew westward, as if urging them forward.

Margarete sat close beside Jo, one arm tucked gently around her shoulders. Jo leaned into her without words. Her hand lay atop her belly, still and warm. The child had not stirred for hours, though the road was uneven.

Ahead, Emilie rode with Roger. Nicholas kept to the side, alert but distant. They had said little since leaving Lambeth.

Jo finally broke the silence.

"Do you think he regrets it?"

Margarete did not answer at once. Her eyes remained on the road ahead. "I think he always regrets when he acts in fear."

Jo nodded. "He's always tried to choose love. But it hasn't always been clear—to him or to others."

"No," Margarete agreed. "But truth mattered to him. Even when it cost him. Even when he was slow to grasp it."

Jo shifted, adjusting her weight. "He knew the gospel. Not just in words, but in shape. In how it unfolds."

Margarete looked at her then, her eyes gentler than the sky above them. "Yes. And I believe he will still cling to that. Even here. Even now."

The cart jostled over a stone. Jo winced, then smiled faintly.

"He taught us all how to listen," she said, "even when he didn't know quite what he heard."

Margarete smiled too—tired, but true. "And how to hold fast to what we've heard, even when others demand silence."

They rode on in quiet again, the breeze brushing their cheeks like an unseen prayer.

They did not speak of the flames.

Only of the man.

And of the God they still believed he would remember.

The road bent at last toward Oxford, its steeples rising above the patchwork of roofs and trees like solemn sentinels. The sun had begun to lower in the west, casting long shadows over the streets as Roger reined the cart to a slow roll.

They found rooms on the north side of town—plain but clean, and with enough space for all of them. Margarete helped Jo from the cart while Emilie stepped in to unpack what they'd brought. Nicholas, restless and tight-lipped, glanced toward the center of town.

Roger met his eye. "Let's go."

They left the others and made their way through the winding lanes until they reached the building where Cranmer was held—a plain structure, half monastery, half prison, its gates reinforced with iron and men.

Roger stepped forward and knocked.

After a long pause, a guard opened the door halfway. "No visitors."

"I need to speak with someone inside. The man you're holding—he is my friend. I've come to—"

The door shifted as if to shut.

But then it pulled open wide.

A man stepped forward, ready to bark dismissal—until his eyes met Roger's.

Will froze.

His jaw clenched, and his posture stiffened—but he did not speak the rebuke he had prepared. Instead, he stepped out, closing the door quietly behind him.

"What are you doing here?" he asked in a hushed voice.

Roger met his son's gaze. "We had to come."

Will looked from him to Nicholas. His face softened, barely.

"You can't come in. No family. That's the queen's order."

Roger started to protest, but Will raised a hand. "I didn't say there was no way to see him."

He turned and motioned them to follow. Around the side of the building, they came to a narrow garden walk. Vines choked the old stones, and a shuttered window rested high along the rear wall. Will pointed.

"That's his room," he said. "Come at dusk. All of you. I'll have him there."

Roger's voice cracked. "Will—"

Will was already turning back.

"Dusk," he repeated.

They returned to the lodging. Jo rose when she saw them, hand on her belly, her eyes full of questions. Margarete reached for Roger's arm.

"Well?"

He nodded. "There's a way. Will found one."

And as the shadows deepened and the sky turned rose-gold, the five of them walked the garden path in silence.

Cranmer stood at the window, framed by candlelight, thinner than they remembered, more bent than he had ever been.

He saw them.

His hand lifted—slow, trembling, but sure.

One by one, they raised theirs in return. No words. Just hands reaching across the dusk. Just tears. Just nearness.

And for a moment, no walls.

Only love.

A knock at the door brought the quiet morning to a halt.

Roger moved first, then paused as Jo shifted uncomfortably in her chair. Nicholas rose instead, crossing to open it.

Will stood there, cloaked against the wind, hair mussed from the early chill. "It's today," he said simply. "He'll speak at St. Mary's. Mid-morning."

No one spoke for a breath.

"Speak?" Emilie asked. "What does that mean?"

"Testify," Will replied, but his voice carried no clarity. "They will read his confession publicly, and he is expected to affirm it. Before . . ." He stopped himself.

Margarete nodded. "We'll go."

"It will be crowded," Will said. "But there will be space in the gallery. I'll see that you're let in."

Roger glanced at Jo. "Can you manage it?"

She drew in a breath, then pushed herself upright with care. "I can walk. I want to hear him."

Will's eyes lingered on her a moment. Then he gave a single nod. "Be ready soon. I'll return to walk you there."

He left without another word.

The room stayed hushed for several heartbeats longer. Then the quiet bustle began—cloaks retrieved, boots laced, shawls tied more firmly. No one spoke of what came after. Only of walking, and listening.

And of standing near, if only from above.

The gallery was full but hushed. Jo leaned forward slightly, both hands resting on the worn wood rail. Margarete sat beside her, jaw set, eyes locked on the pulpit. Roger and Emilie, to the left. Nicholas, close to Jo's side.

The nave below held a crowded solemnity—city folk, officials, clergy. A few noble faces. All eyes drawn toward the platform.

Then, from a side door, they led him in.

Cranmer moved slowly, thin and stooped, draped in the scholar's black. His white beard had grown unkempt, and his eyes searched the room not with fear but with a weary ache. When he reached the pulpit, he took it with both hands and steadied himself.

A bishop stepped forward, unrolling a scroll.

"Thomas Cranmer, former Archbishop of Canterbury, has recanted his errors and hereby affirms the true and apostolic faith of the holy mother Church, as given in this written confession. . . ."

The words rolled on—carefully penned, doctrinally precise, undoing all he had once taught. The air grew stifled with the sound.

Jo felt her fingers clutch tighter to the rail.

Then Cranmer raised a hand.

The bishop faltered.

"I will speak," Cranmer said. His voice was soft but resolute.

The bishop glanced aside. There was hesitation, confusion. But at last he stepped back.

Cranmer stood straighter.

"What was read to you—I wrote. I did. And I signed it. But it was not true."

A ripple moved through the room.

"I was afraid. Not for my body only, but for my soul—afraid that I had led others astray. Afraid that I might be wrong. Afraid of flames. Afraid of God.

"But I was wrong about my fear.

"For the fear of God is not terror. It is not trembling under whip or threat. It is awe. It is trust. It is knowing that the One who made me—who made us—did so not to rule as tyrant, but to walk with us as Father, Brother, Comforter. Creator. Savior."

He looked up to the gallery. Found them.

Margarete's hand rose to her lips. Jo's eyes brimmed.

"I recant my recantations," he said clearly. "I reject them all."

Another murmur, louder this time.

Cranmer's voice strengthened.

"I believe in the mercy of God. I believe in Jesus Christ, crucified for love, raised in glory. I believe he is near to the broken, present in the cell and the fire alike. He does not demand words to earn his love. He is love. Always has been. Always will be."

He reached out a trembling hand toward the gallery.

"To my family—hold to our God. Not because he rules in power. But because he remains in love. He cares for you. He cares for me."

A silence fell.

Then movement. Guards approached. A few in the crowd cried out—some in protest, some in prayer. A young priest turned away, hiding tears.

Cranmer did not resist. He stepped down, steady now, head lifted. And as they led him out, he passed the scroll that bore his final recantation. He did not look at it.

The square had filled.

The bells of St. Mary's had not yet ceased their tolling, but already the crowd pressed into every vantage, their faces upturned toward the wooden platform at center. Those who had crowded the church now poured into the open air, speaking in low murmurs, unsure whether they had witnessed rebellion or redemption.

A cold wind tore through the streets. The sun, pale with smoke, hung low.

Cranmer was brought forward.

The guards led him slowly, allowing the aged man to keep his footing on the uneven stones. His step was feeble but unhesitating. The hush of the crowd grew thicker with every footfall. The pyre, already ringed with dried faggots and pitch, loomed ahead like a waiting altar.

From the far side of the square, the family group emerged from the church in silence.

They paused.

Margarete steadied herself on Roger's arm. Jo, now heavy with child, stood as if transfixed, staring at the figure being helped to the stake. Nicholas reached for her hand.

"We should go," he said.

Emilie nodded, blinking fast. "He wouldn't want us to see this."

Still they stood.

Will was near the edge of the platform, his face pale, unreadable. He turned slightly as he saw the others in the distance, and his eyes met Jo's.

She nodded once, then gripped her side.

"Jo?" Nicholas turned sharply. She staggered.

"I'm fine—just help me."

They turned from the square. As Cranmer mounted the steps, the group pushed into the side street and began the hurried walk back to the house. The wind picked up, snapping the ends of cloaks and catching Jo's hair in tangled streaks. Margarete wept silently. Emilie murmured a prayer. Roger walked with his head down.

Another pain seized Jo.

She cried out, nearly crumpling.

Nicholas lifted her into his arms without a word. The others moved quickly ahead to open the door, to gather linens, to heat water for cloths and comfort. Emilie told Roger to find a midwife, and he rushed out.

In the square, the stake had been set.

Cranmer looked out at the sea of faces. He did not weep. His voice, when he spoke, was clear.

"I come, as I have long wished, to the end of my wandering."

A murmur passed through the crowd.

"What I have written, I now disown. What I have signed, I now renounce. I have offended not only men, but my God—and I return to him now not with cleverness, but with contrition."

He raised his right hand.

"This hand that signed—unworthy, trembling, false—shall burn first."

A gasp. Then silence.

The torches were lowered.

Flames caught quickly, licking upward with sudden ferocity. Cranmer held his arm steady in the rising blaze. He did not pull back.

"Lord Jesus," he called, "receive my spirit."

The fire roared. And at the house, Jo screamed.

Nicholas held her hand; Margarete wiped her brow.

Roger returned with a midwife, sharp, efficient, commanding. Emilie carried water. Roger stood in the doorway, praying aloud.

Another cry. Another rush.

And then—

A child's cry joined hers.

Nicholas, overcome, kissed Jo's hand.

"He's perfect," the midwife said. "Strong lungs. A boy."

Jo turned to Nicholas, her face streaked with tears and sweat and radiant joy.

"His name is Thomas," she whispered. "Our gift from God."

Two days passed. The March winds had quieted, and the trees beyond the Oxford house bent only slightly now, as if sighing in the long silence after the storm.

Inside, the family had just finished preparations to depart. Robes were folded. Saddlebags filled. The fire was low, embers soft. Margarete moved slowly, stuffing a final bag with swaddling cloths; Nicholas checked the straps on the cart; Roger and Emilie whispered together by the window.

Jo stood near the hearth with her son in her arms. She rocked gently, humming low, her eyes half-lost in the embers.

Then the door opened. Will stood there, his cloak dusted from the road, his face lined deeper than it had been two days before.

Jo turned. "You came."

He nodded, stepped in, and looked around at them all—at Margarete's tired smile, at Emilie's tentative warmth, at Nicholas's watchful guard. Then his eyes returned to Jo.

"I watched it all," he said, voice tight. "The fire. The people. The silence." Will paused fighting within himself. His voice cracked. "I told him to sign. I helped her break him."

Jo moved closer, reaching out one arm as the other cradled the baby. Will sank to his knees. His face twisted, and the tears came freely. "I don't know who I am," he whispered. "Maybe I never meant to save him. Maybe I just wanted her favor."

Jo knelt too, lowering herself gently beside him, the child between them. She didn't speak. She only rested her forehead to his and let his weeping fill the silence.

A knock at the door broke the stillness. Roger opened it.

A royal page stood there, breathless. "William Cressy. The queen expects your report."

Will lifted his head. His eyes flicked to the child, to Jo, to Nicholas and Margarete behind them. He stood slowly. His voice, when it came, was low but clear.

"No," he said. "Tell her I have nothing to add."

The page hesitated, then bowed and left.

Jo rose and reached for his hand. So did Nicholas. Will stood between them, their fingers closing around his.

They stepped outside.

The sun sat high behind a veil of cloud. The air was cold but clean.

Without a word, they began the walk eastward—toward Walthamstow. The child slept in Jo's arms. Will walked beside her, head bowed. Behind them, the others followed, a slow procession moving homeward.

No trumpets. No grand declarations.

Only the wind and the road ahead.

And the quiet hope waiting beyond the fire.

www.ingramcontent.com/pod-product-compliance
Lightning Source LLC
Chambersburg PA
CBHW060308100726
47907CB00002B/330